THE DEVIL'S BONEYARD

THE DEVIL'S BONEYARD

A BEN SAVAGE, SALOON RANGER WESTERN

WILLIAM W. JOHNSTONE

AND J. A. JOHNSTONE

PINNACLE BOOKS
Kensington Publishing Corp.
www.kensingtonbooks.com

PINNACLE BOOKS are published by

Kensington Publishing Corp.
119 West 40th Street
New York, NY 10018

PUBLISHER'S NOTE

Following the death of William W. Johnstone, the Johnstone family is working with a carefully selected writer to organize and complete Mr. Johnstone's outlines and many unfinished manuscripts to create additional novels in all of his series like The Last Gunfighter, Mountain Man, and Eagles, among others. This novel was inspired by Mr. Johnstone's superb storytelling.

All Kensington titles, imprints, and distributed lines are available at special quantity discounts for bulk purchases for sales promotions, premiums, fund-raising, educational, or institutional use. Special book excerpts or customized printings can also be created to fit specific needs. For details, write or phone the office of the Kensington sales manager: Kensington Publishing Corp., 119 West 40th Street, New York, NY 10018, attn: Sales Department; phone 1-800-221-2647.

PINNACLE BOOKS, the Pinnacle logo, and the WWJ steer head logo are Reg. U.S. Pat. & TM Off.

ISBN-13: 978-0-7860-4591-4
ISBN-10: 0-7860-4591-4

First printing: November 2020

10 9 8 7 6 5 4 3 2 1

Printed in the United States of America

Electronic edition:
ISBN-13: 978-0-7860-4592-1 (e-book)
ISBN-10: 0-7860-4592-2 (e-book)

CHAPTER 1

"It ain't every day the warden comes down here to say good-bye to a prisoner who's served his time," guard Roland Thomas said. "Out the front door, too, instead of the gate where most of the other inmates walk out." He had been inspired to comment when they saw Warden Mathew Wheeler waiting by the front door of the main prison administration building.

Malcolm Hazzard was very much aware of that fact, but he was not surprised to see the warden. He had participated in many heart-to-heart talks with Warden Wheeler about the paths in life that lead men to evil endings. Hazzard was fortunate to have been incarcerated in the Texas State Prison at a time when Wheeler was warden. "I praise the Lord that they sent me to this prison where a Christian man was in charge, a man who was dedicated to saving the souls of those who had strayed to do the work of the devil." He looked at the guard and smiled. "I wish that you had come to some of our prayer meetings. It might have enlightened your soul. I hope you'll consider doin' that sometime."

Thomas chuckled. "I don't know about that, Hazzard. Don't know if they'll even keep it up after you've gone." Like most of the other guards, he wasn't totally convinced that Malcolm Hazzard had truly been saved. He had to allow, however, that Hazzard wouldn't be the first inmate who decided to walk the straight and narrow after serving his time. In Hazzard's case, it had resulted in an early release after serving only five years of a fifteen-year sentence. But Thomas was convinced that Hazzard had played the warden like a fiddle. For the warden's sake, he hoped Hazzard continued to walk the straight path after he left there.

"Well, Malcolm, the big day has finally come," the warden said as he walked to meet Hazzard, his hand outstretched. "I wanted to be here to walk out that door with you to the first day of the rest of your life. I feel like you are the perfect example of what can be accomplished to rehabilitate an inmate during his prison sentence. I think I can count on you to make our work here at Huntsville proud."

"Thank you, sir," Malcolm replied humbly. "I have you to thank for putting me on the right path for the rest of my life and I hope to bring the Word of the Lord to as many miserable and confused souls as I can." He glanced down at the Bible he was carrying. "I know I have my guide to rely on. And I know, if a miserable soul like mine can be shown the true light, then there's hope for everyone. I only hope you know how grateful I am to you for helping me see that light."

Wheeler smiled, pleased. "We can all be beacons of light for the unsaved. I know you will be a powerful servant of the Lord." He nodded toward Roland Thomas, and Thomas went to the door and held it open as the warden and Hazzard walked through. "God be with you, Malcolm."

"And with you and the staff here at the prison," Hazzard responded.

As soon as they stepped outside, Hazzard was hailed by two men waiting in the street in front of the prison building. They were holding the reins of three saddled horses, as well as lead ropes for two pack-horses. Malcolm returned their greetings and briefly explained to Wheeler that one of them, the heavyset man with the dark beard and the ill-fitting morning coat, was his brother, Ormond. The man with him was a family friend by the name of Pete Russell. When he read the question in the warden's eyes, he said, "I know they're rough-lookin' men, but that's just because they're hardworking men of the soil. But rest assured they're God-fearin' men who have encouraged me to keep my faith durin' these years I've spent inside these walls."

Wheeler hesitated but decided there was no point in having second thoughts based on the appearance of the men who came to meet Malcolm. "It's not important what we look like on the outside," he declared. "It's what's written in a man's heart that counts."

"Amen, Warden," Malcolm replied, turned and walked down the steps to the street where he was greeted in rugged fashion, with a hug from his brother and some backslapping from Pete Russell.

"Come on, Reverend," brother Ormond japed. "I brought you a gray geldin', just like the one they shot out from under you five years ago." He stood back and grinned while he watched Malcolm climb up into the saddle. "I swear, I gotta admit, I didn't think you'd pull it off."

"Well, it sure as hell weren't easy," Malcolm remarked, "but I'da done it for another five years, if it didn't get me out but one day short of my sentence." He jerked the gray's head around and gave it a kick of his heels. "Come on, let's get the hell outta here before they change their minds." Feeling his freedom, he kicked the gray into a gallop on the Madisonville road until well out of sight of Huntsville before he slowed the horse down to a walk. Then he threw his Bible as far as he could sling it into the woods beside the road.

"Yee haw!" Ormond responded when he saw the Bible flying into the bushes. In like fashion, he pulled the morning coat off and threw it as well. Unable to fling the coat as far as Malcolm threw the Bible, he settled for a throw that left it hanging on a tree branch right beside the road. "I stole that coat just so I'd look like a preacher when we picked you up," he told Malcolm. "It was about two sizes too small."

"I'm gonna need to go somewhere to get some clothes," Malcolm said, "boots, hat, ridin' clothes, a weapon, too. Did you bring me money for everything I need?"

"Like I told you when I came to see you last

month," Ormond answered. "I've been saving you a share outta every job we've done. Your money's in the saddlebags of that saddle you're settin' on. It oughta be enough to fix you up. We can ride over to Bryan. It's a good-sized town now and it ain't but about forty miles from here."

"Bryan?" Malcolm repeated. "I've heard the guards talk about Madisonville and it's only twenty miles from here. Let's go there."

Ormond looked at Pete and they both grinned. "Rather not," Ormond said. "That's where I stole the coat. Better off goin' to Bryan. We ain't had no dealin's with anybody there, but the saloon. And there weren't no trouble there. We've been kinda layin' low for the last six months around this part of Texas, waitin' for you to get out."

When they came to a crossroad, Ormond pulled his horse to a stop. "This here is the trail to Bryan." He looked at Malcolm to see if he was going to insist on continuing to Madisonville. When he did not, Ormond turned onto the trail heading west. They rode on for a few minutes before Ormond commented. "Reckon you're wantin' to head on down to Giddings after you get fixed up with some clothes."

"I reckon," Malcolm said. Giddings was the town where their younger brother, William, was killed by a deputy sheriff. The determination to seek vengeance for his brother's death was the driving force that enabled him to maintain his religious charade for so long. During the long dreary days, locked in a two-man cell, it was all he would think about, a chance to see that deputy sheriff beyond the front sight of his

.44. William was only fifteen when he was gunned down in the middle of the street in their foiled attempt to rob the Houston & Texas Central Railroad in Giddings.

His mind raced back to that day. Unknown to Malcolm, his two brothers, and Pete Russell, they picked the very day a big money shipment was on the train, meant for a bank in Houston. There were half a dozen guards escorting that money shipment to Houston. When Malcolm and the others saw the reception awaiting them in the mail car, they made a run for it, and all four of them might have gotten away but for a local deputy sheriff. He had no connections with the railroad. He was just a deputy sheriff who happened to be in a position to take a shot at the fleeing outlaws. The image was still vivid in Malcolm's mind, of the four of them galloping hell-bent-for-leather away from the railroad station, the angry snap of bullets passing all around them. Pete Russell was in the lead, with Malcolm and Ormond right behind him. His younger brother, William, was bringing up the rear.

They were clear of the railroad agents' fire when they reached the main street. It was then that he heard the shot that knocked William out of the saddle. He couldn't see where the shot had come from, but he pulled his horse to a stop, with not much time to pick up his brother. Wheeling the gray gelding around, Malcolm looked down at his brother, just long enough to know William was dead. He gave the gray his heels again at the same instant the willing horse was cut down by rifle fire from a shopkeeper. When his horse stumbled, Malcolm was thrown from the saddle to land on his back, the wind knocked out of him. The thoughts burned bitter in his mind when he remembered lying helpless in the street, covered by two of the merchants wielding shotguns. Ormond and Pete were already out the end of the street. And had it not been for one lucky shot from the deputy sheriff, he and William would have been with them.

Bringing his thoughts back to the present, he responded to Ormond's question. "Yeah, goin' back to Giddings is my number one priority. A feller I talked to in prison is from Giddings and he told me that deputy's name is Mack Bragg. And I've been seein' that name in my sleep at night." He felt both Ormond and Pete staring at him, so he turned to look at them. "First, I'm gonna need to get acquainted with a six-gun again. I don't wanna take any chances. I wanna be ready when I find that lowdown backshooter." A question that had often come to his mind came to him again at this point. Looking at his brother, he asked, "How come you ain't tellin' me that Mack Bragg is already dead?"

"Because he ain't in Giddings no more." Ormond was quick to defend his lack of retaliation against his brother's killer. "We sure as hell couldn't go near the town for over a year in case somebody recognized us, even if we did have our bandannas tied over our faces." He looked at Pete for confirmation.

"That's a fact, Malcolm," Pete backed him up. "But we did go back into town one night and asked the bartender at the Cotton Gin Saloon if he'd seen that deputy in there lately."

Ormond interrupted. "He told us he weren't a

deputy in Giddings no more. Said he'd moved on, but he didn't know where he mighta lit."

"Damn," Malcolm uttered. This was news he hadn't expected to hear, and he had to take a few moments to decide what to do. The killing of Mack Bragg was something that had to be taken care of. It was almost all he had thought about for the last five years. "An eye for an eye," he recited from his prison Bible sessions. William had not even participated in the actual robbery attempt. He only held the horses for his older brothers and Pete. "We'll go to Giddings, anyway," he decided. "That's the only place we've got to start from. Somebody there might know where Bragg went after he left there. We'll just have to be careful who we talk to and make sure nobody recognizes us." Then it occurred to him. "You two are gonna have to make sure nobody gets a good look at you. I don't have to hide. I've served my sentence."

"Like I just told you," Ormond said, "nobody recognized me and Pete when we came back here. As long as we stay away from the train depot, we ought not have to worry." So, with that decision made, they continued on the road to Bryan, some forty miles away.

After one stop to rest their horses, the three men rode into Bryan and went straight to Riker's Saloon to get a bite to eat as well as to satisfy Malcolm's powerful urge for a drink of whiskey, after doin' without for so long. "Ain't seen you boys in here in a while," the bartender said, talking to Ormond. As far as he could recall, he had never seen Malcolm.

"That's a fact," Ormond replied. "We've been workin' over toward San Antone. You still got a cook workin' here?"

"That I do," the bartender said, "and it's beef stew and biscuits tonight."

"That suits my taste," Pete responded, quickly seconded by the Hazzard brothers.

"Curly!" the bartender yelled. "You got three plates of stew out here." Back to them, he said, "He'll fix you up in a minute or two. You want coffee with that?" Getting three nods from them, he yelled again. "They're wantin' coffee with that." Back to them again, he said, "My name's Sid. I swear, I can't remember your names."

"Good," Malcolm responded. "We was hopin' we'd run into a friend of ours. Mack Bragg, has he been in lately?" He had no particular reason to think Bragg was in Bryan, but he figured he might as well ask.

"Can't say," Sid answered. "If he has, he didn't give his name." When Malcolm nodded, Sid said, "'Course, we ain't the only saloon in town."

After supper, they rode out of town but stopped as soon as they came to a creek. They made camp for the night there, since Malcolm wanted to buy some new clothes before going on to Giddings. With only a little bit of daylight remaining, he used it to practice with the Colt .44 Ormond had brought him. Pete and Ormond stood by watching as Malcolm sought to become closely acquainted with the handgun. After a box of cartridges was emptied into trees at various distances, Malcolm declared himself ready. Accuracy was his goal with his new firearm as opposed to fast-draw expertise, for he had no thoughts toward a fast-draw showdown. He planned to simply catch Bragg by surprise and assassinate him without warning. But it was important to him that Bragg should know who it was that killed him and why.

The next morning, they were at the general merchandise store when it opened for business. Malcolm was soon fitted out with pants and shirt, plus a vest, and a hat. He could not find boots to fit, so he had to continue to wear his prison work shoes and hope to find boots in another town. Feeling more comfortable to be out of prison issue, he started breaking in his new clothes on the fifty-mile trip to Giddings.

Unique among Texas towns for its extra wide streets, Giddings served to impress Malcolm with its obvious growth since he had last been there. When they rode into town late in the afternoon, he saw nearly double the number of shops and businesses. One in particular caught his eye, the newly opened Bank of Lee County. "When we're finished here," he said to Ormond, "I expect we'd do well to stop by the bank and draw out some money. We need to get back in business."

"Glad to hear you say that," Ormond replied, "cause we'll be runnin' outta money."

"We got enough to stay in the hotel and stable the horses for a couple of nights," Malcolm said. "I wanna watch that bank for a day or two, so we can decide what's the best time to open our accounts."

His remarks brought a chuckle from Pete, and Ormond commented. "Looks to me like the best place to watch it is from the Texas Rose Saloon. It's right across the street from the bank."

"Might as well make that our first stop," Malcolm

said. "I could use a little drink to cut the dust." They guided their horses to the Texas Rose and tied them at the rail.

"Howdy, gents," Saul Morris greeted them. "What's your pleasure?" They ordered a shot of rye each and tossed them back before engaging the bartender in conversation. "Don't recall seein' you boys in the Texas Rose before. Just passin' through?"

"That's right," Malcolm answered. "Ain't been here in a long time. Thought it was time to take a look and see how the town is growin'. So, I reckon we'll take a room in the hotel for a couple of nights, so we can take a good look."

"Hell," Saul asked, "why go to the hotel? We got rooms here that are just as nice as the hotel and cheaper, too. And you're a helluva lot closer to the whiskey and the women."

"I don't know," Malcolm replied. "Whaddaya think, boys? Wanna take him up on it?"

"All right with me," Ormond said. Pete just shrugged, not really caring.

"We'll take a look at the rooms," Malcolm said.

"Sadie!" Saul yelled, and in a few minutes, a tired-looking woman of uncertain age stuck her head out the kitchen door. "These fellers wanna take a look at the rooms upstairs."

"Well, tell 'em to go on upstairs and look," Sadie responded. "Ain't nobody in 'em." She paused to take a look at the three. "The empty rooms ain't locked." She took a harder look at Pete. "I can take you up-stairs and show you my room, but it'll cost you three dollars," she added with a sly smile.

"We'll keep that in mind," Malcolm spoke for Pete.

As Sadie suggested, they went upstairs and checked out the rooms and decided they were better than they expected. The price was reasonable enough, so they got their saddlebags and war bags off the horses and carried them upstairs. When Saul was giving them their room keys, Malcolm asked casually, "You know, there is a feller I'd like to see, come to think of it. Mack Bragg used to be a deputy sheriff here. Is he still in town?"

"Nah," Saul replied. "He left here more than four years ago."

"Is that a fact?" Malcolm responded. "Well, that's a shame. Where'd he go?"

"I swear, I don't have no idea," Saul answered. "He just moved on somewhere." He failed to notice the frown on Malcolm's face when he gave Ormond a quick look.

"I need to buy some boots," Malcolm said. "Where's the best place for that?

"Well, there's a couple of stores in town that sell shoes and boots," Saul said. "If it was me, though, I'd take a look in Bill Tilton's saddle and harness shop. He makes a fine pair of boots. I got on a pair of 'em, myself." He pulled up a trouser leg to show him. "'Course, he's got ridin' boots, too, which I reckon is what you're lookin' for."

"Much obliged," Malcolm said. "That's where I'll go in the mornin'. Right now, I expect we'd best get our horses to the stable, then we'll see about some supper."

* * *

After supper in the hotel dining room, the three drifters returned to the Texas Rose to take advantage of whatever pleasures were available. They were encouraged when they discovered that poor, tired old Sadie was not the only woman in the entertainment department. When these ladies compared notes the following morning, they could have easily identified which one of the three had been in prison for five years.

Breakfast in the hotel was followed by a visit to the harness shop to look at Bill Tilton's handmade boots. As luck would have it, he had a pair that were Malcolm's size, and Malcolm tried them on. Ormond and Pete grinned as he walked around Tilton's shop for a couple of minutes to get the feel of the boots. "How much you want for these boots?" Malcolm asked. "'Cause I ain't takin' 'em off." When Tilton told him the asking price, Malcolm came back. "Fifty dollars? Hell, I can buy a good pair of boots at the store for half that price."

"Not like those boots, you can't," Tilton said. "I have to charge for all the work I did on that fancy desert cactus design and the handwork on that leather." He glanced down at the work boots Malcolm had just taken off. In addition to the obviously new clothes, Tilton formed a picture of a newly released prison inmate. He had to wonder if they were planning to take the boots without paying a cent.

"He's right," Ormond remarked. "That really ain't too bad a price. Things have gone up since you've been away."

To Tilton's surprise, Malcolm pulled a roll of bills

out of his pocket and counted out fifty dollars. "I used to know a feller here who was the deputy sheriff, name of Mack Bragg, but he's gone from here now."

"Mack Bragg," Tilton repeated. "He ain't a deputy no more. He's the sheriff in a little town called Buzzard's Bluff." He blurted it out before he thought better of giving out that information.

Malcolm sensed Tilton's sudden wariness. "Yeah, that's right. He wrote me a letter and told me he was in Buzzard's Bluff and said to come see him. Only problem is, I don't have no idea where Buzzard's Bluff is and the son of a gun forgot to tell me that in the letter." He looked over at Ormond and shook his head. "That's just like ol' Mack, ain't it?" Both Ormond and Pete laughed with him. "I swear, I'd like to see him again, but I ain't got time to hunt all over Texas for a little town I never heard of."

"Buzzard's Bluff's on the Navasota River, west of Madisonville," Tilton said, having been paid for the boots and no longer afraid he might be betraying Mack Bragg.

"Well, I'll be . . ." Malcolm started, then just shook his head as he looked at Ormond in disbelief. They must have been no more than half a day's ride from Buzzard's Bluff when they left Huntsville. He knew Pete and Ormond were thinking the same thing.

Outside the saddle and harness shop, they stood on the side of the street and discussed their situation. Frustrated at first to think they had traveled this far south of Buzzard's Bluff, Malcolm soon saw the positive aspects of the mistake. "We had to come here to find out where that son of a gun was, so it was worth it for that. But we also found a prime-lookin' bank that's just waitin' for us to call. And it's far enough away from where we're headin' to discourage any posse they raise to come after us. After the way the railroad treated us here, the bank oughta be willin' to make it worth our while." He almost laughed when he thought of Warden Wheeler and what he would think of his model prisoner now. *Everything's working out to make sure Mack Bragg is a dead man,* he thought. "Yes, sir," he boasted, "we had to come down here to find Mack Bragg."

"That's right," Pete said, "and we had to come down here to get them fancy boots you got on." That brought a laugh from all three.

"Let's go back to the Texas Rose and set in them chairs out front, so we can watch the goings-on at that bank," Malcolm said.

The rest of the morning and a part of the afternoon was spent watching the activity at the bank. Satisfied with the peaceful setting of the town, they decided to strike the bank that afternoon. They settled on where they would tie the horses for the best possible route of escape, remembering the rifle fire from one of the stores that ended William's life. Malcolm and Ormond would enter the bank, Pete would stand with the horses and provide cover fire when the brothers came out of the bank. "Let one of them do-gooder storekeepers stick his head out this time. He's gonna get a little surprise," Malcolm declared.

CHAPTER 2

"One of these mornings I'm gonna come in here and find my stove cold and no coffee ready," Annie Grey remarked to the big man seated at the kitchen table, holding a cup of coffee between his hands. "And when I do, I'm gonna come roust you outta the bed for sure."

"It's the only way I can be sure I get a decent cup of coffee to start the day," Ben Savage joked. "Besides, I have to make sure you get cranked up proper." The good-natured bantering between the cook and her employer didn't vary much day after day. The very first morning Ben had awakened in the saloon he had inherited from his old Ranger friend, Jim Vickers, found him wide awake at five-thirty. His long years of waking up before sunup, while on the trail of some wanted individual, had ingrained the habit in his mind. It had now become a ritual that he looked forward to each morning. First, Annie would arrive at six, or a little before, and he usually had the fire going in her stove and a fresh pot of coffee made. Then about the time she had her stove hot enough to bake biscuits, her husband, Johnny, showed up for breakfast. It would be closer to seven when Ben's partner in the business, Rachel Baskin, would join the morning meeting. It would be later, still, before Tiny Davis, the bartender, and Clarice and Ruby showed up.

There wasn't much to discuss at the Lost Coyote on this Sunday morning. Things were pretty peaceful in the little town of Buzzard's Bluff and had been for quite some time. The only thing new to discuss was the first worship service of the new Methodist Church, scheduled for this day. The early arrivals at Annie Grey's breakfast table were unaware of the occasion until Rachel appeared in the kitchen and reminded them. "I'm thinking about attending the town's first church service," she announced. "I think it would be nice to try to show a little welcome to Reverend Gillespie and his wife. Anybody wanna go with me?" She concentrated her gaze on Ben's face. The broad smile on her face was wicked enough to give away the reaction she anticipated.

"I was just thinkin' about that, myself," he japed. "And I'm mighty pleased to know you're goin' to represent the Coyote. But I'm afraid I'll have to stay and watch the saloon. Our hired help is liable to steal us blind if both owners are away. If you need somebody to escort you, I expect Tuck Tucker will be showin' up here for breakfast in a little while. I'll bet Tuck would like to go with you—give him a chance to check on the preacher's knowledge of the scripture." He couldn't hide the smile a picture of the fiery little red-headed gnome brought to mind, but when he looked up at Annie, he saw a deep frown on her face. "What's the matter, Annie, does it bother you if I'm japin' about the church? I apologize, if it does."

"No," she shook her head and spooned out some scrambled eggs on Rachel's plate. "Your silly gabbing don't bother me none. I just feel like something ain't right." Her remark caused Rachel to give her a close look, wondering if Annie was having another one of her "bad feelings." It was a topic often discussed between Ben and Rachel. And while they both agreed it was just coincidence that Annie's feelings of dread were most often followed by some threat of danger, still it was hard to explain. Annie never claimed any special warnings, herself, and would most likely deny any such notion others might have of her.

If you put any stock in what Tuck Tucker had to say about the energetic little woman, you might agree that she's as normal as night following day, maybe just touched in the head a little. "But, hell," Tuck would declare, "who of us ain't, one way or another?"

Rachel's curiosity about Annie's uneasy feelings was quickly forgotten when Tuck and Henry Barnes came in. They were usual breakfast customers, both men single. Henry, owner of the stable, asked Rachel if she still wanted him to hitch up her buggy this morning. "You said you was gonna need it this mornin'," Henry said. "But I didn't know if you wanted it this early or not."

"I'm gonna need it," she told him, "but not till a little later. I'm gonna go to church this morning, and church doesn't start till eleven."

"That's right," Henry remarked. "Reverend Gillespie is openin' his doors this mornin'. I'll have your rig hitched up and ready to go." He looked around the table then, grinning. "Maybe I oughta hitch up a wagon, instead, and you could haul a whole load of sinners with you."

Ham Greeley arrived just in time to hear Henry's remark. "I don't know about that," he said, "I built that church buildin' to handle ordinary sinners. Preacher Gillespie didn't tell me to build it strong enough to hold up under the strain you people would put on it."

"He's got a point there," Ben said. "Better just hitch up the buggy. I'll come get it when Rachel's ready to go."

"Why, thank you, partner, I'd appreciate that," Rachel said to him. The cheerful banter continued with no further thought of Annie's uneasy feeling.

About ten-thirty, Ben walked up the street to the stable to get Rachel's buggy. He pulled it around behind the saloon and tied it to the back step. Annie kept her horse back of the saloon, and Ben was taking a look at the little sorrel to see what kind of shape it was in when Rachel came out the back door. "Well, now don't you look nice," he remarked. "You'll represent the Lost Coyote well."

"Thank you, sir," she responded with a little curtsy. "I don't know if the proper ladies might think I'm representing the devil, though. They might not let me in."

"You might remind them that jealousy is a sin they might wanna think about," Ben replied.

"While I'm all hitched up, I might take a little ride after church," she said. "It's been so long since I've driven this horse, I'm afraid she mighta forgotten what she's supposed to do."

Ben understood why she said it. Her drive to the church was only to the south end of the main street. Ham Greeley and his two helpers had built the church on a piece of land directly across the road from Dr. John Tatum's house and office. "If you want me to, I'll saddle Cousin and ride along with you after church, if you're thinkin' about takin' a long ride."

"Thanks for the offer, but I doubt I'll go far enough to bother saddling your horse." She paused, then continued, "If I go at all." She appreciated his concern for her safety, but things had been so peaceful in Buzzard's Bluff, she didn't think it necessary.

He was sincere in his offer to escort her but glad she didn't accept. Cousin needed some exercise, but he didn't want to be hampered by the slow pace of Rachel's buggy. He assisted her when she climbed up in her buggy, then he stood back and watched her drive away.

She drove the little mare between the saloon and Tuck Tucker's harness shop, out to the street, and turned right toward the south. Passing their competitor, the Golden Rail Saloon, she saw no activity there. The only sign of life on a Sunday morning was the drunk slumped over in a chair out front, a typical sight. Approaching the hotel, which was the last building before reaching the new church, she met three riders coming into town. They weren't anyone she had seen before and obviously not cowhands by their dress. She avoided meeting their stares as they blatantly looked her over, and Annie's look of dread immediately popped back into her mind. Hopefully, they were heading to the Golden Rail, where most of the drifters and outlaws still congregated.

"That's a right pretty little woman drivin' that buggy all by herself," Pete Russell commented as he turned around in the saddle to continue ogling Rachel. "She's turnin' up that path to the church."

Ormond chuckled. "Maybe we oughta stop there, Malcolm, and you could do some of that preachin' you got so good at in prison."

"Yeah," Pete said, "and we could make 'em think their prayers had been answered, if we was to throw in some of the bank's money when they passed the plate."

"I think the bank would druther have us spend that money on whiskey and women, instead of on them pitiful church folks," Malcolm commented. He unconsciously took a glance behind him as if to make sure there was still no sign of a posse. This, in spite of the fact they had run their horses almost to death to ensure there was no possibility of being overtaken. It had been a good score. They rode away from Giddings with over twenty-two thousand dollars. It had been necessary to shoot the bank manager when he attempted to resist, but it served to inspire the tellers to gather up the money as quickly as they could empty the drawers. So now, they were going to have to wait for their horses to rest before settling with Mack Bragg. It always paid to have a good horse under you and it was almost certain they would need a fast departure when the business with the sheriff was done. After talking it over with Ormond and Pete, Malcolm made the decision. "We'll take the horses to that stable up at the end of the street, so they can get watered and fed, and load 'em up again when we're ready to take care of Mack Bragg. That'll give us time to spot Bragg and figure out the best way to take him down, so we don't run into no trouble gettin' the hell outta here."

They continued along the street, holding their weary horses to a slow walk, all three men with their eyes locked on the sheriff's office and jail as they approached it. Ready to shoot in the event he might suddenly recognize them from the attempted train robbery, they believed it highly unlikely since they had been wearing masks. Remembering how fast it had all blown up around them, they knew they could not recognize Bragg if they saw him. He would have to be identified to be sure. For that reason, Malcolm, halfway wished the sheriff would come walking out of his office as they passed by.

"The Golden Rail," Ormond announced when they rode by. "Maybe we could stop in there while we're waitin' for our horses to rest up."

"There's another'n up ahead," Pete said. "That sounds like the place for you, Ormond, the Lost Coyote."

"We'll take care of the horses before we even think about the saloons," Malcolm reminded them. "And if you two think we rode all the way back here to spend our money in a saloon, then I'll be better off huntin' Bragg down by myself."

"Don't get your underdrawers all in a tangle, brother," Ormond reacted. "Me and Pete know what we're here for." He looked over at Pete. "We ain't gonna get drunk. Right, Pete?"

"Right," Pete replied. "We'll take care of Bragg, then we'll go somewhere else and get drunk." He pushed on ahead of them and headed for the stable.

Henry Barnes watched the three riders from the hayloft until they headed toward his barn before he went down the ladder to the barn floor. As they pulled up to the door, he walked out to meet them. "Howdy, fellers, you lookin' to board them horses?"

"That's a fact," Malcolm answered. "They're plum wore out, and we've got a long way to go yet. So, we need to rest 'em up good, water and feed 'em."

"How long you thinkin' about leavin' 'em here?"

"Like I just said," Malcolm replied, "we're in a hurry to get somewhere, so we might leave 'em all night, but if they get rested up enough, we might not stay tonight."

That seemed a little odd to Henry, so he said as much. "I'm always glad to charge you for takin' care of your horses. But no longer'n you boys are talkin' about stayin' in town, looks like you'd ride about half a mile down the creek where there's good grass and let 'em graze there while they're restin'. That way, it wouldn't cost you nothin'."

Malcolm forced a patient smile. "Well, you see, it's like this. We've been ridin' for days, so we're ready to have ourselves a good meal and a couple of drinks. We've got some things on them packhorses that we don't wanna lose. So it's worth it to us to pay you to watch our packs and our horses, so we don't have to. We've got the money to pay for havin' 'em right handy here, instead of half a mile down the creek and one of us havin' to watch 'em."

"Oh," Henry replied. "Well, I reckon that does make sense. I'll take care of 'em."

"Good," Malcolm said. "We'll help you unsaddle 'em, then we're gonna go find somethin' to eat. Where's a good place to buy some dinner?"

"Ordinarily, I'd say the Lost Coyote, right next door. But today's Sunday, and Annie don't cook dinner on Sundays. But you can always get a good meal at the hotel in the dinin' room."

"That sounds more to my likin'," Pete said.

Henry looked at his pocket watch. "They oughta be open for dinner now. It's right at noon."

"What about that other saloon between the Lost Coyote and the hotel?" Malcolm asked. "Have they got a cook on Sunday?" He was set on having a couple of drinks before he ate. And he was also considering the fact that the Golden Rail was closer to the jail.

"Yeah, they've got a cook. The food ain't as good as the hotel's, but you can get somethin' to eat there."

"We'll take a look," Malcolm decided. "I want a drink of likker, whether we eat there or not." They thanked Henry and started walking back toward the Golden Rail down the street.

"It must be Sunday," Lacy James exclaimed. "Ben Savage is here for the noon meal."

"Howdy, Lacy," Ben greeted her patiently, long accustomed to her usual teasing. "You know it would hurt Annie's feelin's if I ate dinner here every day. Besides, I don't have to pay for it at the Coyote." He started to unbuckle his gun belt as usual, but decided to leave it on, drew his six-gun, and placed it on the table provided for that purpose.

Lacy laughed. "I guess that is a strong point to consider, but you're not remembering the classy company you get here at the River House Hotel."

"Well, now, that is a fact I'd forgotten about. Where is Cindy, anyway?" He pretended to look around the room for Lacy's young waitress.

Lacy threw her head back and chuckled. "Cindy," she called out then and a few seconds later, the young lady stuck her head out the kitchen door. "You've got a customer out here."

"Afternoon, Ben," she greeted him. "Coffee?" She asked, knowing it unnecessary. He always wanted coffee. He confirmed it with a nod. "Be right back," she said and popped back into the kitchen.

He indulged in a couple of minutes more small talk with Lacy until Cindy reappeared, carrying a cup of coffee for him. "Today you've got two choices for your Sunday dinner," she said, "roast beef or fried ham."

"There you go," Lacy commented, still teasing. "At the River House Dining Room, you get two choices."

Ben grinned at her. "You get two choices at the Coyote," he said. "Eat what Annie cooks, or don't eat what Annie cooks." It was good for a hearty chortle out of Lacy before she left him to seat another customer. He told Cindy he'd take the roast beef. "I had ham for breakfast." She left to get his food and he turned his attention to the cup of hot coffee. It was only for a few moments, however, before he became aware of the conversation between Lacy and the customer at the door. *A stranger,* he thought, *and Lacy's having to explain the "no guns" rule in the dining room.*

He would have been more interested had he been able to understand what they were saying.

"No, ma'am," Pete Russell said, "I think I'll just keep my gun on. I feel right nekkid without it. Who's the big feller settin' in the back, there? Is that the sheriff?" Pete had never gotten even a glimpse of the man who shot William Hazzard.

"No," Lacy answered. "That's Ben Savage. He owns the Lost Coyote. I'm afraid you're gonna have to leave that gun on the table, if you want us to serve you," she insisted.

"Lady, I ain't takin' my gun off. I don't give a damn about your rules." He was thinking that Malcolm and Ormond would be there before he finished eating and he knew they would have a good laugh at his expense, if he let this woman take his gun. "I got two friends comin' behind me and they ain't gonna take their guns off, neither, so that's that."

"I'm afraid we can't serve you and your friends, if you're gonna insist on wearing firearms in this dining room. Look around you, no one else is wearing a firearm, are they?"

The tone of the discussion at the door became a little more tense and louder, to the point where it attracted Ben's attention. He heard Pete's next question for Lacy. "What are you gonna do about it, if I don't take my gun off, throw me out?"

Ever the sassy one, even with someone of obvious self-assurance, Lacy answered. "Well, we'll seat you outside the door where you won't likely shoot any of our sensible customers. We won't serve you any food or coffee. Then when it's time to close, we'll lock the door and clean up the dining room and say goodnight to you when we all go home."

"You got a right sassy mouth on you, ain't you, bitch?" Pete growled.

"Yes, I guess I have," she responded. "You're not the first to let me know that. Right now, this sassy mouth is telling you we refuse to serve you. So, you and your guns can go on down to the Golden Rail with the rest of your crowd. They sell food. It ain't as good as ours, but they'll let you wear your guns while you're eating it."

Knowing he had to help her, Ben laid his napkin beside his plate and got up. He walked unhurriedly toward the door. About to come back at Lacy, Pete paused when he saw Ben approaching. He dropped his hand to rest on the handle of his .44 and turned to face Ben. "What the hell do you want?" Pete demanded.

"Couldn't help overhearin' the conversation between you and the lady," Ben said. "It's plain to see you're new in town, so I thought I could give you some help. I'll walk outside with you and show you the place where you can eat with your gun and nobody will bother you."

"If I wanted to hear anything outta you, I'da told you, so you'd best get your ass back to that table before I put another airhole in your head." He closed his hand around the handle of his .44.

"I figured you were too shy to ask for help in findin' your kind of eatin' place," Ben said as he clamped down on Pete's hand, trapping it on the holstered gun. With his other hand, he grabbed the back of

Pete's coat and started walking him toward the door. Quick to assist, Lacy opened the door and held it for him. With her free hand, she picked his six-gun off the table beside the door and slipped it into his empty holster as he passed by her. Ben nodded to her in response. Overpowered by the bigger man, Pete had no choice but to stumble ahead of him until they were outside the building and he was released. Flustered and mad as hell, he spun around to find himself staring at the Colt six-gun in Ben's hand, leveled at his belly. With his gun not halfway out of his holster at that point, he wisely released it to let it drop back in.

"This ain't none of your business," was all Pete could think of to say at that moment.

With no desire to see this confrontation develop into anything further than it already had, Ben made an attempt to defuse it. "I know how you feel. I objected to leavin' my gun on the table when I first started eatin' here, but I got used to it. A lot of the local citizens eat here with their families, so they want 'em to feel safe." He pointed to the Golden Rail up the street. "You'd be more satisfied at the Golden Rail." He paused while Pete was making up his mind what to do. "I'm just tryin' to lend a helpin' hand to a stranger, that's all." Ben said.

After a few more moments, Pete made an effort to save face. "This wasn't none of your business to stick your nose in. But you're lucky I'm in a good mood and I'd already decided I didn't wanna eat in there, nohow. But I didn't like her snotty attitude. I'll let this business between you and me drop, and I'll try that Golden Rail."

"It takes a big man to do that. I know the town of Buzzard's Bluff appreciates it." He stood there watching Pete as he turned and walked up the street. When he was satisfied the stranger was not going to turn around, he went back inside to find Lacy standing by the window. "He said you had a snotty attitude," he japed and started to remove his pistol.

"Keep it," she said. "He might come back." He raised his eyebrows in surprise as he dropped the weapon back in his holster. "Thanks, Ben," she said.

CHAPTER 3

"Thought you was in a big hurry to eat," Ormond Hazzard said when Pete walked back into the Golden Rail.

"I was," Pete replied, "but I ran into a little bit of trouble in that damn dinin' room."

"What kinda trouble?" Malcolm asked at once, having already warned his brother and Pete not to do anything that might tip anybody off that they were gunning for the sheriff.

"I know what you said," Pete assured him at once. "It didn't have nothin' to do with the sheriff. I got into it with the woman that runs the dinin' room and some big jasper that was eatin' there." He went on to explain the altercation with Ben Savage.

Mickey Dupree, the bartender, called out to ask if Pete wanted a drink. When Pete said he did, Mickey brought it over to him, then remained to listen to Pete's accounting of his confrontation with Lacy James. He chuckled when Pete told them what Lacy had said, then he commented. "She's a sassy little bitch, all right. She won't let nobody eat there till they park their guns on the table. I don't know why you just don't eat here. Peggy's got some kinda stew cooked up. I tried it and it ain't bad." Getting back to Pete's story then he asked, "You say some feller stepped in to argue with you? Who was it? Freeman Brown, the feller that owns the hotel?"

"No," Pete answered. "The woman said he owned the saloon up the street." He didn't go into the part of the argument where he was hustled out the door by the nape of his neck and faced a drawn .44 in the street.

"Big feller?" Mickey asked, Pete nodded. "That was Ben Savage. He owns the Lost Coyote in partnership with a woman, Rachel Baskin. He was a Texas Ranger before he got that saloon and he's been known to have a fast hand with a six-gun. Back when Estelle Dalton decided to sell the Golden Rail, she offered it to Savage and Rachel Baskin, but they decided they didn't want it. So that's how her manager, Wilson Bishop, wound up with it."

"It's a good thing you decided to let it go and come on back here," Malcolm said. "We sure as hell didn't come to town lookin' for trouble." He gave him a stern look to remind him. "We've been talkin' to Mickey, here, about Buzzard's Bluff. He says it's a right peaceful little town. I told him they must have a good sheriff."

"That's a fact," Mickey interrupted. "And we ain't always been on good terms with him here at the Golden Rail, on account of we get some rough customers from time to time. But I have to say he's tryin' to do his job. He ain't no friend of the Golden

Rail, but he don't hassle us any more'n he does the Lost Coyote."

"Give us some of that stew you've been braggin' about," Ormond said. He didn't see any point in going to the hotel when there was food right there.

"Me, too," Malcolm said and looked at Pete only to get a shrug in reply. "Make it three." He waited for Mickey to yell the order out for Peggy to hear in the kitchen before he continued his conversation with him. "I'd like to meet this sheriff of yours," Malcolm started. "What's his hole card?" When Mickey looked confused by the question, Malcolm asked, "What's his thing? Fast draw? Strong and tough as nails, what?"

Mickey shrugged. "I don't know. He's tough enough, I reckon. I ain't ever seen him draw against anybody. He just works hard at the job. If I had to say, I'd bet against him, if he ever had to come up against Ben Savage." He shrugged again. "But I don't reckon that'll ever happen. Him and Savage are friends."

When a couple of cowhands came in the saloon, causing Mickey to return to the bar, Ormond was inspired to comment. "After we settle with the sheriff, it'd be kind of interestin' to see if this Ben Savage feller has all the starch in him that Mickey thinks he has, wouldn't it?"

"Might at that," Malcolm responded. "Sounds like we'd own the whole town if we got rid of both of 'em, don't it? Whaddaya think, Pete? You saw Ben Savage. Think you could take him in a fair fight?"

Concerned that Malcolm might try to stage a fast-draw competition between him and Savage, Pete decided to be honest. "I don't know. I couldn't say." He thought back at how quickly the big man had his gun on him when he turned around to face him. "Ormond's faster'n me. He might take him."

His answer caused Malcolm to nod thoughtfully. "Well, we all know I'm a little rusty. Maybe we better just shoot the son of a gun in the back, if he causes us any trouble."

"That's always the safest," Ormond said with a chuckle. "First, we've gotta find the sheriff. Looks like we're gonna have to go to the damn jailhouse to find him." He looked toward the bar. "Hey, Mickey, where's the sheriff? Don't he ever take a walk around town?"

"I'm damned if I know," Mickey answered. "You usually see him around town, keepin' an eye on things." He turned to a scruffy-looking man, sitting alone at a table, eating a bowl of Peggy's stew. "Hey, Stump, where's the sheriff?"

Stump Jones, who served as general handyman for the owner of the Golden Rail, Wilson Bishop, looked up from his bowl only long enough to answer, "Gone to church."

"Gone to church?" Ormond asked and looked at Malcolm and whispered, "He musta got a feelin' somebody was comin' after him."

"I forgot about that," Mickey answered him. "There's a new preacher in town and a new church. If you came into town on the south end, you passed right by it. Today's the first service in the church. I expect there's a lotta folks goin' to hear the preachin' today that ain't ever goin' back for seconds." He chuckled in appreciation of his own wit.

"Maybe we oughta go to the church," Ormond joked. "Give the preacher somethin' to preach about."

Hearing his comment, Mickey said, "You're too late. I expect the service is about over by now."

"I reckon you're right," Malcolm remarked. "I'll tell you what, boys, it's a fine Sunday mornin'. Why don't we take this bottle out on the front porch and watch the town folks comin' back from church?" When Ormond said he'd just as soon sit inside at the table, Malcolm gave him a sly look and commented softly, "Maybe we'll see if somebody goes in the sheriff's office."

"Oh," Ormond replied, "that's a good idea. Why don't we do that?" He picked up the bottle and followed Malcolm out the door. There were four chairs on the short porch of the saloon. So they pulled three of them on one side of the front door, close enough to pass the bottle back and forth without anyone having to get up. It wasn't long before some people came into town. They were only a few, since most of the merchants didn't open their shops on Sunday. "Lookee yonder," Ormond said. "There's that little filly drivin' the buggy." There was a man on horseback keeping pace with the buggy and talking to the woman as they came up from the south end of the street. When they reached the jail, just short of the Golden Rail, the rider broke away from the buggy and reined his horse to a stop at the sheriff's office.

"Uh-oh," Malcolm grunted and sat up straight in his chair, straining to get a good look at the man. "It's him! It's the sheriff!" he exclaimed when the man took out his keys and unlocked the office door. "That's Mack Bragg, the devil that shot William down," he growled, the knuckles of his fingers white as a result of the strain of his clenched fists. The urge to take a shot at him was overpowering as he unlocked the door, his back turned toward them.

Sensing Malcolm's tension, Ormond cautioned. "Too bad we ain't got a rifle handy. It's a little too far to be sure of with a pistol."

"Yeah, it's too far," Malcolm agreed and reminded himself that he wanted Bragg to know who killed him and why. "I want him to know." He got up from his chair.

"Now?" Pete blurted.

"As good a time as any," Malcolm replied.

"Hold on a minute!" Ormond exclaimed. "Let's make sure we don't set ourselves up in a turkey shoot, where we'd be the turkeys. It's broad daylight, and we ain't got our horses ready to go. They ain't hardly had as much time to rest as they need. Every jasper in town might be takin' shots at us. It'd be just like it was in Giddings when he shot William."

Malcolm cooled down enough to hear what his brother was telling him. Still, he was not willing to pass up the chance to take his vengeance now, while Bragg was in his office. Seeing his indecision, Ormond insisted, "We have to be ready to ride like hell as soon as we kill him. Damn it, I wanna be sure I'm alive after we take care of him." Malcolm nodded rapidly while biting his lower lip in his frustration, knowing Ormond was right. It turned out to be a moot point, anyway, for while they discussed it, Bragg came out of his office, climbed on his horse, and rode past them on his way toward the stable.

"Damn!" Malcolm swore, afraid they might not get another chance like the one just missed. His next thought was to go to the stable and corner Bragg there, but even if they were able to do the job there in the stable, there would be the time factor involved in packing up the two packhorses and saddling their mounts before they could get away.

Pete got up from his chair and walked to the end of the narrow porch to watch Bragg ride up the street. "He ain't goin' to the stable," he suddenly announced. "He's goin' in that other saloon up the street."

"Howdy, Sheriff," Tiny Davis called out from behind the bar when Mack walked into the Lost Coyote. "What's your pleasure?"

"Nothin' right now, Tiny, I'm fixin' to go down to the hotel to dinner. I just got back from church. Thought I'd be one of the ones to welcome Ronald Gillespie and his wife, Marva, to our little town. He laid down a powerful sermon. It was a little too long to suit me, though. I was sittin' next to Rachel, and we thought Gillespie was gonna starve us to death before he finally let ol' Satan loose. I was afraid for a while he was gonna preach us right through dinnertime at the hotel. We still got time, though, so I was gonna take my horse to the stable. Then I thought I'd ask Rachel if she was gonna go eat and I'd walk her to the hotel." He looked over at Ben, standing at the end of the bar. "How 'bout you, Ben? You wanna go get some dinner?"

"Nope," Ben replied. "I just got back from there. Rachel's in the office. I'll get her for you." He left Mack to pass the time of day with Tiny. In a couple of minutes, he returned with Rachel right behind him.

"I'm surprised you didn't stop at the hotel when

we were down at that end of the street," Rachel said. "You said you were starving."

"So did you. That's why I stopped to see if you'd like an escort to the hotel," Bragg said.

"Well, I appreciate the offer," she responded, "but I'm just gonna make myself some coffee and biscuits and call that dinner. You're welcome to join me for that, if you like."

"I reckon not," Bragg replied. "Thanks for the offer, but after Reverend Gillespie's sermon this mornin', I'm gonna need some meat and beans." He turned to leave just as the three strangers Rachel had seen earlier walked in the door.

As a matter of habit, Ben took an extra-long look at the three, especially interested when he recognized Pete Russell as the man he had escorted out of the dining room less than an hour earlier. *This looks like trouble,* he thought.

Bragg, on the other hand, was concentrating on something to fill his stomach, so he gave the three strangers a wide berth and started to walk around them, heading for the door. Malcolm stepped in front of him, however. "Say, ain't you the sheriff?"

"That's right, I'm Sheriff Bragg. What can I do for you?"

Malcolm found himself face-to-face with the man he had sworn to kill and all the previous talk he had just had with Ormond and Pete about being smart in his revenge left his mind blank. The only thing in his mind now was the fact that he was looking his brother's killer in the eye. He could feel a slight twitching in the fingers of his right hand and the tensing of the muscles in his arm. Puzzled by the strange behavior of the man staring blankly at him, Mack Bragg started to step around him when Malcolm found his voice. "Five years ago, you shot my brother down." That was all that was said before he made his move.

Watching closely, ever since the three suspicious-looking strangers walked into the saloon, only Ben Savage noticed the slight tensing in Malcolm Hazzard's arm and Ben's six-gun was already out when Malcolm pulled his pistol. The muzzle never cleared his holster before he was struck in the chest by Ben's first shot, followed by his second to the gut. The shots ignited a chaotic exchange of gunshots. As Malcolm collapsed to the floor, both Ormond and Pete drew their weapons and fired wildly as Mack dived behind a table, his gun in hand now and firing in the direction of Ormond and Pete. Another shot from Ben clipped Pete's shoulder as he and Ormond backed out the door, firing as fast as they could.

Concerned now with the safety of his people, Ben looked around at the toppled tables where the few customers who were in at that time of day had taken cover when the bullets were flying. "Rachel!" he called out.

"Over here!" He heard the muffled voice behind the bar. After a quick look at the door to make sure they were gone, he looked over behind the bar where he found Rachel shoved up under the bar behind Tiny, who was protecting her with his huge body. Seeing they were all right, he called out, "Mack?"

"Yeah, I'm okay," Mack answered from behind a table, "just shook up a little bit. I ain't lyin', I sure as hell didn't see that comin'." He got up from the table and looked down at the body. "I ain't ever seen the man before."

"You don't know who he is?" Ben asked.

"No, I don't . . ." He started, then stopped as he put it all together in his mind. "Wait, he said I killed his brother five years ago. Five years ago, I was a deputy sheriff in Giddings, Texas, when four men tried to hold up the train in the station. I wasn't at the station, but I threw a couple of shots at them when they made a run for it through the center of town. One of 'em hit this fellow's brother and this one got his horse shot out from under him. The railroad men captured him. His name's Malcolm Hazzard."

Ben looked down at the body and commented, "He musta just got outta prison, by the look of those new clothes he's wearin." He looked up at Bragg then. "Instead of standin' here gawkin' at him, I expect you wanna get after the other two. I'll give you a hand."

"I appreciate it," Bragg said, then paused when he looked at his hand to discover blood running out of his shirtsleeve. "I think I'm shot." He looked up at Ben in disbelief. "I think I'm shot," he repeated.

"You sure are," Rachel said and hurried over to help. There was a hole in the sleeve of his coat, just over his elbow. "Take your coat off," she instructed him. Then she turned to the two women standing there gawking at the bloody shirtsleeve when his coat was off. "Clarice, go get a pan of water and some cloth." Clarice, the older of the two saloon girls, went at once to do her bidding. Back to Bragg then, she asked, "You didn't even know you were shot?"

"No, I sure didn't," he answered. "It all happened so fast, with bullets flyin' all around me. I reckon when I dived over behind that table, I was too excited to know what hit me, between knockin' the table over and takin' a bullet. I'm startin' to feel it now." He stared at the crease in his upper arm after Rachel rolled his sleeve up over it. "I'd best get after those two."

"Not till I stop that bleeding," Rachel insisted. She took one of the cloths Clarice brought and soaked it in the pan of water. "Sorry we don't have time to heat the water," she said as she cleaned most of the blood away. It continued to bleed, so she wrapped the wound nice and tight. "Maybe that'll hold you till you can see Doc Tatum."

Bragg, with Ben close behind him, headed for the door, almost colliding with Tuck Tucker, who had heard the shooting. "Two fellers ran toward the stable!" Tuck blurted. "I ran back to my shop to fetch my shotgun!" When they immediately started running toward the stable, he followed.

They were met at the stable door by Henry Barnes, who was still somewhat shaken by the events of the last few minutes. "They're gone!" Henry exclaimed. "Saddled up, threw some stuff on one packhorse and took off. Rode out the north road." His report was for the sheriff, but his eyes were on Ben. "You're too late to catch 'em."

"It's my fault," Bragg said. "We lost too much time fussin' with my wound."

"Probably a good idea to stop that bleedin'," Ben commented. "You thinkin' about roundin' up a posse to go after 'em?"

"If you are, I'll ride with ya," Tuck volunteered.

"I know you would," Bragg said, accustomed to the

gnome-like little man's show of bravado. "I don't know that it would be worth it. I don't think those two will ever be back to Buzzard's Bluff. And we got the man who tried to kill me." He turned to look at Ben. "I've got you to thank for that. I reckon I owe you for that. He took me completely by surprise." Back to Henry again, he asked, "They on fresh horses?" Henry said they were. "Not much sense in even tryin' to round up a posse to go after 'em."

"I expect you're right," Ben agreed. "I don't think they'll be back." It was his honest opinion. He didn't expect to see them making another attempt on Bragg's life. He looked at Henry, who still seemed to be shaken up about it. "You said they took fresh horses, right?"

Henry nodded but hesitated before answering. "One of 'em was your dun."

Henry's simple statement delivered a blow to Ben's mind. "They took Cousin?" He demanded. The thought was almost staggering. "They took my horse?" He asked again. "How the hell did you let that happen?"

Henry shrank back against the stable door, afraid the big man was going to explode. "I couldn't do nothin' to stop 'em, Ben. They held a gun on me the whole time while they took their pick of the horses in the corral. They was desperate. One of 'em was shot and they didn't even take time to try to fix him up. I was afraid they was gonna shoot me. They took your horse and Cecil Howard's black Morgan and one of the packhorses they brought with 'em."

I wish to hell we hadn't taken time to take care of Mack's wound, Ben thought. *We might have gotten here soon enough to stop them.* Everything changed with Henry's confession. Satisfied before to let the two would-be assassins run, since he foresaw no additional harm for the town, there was no choice in the matter now. Stealing Cousin was the same to him as the kidnapping of a member of his family. "I'm gonna need a horse," he said to Henry. "And I mean a good horse."

"Take my red roan," Henry offered. "He's a good horse for a man your size, and he won't let you down." He shook his head slowly. "I reckon that's the least I can do. I'm sorry about this, Ben."

Angry at him moments before, Ben realized he had no right to be. "It ain't your fault, Henry. You didn't have any choice in the matter. I 'preciate the use of your horse. I'll treat him just the same as I treat Cousin. Did they take my saddle?"

"No, they took their saddles," Henry answered.

"Well, I guess that's good," Ben remarked. "At least my fanny will feel at home. I'm gonna go back to the Coyote and get some things I'll need. Then I'll be right back here for the horse."

"He'll be ready," Henry promised, "saddled and waitin'."

Mack Bragg and Tuck Tucker were silent witnesses to the conversation just exchanged between Ben and Henry. Finally, Bragg asked, "You gonna want some help to go after those two?"

"No, I spent twelve years trailin' no-good saddle trash like these two without any help. I'd best go alone. Thanks for the offer, but you have to take care of the town of Buzzard's Bluff. And I don't know how long this is gonna take."

Since Ben appeared to be quite firm in his preference to ride alone, Tuck felt confident that if he volunteered, his help would also be refused, so he spoke up. "I can close my shop up and go with you to hunt those jaspers down. By Ned, we'll run 'em to ground in no time."

Even in this moment of concern for Cousin, Ben couldn't help being amused by the typical boastful talk from the red-headed little man. "You're probably right, Tuck, but you'd be more useful in town, since the sheriff is wounded. And these two jaspers might double back on me and come back here. I figured you'd be willin', though." Out of the corner of his eye, he caught Bragg shaking his head. "All right, time's a-wastin'," he said to Henry. "I'll be back for your horse in a few minutes."

When they returned to the Lost Coyote, they found Merle Baker had already arrived to take care of the body. "This fellow was carrying a big roll of money, Mack," he said to the sheriff. "I'll bet he's wanted somewhere."

"I wouldn't be surprised," Bragg replied. "I'll look through my files and see if I've got any paper on him and his two friends."

Ben went straight through the barroom and into the back hall to his room. Rachel paused long enough to remind Bragg, "You need to go see Doc Tatum and let him take a look at that wound. I know it doesn't look too bad, but you don't want to get it infected." She followed Ben through the back door then.

When she found the door to his room open, she stood in the doorway and rapped on the wall. "I had a feeling," she said when he turned around, his saddlebags in one hand and his rifle in the other. "You and Mack going after those two?"

"No, just me," he answered and started looking

around for his war bag. When he spotted it on the floor beside the bed, he laid the rifle on the bed and picked up the bag. Thinking to change the subject, he said, "You never took that buggy ride you were gonna take after church. If you had, you wouldn't have had to crawl under the bar to keep from gettin' shot."

She ignored his effort to sidetrack her and continued to lecture him. "Ben, you know you're no longer in the Rangers. That's Mack's job to go after outlaws. Your business is here in Buzzard's Bluff. Let the sheriff handle the sheriff's business."

"The sheriff's place is here to protect the town, so that's what he's gonna do. You don't understand, Rachel. Those bastards took my horse. I don't give a damn about puttin' those two in jail. I'm goin' after my horse." He gave her a grin. "I've known Cousin longer'n I've known you and everybody else here in the Coyote. If it was one of you, I'd go after you, too." He paused to grin again. "At least, I'd think about it. If it was Tuck, I'd just let him talk his way out of it." He threw his saddlebags over his shoulder and picked up his war bag in one hand and his rifle in the other. When he walked through the door, he said, "Lock the door for me, will you? And by the way, according to Captain Randolph Mitchell, I am still an official Texas Ranger on special assignment."

"Well, if you go out there and get yourself killed, don't come back here looking for sympathy," she said before she thought it through.

"I expect, if that happens, I can guarantee you I won't come back here lookin' for sympathy."

"Damn it, you know what I meant," she responded. "You be careful. I've gotten used to having you around."

She followed him back up the hall to the saloon. "And Annie's gonna wanna know why there's no fire in her stove in the morning."

"Maybe you could handle that for me tomorrow," he joked, as he went in the door.

Seeing him carrying his gear, Tuck declared, "I'll kinda keep an eye on things till you get back."

"'Preciate it, Tuck. I know Rachel does, too," Ben said.

"How long you gonna be gone?" Tuck asked.

"Till I catch up with my horse, I reckon," Ben answered and went out the front door to the street.

When he got back to the stable, Henry had his horse saddled and had put the packsaddle on the other horse. Since he figured enough time had already been wasted, that was all that was said before Ben climbed up into the saddle and loped out along the road after Cousin's abductors.

CHAPTER 4

The first decision he was required to make came up less than a quarter of a mile out of town, when he reached the fork that turned off toward Waco, which was about seventy miles northwest of Buzzard's Bluff. Although he figured the fork toward Waco was more than likely the road they took, he pulled the roan up to make sure. The trail that continued on straight north only led to a couple of small ranches and would not likely be their objective. When he reined the roan to a stop, he found it unnecessary to dismount, for he could plainly see the tracks confirming his assumption. So, he gave the roan a touch of his heels and they were off at an easy lope.

The tracks he followed were the only new ones on the road, and from the spacing of them, he could see the horses were being pushed hard. The thought of the two outlaws overworking Cousin was weighing heavily on his mind, and he was hampered by his reluctance to overwork Henry's red roan. So, there was no thought of overtaking the two outlaws. They would have to stop sometime to rest the horses. He was just hoping he was not too far behind them to catch them when they stopped. He continued on, holding the roan to a pace he could maintain for a long time.

After riding for what he figured to be close to twenty-five miles, during which he crossed several streams that would have been suitable to rest the horses, he became more and more worried about Cousin. Still, the tracks he followed never veered from the wagon road. Finally, he made the decision to stop when he came to a small stream, feeling he had pushed the roan far enough. "It'll just take us a little longer, Red," he addressed the horse, "but as long as they leave tracks, we'll catch 'em."

During his twelve years in the law enforcement business, he had learned to have patience when on the trail of an outlaw. But this was the first time he had been on a mission to rescue his horse, and he was having a great deal of trouble trying to be patient. On other occasions, he would most likely have used the opportunity to build a little fire and make himself a cup of coffee. This time, there was no desire to do so—he just sat and waited until the horses appeared to be rested enough to continue. Then he was back in the saddle.

He had never ridden the Waco trail before, never had any occasion to since his arrival in Buzzard's Bluff. For that reason, he was surprised to come to a healthy creek with a cabin and several outbuildings perched on the bank approximately ten miles past the spot where he had rested his horses. It was the first place the tracks he followed left the road. Evidently, the two men he chased were more familiar with the territory than he was. He speculated that they might have had this cabin in mind all along and pushed the horses hard to reach it before stopping. He was struck with a feeling of caution. Maybe there was a reason they came to this place, which he could now see was some sort of trading post. When he came to a path leading from the road to the cabin, he stopped to look it over before approaching it. There were no horses at the hitching rail in front of the porch. And even had there been, he knew the two he followed had come and gone. For he could see their tracks coming back up the path to return to the road. He decided to take the time to stop briefly in case he might learn something that would help his cause.

He was halfway down the path before he noticed a woman sitting in a rocking chair on one side of the narrow porch. She had been hidden from his sight by what looked like a mulberry bush in front of the porch. Smoking a corncob pipe, she casually watched him as he approached. "Evenin'," he called out as he pulled up by the rail.

"Evenin'," she returned and he realized she was not a young woman. "I reckon you'd be chasin' them two fellers that was here a while ago."

"I might be at that," he replied.

"One of 'em was gunshot," she said. "Was you the one that shot him?"

"I don't know. Two or three of us shot at him. I don't know whose shot was the one that hit him."

She paused to knock the ashes from her pipe. "They come here so's I could doctor his shoulder. I cut the bullet outta his shoulder and give him a poultice to put on it. What are you chasin' 'em for? Are you a lawman?"

"I'm chasin' 'em 'cause they stole my horse," Ben answered.

She considered that for a moment before calling out. "Cletus! He said they stole his horse."

A grizzled old man stepped out on the porch from where he had been standing just inside the door. He was holding a shotgun. "Is that a fact?" he asked. "Which one of them horses was yours?"

"The dun," Ben answered. "He goes by the name of Cousin, and he's the reason I wanna catch up with those two. They also attempted to kill the sheriff in Buzzard's Bluff and that's almost as bad as stealin' my horse."

"Mack Bragg?" Cletus asked.

"That's right," Ben replied. "They wounded him, but he ain't hurt bad. How big a head start have they got on me?"

Cletus ignored his question, still holding his shotgun at the ready. "They said there might be a crazy gunman after 'em. Said he kilt one of 'em's brother and now he's after them."

"I reckon I'm the crazy gunman," Ben declared, reached in his pocket and pulled out his badge. "I'm a Texas Ranger, and they're right, you gotta be crazy to be a Ranger."

"They left that Ranger part out," Cletus said and propped his shotgun against the wall. "They left here a little over an hour ago. They were here long enough for Jenny to doctor that one feller's shoulder and rest their horses." He paused, then said, "Reckon I shoulda said they rested your horse."

"I don't reckon they did any talkin' about where they were headin'," Ben said.

"Not directly to me," Cletus said, "but I heard 'em a couple of times sayin' somethin' to each other about goin to church." When Ben questioned that, Cletus looked at his wife and asked, "You heard 'em sayin' somethin' about goin' to church when they was gettin' on their horses, didn't you? Goin' to church in Waco, wasn't it?"

"I don't recollect for sure," Jenny answered. "Maybe it was more like they was goin' *to* the church."

Ben figured that highly unlikely and just figured it was the weakness of two old minds. They weren't much help, but at least they were able to point him to Waco. Their little store looked to be in petty shabby condition, and he felt the urge to give them a little help, since they seemed willing to help him. "When I left Buzzard's Bluff, I didn't take time to get some supplies I might be needin' before I get home again. You got any coffee beans and maybe some flour? And I'm gonna need some salt."

"Yes, sir, I can fix you up with all them things. And I can grind them coffee beans for you," Cletus said. By the time Ben was ready to go, he had run up a nice little order for them. When he turned the red roan back up the path, both Cletus and Jenny were telling him to come back to see them next time he was up that way.

If he could trust Cletus and Jenny's memories, he could now assume Ormond and Pete were on this road because they intended to go to Waco, instead of just running in any direction. The part about the church was hard to believe, however. He figured the two men must have talked about going someplace that the old couple mistook for "church." It was still about thirty-five miles to Waco, but it wasn't the first time he had tracked men solely on their hoofprints on a common road to keep him on track. If they led him straight into the town of Waco, there would be too many tracks to determine which were theirs. His job was going to become a door-to-door search and depend a large part on blind luck. It had been quite some time, but the last time he had been to Waco, it was already a sizable town. At that time, he was sure there was more than one church there, but he wasn't concerned with counting churches at the time.

It was not long before he had to admit darkness was setting in and he should bed his horses down for the night. He relieved the horses of their burdens and hobbled them in a good grazing area. "Might as well eat something, myself, since it's been a while since that big Sunday dinner at the hotel." He looked through the sacks he had gotten at Cletus's store. After setting his little coffeepot on a hastily built fire, he took a look in the sack of flour he had just purchased. Thinking he might make his version of pan biscuits to go with his bacon, he continued staring at it when it appeared the flour was moving. Even as dark as it now was, he knew full well what caused that quivering, he reached in with his fingers and stirred it up, agitating the residents within. "I swear," he muttered, "it's a wonder ol' Cletus didn't charge me for the meat." He decided he didn't want to bother sifting all the weevils out, so he rolled the bag back up and left them undisturbed. Then he got some hardtack out of his packs to have with his bacon and coffee. Sleep wasn't long in coming.

When still about ten miles short of Waco, the tracks led off the road by a busy stream bordered by a line of oak trees. When he followed them, he found a campsite where a fire had been built. It was obvious the two outlaws were no longer worried about being chased, if they stopped to rest their horses when Waco was only ten more miles. "I reckon I should do the same for you, Red," he said to the roan as he stepped down from the saddle. Just to make sure he had found their camp, he checked the ashes and found them still warm.

By the time he reached Waco, his earlier presumption proved to be accurate even before he entered the town itself. For Ormond and Pete's tracks were soon lost in the many tracks of horses, oxen, and wagon wheels entering the busy town on the west bank of the Brazos River. Some years back, the leading citizens of Waco organized a program to build the first bridge across the Brazos, and completion of the bridge brought new prosperity to the town. Settlers moving west could now cross the river in Waco, many of them remaining in the area. The town continued to grow, and the last time Ben had been in town, there were two stables, one on each end of town. Depending on a blind search and dumb luck, he decided to check with the stables first on the chance his two outlaws decided to board their horses. If they were as well fixed for cash as their recently departed partner had been, they might well decide to do so. With that in mind, he pulled the roan to a stop at the first stable he came to.

"How do?" Thomas Holms greeted him when he stepped down. Then waited for Ben to state his business.

Ben decided he might get a lot more cooperation from the honest folk in town if he made use of his status as a ranger. So he showed Holms his badge and said, "I'm hopin' you can give me a little information on two outlaws I'm trailin'." Thomas looked receptive, so Ben continued. "The men I'm after should have hit town earlier today. They're ridin' a dun and a black Morgan. One of the men has his arm in a sling."

Holms shook his head. "No, sir, they didn't stop here. I ain't had nobody stop in here since about noon, and I reckon I sure as hell woulda remembered those two."

"So I ain't likely to find two horses like those two in your stable if I was to take a look?"

"You're sure as hell welcome to take a look. I've got a couple of dun horses, but I don't have a Morgan in here right now," Holms said.

Ben felt sure the man was telling him the truth. "I'll take your word for it. I 'preciate your help. If somebody like that shows up, I'd appreciate it if you'd let the sheriff know." He climbed back up into the saddle and headed toward the other stable.

Looking at the horses tied up at the stores and saloons he passed, he saw no sign of the ones he sought. Near the middle of the main street, he came to the sheriff's office. He rode on past, but he thought it a wise move to alert the sheriff in his capacity as a

Texas Ranger and let him know what had brought him to Waco. The sheriff could be a source of information on where he should look for the fugitives. With that thought in mind, he reached in his pocket, pulled out his badge again, and pinned it on his vest.

When he reached the other stable, he didn't see anyone around, so he dismounted and walked over to the corral and looked at the horses. There was no sign of Cousin, so he went into the stable to see if there were any in the stalls. "Somethin' I can do for you?" He turned around to find the owner standing in the alleyway behind him.

"Yes, sir," Ben answered and pulled his coat aside to reveal his badge. "I'm Ben Savage, Texas Ranger." Then he told him the same thing he had told Thomas Holms on the other end of town and received the same response.

"No, sir, I'm sorry I can't help you, Savage. My name's Bob Graham. I'd surely help you if I could, but there ain't been nobody here like them two."

"Much obliged, Mr. Graham. I might be back to board my horses, but I don't know for sure right now." He left the stable then and went back to the sheriff's office.

Walt Murphy took a serious look at the big man tying his horse at the hitching rail in front of his office. A stranger, Walt was certain he had never seen him before. He walked outside to meet him. "Howdy. What can I do for you?"

"Howdy," Ben returned. "Are you the sheriff?"

"I am. Walt Murphy, what can I do for you?" he asked again.

"Ben Savage, Walt," he answered. "I'm a Texas Ranger,

F-Company, outta Austin. I trailed two men to Waco. They're wanted for attempted murder and horse thievin' in Buzzard's Bluff. I just thought I'd check with you first before I started looking for 'em here. And I'd appreciate any help you might wanna give me, since I don't know your town that well."

Walt extended his hand. "I'll be glad to help you any way I can. Give me a description of these two. Maybe I've already seen 'em." After Ben gave him their descriptions, the sheriff said, "Well, I'm sure I haven't seen those two, but you say they just hit town today, right?"

"That's right," Ben replied. "And I've got reason to believe they might be carryin' a good bit of money. At least the one shot in Buzzard's Bluff was, and I wouldn't be surprised if a notice came out on three men involved in a robbery somewhere. My point is, they've got money to spend, so where in Waco would an outlaw likely go to spend that money?"

"I expect the first place I'd look, if I was you, would be in the Reservation." Seeing the puzzled expression on Ben's face, Walt explained. "That's a section of town where most of the prostitution and dance halls are. It's a regular red-light district, but we keep a pretty good eye on it, so it don't get too outta hand."

"The Reservation, huh?" Ben replied. "Sounds like the place to start, all right. Where is it?"

Sheriff Murphy told him where the Reservation was and the most likely saloons to check on. "I'd start with the Hog's Breath Saloon. That's the biggest and the one that attracts the most customers. Brady John's the owner's name. I'll take a look around this part of town for you." When Ben started to leave, Walt asked one more question. "If you're ridin' outta Austin, how'd you get onto these jaspers so quick?"

"I'm based in Buzzard's Bluff," Ben told him, "and I got on their tails so quick because that dun geldin' one of 'em's ridin' belongs to me. The son of a gun stole my horse outta the stable when they made a run for it."

Walt couldn't help a chuckle upon hearing that. "I reckon you are anxious to catch up with 'em. If you wanna go ahead and take a little tour of the Reservation, I'll talk to some of the spots they coulda landed in on this part of town. I'll see if my deputy's seen anything when he gets back."

"'Preciate it, Sheriff," Ben responded. He was glad to get his help. He untied the roan and headed to the Reservation, his packhorse following along behind.

Walt Murphy stood in front of his office and watched until Ben turned at the corner of the street, then he walked over to the railroad depot and went in the telegraph office. "Hey, Floyd, I need to have you wire the Ranger headquarters, F-Company, in Austin. I need some information on a fellow as soon as I can get it." He had some doubts as to why the Rangers would station a man in the little town of Buzzard's Bluff, so he dictated a telegram to inquire about a Ranger, Ben Savage. "And, Floyd, as soon as you get an answer, send somebody to find me."

"Will do, Sheriff, but I don't know how long that'll be."

Walt walked back to his office then, thinking about the big man claiming to be a Texas Ranger. "Maybe he'll run into Peewee," he said aloud and laughed when he pictured it.

CHAPTER 5

The hitching rail was fairly crowded at the Hog's Breath Saloon. The sheriff was right when he said it would be easy to find. There was a big picture of a hog's head painted over the door. Before tying his horses at the rail, however, Ben took a quick look at those already tied there to make sure Cousin wasn't one of them. Then he rode down the street to make sure his horse wasn't in front of any of the other saloons before he returned to the Hog's Breath. He paused to think about it, then decided to pull his rifle out of the saddle sling.

It wasn't hard to guess what the Hog's Breath's main source of business was when he walked inside. The saloon was crowded, but even so, there were four soiled doves sitting around a table right at the front door, while others mingled with the boisterous crowd of men. One of the women at the table looked up at Ben and said, "Hey, sweetie, I've been waitin' for you to come in. You lookin' for some gentle company, or are you a bronc buster?"

He couldn't help thinking about Clarice and Ruby

back at the Lost Coyote. They could surely show these women some class. It struck him as odd then that he never really thought about Ruby and Clarice as whores. "I'm lookin' for two fellows that mighta come by here earlier today. One of 'em's nursin' a shoulder wound, might have his arm in a sling. You see anybody like that?" Even as he was asking the question, he realized he was wasting his time. It struck him then, that if he found the two men he searched for, it would strictly be luck. There were too many places to disappear, too many saloons, too many whorehouses, too many dance halls. When the prostitute answered his question, she confirmed his thoughts.

She looked at one of the other women seated at the table. "He wants to know if we've seen two fellers and one of 'em's wearin' a bandage on his shoulder," she announced, followed by a loud cackle of contempt. Back at Ben then, she said. "Hellfire, sweetie, I've seen a man with his whole head bandaged and another'n with a wooden leg. Both of 'em paid to go upstairs with me. What's your problem? Don't you like girls?" He didn't bother to answer, just turned away and walked toward the bar. Behind him, he heard one of the women say, "Well, ain't he the high-and-mighty one? Maybe he'll talk to Peewee." Her comment was followed by a chorus of chuckles from her three female companions.

Finding a space, he moved up to the bar and waited until the bartender finished pouring drinks for a couple of cowhands and moved down to him. "Whaddaya drinkin'?" the bartender asked.

He was a rather small man with a bald head. Ben figured he might be the man the woman referred to as Peewee. "I could use a shot of whiskey right now," Ben answered. "Rye, if you've got it." The bartender reached for a bottle and poured a shot. "Where would I find Brady John?" Ben asked.

"Whaddaya wanna talk to him about?" the bartender asked.

"Well, I reckon that would be between me and him. I just wanna ask him a question."

"Brady don't like to answer no questions. I answer most of the questions in here. Brady ain't got time to talk to every drifter comin' in here lookin' for a job or a handout."

Ben considered that for a few seconds before responding. The bartender would logically be the one most qualified to know if his two fugitives had come in. "All right," he said. "I'll ask you. Have two men come in the saloon in the last couple of hours, one of 'em with his arm bandaged up?"

"Do you see two men like that in here?" the bartender asked sarcastically.

"No, but I can't see who's upstairs with one of your classy ladies," Ben answered.

"Ain't nobody you're lookin' for upstairs," the bartender said. "I wouldn't tell you if there was."

"What if I told you I'm a Texas Ranger and those men are wanted for attempted murder?"

"Then I damn-sure wouldn't tell you," the bartender declared. "That'll be fifty cents for that rye whiskey."

"The price of whiskey is pretty high in this part of town, ain't it?" Ben asked, expecting to pay a quarter.

"That's the price we charge lawmen who come in here to hassle our customers," the bartender responded defiantly. By this time, much of the conversation at the crowded bar died away when the customers nearby became interested in what was being said between the wiry little bartender and the big stranger.

Aware of that, Ben turned and looked directly at a man farther down the bar who was dressed in a morning coat with vest and tie. He had been in casual conversation with two of the other drinkers before pausing to listen to Ben's questions. "How about you, Mr. John?" Ben asked. "Were you too busy to notice if those men went upstairs?"

He stared at Ben, a wry smile on his face, and asked, "How do you know I'm Brady John?"

"I figured you'd better be when I saw you reach over the bar and pour yourself a drink of whiskey that's priced higher than it oughta be."

"That's just the rye whiskey," John said in defense of his price, for the benefit of the customers close enough to hear. "Rye costs me more. And our policy here at the Hog's Breath is not to give out any information on any of our customers, especially to those who come in here carrying a rifle. So I believe that'll about take care of your business with this saloon." He looked at the bartender then and said, "Buddy, he's a pretty big man, better get Peewee to show this damn lawman to the door."

Upon hearing the order, Buddy grinned, but made no move to leave the bar. Instead, he threw his head back and yelled out, "Peewee!" As if responding to a rehearsed procedure. The customers standing near the bar parted to form an alley. And in a few seconds, the path was virtually filled by one of the biggest men Ben had ever seen. At least, Ben thought he was a man. At the moment, however, he resembled possibly a crossbreed between a bull and an ape. "Peewee." Buddy nodded toward Ben and ordered, "Mr. John said to throw this feller out the door."

This immediately brought a foolish smile to the monster's face, revealing teeth with large gaps between them, and he came at once toward Ben, eager to do his master's bidding. All conversation in the crowded saloon stopped then and the customers pushed forward to watch the fun. *How the hell did it come to this?* Ben thought, as he watched the grinning menace advancing toward him, his hands outstretched as if to grab him by the throat. Trying to decide his best chance to keep from being handled like a sack of potatoes, Ben stood ready, his rifle in both hands. *If he just keeps his hands raised,* he thought moments before Peewee lunged for him. There was no time left for conscious thought after that. His reflexes took over and he dropped into a low crouch to dip under the outstretched arms that left the monster's rib cage unprotected. With all the force he could summon, he jammed his rifle butt into Peewee's ribs.

The huge man doubled over with a loud grunt as the air was forced from his lungs. Still, he tried to reach out for Ben, even with the pain it caused. Given no choice, Ben dodged the outstretched arm and laid the rifle butt hard against Peewee's face as hard as he could swing it. The dazed giant took two more uncertain steps before crashing to the floor before a stunned audience of spectators. Seeing his monster disabled, Brady John pulled his coat aside and reached for the .44 he wore. Before he could pull it, Ben spun around to face him, his six-gun already aimed. Angry now for having been subjected to John's attempt to have him manhandled, he snapped, "Go ahead and pull it! It'll be a pleasure to accommodate you." John immediately released the pistol and held both hands up, palms out.

Ben looked down at the fallen man. Blood was running down the side of his face, and he was heaving as he tried to recover his breath. He almost felt sorry for the beast, but nothing but contempt for the man who would use him as one. With his six-gun in his hand, he backed slowly to the door. When he got to the table where the four prostitutes had been sitting, he found them all standing. As he passed by them on his way to the door, the one who had talked to him before, spoke. "If you ever come back in here again when you ain't lookin' to kick somebody's behind, ask for Deloris. I would dearly love to entertain you."

"I'll keep it in mind," he replied.

Outside, he was met by a young man wearing a badge. "Are you Ben Savage? The young man asked. When Ben said that he was, the young man said, "I'm Deputy Sheriff Wayne Price. Sheriff Murphy told me I might find you here." He motioned toward the door of the saloon. "You run into some trouble in there?"

"Yeah, but nothin' that couldn't be handled.

"I'll go inside and take a quick look," Wayne said. "Walt told me what you were in town for. Let me know if I can help you."

"'Preciate it, Deputy. I'll head back to the jail as soon as I take another look around this street." He climbed back on the roan and rode the length of the street one more time, looking for Cousin and a black

Morgan. When that failed to produce any sign of his horse, he headed back toward the sheriff's office.

Walt Murphy was waiting for him at his office, having gotten an almost immediate reply from the telegram he had sent, as well as a report on Ben's visit to the Hog's Breath from his deputy. Before he could speak, Ben beat him to it. "You coulda told me a helluva lot more about what to expect at the Hog's Breath," he charged. "Was that your special little reception for every law officer that comes to town, or is that reserved for Rangers only?"

"I apologize," Walt said, "but that was the first place to look. Every outlaw that hits town usually heads straight for the Hog's Breath. Wayne will tell you that." He glanced at his deputy and received an affirmative nod. "And to tell you the truth, I thought you looked like you could handle most anything. Wayne told me about your little meetin' with Peewee, so it looks like I was right about that. No hard feelin's?"

"I reckon," Ben allowed reluctantly, still thinking he had rather have done the job on Brady John than the poor dumb beast Brady sicced on him.

"Good," Walt declared. Then, looking at his deputy again, he said, "Wayne, go on back to the Hog's Breath and make sure Brady John ain't gettin' hisself all worked up about the whuppin' Peewee just took." Wayne responded, and once he was out the door, Walt got back to Ben. "Now, I reckon I need to apologize again. To tell you the truth, I wasn't sure I bought your story. I mean, the part about bein' stationed in Buzzard's Bluff. So I wired Austin for confirmation. They got back to me right away, confirmin' everything you told me, plus, they gave me some more news you oughta be interested in hearin'. Three men robbed the Bank of Lee County in Giddings and escaped with over twenty-two thousand dollars. Austin thought we oughta be on the alert, in case they come up this way. And I'm thinkin' the three men you're interested in could be the three that robbed the bank. You said that one you killed was totin' plenty of money."

Walt was right. That was very interesting to Ben, and like him, he considered it possible that Malcolm Hazzard, his brother, and their friend could have very well been the men who robbed that bank. But the important thing, as far as he was concerned, was still the recovery of his horse. And at this point, he was less than optimistic about finding the two men who had stolen Cousin. He pressed Walt for more likely places the pair might show up, but he was sure they would have been sighted by now, if they, in fact, stopped in Waco. "If they're still here," Walt said, "they're camped somewhere outside of town. And if they're totin' all that bank money, campin' out in the bushes ain't likely what they'd do. They'd most likely check in the hotel, so I'll check on that right away. But I expect they might already be on the way to Dallas."

It seemed to Ben that the sheriff was anxious to send him somewhere else to search for the two outlaws. Then he remembered Cletus and Jenny Priest saying the outlaws said something about going to the church. "Where's the church?"

Walt hesitated before answering. "About four miles east of here," he replied. "You've heard about the church, huh? I think people try to make more out of it than what it is. It's kind of a combination saloon and tradin' post. Sometimes it's a hangout for all kinds of drifters, cowhands ridin' the grub line, outlaws on the run, all kinds."

"Why do they call it the church?"

"'Cause that's what it was," Walt said. "A group of religious folks was part of a wagon train headin' west. Some of 'em decided that was good farmland east of Waco, so they stopped right there and built 'em a church. They lasted about three years before somebody brought some smallpox into the community and that eventually killed about half of 'em. And them that could, moved on west. I think the smallpox story keeps most folks away from there, except some men down on their luck." He paused to shake his head. "No, I expect these boys you're lookin' for ain't likely lookin' to hole up in a place like the church. I'm bettin' they're headin' to Dallas."

"How can I find the church?" Ben asked, feeling that was where Ormond and Pete had gone in spite of Walt's downplaying the importance of it.

"Well, I know you saw the bridge across the Brazos when you rode in town. Hell, you can't miss it. Just cross the bridge and follow that road for four miles. It goes right by the church. You'll see it, settin' on a little rise by a creek. Your boys could be there, I reckon, but you might find some other boys on the run. So it ain't the kinda place where you walk in and say, 'Howdy, boys, I'm a Texas Ranger'. It could cost you your life."

Having been a Texas Ranger for twelve years, Ben couldn't understand why he had never heard of such a place. "Why is it allowed to be there? Only four miles from town, how is it possible that no one has informed the Rangers or the Marshal Service?"

"Because they take care of their own. The big boss of it is Reuben Drum. He needs Waco for the stock he sells, and he keeps a pretty tight rein on anybody that uses his church. He's come down hard on a few wild ones who raised hell here in town. It's kind of an arrangement that none of the city council admits knowin' anything about. As long as Reuben doesn't cause trouble for Waco, Waco will look the other way." He paused to give Ben a hard look. "Now I'm tellin' you all this, so you'll know Reuben Drum and his boys ain't folks you wanna fool around with. And if those two fellows you're after really have gone to the church to hide out. Reuben ain't gonna let you come in and arrest 'em. I know what you're thinkin', mount up a company of Rangers and ride in there and clean the place out. You ain't the first one that thinks it's as simple as that. I sat in a meetin' with the mayor and two of the town council when a U.S. marshal came here to investigate the church. What it amounted to was we told the marshal that the church wasn't no trouble at all to the town and we were satisfied to just leave 'em alone. As a matter of fact, it was better for the town to have a place where the drifters could hole up—kept 'em outta town."

Ben sat patiently listening to what he thought was a pretty unlikely story, and he told Walt as much. "I just wanted to tell you how things are at the church," Walt insisted. "You can take it or leave it, but I'd advise you to forget about those two outlaws stoppin' in

Waco. We ain't seen no sign of 'em, and we would have by now."

"I 'preciate what you're tellin' me and maybe it would be best if I was to take your advice and get on the road to Dallas." That was not what he intended to do, not by a long shot. He had no intention to let those two get away with kidnapping Cousin. The possibility that they were connected to the bank robbery in Giddings was secondary. Maybe the story he told him about Reuben Drum and the church was straight up. On the other hand, the sheriff might possibly be in a working arrangement with the outlaw. At any rate, it seemed best not to let Walt know he was going to the church. "Well, I reckon I've about used up this day," he said. "I might as well wait till mornin' to start back. Think I'll leave my horses in the stable tonight and sleep with 'em. I don't wanna lose another horse. I'm ready for a good supper, too. Got any good recommendations?"

"You can't go wrong with Jake's Rib House," Walt said. "Best barbecued ribs in Texas. Jake and his brother Melvin own it and they don't cook but one meal a day—supper. I was thinkin' about eatin' there, myself tonight. Just to show you I'm sorry I didn't warn you about Peewee, I'd like to take supper with you as my guest. Whaddaya say?"

"That sounds like too good an offer to pass up," Ben accepted. "I don't know how long it's been since I've had any good ribs."

"Good," Walt responded. "Which stable are you thinkin' about usin'?" When Ben told him he was figuring on using the one up at that end of town, Walt said,

"Bob Graham, he's a good man. He'll take care of your horses and he won't charge you an arm and a leg. Why don't you go on and take your horses, and when you're done, we'll go to supper. That all right with you?"

"That suits me just fine," Ben replied.

"You decide to leave 'em here with me tonight?" Bob Graham asked when he walked out of his barn just as Ben pulled up before the stable.

"Yep, I thought I would. Sheriff Murphy said you were a good man with horses, and a fair man when it comes to price."

Graham snorted a chuckle. "He did, did he? Well, I reckon I'll have to try to live up to his expectations."

"Right now, I'm just figurin' on bein' in town one night," Ben told him. "I'd like to leave early in the mornin, so I'd like to sleep in the stall with my horses, if you don't charge too much. Any problem with that?"

"Nope, no problem, long as I don't have to feed you extra grain, you're welcome to sleep with 'em. How early are you wantin' to leave in the mornin'. I don't usually open the stable till five o'clock."

"That'll do just fine," Ben said. "I'll leave when you get here. What time are you gonna lock up tonight? I told Sheriff Murphy I'd go to supper with him."

"Jake's Rib House?" Graham asked.

"Matter of fact," Ben answered. "How'd you know that?"

"That's where Walt Murphy always eats. I swear, I believe he's gonna turn into a hog."

"Is the food as good as the sheriff told me it was?" Ben asked.

"Oh, yeah, ain't nothin' wrong with the ribs Jake cooks. If you like ribs, you'll enjoy Jake's." When Ben asked again when he would lock the stable up for the night, Graham replied, "Oh, I'll be here for a good while yet. As long as you don't hit one of the saloons after supper and tie one on, I'll be here till about eight o'clock."

"I don't plan to do any drinkin' tonight, so I'll be back right after supper," Ben assured him. He had a feeling Bob Graham was a man he could trust, so he decided to ask him a question. "You ever hear of a place near here called the church?"

Misunderstanding the question, Graham replied, "Are you wantin' to know where the church is? Which church? There's three of 'em in town."

"No, I ain't talkin' about a real church . . ." Ben started, but that was as far as he got before Graham interrupted him.

"Are you talkin' about that old church about four miles east of town, where an old crook named Reuben Drum runs a saloon and flophouse for drifters?"

"Oh, so you know about that place?"

"Hell, everybody in town knows about the church," Graham replied.

"Talkin' to Sheriff Murphy, I got the idea that there might be some dangerous outlaws there most of the time."

Graham shook his head slowly. "Ain't nobody in town worried about that trash that drifts through the church. And most of us know that ol' Reuben Drum pays Walt Murphy to keep the law from goin' out there and cleanin' those rats outta there. What Drum doesn't know is there ain't a handful of folks in Waco that give a damn if he's runnin' a boardin' house for two-bit outlaws, long as they stay the hell away from town."

After talking with Bob Graham, Ben had an entirely different picture of the church, as well as a more accurate assessment of Sheriff Walt Murphy. It was plain to see why Murphy didn't want him to approach the church. The sheriff's attempts to discourage his snooping around started when he sent him to the Hog's Breath, hoping he would have a confrontation with Peewee. Murphy must have thought that would be enough to discourage him from any further snooping around town. *Might as well go to supper with him, though,* he thought. *Let him think I believe his story—no sense in alienating the law in town. Besides, I like barbecued ribs.*

So, he went back to the jail, and he and Walt went from there to Jake's Rib House. He was not disappointed. The ribs were as good as Walt had claimed. He thanked the sheriff for his hospitality and all the helpful advice he had offered. Walt told him he was always ready to help the ranger service, and to prove it, he volunteered to render another service. "I responded to Austin's wire about the bank robbery. I figured I could handle that for you, since I know those men at the church. Reuben Drum knows I won't stand for no bank robbers hidin' out at the church. I told Austin I'd handle the investigation of the bank robbers and see if the men you've been trackin' are at the church. How's that? Wouldn't that pretty much take care of Austin's problem and yours, too? The main thing you wanna find out is whether or not these two jaspers you've been trailin' are at the church, right? And I can find that out for you. Save you a lotta time, 'cause Drum knows he's in bad trouble if he doesn't shoot straight with me." He didn't wait for Ben's response before continuing. "Tell you what, why don't you stay in town another day and look for any sign of those two you're trackin'? I'll ride out to the church tonight, so I can catch 'em while everybody's there. I'll find out right quick if they are, and if they are, I'll tell you in the mornin', and go with you to arrest 'em."

Ben nodded slowly while thinking to himself, *I wonder if I look as stupid as he evidently thinks I am.* To Walt, he said, "That's askin' a lot for you to take all that time and trouble to help me arrest two men."

"Not at all," Walt insisted. "I can find out in a few minutes if those two men are at the church, and it would take you a helluva lot longer, if you found out at all. Might as well save you the time and trouble."

"I would like to look around in town," Ben told him. "I was gonna ride out to the church in the mornin', though, before I covered the rest of town. If you're sure you wanna do that, it would save me some time."

"I'll be able to let you know first thing in the mornin'," Walt said. "I ain't got nothin' to do in town tonight. Wayne will be here to watch the town, and I'll be back before too much trouble can get started."

"All right, then," Ben said. "I'll have to tell my captain how cooperative you've been." Walt shrugged and gave him a big smile. It didn't take anything more to convince Ben that he was dealing with a sheriff who was as crooked as a snake. What amazed him was the fact that Walt expected him to believe him. No doubt he was thinking about how much of that twenty-two thousand dollars that was stolen from the Giddings bank these two were in possession of. Ben was tempted to ask him if Ormond and Pete were at the church when he dropped in, why would they wait there to be arrested the next day? But he decided to hold such logical questions and agreed, at Walt's suggestion, to meet him for breakfast at the hotel dining room in the morning.

They parted company then, with Walt saying he didn't want to wait any later to make his four-mile ride to the church. Since it was still early, Ben stayed to have one last cup of coffee before retiring to the stable for the night. As he sat there, he replayed his wild day in his mind. He would have been concerned that the men he chased were even now getting farther and farther away, but he was convinced they were at the church. And he intended to confirm that after breakfast the next morning. He shook his head when he thought about Sheriff Walt Murphy. *All I wanted to do was get my damn horse back and go home to Buzzard's Bluff,* he thought. It would have been as simple as that if he was working with an honest sheriff.

"Somebody's comin' up the path from the road," Riley Best called back through the open door of the church. He had not bothered to go any farther than the front steps of the building to answer a call from Mother Nature. And the arrival of a lone man on a horse was not concern enough for him to rush his business. After a few seconds more, he called back again. "It's Walt Murphy." That was enough to generate some interest among those inside, but not enough to stop the card game, or the drinking party two of the men were engaged in with Dora and Pauline. Since it was unusual for the sheriff to call on them this late in the evening, Reuben Drum got up from the table he had been seated at and walked outside to meet him.

"Walt," Reuben greeted the sheriff when he pulled up in front of the church and stepped down from the saddle. "You're out visitin' kinda late, ain'tcha? What's up?"

"Evenin', Reuben," Walt responded. "I thought there's somethin' you might be interested to know, so I thought I'd ride out tonight. I brought a bottle with me to make the talkin' easier."

"Well, in that case, come on in," Reuben invited.

Walt looped his reins around the end of one of the steps. "Riley," he acknowledged as he walked past him and followed Reuben inside. Riley Best had been holed up at the church long enough for Walt to think of him as more or less a permanent resident, along with Reuben's son, Lester. Inside, he received simple nods of greeting from all but two of the current occupants, who in contrast to the others, became wary and nervous. "I see you've got two new faces since I was last out here," Walt noted. "That's the reason I thought I'd best give you a warnin'." The two new faces reacted to his statement with looks of immediate preparation to resist arrest.

"Ain't no need to get nervous, boys," Reuben said.

"Sheriff ain't rode out here tonight to arrest nobody. Ain't that right, Walt?"

"That's a fact," Walt replied. "I came out here to tell you a Texas Ranger hit town today, lookin' for you two fellers. Now, don't go gettin' nervous," he said as Pete and Ormond did just that. "I told him you hadn't showed up in town, and I expected that you didn't stop here 'cause you most likely were tryin' to get to Dallas as fast as you could. No, he don't know about the church," Walt lied in answer to Reuben's question. "And he ain't gonna find out about it from me. There's a notice out from Austin about some outlaws holdin' up a bank in Giddings, and I expect that Ranger's took up a notion it was you two fellers. But I checked with Austin and they said it was three fellers that held up the bank."

Convinced by then that the sheriff was not there to arrest them, Ormond asked, "Why would a Texas Ranger be after me and Pete? Why would he have any idea we had anything to do with a bank holdup?"

"I don't know," Walt answered. "He told me he was trailin' you from Buzzard's Bluff."

"Buzzard's Bluff?" Ormond responded, then hesitated a couple of seconds before blurting, "Ben Savage." He looked at Pete, and Pete nodded slowly in response. Looking back at Walt then, he asked, "Big feller?" Before Walt could reply, Ormond continued. "Ben Savage ain't no Ranger. He used to be one. He owns a saloon in Buzzard's Bluff, now and he shot my brother down. We oughta be the ones chasin' him, not the other way around. Ain't that right, Pete?" Pete said that it was. "It got too hot for us in Buzzard's

Bluff, so we cut out. Ben Savage ain't got no reason to be chasin' us. We sure as hell ain't robbed no bank."

"No need to worry about him," Walt assured Ormond. "I expect he'll be gone from here in the mornin'. I told him you two musta passed right on through town. He took a look around for you. I sent him over to the Reservation, told him if you were in town, you'd most likely be at the Hog's Breath." He paused to shake his head and laugh.

"He run into Peewee?" Riley asked.

"Yeah, he did," Walt answered, "and I can see why you don't want him to catch up with you. He caved Peewee's ribs in and liked to broke his cheekbone, laid ol' Peewee out like an ox shot in the head."

"I reckon we shoulda took care of him before we left Buzzard's Bluff," Ormond said to Pete. "We didn't have no idea he'd come lookin' for us."

"You think we oughta go find him?" Pete asked, thinking that maybe Ormond had lost his mind, but Walt answered him before Ormond could.

"Ain't no need to," Walt told him. "I pretty much sent him on his way to Dallas. I don't want him snoopin' around in my town."

CHAPTER 6

"I was right," Walt Murphy announced when he came into the hotel dining room in the morning to find Ben already sitting at a table there. "Sorry to disappoint you, but they ain't at the church. I didn't really expect 'em to be there. Ol' Drum knows I don't want any bank robbers hidin' out this close to town."

"You want breakfast, Sheriff?" Mary Jane Reynolds asked.

"I sure do, honey," Walt answered and sat down at the table. "What you plannin' on doin' now?" he asked Ben.

"I figured I'd still look around town a little bit before I move on," Ben answered, "maybe look around outside of town to see if I can find a campsite. If I do, I might pick up a trail to follow again."

"Well, good luck to ya," Walt said. "I expect those boys you're chasin' are on their way to Dallas."

"Thanks," Ben said and got up to leave. "And thanks again for your help."

"Glad to help," Walt replied, smiling as he watched the big Ranger walk away.

"You look like you're in a good mood this morning," Mary Jane said as she placed a cup of coffee before him.

"You can say that again, sweetheart," Walt replied. "I feel like it's gonna be a good day." He thought about his visit to Reuben Drum the night just passed. When he had walked into the church, his badge fully on display, several of the men around the long table on the side of the room had paid very little attention when they saw him. Two of them caught his eye at once, however. After he had talked to them about the bank robbery, he asked Reuben who they were. Reuben had told him they were a couple of horse thieves and nothing more. He had to smile when he thought about it, *a couple of horse thieves with probably about fourteen thousand dollars from the bank in Giddings*. That would be about what they were carrying after the three-way split with the third man. "Tell 'em not to worry about it," he had said to Reuben. "There's a Texas Ranger on their trail, but he don't know nothin' about the church." As far as he could tell, Reuben had taken his word for it.

His thoughts were interrupted for a moment when Mary Jane brought his breakfast but were soon back on the money the two outlaws were carrying. Pete Russell and Ormond Hazzard were their names, according to Reuben. The thoughts occupying his mind now were what he was going to do about that money. He could tell Reuben about it, and they could split it. About seven thousand each wasn't a bad payday, but it wasn't as nice as keeping the whole thing for himself. He would have to come up with some story to get Pete and Ormond away from the church. *That shouldn't be too hard,* he thought and smiled again when he thought of the story he had made up for the Ranger. He chuckled before he caught himself, causing Mary Jane to turn toward him and he waved her away. *I hope he gives up pretty soon and heads on out to Dallas or somewhere,* he thought.

Hardly ready to leave Waco, Ben Savage rode across the bridge to the east bank of the Brazos River. He was leading his packhorse because he had no intention of returning to Waco once he finished what he came to do. Ordinarily, he would have intentions to arrest the two outlaws and take them to the Waco jail to be held for transport by a deputy marshal or put on trial there in Waco. It would be simple enough to transport them to Austin on the train, but in this case, he could not trust the sheriff to hold the prisoners. The question of Deputy Wayne Price came to mind and whether or not he could be trusted. Thinking back, he recalled how Walt had sent his deputy back to the Hog's Breath before telling him about the bank money. Wayne might be unaware of the sheriff's arrangement with Drum, and consequently, the sheriff didn't want him to know about the bank money. It was best not to take a chance, so Ben would more likely have to transport them back to Buzzard's Bluff to await a jail wagon from Austin. *First thing,* he reminded himself, *is to capture them.*

He followed the road past several small buildings

and shacks for about a mile before he left all signs of civilization. But the road was well traveled, to judge by the tracks of hoofprints and wagon wheels. He was sure he had traveled nearly four miles when he saw a line of trees that indicated a sizable stream or creek ahead. There, through the trees, he spotted the church. Sitting on a little rise, it was easily seen from the road. A sizeable structure, complete with steeple, but no cross, it had been no doubt situated so it stood like a beacon to those who came to worship. *Too bad,* he thought, *it just calls out to the wicked now.* He decided he was too close to continue on the road, so he turned the roan toward a low line of hills to the north. He continued on that line until he thought he was far enough past the church to cut back to the west to come up behind the church.

He found that by riding along the creek bank, he could get fairly close to the church without being seen. From what he had learned about the notorious hideout, the occupants were not likely to have lookouts posted. When he reached a point about fifty yards from the back of the church, he dismounted and tied his horses in the trees by the creek. He could see no one outside around the church or near the small barn, corral, and outhouse. He made his way closer on foot until he came to a small group of horses grazing near the creek. Anxious now, he moved up closer to the edge of the tree line to get a better look at all the horses. *There!* he thought when he started to count them, for he spotted the dun gelding he searched for. At almost the same instant, the horse raised its head and nickered, its ears pricked and alert. Ben whistled softly and Cousin came to him at once. Cecil Howard's Morgan followed the dun, since it was accustomed to following it now.

The horse came to Ben in the edge of the trees, displaying its excitement at seeing him again. There was a brief reunion between horse and master as Ben hugged Cousin's neck and stroked his face. He was forced to share his affection when the Morgan pushed his nose in for attention as well. The reunion lasted for a few minutes before Ben reminded himself that he had a couple of outlaws to deal with. He paused to count the rest of the horses in an effort to guess how many riders might be inside the building. Fifteen horses were all he could see. Allowing for the fact that one of them was the packhorse Pete and Ormond had taken, that left fourteen. He had no idea how many horses belonged to Reuben Drum and how many were packhorses. He could safely assume there might be as many as eight men inside, in addition to the two he was after. It would be extremely risky for him to attempt any kind of surprise arrest when he wasn't sure how many he would be dealing with. And that was not taking into account if there were women in there who wouldn't hesitate to put a bullet in his back. While he tried to determine what he should do, he decided to get his saddle back on Cousin where it belonged.

Luckily, the two horse thieves had left the bridles on the horses, making Ben's job of handling them a little easier. He led both horses back to the spot where he had left the roan and his packhorse. He tied the Morgan's reins to a tree limb while he went about the business of getting his bridle and saddle off the roan and onto Cousin.

With his major goal accomplished, he felt tempted to turn around and go home and leave the two outlaws to enjoy the bank's money. "Why the hell didn't you buck that son of a gun off, instead of totin' him all the way up here?" he lectured Cousin. Done with wishful thinking, he had to now figure out how to arrest the two he chased without getting shot by however many there were in that church. While he tried to think, his gaze fell on the corral and lingered there for a moment. It occurred to him that the corral was empty with the gate open. They had let all their horses out to graze. It stood to reason that before dark they would drive the horses back in the corral for the night. At that time, they were going to discover that two of the horses were missing. That was going to be his best chance of moving on Pete and Ormond, for they would be more concerned than anyone else, since the missing horses were theirs.

The problem that concerned him now was the time of day. It was still morning, so he was going to have to wait out the day until it was time to put the horses away that evening. There was nothing else to do, so he resigned himself to accept that fact. If he had run them down in a saloon in town, he could have gone in relying on the element of surprise to capture both men. In this case, however, he had to figure every man in there was his enemy and he couldn't cover all of them by himself. His plan to attempt to separate Pete and Ormond from the others was dependent upon a lot of luck, but it was the best he could come up with. So, he moved his horses farther back up the creek to make sure they weren't discovered when the search for the missing horses got underway. With the rest of the day to kill, he took his time to find what he considered to be the best spot to tie them. Then he made his way back closer to the church to pick a spot to wait where he could watch any activity around the building.

As the day dragged by, there was very little activity outside the church. Once in a while, one of the women who resided there would come out the back door and take advantage of the outhouse. He paid more attention whenever a man appeared, usually stopping short of the outhouse before relieving himself. He strived to remember them, hoping to get an accurate count of his potential enemies. He figured, for the length of time he would be waiting, everyone in the church should have to answer nature's call at least once. Occasionally, an older woman, obviously the cook, would come out to the pump to fill a bucket with water, and once she opened the back door to throw a pan of dirty water out. By the end of the day, he had a count of ten men, counting Pete Russell and Ormond Hazzard. One of those, he figured, might be Reuben Drum. He had no way of telling for sure. In addition, he counted three women, including the cook.

There was one more visitor to show up in the middle of the day. This one, Ben recognized right away. "Sheriff Walt Murphy," he murmured softly, as he watched him ride up to the front door of the church. Ben couldn't help admiring the sheriff's horse, a fine-looking buckskin, befitting his position as the sheriff of Waco. He was coming to make sure he hadn't shown up there that morning, Ben figured.

No doubt he assured Pete and Ormond that nobody would know they were there and invited them to stay as long as they wanted. If there was any question about whether or not Walt came with intentions to arrest the two men for bank robbery, it was answered when after about an hour, Walt came back out and rode away. *That means they're staying for a while,* Ben thought. *I'll bet he never mentioned the bank money.*

When the sun finally completed most of its journey across the low hills to the west, he made a quick trip back to the horses and got some jerky out of his saddlebags to tease his stomach with. Back to his lookout spot, he saw two men come out of the church and head toward the horses. *Must be suppertime,* he thought, although his empty stomach had already alerted him to that possibility. *Shouldn't be long now.*

"We got a couple of horses missin'," Slim Dickens reported to Reuben Drum when he came back into the church.

"You sure you counted 'em right?" Drum responded, since Slim wasn't noted for his carefulness.

"Yeah, I'm sure," Slim answered. "Me and Riley rounded 'em up and put 'em in the corral and there's two that ain't there." He looked at Riley for confirmation.

"That's a fact," Riley reported, then looked at Ormond. "All our horses was there, but the two you boys rode in on are missin'. Your packhorse didn't run off with'em, though."

Sitting at the table, working on a bottle of whiskey with Dora and Pauline helping out, Pete Russell and

Ormond Hazzard immediately snapped out of a lazy haze when they realized he was talking about their horses. "What are you talkin' about?" Ormond demanded. "Our horses better not be missin'. They was grazin' right there with the rest of the horses." He looked around frantically as if looking for someone to blame. "What the hell, Reuben? I thought we was safe here."

"Ain't no use to get excited, Ormond," Reuben said. "They musta just wandered off somewhere. They ain't been here long enough to get used to stayin' with our little herd. Don't you expect, Lester?"

"I expect you might be right," Reuben's son, Lester, answered. "They'll most likely wander back to the rest of the horses before dark."

"You sure that crooked sheriff that was in here is on the up-and-up with you?" Pete asked."

"Walt Murphy's been workin' with me for a long time," Reuben assured him. "He may be a lotta things that ain't all good, but he ain't a horse thief. Just give them horses a little time. They'll wander back to the corral."

"I don't know, maybe you're right," Ormond said. It was obvious that nobody else was the least bit concerned about the two missing horses. And while it stood to reason that he and Pete would be the only ones motivated to go and look for them, he was not that enthusiastic about leaving the whiskey and the company of the two women. He looked at Pete and shrugged. "I reckon it ain't nothin' to worry about."

After a while, Pete began to worry a little when the light coming in the windows began to fade rapidly. He looked at Ormond and he could tell right away that Ormond was thinking the same thing he was, so he got up from the table and said he was going to check the corral to see if their horses had wandered back. In a very short time, he returned and reported that there was still no sign of the two horses. "I ain't plannin' to set around this table drinkin' whiskey while my horse is wanderin' up that creek somewhere." He turned to look at his partner. "What about you, Ormond?"

"I'll go with you," Ormond said at once. He was not under any illusion that those stolen horses felt any affinity for either one of them, so they wouldn't be prone to come looking for Pete and him. "We'll borrow a couple of your horses. You can't round up no horses on foot. There ain't no tellin' how far they wandered." He looked directly at Pete when he said it and Pete nodded, for he was thinking along the same lines his partner was. They were both carrying about seventy-five hundred dollars in their saddlebags, their share of the bank money they had split three ways. They needed their horses, but they didn't want to go looking for them while their saddlebags were left there in the church for Reuben and his son to go through.

"Sure," Reuben said, "take any of 'em."

"Any of 'em, but that gray," Lester informed them. "That gray's my horse and don't nobody ride him but me."

"Come on, Pete, let's saddle up a couple of horses and see if we can't find ours," Ormond said.

"Whaddaya need a saddle for?" Riley Best asked. "If it was me, I'd just ride bareback for no farther than you'll be ridin'."

"I don't cotton to ridin' bareback," Ormond said. "I ain't no damn Injun."

"Me, neither," Pete remarked. "You got better control settin' in a saddle. Besides, your horses ain't used to us on their backs. Let's go, Ormond." They walked out of the room that was partitioned off for the saloon, to the back room where they were sleeping. This was where they also had their saddles and saddlebags.

"We'll give you a hand," Lester said and followed them into the back room. Slim and Riley came along as well. The rest of the men remained to work on the whiskey. When they picked up their saddles, Lester was prompted to ask. "Whaddaya takin' your saddlebags for?"

"Oh," Ormond responded and shrugged as if he did it without thinking. "Old habit, I reckon. Pete's the same way. Anyway, a horse don't feel like he's been saddled without the saddlebags. At least, that's the way I was always told."

"Hell," Slim couldn't help remarking, "a horse don't know the difference." He grinned at Riley and asked, "How 'bout all that stuff you had on your packhorse? All that campin' equipment, ain't you gonna take that with you, too?"

"Different folks got different ways, I reckon," Ormond said. "'Stead of wastin' time talkin' about it, lets go find our horses." He picked up his saddle and saddlebags and walked out the back door, heading for the corral. Pete hurried after him before there was any further debate on the subject of saddlebags. There had already been enough discussion to create a strong desire for Reuben's son to see what they might be carrying in them.

The two outlaws picked out a couple of horses, both of which were the property of Reuben Drum. They assured Lester that they would be careful with them as it was beginning to get dark. After talking about the best place to look for the horses, they decided on riding up the creek a short distance, then following it back. Their thinking was that the two horses might have found a place next to the water to wait for morning. Once they were away from the church, they stopped to discuss further options. Still with suspicions about Sheriff Walt Murphy, they thought he might very well have something to do with their missing horses. So they decided, if they didn't find the horses pretty quick, they would just keep on going. They had their money with them and horses and saddles, too. So there was nothing to force them to return to the church.

CHAPTER 7

"We shouldn'ta waited so long before we went after 'em," Ormond complained. "It's gettin' darker every minute. We'll be lucky if we find them horses before daylight."

"Maybe not," Pete replied. "I can't see no reason those horses would wander off like that and not come back. That blame sheriff looked like a horse thief to me. I think that's what happened to our horses. Don't it strike you kinda strange that the two best horses in the bunch was the ones that ain't come home? I'm thinkin' we sure did the right thing when we took our saddlebags with us. If we don't find our horses up this crick pretty soon, I think we'd best keep right on goin'. We got horses. They ain't as good as the ones we lost, but they'll get us to where we can buy better ones—or steal 'em if we run up on somebody's herd."

"That makes sense to me," Ormond responded. "I ain't never felt like I could turn my back on any of that bunch at the church, especially that son of his, and they're all in this business with that sheriff."

They continued following the creek for a few

minutes more before Pete said, "We ain't gonna find them horses on this dark creek. We're just wastin' time before Reuben gets suspicious and they come after us. Let's head on away from here."

"Hold on," Ormond said. "I see 'em." When Pete started craning his head in an effort to see where Ormond was looking, Ormond pointed. "Look yonder on the other side of the crick, back in them trees. They're up in there."

"I don't see nothin'," Pete insisted. "Where?" Ormond kept pointing at a spot where two large trees overhung the creek. Pete stared at the darkness between the two trees for a long moment before he exclaimed, "I see 'em! Least, I saw somethin' move on the other side of those trees. Come on, let's go get 'em."

"Take it slow," Ormond cautioned. "We don't wanna spook 'em and have to chase 'em all over the county."

"Right," Pete replied, "we'll just walk up to 'em nice and easy." They did just that, guiding their horses into the shallow creek to come up downstream of the ones they had spotted. They found the two missing horses standing together and they showed no signs of bolting as Pete and Ormond slowly dismounted and began to walk toward them.

"Easy . . . Easy," Ormond murmured calmly as he and Pete approached the dun and the Morgan. "What tha. . ." He started then. "They ain't runnin' 'cause they're tied to the tree. What tha . . ." He started again.

"One of 'em's saddled!" Pete blurted. "Somethin's goin' on here," he said and started to reach for the .44 at his side.

"Do it and you're dead," Ben warned him. "Get your hands up where I can see 'em, or I'll cut you down where you stand." Then he raised his voice. "Keep your shotgun on 'em, Tuck. If they make a move toward those guns, blast 'em." He took a few steps away from the bushes he had been hiding in to position himself directly behind them, his six-gun in hand. "All right, one at a time, you first, big'un. Very slowly, take your left hand and unbuckle that gun belt and let it drop. Tuck, keep that shotgun on the skinny one. If he makes a move, blow a hole in him." Feeling helplessly trapped, Ormond hesitated before moving to unbuckle his belt. "You're makin' it hard to keep my finger still on this trigger and it's a little touchy as it is," Ben warned.

"I figured you for a yellow-bellied back-shooter when you was here before," Ormond challenged. "Why didn't you call me out face to face when you was here this mornin'?" he asked, trying to stall as long as he could.

Realizing Ormond thought he was Walt Murphy, Ben said, "I thought you might be too fast for me, so I waited till I could bring a little help. "Tuck, if he doesn't drop that belt by the time I count to three, give him a taste of that buckshot. One, two . . ." That was as far as he got before the belt dropped to the ground. "Put your hands behind your back," Ben ordered. Ormond reluctantly obeyed, convinced he would be shot if he didn't. "Watch the other one, Tuck," Ben said as he quickly clamped one of the two pairs of handcuffs he brought with him on Ormond. With thoughts of resistance useless, Pete didn't wait to be told. He unbuckled his gun belt and let it drop to the ground while he strained to peer into the dark bushes on the other side of the horses, trying to make out the man with the shotgun. He flinched slightly when Ben pulled his wounded arm back to handcuff him. With Pete cuffed and on his knees, Ben turned his attention to the bigger man.

He took the coil of rope he always carried on his saddle, fashioned a loop at one end, and threw it over Ormond's head, drawing it tight around his arms. With his arms bound tight against his sides, Ormond could do little to resist being pulled close to a tree and tied there while Ben helped Pete back up on his feet. "You!" Pete gasped when Ben turned him around and he was able to get a look at his captor. "Savage!" He blurted again. "Ormond, it ain't the sheriff! It's that gunslinger that shot Malcolm! Ormond!" He exclaimed again when he didn't answer right away.

"I know it," Ormond answered him. "I can see him." He strained against the rope restraining him as he stared at Ben. "Why are you tailin' us? Ain't you done enough harm to us? You killed my brother. Ain't that enough for you?"

"You stole my horse," Ben answered. "You shouldn't have run off with that dun yonder."

Ben Savage was the last person he expected to see at this particular time. Later on, he had told himself when he and Pete had to run from Buzzard's Bluff, he would return to take his vengeance against the big saloon owner when everything had cooled down. "You're makin' the biggest mistake you ever made in your life, Savage," he warned. "Whaddaya think you're gonna do with us? Take us to the jailhouse?" He hoped that was what Ben intended, since if was unlikely Ben knew of Walt Murphy's partnership with Reuben Drum. "How you gonna take both of us to jail by yourself?"

"What about the jasper with the shotgun, Ormond?" Pete reminded him.

"Pete, you damn idiot, there ain't nobody in the bushes with a shotgun," Ormond said. "He played us for a couple of fools. Ain't that right, Savage? But you've still gotta take us to the jail and that might take some doin'. To start with, you got Pete up on that horse, but I ain't gonna get on my horse. I'm as big as you are, and I ain't gonna get on no horse. You gonna shoot me? 'Cause if you do, you're gonna have half a dozen men comin' outta that church after you. You think about that." He paused briefly to let that soak in, then said, "I'll tell you what. You untie me and get these handcuffs off me and Pete, and we'll let you get on your damn horse and ride outta here and no hard feelins."

"I swear, Ormond," knowing his name now, since Pete called him by it, "that's a mighty considerate offer. Just set you free and you'll just watch me ride away. It'd be even better if I was to set you free and shoot myself, wouldn't it—save you the trouble. Now I was figurin' on helpin' you up on your horse, like I did with your partner. Figured you'd rather sit up on a horse instead of walkin' all the way."

"I ain't walkin' nowhere," Ormond stated flatly, "and that's all there is to it."

"I'm a reasonable man, so if that's your choice, I'm here to accommodate you. You ain't the first man I've arrested that decided he'd rather be dragged by a horse. Tell you the truth, though, I ain't ever had one that didn't change his mind after about half a mile. Draggin' is a little bit harder on the horses, too, but we've got a couple extra, so we can trade off."

Ormond was not sure if Ben was bluffing or not. "Why do you keep talkin' about arrestin' us? You ain't no lawman. You can't arrest nobody."

"Well, that's where you're wrong," Ben told him. He pulled his coat aside and said, "If it ain't too dark for you to see, this is a Texas Ranger badge, and you *are* under arrest. There ain't no doubt about that, for horse stealin', bank robbery, and murder of a bank teller in Giddings. There's also a little matter of attempted murder of the sheriff in Buzzard's Bluff. I'm sure you'll be glad to know he ain't dead. You just nicked him in the arm. I expect we'd best get started. We've got a long way to go."

"It's four miles to Waco," Pete protested. "You ain't really thinkin' about draggin' him all the way to town, are you?"

"No," Ben answered. "We ain't goin' to Waco. I'm plannin' to drag him about seventy miles, back to Buzzard's Bluff. And that's where you'll wait for the marshals to transport you to Austin for trial." Pete stared at him in disbelief. "I'm sorry Ormond is gonna slow us up, but he says he'd rather get dragged that far instead of sittin' in the saddle." The subject of their conversation stood gaping at the two of them discussing his method of transport, as Pete and Ormond were still unable to believe what they were hearing. "Well, we're just wastin' time standin' here jawin'," Ben announced. "Let's get you offa that tree."

He loosened the end of the rope from the limb where he had tied it off, then walked round and round the tree to free Ormond from the trunk. Thinking this was his opportunity to escape and feeling sure Ben didn't want to shoot, because that would bring Reuben and the others, Ormond got set to run. He stood tensed, as each turn of the rope disappeared from around him until, finally, he was free of the tree. With his hands cuffed behind his back, he couldn't remove the one loop still around his arms, but he could run. So, when the last turn of the rope fell away and he was held only by the loop, he didn't hesitate. He took off as fast as he could run toward the berry bushes straight ahead. Ben, expecting just such an attempt, took another quick turn around the tree with the very end of the rope and braced himself. Running for all he was worth, Ormond quickly took all the slack out of the long length of rope. The result was a sudden stop for his upper body while his feet proceeded ahead of him to land him flat on his back. While he tried to recover his breath, Ben was already binding his feet together and tying them securely to his hands. With the length of rope he had left, he tied it to Ormond's saddle.

When he was satisfied that Ormond was securely bound, he said, "Well, boys, I reckon we're ready to start back to Buzzard's Bluff. I'm gonna borrow that rope on your saddle, Pete. I think that's what I heard him call you."

Pete watched him while he rigged up a lead rope that he tied all the reins of the other horses to, then prepared to climb up on Cousin. "I swear," Pete asked, "you ain't really gonna drag him all the way to Buzzard's Bluff, are you?"

"You heard him say that's the way he preferred to

travel," Ben answered. "And one thing I learned ridin' with the Rangers, was to make your prisoner as comfortable as possible. How 'bout you? You comfortable in that saddle?"

Pete didn't answer the question. Instead, he asked, "Who's Tuck, that feller you was talkin' too in the bushes?"

"Tuck?" Ben responded. "He's a fellow who likes to give me a hand whenever he can." It was too dark for Pete to see the smile on Ben's face when he thought about the bandy-legged little keg of dynamite. He'd have to be sure to thank Tuck for his help in capturing the two of them. Up in the saddle then, he looked back at the furious man tied hand and foot on the ground behind him. "It's liable to be a little rough till we get outta these woods, but it'll go a little bit smoother when we get out on the road." With that warning, he gave Cousin a firm nudge, which the horse knew as a signal to jump to a smart pace. Ormond couldn't prevent the bellow that escaped his mouth when his horse followed and jerked him across a tree root.

That was all the sound that came out of the stubborn outlaw's mouth for a few minutes, although the pounding his body was taking could be heard as he was dragged across the rough ground. Ben took a wide circle around the little rise the church was on in case Ormond couldn't keep from yelling. It was Ormand's foolish attempt to show his toughness and determination. Ben was hoping to break his stubborn resistance before riding very far. He had no intention of brutally dragging a man for very long, even a man like Ormond, who disrespected human life. So he was relieved when Ormond finally called it quits. "All right. All right," he yelled shortly after they reached the road below the church. "I'll ride, damn it!"

"What?" Ben yelled back. "What did you say?" He kept the horses moving.

"You win!" Ormond yelled frantically, fearful now that Ben didn't intend to stop. "I'll ride! I'll ride!"

Ben pulled the horses to a stop then. "Well, that sure seems a lot more sensible to me." He dismounted and untied Ormond's feet but left his arms bound to his sides until he had him up in the saddle before freeing them. Once he was settled, Ben took a hard look at Ormond, his clothes torn and little spots of blood showing up through his shirt and trousers. "That's a hard way to travel. I'm gonna tell both of you how it's gonna be from here on out. You don't give me any trouble and I won't give you any. But make no mistake, I will not hesitate to put a bullet in your head, if you give me reason to. I've hauled many an outlaw to court before, so if you try to escape, know this; I will shoot you down. I might as well tell you now, I don't sleep, especially on a ride this short, when we won't stop but one or maybe two nights. My job is to transport the two of you to a holdin' cell in Buzzard's Bluff. The trip will be as easy as you make it. We understand each other?" Neither man answered. "All right, let's move." He nudged Cousin again and looked back over his shoulder. "Sorry about your hat. There wasn't time to stop for it."

He led them back to Waco, but when he crossed the bridge, he turned them to the south to strike the trail he had ridden into the town the day before. His two prisoners rode sullenly along behind him with no recourse but to ride silently, each one thinking of the small fortune riding in their saddlebags. There was no possibility in either man's mind of this journey being completed. There was bound to be an opportunity somewhere between Waco and Buzzard's Bluff when the smug lawman would get careless.

Since he was following a clear wagon track that led to Buzzard's Bluff, Ben continued riding late that night until he decided he had a good lead on anyone who might start out after him. When he came to a little creek that seemed a suitable campsite, he led his prisoners off the road and into a small clearing near the water. "Here's how we're gonna do this," he told them. "Ormond, throw your leg over and I'll keep you from fallin' on your behind. Pete, you just sit right where you are." With his six-gun in hand, he ordered Ormond to walk over to a small tree he pointed out. When Ormond hesitated, obviously weighing his possibilities, Ben fired a shot into the ground between his feet.

Ormond jumped backward in quick reflex. "All right!" He exclaimed, "I'm goin'." He quickly walked over to the tree Ben indicated and stood there.

"You might wanna move around to the other side of the tree, so you'll be facin' the fire when you sit down," Ben suggested and waited until he did so. Then he told him to sit down with his legs on either side of the tree. When he did, Ben quickly tied his feet together. "We'll leave you like that for a while, till I get your partner fixed up." Hearing that, Pete kicked one foot out of the stirrup when the wild thought of jumping off the horse and running struck him. "Keep your gun on him, Tuck," Ben warned.

Pete immediately settled down again without thinking. When he did think about it, he mumbled, "There ain't nobody named Tuck helpin' you."

"Depends on how you look at it," Ben said. "You saw what Ormond just did, so you're gonna do the same thing on that tree." He pointed to another tree about twenty-five feet from the one Ormond straddled. While he got Pete secured to the second tree, he spoke loud enough for both men to hear. "I'll rustle up enough grub to keep us alive till we get to Buzzard's Bluff. I'll free your hands long enough for you to eat. That's always a time when prisoners get an idea about untying their feet and takin' off. So, that's when I'll be watchin' you real close. As long as you both behave, it'll be an easy trip to Buzzard's Bluff. If you give me any trouble, my usual practice is to put a round into your shoulder or leg to hobble you. Just remember, I warned you, if you decide to go that route. You understand?"

"You go to hell," Ormond replied, having somewhat recovered from the ordeal of having been dragged, the worst part of which was his bluff being called. "You'd best keep a sharp eye of us. You still have a debt to pay for killin' my brother." He didn't say it, but in his mind, there was also the matter of settling with Mack Bragg. He had been forced to run from Buzzard's Bluff, but he had every intention of revenging his brother.

"Thanks for the warnin'," Ben responded. "I'll be sure not to take any chances with you." With the two of them sitting snug against a tree, their hands cuffed behind their backs, he felt he could get about the business of taking care of the horses. Then he could build a fire and cook some of the bacon he had left. They should reach Cletus Priest's store in the morning. He could buy supplies there for a little better breakfast for them and give the horses a good rest.

After he fed his prisoners and himself a supper of bacon and coffee, and suffered their complaints about it, he released each of them to take the opportunity to answer nature's call before being locked to the tree all night. "I gotta go, but I can't go while anybody's watchin' me," Ormond complained.

Before Ben could answer, Pete responded. "Since when?" He blurted before thinking. "I remember that time in Houston when you stood out there in the . . ." He stopped before going any further, when it struck him what he was saying. Glancing quickly at Ormond to see the look of painful anger in his face, he said, "That's right, you always was kinda shy about that."

Ben smiled at Ormond and said, "Just pretend I ain't here." After his prisoners relieved themselves, he had them return to their sitting positions at their respective trees. The only difference, their hands cuffed around the tree trunk and their feet untied. He reminded them that he never slept, then he sat down against a tree on the other side of the fire to watch them, his rifle across his lap. Although there was much complaining about having to try to sleep locked to a tree, in time, they both fell asleep from sheer exhaustion. He was not far behind them to slumber, confident that the handcuffs would not fail.

CHAPTER 8

"They coulda gone all the way to Oklahoma lookin' for those horses by now," Lester Drum declared to his father when he walked back into the church. It was the second time he had gone out to the corral to check for any sign of Ormond and Pete, since they supposedly went in search of their missing horses. "I knew damn well they was up to somethin' when they wouldn't go without their saddles and saddlebags. I'll bet they robbed that bank in Giddings that Walt Murphy mentioned. That's why they wouldn't leave their saddlebags here when they went to hunt for them horses."

"I expect you might be right about that," Reuben said. "They weren't takin' no chances on us lookin' in those saddlebags. We're gonna have to talk about that when they come back."

"If they come back," Lester prompted, fully suspicious now.

"But what happened to their horses in the first place?" Slim wondered. "How come their horses was the only ones that wandered off?"

Thoroughly worked up by this time, Lester was working out the plot in his head. "Walt Murphy," he blurted. "He's in it with 'em. Those two horses didn't just happen to wander off from the rest of 'em. I expect Ormond and Pete are slappin' their saddles back on that dun and that Morgan right now, while we're settin' here suckin' our thumbs. They most likely counted out Walt's share of that bank money already."

Reuben was not sure he agreed. "I know that's one way of lookin' at it, Lester. But Walt's been pretty square with me for a long time now."

"There ain't never been a payoff this big before," Lester insisted. "Hell, Pap, it's as plain as the nose on your face." It was all adding up in his mind at this point. "Don't it strike you as kinda strange that he knew those two birds were here at the church before he came over here yesterday? He knew about that bank robbery and he knew they were here."

His father didn't reply for a long few moments while he thought about everything his son had said. When he finally spoke, he said, "I reckon you might be right. I don't know why I didn't see what he was up to." The more he accepted Lester's interpretation of the incident, the angrier he became. "On top of that, he stole two horses from me."

"I'm goin' after that damn snake," Lester declared. "He ain't gettin' away with this." He looked around him for volunteers. Several stepped forward. "Slim, you and Riley, I don't want too many. Let's saddle up." He headed for the door.

"Hold on a minute, Son," Reuben stopped him. "Where are you goin' to look for 'em? We ain't got no idea where they headed when they left here."

"First place I'm gonna look is Sheriff Walt Murphy's office in Waco," Lester answered. "If he ain't there, we'll have to wait till mornin' to find a trail to see which way he left here tonight. He might notta gone back to town, but we'll run him to ground. I'll guarantee you that."

"You be careful," Reuben told him. "And let him tell you his side of it. We've been workin' together for a good while now."

Lester, Slim, and Riley hustled out to the corral to saddle up. With time precious, they didn't waste it, and were soon in the saddle and on the road to Waco and the sheriff's office.

"What tha . . ." Walt Murphy sputtered, startled when the three outlaws from the church suddenly appeared in the doorway of his office. He rushed to the door and took a quick look up and down the street before confronting them. "Lester, what in the hell are you fellers doin' here on this side of town? Does your pa know you boys are in town, on this side of town at that?" His agreement with Reuben was their visits to town would be seldom and only in the Reservation when they did come in.

"I'm thinkin' you oughta be able to guess why we're here," Lester said and walked over to the door to the cell room. "You got anybody in jail?" He asked, "Somebody that ain't really under arrest?"

"Are you drunk?" Walt asked. "What are you talkin' about? No, there ain't nobody in the cells right now. You'd best start makin' sense or you're liable to end up in one of 'em."

"I'm tired of beatin' around the bush with you," Lester said. "Where's Ormond Hazzard and Pete Russell?" As he asked the question, it occurred to him that Walt might not have an arrangement with them. He might have simply killed them and was the sole owner of the bank cash. "Maybe I'd do better askin' you where's the bank money they was carryin in their saddlebags?"

Walt looked at the two men with Lester, their faces questioning him as well. "What the hell are you talkin' about, Lester? Ormond and Pete damn-sure better be at the church. That's where they were the last time I saw 'em. So maybe you'd best tell me where they are."

"You ain't foolin' nobody," Lester came back at him. "How 'bout those two horses?"

"How 'bout what two horses?" Walt asked. The argument went back and forth for several minutes until, finally, Lester related the events that took place earlier, starting with Slim's report of the two missing horses. Walt gradually got a picture of what had really happened, although Lester had not reached that point yet. He paused for a few moments to catch his breath while Lester continued to glare at him accusingly. "I know where the two horses are," he said, his tone calmer now. "I know where Pete and Ormond are, and I know where the money is." This captured their attention right away. "While we're standin' here arguing, they're under arrest and on their way to Buzzard's Bluff." He clenched his teeth together and scowled when he thought about Ben Savage and the way he had played him for a fool. This was the only answer to Pete and Ormond's sudden disappearance. Ben Savage rigged up an ambush and captured them.

After he explained it to the three outlaws from the church, he told them what they must do. "You've got to catch up with Savage before he gets Pete and Ormond to the jailhouse in Buzzard's Bluff. That's all there is to it. If you don't, we'll all lose a share in that money." Lester asked if Walt was going with them, and Walt said, "No, I ain't goin' with you. I can't, not and still be the sheriff of this town. It's up to the three of you to get that money. Whether you set Pete and Ormond free don't matter. Just get the money. Don't waste no more time. Get goin'."

"We shoulda brought a packhorse with some food," Slim said at once.

"They'll be takin' the road that leads to Buzzard's Bluff," Walt replied. "Cletus Priest has a store on that road—you can stop and get you some supplies there. I've got a little coffeepot I don't ever use. You can take that with you, but I want it back." He walked to the door and took a look up and down the street. "Now get on outta here before one of our honest citizens sees you comin' outta my office and starts askin' me who you are."

Up before sunrise the next morning, after a very short night, Ben woke his prisoners and had them on their horses quickly and back on the road to Buzzard's Bluff. Promising them a good breakfast when the horses were ready to rest, he planned that stop to be at Cletus Priest's store.

"I believe you boys know Cletus and Jenny," he said,

as he turned Cousin off the road. They were spotted by Cletus before they reached the cabin.

"Well, I'll be double doggoned," he mumbled, then called out. "Jenny, here comes Ben Savage back and he's got them two fellers with him."

She came out on the porch to see for herself. "I see he ain't wearin' that sling no more," she commented, staring at Pete. "It musta healed up all right."

"Howdy, Ben," Cletus greeted him. "I see you caught up with Mr. Smith and Mr. Jones."

"Howdy, Cletus," Ben returned and tipped his hat in Jenny's direction. "Yep, I found 'em up near Waco, and they've agreed to go back to Buzzard's Bluff with me. I didn't give 'em much supper last night, so I promised 'em I'd give 'em a good breakfast when we got here."

Jenny stepped down from the porch and walked over beside Pete's horse. "How's that arm doin'?" she asked.

"It's comin' along just fine," Pete answered.

"I don't take kindly to liars," she said. "I wouldn'ta bothered doctorin' that arm if I'da knowed you was lyin' about who shot you, it bein' a Texas Ranger and all."

"Yessum," Pete replied contritely. "I'm real sorry about that, but I was afraid you wouldn't doctor my arm if I told you how I got shot."

"Haw," she snorted. "I reckon that's a fact, all right." She turned to Ben then. "Was you talkin' about me cookin' up a breakfast for 'em?"

"Tell you the truth, I didn't figure you did that kinda business," Ben said. "I was just thinkin' I would buy some ham or sowbelly from you, maybe some sugar and apples, if you've got any dried apples."

"We'd be glad to sell you them things, always appreciate the business," she said. "Whaddaya gonna do with them two?"

"I'm plannin' on takin' 'em to Buzzard's Bluff and put 'em in the jail," Ben answered. "Then Sheriff Bragg will hold 'em there till some U.S. marshals pick 'em up and take 'em to Austin for trial."

She appeared to consider that for a few minutes, then she asked, "You expect they'll hang 'em?"

"I don't know," Ben answered. "They tried to kill Mack Bragg, they robbed a bank in Giddings, killed a bank manager . . . and they stole my horse. So I reckon it depends on what the judge and jury think."

"As bad as they are, it seems a shame they can't have one good meal before they're took to jail. That one feller I took care of, he didn't seem so bad. I believe the big one has led him to get mixed up in all them things you say they done. What would you say about me cookin' up a big breakfast for 'em, sausage and taters, biscuits and gravy?"

Ben was surprised. Evidently, Jenny had developed a little soft spot for Pete while she gave him the care he needed. "Well, if you wanted to go to all that trouble, I'd say I'm agreeable on two conditions. One, I'll pay you ten dollars to cook it, and two, I get to have some of it, too." He watched the smile spread across her bony face. "You got to understand, though, these two prisoners are dangerous men. They'll have to be under guard the whole time they're eatin', and in handcuffs while I'm eatin'."

As surprised as Pete and Ormond were by the old lady's compassion for them, her husband was far less compassionate. "Hon, what in the world are you wantin' to cook for the likes of them two for? They ain't nothin' but common outlaws."

"Don't hurt to give a mad dog a bone once in a while, Cletus," she answered. "'Specially when you can make ten dollars doin' it." She cackled gleefully. "Ranger Savage, we've got us a deal. I'd best get started. Good thing I've already got biscuit dough rolled out."

Caught up in her excitement when she heard how much he offered to pay her for the breakfast, Ben said, "I'll tell you what, we'll make it twenty dollars." That served to make Cletus's eyes grow as big as Jenny's. Ben promptly went to Ormond's saddlebags and peeled a twenty-dollar bill from a stack of twenties, courtesy of the Bank of Lee County. He figured it wouldn't make much difference to the bank. It just added to the amount the two outlaws had already spent.

When Jenny hurried to the kitchen, Ben's concerns turned to taking care of the horses, as well as securing his prisoners. When he helped them off the horses, Cletus offered to help. "If you don't particularly want to lock those boys to a tree, you could put 'em in the smokehouse and take the handcuffs off 'em. I built that smokehouse so nobody can get in, and when I put that padlock on the door, can't nobody get out. You take a look at it." Ben did and decided Cletus was right, so his prisoners got a little relief from hugging the trees. Besides that, he thought, there would be very little incentive for escaping at this point, with the promise of the big breakfast coming. "I figure you could use a little time for your horses and have a cup of coffee without havin' to guard those two while Jenny's cookin'.."

That sounded like a workable plan to Ben, so he did as Cletus suggested. Neither Ormond nor Pete gave him any complaints about being locked in the smoke-house. They were glad to have their hands free for a while.

Ben figured the big breakfast Jenny was fixing would cost him time he hadn't figured on, but it might help if Pete and Ormond had full bellies when he left there. Maybe they might be less inspired to escape during the last leg of the journey to Buzzard's Bluff. As he recalled, it was a distance of about thirty-five miles and it was still early in the day, so there was plenty of time left to get home before dark, even if he stopped once more to give the horses a rest. So, while Jenny was cooking, he took the opportunity to spend a little more time checking his horse's condition. He was especially concerned about the condition of the big dun's hooves, and after his inspection, he decided to take Cousin to Jim Bowden for new shoes when he got back to Buzzard's Bluff.

In a short time, Jenny announced that breakfast was ready, so Ben unlocked the smokehouse and told Pete and Ormond to come outside. Jenny was going to serve them at the table in the kitchen, but Ben told her there were too many things in the kitchen to tempt his prisoners to try something desperate. "Better to have them sit down outside on the ground," he told her. "That way, I can watch them while they eat and won't have to worry about them grabbin' a pot or a pan for a weapon. It ain't any hardship on them. It's a lot better than havin' to eat with their legs tied around a tree." So Ben told them to sit down just outside the smokehouse and Jenny placed two plates heaped with food before them while Ben guarded them with his rifle. When they were finished, he let them take a cup of coffee back inside the smokehouse, locked the padlock on the door, and went into the kitchen to eat his breakfast at the table. When he finished, he said, "That was a mighty fine breakfast. Those two in the smokehouse oughta think that breakfast was worth the trip to jail."

"Thank you kindly, sir," Jenny responded with a shallow curtsy. "You certainly paid a fancy price for it."

"Worth every penny," Ben replied and was about to compliment her further when he was interrupted when Cletus stuck his head in the kitchen door.

"We got more company," Cletus announced, "three riders just turned off the road."

"I'd better take a look," Ben said and immediately got to his feet. His initial concern became reality when he looked out the front door. He recognized the riders as three of the men he had seen coming in and out of the church when he was watching it. "This could be trouble," he said to Cletus, "and some I hadn't counted on to land at your door." This had to be Walt Murphy's doing. They must have gone to him. Otherwise why would they immediately head for Buzzard's Bluff? His major priority now was to try to keep Cletus and Jenny out of harm's way.

"You know who they are?" Cletus asked, concerned now as well.

"Yes, I'm afraid I do," Ben answered. "They're friends of those two in your smokehouse and I expect they've come to get 'em. I don't want you and your wife to get involved in this, so I'll meet 'em outside and see if I can keep 'em goin'. The only advantage I have is they've never seen me, even though I know who they are. You and Jenny stay inside, and I'll try to keep them outside." He hurried back to the kitchen to get his unfinished cup of coffee. By the time he got back to the door, the three outlaws were reining their horses to a stop in front of the porch.

Ben walked out on the porch, coffee cup in hand, his left one. "Howdy," he greeted them, as friendly as he could make it sound. "You fellows come down from Waco? I'm headed up that way. How far is it from here?"

Lester Drum looked him up and down before he answered. Looking around him, he saw no horses anywhere. "Is that a fact?" he responded. "It's about thirty-five miles, I reckon. I don't see no horses. You plannin' on walkin'?"

Ben forced a little chuckle and took a little sip of coffee. "Nope. I got a saddle horse and a packhorse down at the creek—givin' 'em a little rest. Where you fellows headin'?" He tried not to look too concerned when Riley and Slim walked their horses a few yards to each side of the store, just to take a look.

"He's right, Lester," Slim said, "there's horses waterin' down the creek a-ways."

"We're tryin' to catch up with some friends of ours," Lester said, answering Ben's question. "We thought we might catch 'em here."

"Three of 'em?" Ben asked. Lester didn't answer

him, but both Slim and Riley nodded in response. "I
passed those fellows a couple of miles south of here.
I expect you'll have to hurry to catch up to 'em." He
thought if he could persuade them to keep going,
he could take his prisoners, leave the road, and go
around them. From the looks of their horses, he
could easily imagine they had been ridden hard.
They would be forced to rest them pretty soon, or
they'd be walking. And he should have no trouble
reaching Buzzard's Bluff before they could catch up.

Lester wasn't sure. He had a suspicious feeling
about the big stranger. He wore a six-gun on his right
hip, but he held his coffee cup in his left hand. That
just struck Lester as odd. He glanced at Cletus, standing in the doorway, saying nothing, but paying close
attention to what was being said. "Is this your store?"
He directed the question at Cletus.

"Yes, sir, it is," Cletus answered. "Can I help you
fellers with somethin'?"

"We're gonna need to get some supplies, ain't we,
Lester?" Slim asked before Lester answered Cletus.

"If what this fellow says is true," Lester answered
him, "we ain't got time to buy supplies." Back to Ben
again, he asked, "You say you met 'em a couple of
miles south of here?"

Ben smiled. "I ain't ever lied to you before, have I?"

Lester couldn't help but smile back at him, but he
said nothing more to Ben. To Cletus, he said, "I'm in
a hurry. You got anything to eat in there that's ready
to go right now?"

"Beef jerky and there might be some biscuits left
over from breakfast," Cletus answered. "We've got
some dried apples. Come on in the store and we'll fix

you up." They climbed down from their saddles and Slim led the way into the store. Ben followed along behind Lester.

Jenny left the front window, where she had been listening to the conversation, and went into the kitchen at once. She met them back at the front counter of the store with the half-filled tray of biscuits. She placed it on the counter, then moved down to the end of the counter while Cletus broke out the beef jerky. "You wanna wait around for Jenny to make a pot of coffee?" Cletus asked, hoping they'd say no.

Lester said they didn't have the time to wait for coffee to boil. He paid Cletus, picked up the dried apples, and told Riley and Slim to pick up the rest. Already a step ahead of him, Slim took a bite out of a biscuit and picked up the sack of jerky Cletus had filled. "Maybe we'll have time for that coffee on our way back to Waco," Lester said. He turned to leave but stopped after taking only two steps, stopped by something he heard. He held up his hand and stood there listening. Then they all became aware of what had caught his attention. It was a steady bumping sound from outside the store that became louder by the second. "What the hell is that?" Lester asked as Ben set his coffee cup down very carefully on the counter. In answer to his question, they heard the distinct sound of a man's voice, even though it was muffled.

"Ben Savage! Let us out! Ben Savage!" the voice repeated frantically and was joined by another voice.

"Ben Savage," Lester repeated, suddenly realizing. He dropped the dried apples and reached for his revolver the same time Ben drew his Colt. Already guessing what was coming next, when he first heard the muffled cry from the smokehouse, Ben was a second ahead of Lester on the draw. The result was a .44 slug in Lester's chest before he had a chance to level his weapon. Lester pulled the trigger, but the bullet went into the floor. The sudden exchange of shots caught Slim and Riley by surprise, but both dropped their packages and reached for their weapons. Ben knew he wasn't fast enough to get both of them, so he threw his next shot at Riley, who appeared to be ahead of Slim. Riley went down with Ben's second shot, but Slim already had his .44 leveled and ready to fire before Ben could pull the hammer back for a third shot. He dropped to his knee while he cocked his pistol, hoping to present a smaller target to throw Slim's aim off. The sudden explosion of a double-barrel shotgun knocked Slim backward to land on the floor, his chest torn apart by the buckshot at that range. The shot had come from behind the counter, but when Ben looked up, there was no one there. He scrambled up on his feet and looked over the counter to see Jenny Priest lying flat on her back, the shotgun pointed straight up at the ceiling. Cletus was at her side, trying to help her up.

Throughout the whole incident, the frantic clamor from the smokehouse continued, pausing only when the explosion of gunfire occurred. "Is Jenny all right?" Ben asked.

"Yeah, she's all right," Cletus answered. "She just got knocked on her backside when she pulled both of them triggers at the same time."

"I'm all right," Jenny confirmed. "I'm just gonna have a beauty of a bruise on my shoulder."

"Well, you just saved my bacon when you shot that

fellow," Ben said. "He was just gettin' ready to cut loose on me. If you're all right, I'm gonna go see what's goin' on in the smokehouse."

We almost pulled it off, was what he was thinking as he walked around the back of the store on his way to the smokehouse. Reuben Drum's men were in the act of leaving when the two in the smokehouse gave it all away. Now, he was wary of some kind of surprise Pete and Ormond had cooked up for him when he reached the door. "Shut up, damn it!" he ordered, "if you want this door unlocked."

"Hurry up!" Ormond came back. "You locked us up in a damn nest of snakes!"

"He ain't lyin', Savage," Pete blurted. "There's snakes in here."

"All right, I'm unlockin' this padlock, but before I pull this lock out of the latch, you think about something. I'll be standin' here with my six-gun aimed at that door and I'll start shootin' at the first move that doesn't look right from either one of you. Is that clear?"

"Yeah, yeah," Ormond replied, impatiently, "we ain't gonna try nothin'. Just let us the hell outta here!"

Ben removed the padlock and stepped back, his pistol in hand. "Come on out. It's open." The door swung open so hard it banged against the front wall of the smokehouse and both men squeezed through the doorway at the same time. "Down on your knees, hands behind your back." They both responded at once, almost eagerly, he thought. He handcuffed both of them, then looked around for someplace to park them while he went back to help clear the bodies from the store. He settled on the two posts that supported the roof over Cletus's back steps. After cuffing each one of them to the posts, he tested the posts to make sure they were solid.

Satisfied his prisoners were secure, he went back to the smokehouse to take a look inside, thinking Cletus would like to know about any rattlesnakes in there. With the door open, he spotted movement near a back corner of the smokehouse. He stood still until the snake slithered across the back of the floor, then he went inside. Watching from their posts by the steps Ormond and Pete waited to hear the gunshot they knew would come. But there was none. "He went in there!" Pete said. "The crazy fool, he oughtn'ta not gone in there."

"I hope it bit him," Ormond said.

In a minute, Ben came back outside, holding the snake at arm's length. Approximately four and a half to five feet, the reptile wiggled and curled as he held it just behind its head. "It ain't nothin' but a rat snake," he said. "It ain't gonna hurt you."

"What was all the shootin' in the store?" Pete asked. "It sounded like a war broke out in there."

"That was the end of three fellows I reckon Reuben Drum sent to rescue you boys, but you managed to get 'em all killed when you started cryin' like a couple of schoolgirls. They were fixin' to leave when you two started hollerin'. I reckon they found out about all that bank money you were carryin.'"

He left them to wonder who the three men were who came after them while he went back in the store to help Cletus and Jenny. When he went inside, he found them kneeling beside Riley Best. Jenny looked up at him and said, "He ain't dead. He's bad hurt, though, shot through the shoulder, right through the base of his neck."

"The other two are dead," Cletus said. "I reckon we've got some holes to dig. Whaddaya think we oughta do about this one?"

Ben knelt down beside the wounded man to see the extent of his wound himself. Riley made not a sound, but his eyes were wide with fear as he looked up at the powerful man seeming to hover over him. "Reckon it's my fault," Ben said as he examined the wound, "but I didn't have time to take good aim at you. If we bandage you up, you think you can make it back to the church?"

Confused by the question, not sure if he was being given the option of living or not, Riley nevertheless blurted, "I sure as hell can!"

Ben looked up at Cletus, who was now standing over him. "Let's see if we can bandage him up, so he'll stop bleedin', give him something to eat, put him on his horse, and let him go." He looked back down at Riley again. "Is that all right with you? Or do you want me to put you outta your misery?"

"Yes, sir, that's all right with me, and I'll thank you for sparin' my life. You're a good man, Ben Savage, 'cause I woulda shot you, if I was faster. I ain't never gonna forget this."

"Better let me do the bandagin'," Jenny said. "He's liable to end up with something that looks like a horse collar, if one of you do it." She went to the pantry where she kept the old sheets she used to make bandages, then poured some water in a basin to heat on the stove. When it had warmed to her satisfaction, she cleaned the area around his wound as best she could.

When she had finished, she said, "If you're careful, maybe that'll keep the dirt out of it. You need to see a doctor soon as you can." Then she felt inspired to comment. "He's a hard man to figure out," she said, referring to Ben, who was waiting to put Riley on his horse. "Cut your partner down and coulda finished you off, too."

CHAPTER 9

Still harboring the fear that he might suddenly feel the impact of a fatal bullet in his back, Riley Best walked cautiously down the front steps. Ben walked behind him, and when he got to his horse, Ben helped him up in the saddle. Then he drew the Winchester rifle out of Riley's saddle sling. "I expect I can trust you at your word," Ben said, "but I'm tradin' you your life for this rifle. That way, you won't get to thinkin' about changin' your mind when you get outta pistol range."

"Oh, I swear, I ain't gonna go back on my word," Riley insisted at once. "I'm gonna get back to Waco just as fast as I can. Like I said, I owe you for this."

"All right," Ben replied, "but don't go too far before you rest that horse. You and your friends dang-near killed 'em on the way down here."

"Yes, sir, I'll give him a good rest, soon as I find a good spot." He turned the horse back toward the wagon road and headed back north toward Waco.

"You don't reckon he'll double back after he gets outta sight, do you?" Cletus wondered.

"I don't think so," Ben gave his honest opinion, "but I ain't always right. Let's get to work diggin' a hole to dump those bodies in."

"He went off and left his pals' horses," Cletus said.

"He wasn't in any position to make any demands about who got the horses," Ben told him. "So, I thought it would help repay you for the trouble they caused, if you kept the horses and tack."

"That's mighty generous of you, Ben," Cletus responded. "Yessir, that's mighty generous."

Cletus supplied a pick and shovel, selected the spot, and did a little of the labor, but as he had a tendency to do, Ben did most of the digging for the two bodies. Cletus had suggested that Pete and Ormond should do the work of digging the grave, but Ben preferred to jump on the task and get it done. He was already delayed in getting back to Buzzard's Bluff, and he didn't want to stand around guarding two reluctant prisoners. The two of them had the nerve to complain about having to sit handcuffed to the posts, causing Ben to remind them that it was their fault, since they had been so frightened by a rat snake. "We woulda been halfway to Buzzard's Bluff and a comfortable cot in Mack Bragg's jailhouse by now, if you hadn't got squirrelly over a common rat snake."

"A snake's a snake," Ormond said, "and I ain't got no use for none of 'em. I don't care what brand he is."

It was the middle of the afternoon by the time Ben led his prisoners up the path to the wagon road to Buzzard's Bluff, on horses watered, fed, and well rested. "I declare," Cletus said, "I don't know what we'll do for excitement around here with you leaving.

Come back to see us when you ain't got nothin' on your mind but visiting."

"That's right," Jenny spoke up, "sometime when you don't need my hospital. And I guarantee you, I'll remember you for as long as it takes that blue spot on my shoulder to go away."

"You're lucky you've got a woman that's handy with a shotgun to take care of you, Cletus," Ben japed. "If you ever have occasion to come to Buzzard's Bluff, drop in the Lost Coyote. We ain't as rough as other saloons. We got a right respectable lady managing the place." He extended the invitation, knowing no respectable woman would enter a saloon, even with her husband.

Henry Barnes was standing outside his stable talking to Jim Bowden when Ben approached the north end of Buzzard's Bluff's main street. They both turned to wait for him when they saw who it was, and the two riders behind him told them he had accomplished what he had set out to do. It was not surprising to either man. "Henry, Jim," Ben nodded to each of them in turn.

"Good to see you're ridin' Cousin," Henry said.

"Yep," Ben commented, "and I brought your red roan and Cecil's Morgan back with me. They're all in good shape and I'll bring 'em back here to the stable soon as I get their riders settled in Mack Bragg's hotel." He looked at Bowden then. "In a day or two, I'm gonna need to let you put some new shoes on Cousin, Jim."

"Sure thing, Ben," Bowden answered, "any time you want."

Gazing at the two sullen prisoners, sitting stiffly in the saddle, Henry was eager to hear Ben's account of the incidents that led up to their capture. But he was reluctant to press him in front of his captives. Jim Bowden, on the other hand, suffered no such reluctance. "I see you caught up with these two jaspers. They give you any trouble?"

"Some," Ben replied simply before giving Cousin a slight nudge with his heels and proceeding toward the jail. He didn't get past the harness shop before Tuck saw him through the open door and dropped the bridle he was mending to chase after him. He arrived at the sheriff's office seconds after Ben pulled up in front and climbed down from the saddle.

Seeing Ben and his prisoners through his office window, Mack Bragg stepped outside to meet him. "Sheriff," Tuck announced as he hustled up to the horses, "Ben's back."

Mack glanced at Tuck, then back at Ben and grinned. "I see he is, Tuck. Thanks for lettin' me know." Turning his full attention to Ben and his prisoners then, he said, "I've got a nice clean cell ready for you. I expect you'll be glad to get 'em off your hands. I'll give you a hand gettin' 'em down off those horses."

Together, they pulled Pete and Ormond off the horses and marched them into the sheriff's office. Tuck drew his .44 and proceeded to help guard them as they went through the door. "Tuck," Mack suggested, "how 'bout goin' up to the hotel and tell Lacy I'm gonna need two supper plates for these two? She'll know what time to send 'em up here."

"Right, Sheriff," Tuck responded, "if you're sure you don't need an extra gun to lock these polecats up."

"I think Ben and I can handle it," Mack said. "'Preciate your help." He walked Pete and Ormond into a cell and locked it, then had them back up to the bars, and Ben unlocked their handcuffs. Only then did Tuck give a little snort and go out the door. "I could just as easy have told Lacy when I went up to supper," Mack confessed. "But I wanted to get Tuck outta here, so you can tell me why you brought these birds all the way back here, instead of turnin' 'em over to the sheriff in Waco."

"It's a long story, but there was a damn good reason not to turn 'em over to Sheriff Walt Murphy. Before we get into that, you need to know the saddlebags on two horses out there are carryin' a lot of money. And I think, if you add it up with that money you found on Malcolm Hazzard, you're gonna find you've got the biggest portion of that twenty-two thousand dollars that belongs to the bank in Giddings."

"So, it was those three that robbed the bank, just like we figured," Mack said. "We'd best carry it inside and put it in the safe-box with the rest of the money. I ain't real easy about havin' all that money in here. I'm gonna have to ride over to Madisonville to wire Austin that we're holdin' two of the bank robbers and what's left of the money."

"I expect so, and if you're worried about it, you could let Tuck sit on top of that safe-box till the marshal sends somebody to get it," Ben said. "Maybe I can ride over to Madisonville to send the wire."

Mack laughed at Ben's crack about Tuck. "That

might not be such a bad idea," he said, "if Tuck ain't too busy and I'll take you up on that offer to ride to Madisonville. Now, let's get that money off those horses before he gets back. He'd have the news all over town before supper."

When they finished packing all the money into Mack's safe-box, Ben said he might see him at the hotel for supper after he took the horses back to the stable. Mack confessed that he was feeling a little uneasy about leaving the jail unguarded with that amount of money in the office. "I don't think you'll have to worry about it," Ben told him. "It's locked in a pretty good safe-box. When you go to supper, lock the office like you always do. Nobody's liable to get suspicious unless you change your normal habits."

"I suppose you're right," Mack decided. "I just don't want anything to happen to that money while it's in my possession." He walked outside and watched while Ben climbed aboard Cousin and led the other horses to the stable.

"Ben's back!" Tuck Tucker announced loudly as he walked in the door of the Lost Coyote. "Brought them two saddle tramps with him. We put 'em in jail. He's at the stable, takin' care of the horses now."

Ham Greeley turned around in his chair to look at Tuck. "Is that a fact? Well, thanks for tellin' us. What color underwear is he wearin' today?"

Not realizing he was being japed by his poker pal, Tuck answered. "How the heck do I know? White, same color as he always wears, I reckon. What difference does that make?"

Ham looked over at the bar to see Tiny's grinning face. "Dumb as a stump," he muttered. Back to Tuck then, he said, "Set yourself down and get ready to lose every dime you're totin'. Tiny, bring him a shot of the cheap whiskey." He dealt two hands on the table. "Read 'em and weep," he challenged.

"I'll be dad-burned," Tuck charged, "not till I give them cards a shuffle."

Tiny looked at Clarice and shook his head, then grinned at Rachel when she came out of the office. Now that Ben was back in town, everything could get back to normal, and when he came in the front door, Rachel met him. "Welcome home, partner. Tuck said you brought those two men back, and I suppose you rescued Cousin."

"I did," Ben replied, "and as soon as I throw my saddlebags in my room, I'm headin' for the hotel dinin' room. I told Mack I'd go eat with him. You wanna come along?"

"No, I expect not," she said. "You and the sheriff probably have a lot to talk over about what you're gonna do with the two you brought back. I suppose you're gonna transport them to Austin."

"No, ma'am," he answered. "If the U.S. marshal in Austin wants 'em, he can send somebody to pick 'em up. I ain't got time to ride all over Texas, anyway. I've got a saloon to run."

"That's right, you do," she said, knowing he was japing. "You'd better stick around to make sure your partner isn't stealing you blind."

* * *

Another reunion that had taken place, this one over seventy miles from Buzzard's Bluff, was not nearly so joyous. Riley Best turned his weary horse off the road and onto the path leading up to the church. Barely able to stay in the saddle, he had wondered if he was ever to reach the church again. As Ben Savage had advised, Riley had stopped and rested the horse but had ridden it into weariness again. At this point, he didn't care if the horse died, he had made it back. He rode up to the front steps and stopped, not sure if he could get down without collapsing.

Inside the church, Booth Brayer was standing near the front door when he heard a horse whinny, so he opened the door to investigate. At first, he wasn't sure who it was and he squinted to adjust his eyes to the darkness outside the church. "Damn," he uttered an oath then. "Riley?" Without waiting for Riley to answer, he turned back toward the others in the room. "It's Riley! And he's by hisself, and it looks like he's been shot or somethin'." His announcement brought the others to their feet and rushing to the door.

"What tha hell, Riley?" Reuben Drum blurted as they gathered around him. Reuben looked back down the path for the others. "Where's Lester and Slim? What happened?"

"He's been shot, Reuben, we need to get him offa that horse," Charlie Taylor said. "Gimme a hand, Booth." They pulled Riley off his horse and carried him into the church. Reuben walked at his side as they went up the steps, asking him where Lester was.

Riley looked up at him mournfully and finally spoke. "Lester's dead. Slim's dead, too—Ben Savage." That was all he could say, so they carried him in and laid him on his cot.

Reuben Drum stood frozen, unable to speak upon hearing his son was dead. When Booth saw Reuben's sudden ineptness, he took charge of the wounded man. "Dora," he said to Dora Cox, "you and Paulene get a pan of water and some rags from Frances. He's been bleedin' pretty bad. Let's see if we can clean him up a little and try to stop him from bleedin' more." He began to unwrap the bandage Jenny Priest had put on the wounds, so he could see just how bad they were. When the two women came back, the cook, Frances Wright, was with them. The three women took over the cleanup while the men stood around to watch. "Looks like there's two holes," Booth said when they were clean enough to see, "one where the bullet went in and one where it came out."

By the time the women had Riley cleaned up and re-bandaged, Reuben had taken control of his emotions. He took a closer look at Riley's wounds and determined they were not as serious as first assumed. For his part, Riley began to feel that he was going to survive, after having feared he was going to bleed to death before he reached the sanctity of the church. His eyes blinked open in a little while to stare up at the circle of faces gathered around him. "I thought I was a goner," he muttered.

"What happened, Riley?" Reuben asked for the second time. "Lester, Slim, and Pete and Ormond, what happened?"

"Why don't you let him rest up some before you ask him all them questions?" Paulene interrupted.

Reuben turned to glare at her and snapped, "'Cause I wanna know right now, damn it." He turned back to the wounded man. "Tell me what happened. You said somethin' about Ben Savage."

"I need some coffee and somethin' to eat," Riley said. While Frances went to the kitchen to scare up something for him, he told Reuben about their pursuit of Savage and his prisoners. "We didn't even know we'd caught up with him at that old man's store 'bout halfway to Buzzard's Bluff. None of us ever saw Ben Savage before, so he had the drop on us. We'da gone on to Buzzard's Bluff if Pete and Ormond hadn't started hollerin'. He had 'em locked up in the smokehouse. That's when the shootin' started. Savage shot Lester and me. Slim got blasted with a shotgun and Savage let me go."

"He let you go? Why'd he let you go?" Reuben reacted, at once suspicious.

"I don't know for sure," Riley replied. "I think maybe he figured I weren't gonna make it, anyway."

After hearing the whole story, Reuben was devastated. Sheriff Walt Murphy had come out to the church that morning to set him straight on the disappearance of Pete Russell and Ormond Hazzard. Now, with Riley's return to report that everything went wrong, he was struck with the death of his only son. Of lesser importance to him, but of major concern to the other men at the church, was the loss of somewhere around fourteen thousand dollars. The capture of Pete and Ormond was of no concern to anyone. Reuben's focus turned to thoughts of vengeance for the death of his son. He knew he was not too old to take revenge into his own hands, but he was in a position to put a price on the head of Ben Savage, so he might as well pay one of the younger men to do it. He would wait, however, before announcing it until he decided how much he was willing to part with.

As Reuben expected, Walt Murphy showed up the next morning to see if the three men sent after Ben Savage had returned. The news of their demise was equally disastrous to him as it had been to Reuben, but not for the same reason. His loss was that of the stolen bank money Ormond and Pete had been carrying. He questioned Riley Best about everything that happened and Walt was not convinced that Savage had no designs on that money for himself. He doubted Ben was going to turn it over to the authorities. And it almost sickened him that the money had been right there in the church. "What a waste." He blurted.

When he realized his outburst had garnered everyone's attention, he went on to create a plan. "Listen," he said, "I feel bad for Reuben for losin' his son. We all do. We feel bad about Slim and Riley, too. Ben Savage needs to pay for what he did to those boys. But I'm thinkin' there's somethin' else to do while we're at it. Ben Savage told me he was intendin' to hold Ormond and Pete in the Buzzard's Bluff jail till the federal agents could come and get 'em. And after what Riley, here, said, I believe that's what Savage is really gonna do. Them two fellers ain't the only thing he's holdin' in that little jail of theirs. There's also about fourteen thousand dollars those boys left here with, and maybe more, because the third man on that bank job was killed in Buzzard's Bluff. So what happened to his share of the money?" He paused to look around at the faces captured by his words. "My bet is that it's right there with the rest of the money now."

Satisfied that he had everyone's attention, he continued. "There ain't no telegraph in Buzzard's Bluff. So somebody's gonna have to go to the nearest town that does have one just so they can wire Austin to come get the prisoners and the money. Then it'll take some time to send some marshals to Buzzard's Bluff to pick 'em up." He paused again to see if anyone could see what he was getting at.

"All that ain't gonna happen overnight," Booth commented, "more like three or four days."

"Those agencies don't move that fast," Walt replied. "I expect it might be a week before anybody shows up in Buzzard's Bluff. So, what I'm sayin' is we've got plenty of time to get down there, settle with Ben Savage for the killin's, and rob the sheriff's office of all that money. It's too good a chance to pass up." He paused again to watch their reaction, and it was obvious to the eye that everyone was considering the likelihood that it could succeed.

"We'd need to get there before the marshals get to town," Charlie Taylor commented, "when we won't have to worry about anybody but the sheriff and Ben Savage."

Sitting at the table now that his wounds felt a little better, Riley was quick to give them warning. "If we decide to do what you're talkin' about, we'd best take care of Ben Savage before we try anything at the sheriff's office."

"If we plan it right, we oughta be able to hit 'em both at the same time," Booth said, already enthusiastic about the planned raid. "Does he hang out at the sheriff's office?"

"No," Walt said. "He hangs out at the Lost Coyote Saloon. The best thing to do is to split up. We've got four men, so two can hit the saloon and two at the sheriff's office. Shoot Savage first and anybody else that gets in the way in the saloon. When the sheriff hears the shots and comes runnin', the two outside the office can nail him before he can lock up."

"Two at the Lost Coyote and two at the sheriff's office," Dick Flynn commented. "That ain't but four, and I count six of us here. 'Course I ain't countin' Riley. He's wounded, so that sounds to me like four of us are gonna stick our butts out there to risk gettin' shot, then split the money six ways. Am I the only one that thinks that don't sound right?"

Walt Murphy answered him. "Reuben ain't hardly fit to ride down there and get into the middle of it at his age. He needs to stay here and take care of this place."

"I reckon that's right," Dick replied, "so I reckon that leaves you. How come you're supposed to get an even split, if you ain't gonna stick your behind out where the bullets are flyin'?"

Walt's eyes narrowed as he concentrated a dark scowl in Dick's direction. "Flynn, you and John Temple ain't been here at the church but a week or two. So I reckon nobody's told you that if it wasn't for my deal with Reuben Drum, your ass would likely be shinin' one of the bunks in my jail right now, instead of layin' around out here in a private saloon. You see, I know that you and John Temple are wanted in Kansas for armed robbery, but I don't pass that information on to the marshals or the Rangers while you're takin' your ease right on my doorstep. Me and Reuben think that's worth somethin' and that's the reason I get an equal share. The other thing you ain't thought out yet is I'm the reason you know those two boys was carryin' all that money. I don't believe they volunteered that information when they lit here, did they?" He continued to lock eyes with Flynn, who stared back sullenly, so Walt made one more statement. "You don't have to go on this little job if you don't want to. But if you don't, you know too much, so you're gonna have to sit it out in one of my jail cells till we're all back here."

"Too many folks know Walt's the sheriff in Waco," Booth said to Flynn. "He can't take a chance on bustin' in the jail in Buzzard's Bluff. It'd be all over the state by the time we got back here."

"Yeah, I reckon I wasn't thinkin' about that," Dick said. "No hard feelin's, all right?"

Walt answered with only a nod, then got back to business. "Let's decide how we're gonna hit 'em. We can decide who's gonna do what tonight and get on the road in the mornin'. That'll still give us plenty of time," he said when he saw questioning glances. "They'll have to send somebody to the telegraph office, most likely in Madisonville. We'll give 'em tomorrow to do that, in case Ben Savage decides he's gonna do it. We need to make sure he's in town." He glanced over at Reuben and gave him a reassuring nod. "He's got to pay." He didn't express it, but he was still needing a little payback himself for the way Savage played him for a fool.

The planning and the preparation for the big raid on the small town of Buzzard's Bluff went on for some time before they finally called it off until morning. Walt decided it too important not to be back in the morning before they set out. "I'll tell my deputy I've got some repair work on the roof of my cabin I have to tend to and I'll be late comin' in tomorrow." He grinned at Brayer and said, "A payday like this don't come along every day, does it, Booth?"

CHAPTER 10

Walt was back at the church early the following morning, arriving while the outlaws were still eating breakfast. "I thought you mighta already been gone," he said. "I expected to meet you on the road between here and Waco."

"We decided we might as well eat breakfast before we left," Booth told him, "since we're gonna make it a two-day ride, anyway. Ain't no sense in gettin' to Buzzard's Bluff on wore-out horses, is there?"

"You're right about that," Walt replied. "There's somethin' else we didn't say anything about last night, and I figured I'd better say somethin' about it this mornin'. If you came up this way from the south, you might remember there's a little store settin' on a creek about halfway between Buzzard's Bluff and Waco. That's the place Lester and Slim got killed by Ben Savage. You boys best ride around that store, so the man and his wife that owns it can't say they saw you on the trail to Buzzard's Bluff."

Booth grinned when he answered. "I expect so,

Walt. Don't worry, we know what we're doin'. You and Reuben just be ready to help us count up the money when we come back."

Walt pulled him off to the side and quietly asked, "You think those two new ones can be depended on to do the job?" He was referring to Dick Flynn and John Temple, who had just recently joined the group at the church. "That Flynn feller strikes me as somebody who's liable to decide he's gonna play a different game, if he sees an edge for himself—him and his partner both."

"Don't worry, me and Charlie will keep an eye on 'em," Booth assured him. "We talked about it last night after you left and decided to split 'em up. Me and Flynn are gonna go to the saloon to get the party started. And Charlie and Temple are gonna be at the sheriff's office." He looked over his shoulder to make sure no one could hear before saying, "One false move and I'll shoot the sorry dog, if him and Temple get any ideas about takin' the whole pot and cuttin' the rest of us out."

"Good man," Walt said. "I told Reuben we could depend on you to get that money back here." Even as he said it, he was concerned that the temptation might be just enough for Booth to forget the way back to the church, especially if his partners in the robbery were killed. One man could set himself up for the rest of his life with that much money. And that was the reason he had told his deputy, Wayne Price, that he was taking a few days off to check on an uncle who was ill. Of the men still there at the church, he felt that Booth and Charlie were the most dependable to honor their given word. But they were outlaws and had killed before, especially Booth, who was exceptionally fast with a sidearm.

When everyone had finished eating, Walt drank a cup of coffee while he watched them bringing their horses, already saddled and packed, to the front of the church. Along with Reuben and Riley, who was on his feet again, but still weak, he wished the men good luck. They remained there on the steps until the gang of four assassins rode out of sight on the Waco road. "Well," Walt said, as he turned to take his cup back to the kitchen, "I reckon I'd best get back to town before Wayne sends out a search party for me. Maybe we'll all be rich when we see those boys again."

"I'm just sorry I ain't gonna be able to attend the funeral," Reuben said, referring to the one that would probably be held for Ben Savage.

Walt climbed on his horse and turned the buckskin back toward the Waco road. He rode for only a quarter of a mile before turning off the road when it crossed a tiny stream that cut through a small patch of trees. Following the stream, he rode into the trees until he came to a packhorse tied next to the water, untied the packhorse's reins, and led it back to the road. He set out then, trailing the four outlaws. He could not risk participating in the ambitious plan to kill Ben Savage, and possibly the sheriff as well, because he could be identified too easily. But he was not willing to gamble on the job ending as planned with all the money brought to the church to be split equally. For that reason, he was going to tail the party of four to protect his interest in the deal. He couldn't participate in the robbery, but he could keep an eye on the ones who did.

With no reason to hurry, Walt walked the buckskin along the road to Buzzard's Bluff, and after he had ridden close to twenty miles, he cautioned himself to be more alert. Having already picked up tracks that he felt sure were left by the party he trailed, he watched the road more closely, especially when approaching a stream. If they were intent upon taking it easy on their horses, they should be thinking to rest them after riding this far. Suddenly the buckskin nickered, telling him the horse sensed other horses. Walt reined him to a halt and turned him off the road to take a wide circle until reaching the stream he assumed to be ahead. When he struck it, he knew the riders he followed were somewhere between him and the road. He decided to tie his horses there and make his way back along the stream on foot to make sure the buckskin hadn't nickered at a deer or some other animal.

He walked for what he estimated to be about fifty yards when he caught sight of a thin ribbon of smoke drifting up through the trees. He knew then he was right. There was no need to get any closer and take a chance on being spotted. He returned to his horses and sat down to wait them out. He envied the four outlaws and their fire, but he didn't chance building one of his own and having to explain his existence there. He settled for some beef jerky and water.

When he figured it had been plenty of time to rest the horses, he walked back down the stream, past the point where he had turned back before, until he could see where they had camped close to the road.

They were gone, and from the feel of the wet remains of their fire, it had not been long since it had been extinguished. With still no cause to hurry, he led his horses back to the road and climbed up into the saddle again. In about ten or fifteen miles, he would circle wide to miss Cletus Priest's store, then continue on until time to camp for the night. Tomorrow, he would continue the same routine until reaching the little town of Buzzard's Bluff. At that point, he would have to find a spot to watch the sheriff's office, for that was where the money had to be.

The four riders walked their horses past Henry Barnes's stable and continued on past the blacksmith shop where Jim Bowden was fitting a dun gelding with new shoes. "Nice quiet little town, ain't it?" Charlie Taylor remarked to no response from his companions.

"Yonder's the Lost Coyote," Booth pointed out. "Jail's down there on the left, across from that other saloon. Everything's just like Walt said it was. Everybody know what to do?"

"Yeah," Flynn replied, "as long as they know what they're supposed to do. It might be that Ben Savage don't know he's supposed to be in that saloon right now."

"If he ain't, then we'll wait till he shows up," Booth said. "We'll ask the bartender where Savage is and when he's comin' back. But it's important that we put him down first. We don't want him sneakin' around after we get the party started."

"I swear, you and that yellow-bellied sheriff sure are

worried about that one man," Flynn crowed. "He must be hell on a stick."

"I reckon you could ask Lester Drum and Slim Dickens and Riley Best," Booth answered, "three pretty good men." He turned his attention to Charlie then. "You and Temple find you a spot to watch the sheriff's office. The front porch of that saloon down the street looks like a good place. Just wait for me and Flynn to start the dance, and as soon as you hear the shootin', get over to the jail to catch the sheriff. Take your horses with you, and we'll all take off across that creek after we've got the money."

"We can handle that, can't we, John?" Charlie asked, and Temple said they sure could. So Booth and Flynn pulled over in front of the Lost Coyote while Charlie and Temple rode down to the Golden Rail.

"Howdy, men," Tiny greeted the two strangers when they walked up to the bar. "What's your pleasure?" They both seemed to scan the saloon from one side to the other, as if someone might be waiting in ambush. Tiny's first thought was they were most likely men on the run from the law and would have been more in their element in the Golden Rail.

"I'll have a whiskey," Booth said.

"Gimme one, too," Flynn ordered. "You ain't too busy in here today. It ain't Sunday, is it?"

Tiny chuckled as he poured a shot for each of them. "Nope, today's Thursday, I think, and this is about normal for a Thursday." He corked the bottle and asked, "This your first time in Buzzard's Bluff?"

"That's right," Booth answered. "Who owns this place?"

Tiny shrugged and said, "That's one of 'em sittin' at the table by the kitchen door, eatin'." He nodded in Rachel's direction. "Her partner's Ben Savage."

"I've heard of him," Booth said. "I'd sure like to meet him." He looked across the room again. "Is he in here?"

"No, sir, not right now," Tiny answered. He thought he read disappointment in the faces of both men. "If you're wantin' to meet him, he just took his horse to get new shoes. He oughta be back in a few minutes."

"Good," Booth declared. "I'll have another shot of that whiskey. How 'bout you, Dick?" Flynn said he would, so Tiny poured a couple more. Then he moved down the bar to pour a drink for a young cowhand who had come into town to see Ruby. He paused to talk to them for a few minutes until the young man paid for his drink, then Ruby took his hand and led him upstairs. Tiny came back to the two strangers and asked if they wanted another drink. "Not right now," Booth answered. "Maybe we might have a drink with Ben Savage when he gets back."

"Might at that," Tiny said cheerfully, even though he suddenly realized he had an odd feeling about the two men, and he wondered why they were so keen on meeting Ben. It didn't help when he looked over at the table where Rachel was eating because he saw Annie staring back at him, a deep frown etched on her face. It was only for a few moments, however, then she filled Rachel's cup from the big pot she was holding and returned to the kitchen. Tiny shook his head to clear it of a thought. *Clarice and Ruby, now they've got me thinking that Annie's a spook.* "What?" he blurted when he realized one of the men had said something. "Sorry, I think my mind wandered off somewhere for a second. What did you say?"

"I said I'd appreciate it if you'll tell me when you see Ben Savage come in," Booth said. "I've got somethin' I'd like to talk to him about."

"Oh . . ." Tiny responded. "Sure thing, I'll let you know." He reached under the bar and started drying some shot glasses from a bucket of rinse water. It wasn't but a few minutes after that when Ben walked in. "There's Ben now." He barely got the words out before Booth spun around, his pistol out of his holster. "Ben!" Tiny yelled and grabbed the heavy oak club he kept under the counter. He swung it against Booth's shoulder at the same time Booth pulled the trigger, causing his shot to miss Ben, who was only a fraction of a second behind with a shot that doubled Booth over. Before he hit the floor, Flynn stepped aside to give himself a clear shot, only to stagger backward from the impact of Ben's second shot in his chest. He howled with the knowledge that he was a dead man. But, determined to take Ben with him, he refused to go down and defied the pain that filled his chest as he aimed his pistol at him. A hammer-like blow from Tiny's oak club on his forearm forced Flynn's aim to point to the floor. There was no shot fired, since he died before he could pull the trigger.

The sudden explosion of gunfire stunned everyone in the saloon, including Ben, but only for a moment. It struck him that it had to do with the money, and he had to believe these two men were only a part of it.

Without a word to anyone, he turned around and ran out the door, certain the two men were done for. His six-gun still in hand, he ran toward the jail, looking right and left for threats from any more suspicious strangers. He paid little attention to the two men sitting on the porch of the Golden Rail.

"What tha hell . . . ?" Charlie Taylor blurted when he saw the big man bound up the steps at the sheriff's office with his gun in hand. Having heard shots fired in the saloon up the street, he and John Temple were both on the edge of their chairs, ready to spring out of them as soon as they saw the sheriff come out of his office. Charlie leaned forward and craned his neck to look up the street toward the Lost Coyote for any sign of Booth or Flynn. "This don't look too good," he declared. "And I've got a feelin' that big jasper that just ran in the sheriff's office might be Ben Savage."

"Whaddaya think we oughta do?" Temple asked. "We heard them shots. Somebody musta got shot, and it don't look like it was Ben Savage. Him and the sheriff might be lookin' for us next."

"Maybe," Charlie replied. "But maybe, if they shot Booth and Flynn, they don't know about us. If they did, they'da come here lookin' for us. I'm thinkin' this whole deal has got boogered up and the best thing for us is to get on our horses and ride outta here."

"I'm thinkin' the same thing, partner. I hate to pass up a chance to get a-holt of a bunch of that money, but I doubt there's any place to spend it in hell. If Booth and Flynn weren't dead, they'da been chasin' that feller to the jailhouse."

"Well, there ain't much use in hangin' around any longer," Charlie commented. "Let's just take our time climbin' on our horses, so nobody gets a notion we're anxious to get outta town." Temple nodded in agreement. So they got up from their chairs and went to their horses as casually as they could affect. Then with hardly a glance toward the sheriff's office, they turned away from the rail and slow-walked their horses back up the street, returning to the road they had ridden in on that morning.

"I swear . . ." Temple uttered involuntarily as they plodded past the Lost Coyote, for the bodies of Booth and Flynn were already being carried out of the saloon and laid on the porch for the undertaker. It was a sobering sight.

"What tha hell . . .?" Another observer blurted his reaction to the scene he was witnessing. From a natural blind of laurel bushes near the creek bank, Walt Murphy adjusted his field glass to focus on the two riders casually riding up the street. "They're cuttin' out!" He shifted his glass back to the sheriff's office and when he saw no activity there, he shifted his focus back on the two riders. When he did, he also saw the bodies when they passed the saloon. "Ben Savage," he spat, as if cursing. He had seen Ben running to the sheriff's office. And while he could not know the reason, he had hoped he was running for his life. Now, he knew what the shots had been. Savage killed them, and he couldn't understand how that could have happened. The plan had been a simple assassination, shoot on sight, with no warning whatsoever. How could they have messed that up? Then they passed on a second chance to put Savage down when he ran out in the street, right by Temple and Charlie Taylor. *Why didn't they shoot him down?* Walt was beside himself with frustration. He left his post in the laurels and ran to his horse, anxious to intercept the two retreating outlaws.

Once they were out of sight of the town, they increased their pace to a fast walk, thinking to put distance between themselves and Buzzard's Bluff. They had gone no farther than a few hundred yards when a rider leading a packhorse suddenly cut across in front of them and pulled his horse to a stop in the middle of the road. They both reached for their guns before they realized it was Walt Murphy. "Why didn't you reach for your guns back there when Ben Savage ran right in front of you?" he demanded.

"Walt!" Charlie Taylor exclaimed. "What are you doin' here?"

"Tryin' to make sure we don't just kiss an opportunity to get rich good-bye," Walt answered. "Where the hell are you two goin'? What happened back there?"

"I don't know, Walt," Charlie replied. "We did exactly like we talked about back at the church. Booth and Flynn said they'd gun Savage down and me and Temple were ready to jump the sheriff as soon as he came out the door. Well, we done our part. We was ready, but somethin' went wrong in that saloon."

"Somethin' went wrong, all right," Walt complained. "What did Booth do? Did he go in there and call Savage out? The plan was to shoot Savage on sight, not have a duel with him."

"He never said he was gonna call him out," Temple

said. "He said he was gonna shoot him without even a howdy-do."

"Why didn't you shoot Savage when he walked down the street?" Walt demanded. "You couldn'ta got a much easier shot."

"That weren't supposed to be our part in the plan," Charlie insisted. "They was supposed to shoot Savage, and we was supposed to jump the sheriff when he came out to do somethin' about it."

"So you just decided to just stick your tail between your legs and slink off, did you?" Walt scoffed. "And leave over twenty thousand dollars in the sheriff's office to let Ben Savage and Mack Bragg split it between 'em."

"I don't see what else we coulda done," Charlie maintained. "Me and Temple woulda more'n likely got ourselves shot tryin' to go up against the two of them."

"Well, there's three of us now, and I ain't ready to leave all that money for Savage and Bragg to retire on without tryin' to get a piece of it for myself. We'll circle back to that spot I was watchin' from. They gotta eat sometime. Both of 'em ain't gonna be settin' on that money all the time. Come to think of it, Savage wasn't helpin' guard it anyway. He was in the saloon when Booth and Flynn went in there after him. We might just raid that jailhouse tonight."

"I thought you couldn't come on this job because you were afraid somebody would recognize you," Temple remarked.

"That was true for the plan we had that Booth and Flynn messed up. This is gonna be at night, and I'll bet you Ben Savage ain't gonna be settin' in that jail tonight guardin' that money. I had a feelin' there'd be a screwup on this plan. That's why I showed up, and that's why I brought this." He reached in his saddlebag and pulled out a sack with eye and mouth holes in it to pull over his head. "I won't be takin' any chances on somebody here seein' me." He held it up for them to see. "Now, whaddaya say we get ourselves outta the middle of the road before somebody comes along? I've got coffee and hardtack on my packhorse." That brought a question to mind. "Where's that packhorse you left the church with?"

"Booth and Flynn had it with them," Charlie replied.

"Good thing I came along, ain't it?" Walt cracked. "You two mighta got pretty hungry by the time you got back."

"What made you think they were gonna try to steal that money?" Mack Bragg asked Ben. "Hell, they went in the saloon lookin' for you. You sure they weren't two fellows you mighta sent to prison when you were a Ranger?"

"My memory ain't that bad," Ben replied. "I never saw those two men before the other day when I saw 'em outside that church. And I'm willin' to bet they may or may not have known those two you're holdin' in that cell in there had all that bank money. I know who did know they had it."

"Walt Murphy," Mack said. "I know you said he was in with that bunch at that place they call the church, but he's the town sheriff. Besides, why would he wanna have you killed?"

"Because he knows I know, and he's worried that I might call the Rangers down on him and his little business with Reuben Drum. I think the out-and-out attempt to shoot me was for another reason as well. One of those men I shot at Cletus Priest's store was Lester Drum, Reuben's son."

Mack slowly shook his head as he looked at Ben. "I swear, you do have a knack for makin' enemies. Buzzard's Bluff didn't have any idea of the trouble you were gonna attract when you inherited that saloon. If we'd known, we mighta took up a collection to buy out your interest."

"I'm so good at managin' that saloon that even if you had, Rachel mighta hired me back on salary," Ben joked. Then he got serious again. "Mack, you'd best watch your back till they send somebody to pick up your prisoners. And I don't know if those two that came after me at the Coyote just now are in this with somebody else, or not, but I think you oughta play it like they are. Might be a good idea if I come in and watch the jail when you wanna go to the dinin' room to eat. Wouldn't be any trouble for me. Just tell me what time you wanna go for supper and I'll be here then. All right?"

"Well, I hate to impose on you," Mack answered, "but I have been kinda uneasy when I leave this place and those two prisoners unguarded."

"It's a deal, then. What time do you want me here?" When Mack said five-thirty, Ben said, "I'll be here. Right now, I expect I'd best go back to the Coyote. My folks will be wonderin' what happened to me, and I imagine Tuck Tucker has about drove all of 'em crazy by now."

By the time Ben returned to the Lost Coyote, Merle Baker's handcart was parked in front of the saloon. "I was wonderin' when you were gonna show up," the undertaker greeted him. "Didn't take you long to drum up some business for me. Who are these two? You think anybody will be coming to claim the bodies?"

"I don't know their names," Ben answered, "and there won't be anybody showin' up to claim 'em, that's for sure. They were just two of a gang of outlaws that are holed up about four miles across the river from Waco. Stick 'em in the ground where you buried the rest of the no-names. I expect it'll be under the same arrangement as before." Merle usually received two dollars from the town council to take care of the bodies of no-name drifters and outlaws. Merle was glad to do it at that price because he often received a bonus, depending on the dead man's possessions and their value.

Ben went inside then, where the discussion about the recent shootings was still very much underway. "Ben!" Tuck Tucker announced loudly when he saw him. "We was wonderin' where you took off to. Tiny said you just stepped inside long enough to shoot them fellers, then turned around and left. I was in the outhouse when I heard the shots, but I got here as quick as I could. We ain't been able to figure out what's goin' on."

"There ain't much more I can tell you," Ben replied.

"I was just as surprised as you were, so I went to the jail right away to see if they mighta been creating a distraction while somebody else was makin' an attempt to free Mack's prisoners." He remembered that he had wondered at the time why he hadn't bumped into Tuck on his way to the jail. He walked over to the bar where Tiny was talking to Rachel. "Are you all right?" He asked Rachel.

"Oh, yes, I'm all right," she said facetiously, "just another day at the Lost Coyote. I've gotten quite used to it ever since you decided to retire from the violent world of the Texas Rangers and join the peaceful citizens of Buzzard's Bluff." Sensing he was about to ask if she would like him to leave, she quickly added, "But don't you get any notions about leaving me with this business."

"You heard her say that, didn't you?" Ben asked Tiny. Tiny said that he did and that he would remember it. "The only reason I'm still here right now," Ben went on, "is because you're so handy with that oak club of yours. So, I wanna thank you again." Tiny grinned, reached under the counter, and pulled his club up for them to see.

"Are you calm enough to eat your dinner now?" Rachel asked. "Because Annie isn't going to leave until she sees that you get fed." He said that he was ready to eat, so she told him to sit down at the table next to the kitchen where she generally ate. He obeyed, and Tiny moved back up the bar to talk to a customer. After Ben was seated, Rachel joined him, bringing cups and the coffeepot with her. "Annie's fixin' your plate. I told her to put a piece of ham and a biscuit on another plate for me. I wasn't halfway through my dinner when you came in and those men started shooting. Is it any wonder I couldn't think about eating until after Merle Baker and Tiny carried those dead men out of here?" She frowned as she stared at him in distress. I swear, for a minute there, I thought I'd lost my partner."

"Like I said, if it hadn't been for Tiny's quick thinkin', I expect you mighta had."

In a couple of minutes, Annie brought the food to the table and took the coffeepot back to the kitchen with her. "I'm gonna get my kitchen cleaned up now," she said to Rachel. "There's still some biscuits left, if you get hungry later."

"Don't worry about it, Annie, I'll clean up what mess we make. You run along home before Johnny starts worrying about you." After Annie returned to the kitchen, Rachel gave Ben a knowing gaze and said, "When those two men came in and started talking to Tiny, he said they seemed friendly as could be. But Tiny said he looked at Annie and she had one of those worried looks on her face."

Ben shook his head and chuckled. "I swear, Rachel, you and Clarice have got everybody thinkin' Annie's some kind of fortune-teller, or something."

"She knew!" Rachel insisted. "Maybe she didn't know those two men were gonna try to shoot you. I'll give you that. But she knew they were evil and something bad was gonna happen."

"If you say so," Ben replied, "all I know for sure is she's gettin' to be a better cook than she was when

I first got here. If we ever start servin' supper here, I might have to say good-bye to the hotel dinin' room."

"She knew!" Rachel insisted again, unwilling to concede. When he just chuckled, she said, "And you oughta tell her what you just told me about her cookin'. It would tickle her to think she was pleasing you."

CHAPTER 11

At five-thirty, Ben walked up the steps to the front door of the sheriff's office and knocked. He heard the bolt slide almost immediately, and Mack opened the door. "You must be hungry," Ben said. "You opened the door so quick. It might notta been me."

"I was lookin' out the window and saw you comin'," Mack said. "I'll bring my prisoners their supper when I come back. And like I said, I appreciate you helpin' me out."

"I figure I oughta," Ben said with a chuckle, "since I'm the one who dumped 'em on you. I'll go up to eat later. I didn't eat dinner till late, anyway. In the mornin', I'll ride over to Madisonville and wire my boss in Austin to send somebody to get 'em." He walked outside with Mack and stood on the steps for a while after Mack left for the hotel. Looking up and down the street, he saw nothing that seemed suspicious. *There probably was no one else with those two who came after me,* he thought and went back inside the office, locking the door behind him. "But it doesn't pay to be careless," he said aloud, unaware he was being watched from the bank of the creek.

"I was wonderin' how long it was gonna be before he showed up at the sheriff's office," Walt Murphy commented to his two partners. "Him and the sheriff are takin' turns watchin' Pete and Ormond—looks like—and that chunk of money, too. Well, that's just dandy. Makes our job that much easier, to catch both of 'em in the same place, the money and Savage." He planned to take care of the sheriff as well, but the most important job was to get that money. Second to that was to kill Ben Savage to compensate Reuben Drum for the loss of his son and to prevent any question of his connection to the church.

"I don't know, Walt," Charlie Taylor questioned. "It don't look like an easy thing to break into that sheriff's office. It looks to me like they're ready for somethin' to happen. How are you thinkin' about doin' it? Just charge in there and break the door down?"

"And get shot when we run in the door," John Temple finished for him. He and Charlie had already talked about Walt's determination to get his hands on that money, and they viewed it as a simple suicide plan.

Walt looked at his two companions in crime and smiled. "What's the matter, boys, gettin' cold feet? We're gonna need a little help, and I plan to get it from inside." When both Charlie and Temple looked puzzled by that, he explained. "I've been studyin' that jail section and there's two little windows on that back wall. I figure those windows are up close to the ceilin' in two separate cells. If we can find out if Pete and Ormond are in one of those cells, we can drop a gun through the window. I've got an extra pistol. If one of you has an extra, we can drop a gun for both of 'em. They might be able to do the killin' for us, and all we'd have to do is bust the door open and find the money."

"Damn," Charlie swore, "that might work. Might even give Ormond the chance to square up his account with both the jaspers that killed his brothers." Looking at it in that light, it seemed to him like the perfect vengeance against Ben Savage and Mack Bragg, poetic justice, even. "Let's do it," he said. "I'll ride up behind the jail and drop the gun in the window, but I'll have to drop your extra gun. I ain't got one, myself."

"I swear, I ain't got one, either," Temple confessed.

Walt looked from one of them to the other, plainly disappointed, for he couldn't conceive of any man who made his living with a gun, on either side of the law, not carrying a spare. "Well," he finally said, "it won't make that much difference, I reckon. One gun might be all they need, since they'll have the element of surprise." When Charlie got up from his position seated on the bank as if to go get his horse, Walt stopped him. "You'd best wait till it starts to get a little darker, so you won't be so noticeable from the street. It'll pay us to wait till after supper before we go marchin' up to that jail, anyway."

"What if Savage leaves when the sheriff comes back?" Temple asked. "We need to catch both of 'em together."

Walt didn't answer right away, since he hadn't considered that. After thinking the situation over, he said, "You're right. We need to catch 'em both in there, so we best not wait till dark." He was not comfortable operating in broad daylight, since he might be recognized as the sheriff of Waco. But the lure of twenty thousand dollars waiting just inside that jail was enough to persuade him to risk it. *That's the reason I brought the mask,* he told himself. His mind made up, he handed his extra handgun to Charley. "All right, if you're still wantin' to do it, ride on up behind the jail and see if you can get the gun in the window. From here, it don't look like there's any glass in it. Mack Bragg oughta be back from supper before much longer. I expect that's where he went, since he walked up toward the hotel. Tell Ormond to open fire as soon as Bragg comes in. If we're lucky, Savage will walk back in the cell room with him and he can get both of 'em. If he doesn't, we'll get whichever one he misses, because we'll be comin' in the front door. As soon as they're both down, we'll tear that place apart and find that money. If we work quick enough, we'll get what we came for and be on our way outta town before anybody knows what's goin' on."

Walt and Temple stood at the edge of the trees along the creek and watched as Charlie's horse loped across the open strip between the creek and the back of the buildings. From where they stood, they could see him ride up to the back of the jail. "I reckon we might as well bring our horses up here, ready to ride," Walt said. "We need to be ready to ride as soon as we hear any shootin' inside the jail."

Standing up in the stirrups, Charlie was just high enough to see in the tiny window. "Ormond?" he whispered. "Pete?"

Inside the jail cell, Ormond sat up on his bunk and

looked at Pete, thinking it was he who had whispered. Then the whispered names came again, and he realized it had come from the window above his bunk. "Yeah," he whispered. "Who's that?"

"It's me, Charlie," he answered. "I'm at the window. I can see in it, but I can't raise high enough to look down into the room. Am I over your cell?"

"Yeah, that window's right over my bunk," Ormond said. "Whaddaya doin' up there?"

"We've come to bust you and Pete outta there. I've got a pistol for ya. If I push it through this window, can you catch it?"

"Hell, yeah, drop it," Ormond eagerly replied. "Who's with you? We heard two of the boys tried to gun down Ben Savage and got killed theirselves. Who was it?"

"It was Booth Brayer and Dick Flynn," Pete answered him. "Is there anybody else with you?"

"Walt Murphy and John Temple," Charlie said. "You oughta make it a whole lot easier to get you outta there. You're bound to get a shot off before they know what's happenin'. Maybe get both of 'em. But we'll be comin' in the front door, in case you don't. Do you know where they put the money?"

"Yeah," Ormond replied. "They stuck it in a strongbox like they use on the stagecoaches, and it's settin' on the floor behind the sheriff's desk. Did you say Walt Murphy?" He asked, thinking it unlikely the sheriff would stick his neck out.

"That's what I said, Walt Murphy. All right, look up. I'm fixin' to drop this gun. It's loaded with six rounds." When Ormond said he was ready, Charlie dropped it. Then he went on to tell the two prisoners what the plan was and that they were to wait until Mack Bragg returned. "When he does, cut 'em both down, if you can. As soon as we hear you shootin', we'll bust in the door." They assured him that they understood what to do. "Okay, then," Charlie said, "I reckon we'll see you pretty quick now. I'm gone." He sat down in the saddle, wheeled his horse away from the rear of the jail, and loped back to the cover of the creek to wait and watch for Bragg's return.

In the original plan, they figured to recover Pete and Ormond's horses once Ben Savage and Mack Bragg were out of the picture. Now, however, Walt figured a stray bullet or two in the jailbreak would result in the death of the prisoners and cancel the need for their horses. And once they were clear of Buzzard's Bluff, he could consider the possibility of eliminating Charlie and Temple from sharing in the bank money.

"Here you go," Cindy Moore announced when she came to the table with a large metal tray with two plates of food. "Two suppers for your prisoners. If you keep that dish towel over 'em, they should still be fairly warm by the time you get back to the jail."

"Those two birds oughta appreciate the meals they're gettin' while they're guests at my little hotel," Mack replied. "They ain't gonna get this kind of chuck at their next stop."

"How many more days will we be feeding them?" Lacy James asked.

"I don't know exactly," Mack answered after gulping the last swallow from his cup, "however long it takes 'em to send somebody to transport 'em. We ain't even notified the marshal yet. Ben's gonna ride over to Madisonville in the mornin' to wire Austin, so I can stay here and keep an eye on 'em." He got up from his chair and picked up the tray.

"Don't drop it before you get back to the jail with it," Lacy had to say when it looked like Mack didn't have the tray level.

"I won't," Mack said. "And even if I do, I'll just pick it all up and put it back on the plates. They'll never know the difference, and I guarantee you, they'll eat every bit of it. Ben said he's comin' up here before you close." Cindy held the door open for him as he walked out with his tray of food.

When he got back to the jail, he started to knock on the office door, but almost dropped the big tray when he let go with one hand. "Ben," he yelled. "It's me, open the door." In a few seconds, Ben slid the bolt and opened the door, his six-gun in hand just in case. He took a quick look outside before he holstered his weapon and held the door open for Mack. "I damn-near dropped it when I started to knock on the door," Mack said.

"I'll watch 'em while you take the tray in," Ben said as he closed the door and locked it again. "That grub smells pretty good," he commented as he passed in front of Mack to open the cell room door. When he opened it, he drew his six-gun again and told Pete and Ormond to move to the back of the cell.

Everything was happening just as Ormond had hoped it would. Both Savage and Bragg were in the cell room at the same time. He could feel the six-shooter jammed in his belt behind him, and he battled his emotions in an effort to remain patient, afraid that something would go wrong at any moment. Then, for some reason, Bragg hesitated before the cell door. Without thinking that he might be waiting for Ben to unlock the cell door, Ormond panicked. *They know!* The thought flashed through his mind, and he suddenly reached behind him and pulled the gun out of his belt and fired at Bragg. His shot went through the bars and ricocheted off the big metal tray Mack was holding, sending the two plates and the tray flying and causing Mack to fall back against the bars. Ormond dropped to his knees from the impact of Ben's shot to his chest before he could get off a second shot.

Surprised just as much as Ben and Mack, Pete was stunned and could do nothing but stare at his partner for long seconds until Ormond keeled over sideways. In the critical time it took before he thought to dive for the weapon Ormond had dropped, Ben had time to reconsider his next act. "Get out!" he roared at Mack and hustled out the door after him, instead of putting a bullet in Pete. He slammed the door just as a shot from Pete impacted in the heavy wooden door.

"Son of a gun!" Mack exclaimed. "Why didn't you shoot the other one when you had the chance?"

"I ain't sure," Ben answered honestly. "I thought as lawmen, we oughta turn one of 'em over for trial, if we could." He paused and shrugged. "Besides, after I shot Ormond, Pete waited too long before he made any move for the gun, so it woulda been an out-and-out execution."

Mack thought that over for a few seconds before he said, "I reckon." Then it occurred to him. "Where the hell did they get that gun?" There was no time for speculation on that at the moment, because they were alerted by the sound of someone trying to kick in the front door.

"That's where!" Ben exclaimed. He ran to the gun case to grab the double-barrel shotgun. After he broke it to make sure it was loaded, he got behind the desk where Mack had already taken cover.

Outside the door, Walt Murphy, his sack mask pulled over his head, directed the assault against the office door. Charlie and Temple provided the muscle, thinking the shots they had heard signaled the death of at least one of the lawmen and, since there were two shots fired in quick succession, possibly both of them. Walt was encouraged by the absence of sounds from inside that would indicate any defense. "It's givin', boys," he offered as support for their efforts when the door showed signs of separating from the latch.

Finally, when the door was forced to fly open and bang against the wall, the doorway was filled by Charlie and Temple. The blasts from the shotgun, one barrel for Charlie, the other barrel for Temple, knocked both men backward. Seeing them crumple like rag dolls, Walt needed no time to make a decision. He jumped off the steps, grabbed his horse's reins, and as soon as he got one foot in the stirrup, he whipped the horse to a gallop before he threw his other leg over and landed in the saddle. Ben and Mack both rushed outside but were too late to stop him. They both threw a couple of shots after the masked rider, but he was already out of normal pistol range by then. They could only watch as he disappeared past the stable and out the north end of town. The thought that struck

Ben was the rider rode a fine-looking buckskin horse, and it made him recall the horse that Walt Murphy rode. *Surely not,* he thought, *not even Walt Murphy would stick his neck out that far.* Or would he? It was a lot of money, but would his share be worth the risk just taken by the masked rider? Only if that man had it in mind to eliminate his partners once the job was done. His speculation was interrupted then by a question from Mack.

"What do we do about the situation we've got in that cell now?" Mack asked when they walked back inside the office. "We've got one dead man and one man with a gun in there."

"I reckon, for a start, we could find out if he feels like tossin' that gun outta the cell," Ben said. He looked back out the door when he heard the sounds of the spectators out in the street, now that all the shooting seemed to be over. "Better go ahead and decide before Tuck shows up to take over."

"Well, let's see what he's gonna do," Mack said, referring to Pete. They went to the cell room door and Mack cracked the door just wide enough to talk through. "It's all over now, Pete. I want you to throw that gun out through the bars and you won't get shot. Is Ormond dead?"

"How do I know I can trust you?" Pete answered back. "Damn right, Ormond's dead. I throw my gun away and you'll shoot me, like you did Ormond."

"Ormond didn't give us no choice," Mack replied. "He shot at me first. So I need you to throw that gun on out, all right?"

"What was that shotgun blast?" Pete asked.

"That was some of your gang, I reckon, tryin' to break in the office."

"Are they dead?" Pete asked.

Mack looked at Ben and shrugged before answering. "Well, yeah, they're dead. We didn't have no choice. We had to shoot 'em. So whaddaya say, you ready to throw that gun out?"

Pete was not at all confident that he could believe the sheriff. The more he thought about what just happened, the more it became clear in his mind that the sheriff and Ben Savage had decided to execute all of them, rather than go to the bother of housing them, feeding them, and transporting them to trial. When Bragg pressed him again to throw the weapon through the bars, Pete answered, "I don't think I can trust you. I think I'd best keep this pistol. If you want it, you're just gonna have to come on in here and get it."

Mack and Ben exchanged glances again, both finding it hard to believe the situation they found themselves in. To make matters worse, Tuck Tucker stormed into the office then, after stepping over the two bloodied bodies on the front steps. "I came as quick as I heard the shootin'," he exclaimed, "in case you needed any help. I sent some young'un to fetch Merle Baker. Told him to bring a wagon, 'cause we're gonna have more bodies than he can carry on that little handcart of his." Ben and Mack both turned to shut him up, but it was too late. As was Tuck's usual habit of talking loud to make up for his lack of statue, his booming voice carried into the cell room, further enforcing Pete's conclusion that they intended to kill him.

While a small crowd of spectators milled around

outside the sheriff's office to view Merle Baker's efforts to pick up the mess the shotgun had made, Ben and Mack made an unsuccessful attempt to convince Pete to surrender the gun. "This gun's the only thing I've got to save me from gettin' the same thing Ormond and the others got. So, if you want it, you're gonna have to come in and get it. But I'm warnin' you, I'll shoot the first one sticks his head in that door."

"If you do, you'll still be locked in that cell," Mack replied. "It won't do you any good if you shoot me."

"Maybe so," Pete said, "but it'll be better'n you shootin' me."

"He's kinda got us by the short hairs, ain't he?" Mack speculated. "I ain't about to walk in that door and get shot. Maybe we can catch him when he gets to sleep."

"Maybe," Ben said, "but if he happens to wake up when you're sneakin' in, one of you is gonna have to shoot the other one."

"Well, what am I gonna do?" Mack asked in frustration. "I can't just leave him settin' in there like that."

"Why not?" Ben asked. "Hell, let him sit in that cell with that body, his supper scattered on the floor outside his cell, no fresh water, no emptyin' his thunder mug. Give him time, he'll be ready to come outta there by the time a couple of marshals come to pick him up."

"I'm gonna need to do some work on my front door, though," Mack said after he thought about what Ben said.

"Most likely Ham Greeley's outside with the rest of 'em," Ben said. "Maybe he can fix you up right away."

"He's out there," Tuck chimed in. "I'll go get him."

He started toward the door, then paused long enough to say, "I think that's a good idea to let that son of a gun set there and stew in his own juice."

"Glad you approve," Ben said. When Tuck went outside to get Ham, Ben decided he still had an appetite for supper. "Unless you want me to stay here right now, I'm gonna go up to the hotel and get something to eat before they close. I'll be back afterward, all right?"

"Oh, sure," Mack was quick to reply. "You know I appreciate your help, but I reckon I can watch my jailhouse. You don't have to come back here tonight, if you got things to do at the Coyote." He paused, then said, "I don't reckon that one wearin' the mask will make another try at gettin' him outta here, you think?"

"Well, I can't say for sure, but I wouldn't think so," Ben said. "It's my opinion that he ain't likely to try anything by himself. He was the only one wearin' a mask and it wasn't a bandanna tied around his neck. It was a sack coverin' his whole head. Those two fellows with him didn't even wear bandannas. I figure he's got too much to lose. He's afraid he'd be recognized, and I've got a feelin' he's hightailin' it to Waco right now on that buckskin he likes to ride."

This got Bragg's attention. "You know who he is?"

"No, I'm only guessin', and I ain't got any way to prove it." He changed the subject before having to name a name. "We'll see how ol' Pete likes livin' in there with his partner, especially after his skin changes color and he goes stiff as a board."

* * *

"There's Ben!" Ruby exclaimed, out on the front porch with Rachel, Clarice, and Tiny. After they had heard the shots fired down at the jail, they were straining to see what had happened. When Rachel came over to stand beside her, Ruby pointed toward the small crowd of mostly Golden Rail patrons gathered around the sheriff's office. "There he is," she said again when the crowd parted to let him through.

"I see him," Rachel said, relieved to see that he seemed to be all right. "But where's he going?" She asked when he turned to walk down the street, instead of turning to head toward the Lost Coyote. She walked down the steps then, to stand in the street, so she might see where he was going. "He went in the dining room," she said when he went in the side door of the hotel. She turned to look in amazement at Ruby, who had followed her to the street. When Tiny came down the steps to join them, she turned to him. "It looks like they had a small war down there and Ben went to the dining room at the hotel. That's just like him, isn't it?"

Tiny looked at her and shrugged. She obviously thought Ben should have come at once to the Coyote to let them know what had happened and that he was all right. "Well, it is time for supper, and the dinin' room don't stay open very late," he offered.

Rachel favored him with a look she reserved for small children and most men. She shook her head and said, "I'm going back inside to make sure nobody's in there serving themselves free whiskey while we're out here gaping at the jailhouse." Tiny winked at Ruby and followed Rachel inside.

Ben's firsthand accounting of the incident at the

sheriff's office was delivered to the staff at the hotel dining room as he hurriedly ate his supper. After that, he went back to Mack Bragg's office to see if there had been any progress in the disarming of Mack's prisoner. There had not, but Ham Greeley was already fixing the front door up with a solid bar across it in addition to the lock. And Mack was satisfied to continue the standoff with Pete Russell until the federal marshals came to pick him up, if necessary. Since the sheriff seemed all right with the situation, as unusual as it was, Ben felt no need to stand guard with him. Only then did he return to the Lost Coyote.

He found that everyone in the saloon had already been briefed on the occurrence at the jail by Tuck Tucker. "Did you enjoy your supper?" Rachel asked when he walked over to join her at the end of the bar.

"Yeah, I did," he answered, not finding her question sarcastic at all. "Myrtle cooked pork chops again, but they weren't fried. They were in some kinda heavy gravy—pretty good."

She shook her head patiently, then said, "Well, we're glad to see you're all right. Tuck told us what happened."

"Figured he would," Ben replied. There was no time for further comment, because Henry Barnes joined them at that point.

"Glad to see you're in one piece," Henry greeted him. "When the shootin' started down there, I walked out to the front of the stable and I saw that fellow wearin' a sack on his head when he rode right by me. Scared the devil outta me, but he wasn't payin' me no mind. Ridin' a buckskin, he was flat-out flyin'. I stepped back inside the door, figured he looked like he was too busy to stop and talk." He chuckled at his humor. "Unusual buckskin horse," he commented.

"How so?" Ben asked, interested.

"I don't know why I even noticed it. I mean, with a rider wearin' a mask and gallopin' like hell right by me. You know how a buckskin has black stockings on his lower legs, like that dun you ride? Well, that buckskin's left front leg had only a sock just above the hoof, and the rest of his legs had regular stocking markings."

"Well, that's mighty interestin'," Ben said, thinking he'd give a dollar to get another look at the buckskin Walt Murphy rode. He wished he had been as observant as Henry had been today. When he had seen the horse that day when Walt rode it to the church, he just admired the lines of the horse.

CHAPTER 12

The next morning, Ben waited until after breakfast before saddling Cousin for the twenty-mile trip to Madisonville and the railroad where he wired Captain Randolph Mitchell, his former commanding officer when he rode with F-Company, Texas Rangers. He knew Mitchell would contact the proper person in the marshal service to send a couple of deputies over to transport Pete Russell to trial. It might even be a feather in Mitchell's cap since the capture of the surviving bank robber had been the work of a Ranger. After sending the wire, Ben spent a couple of hours in Madisonville, killing time while he rested his horse, and long enough to get a confirmation wire from Mitchell and eat dinner at the hotel dining room. Mitchell's wire said he might have to hold the prisoner for as long as a week, depending upon the availability of the deputies to do the job. There was also the option of Ben transporting the prisoner to Austin, himself. But he gave that no consideration at all. The only reason he had gone in pursuit of the bank robbers was because they stole his horse. Once he got his horse back, it was the marshals' or the Rangers' business, and they were welcome to it. He was happy to give Mack Bragg a hand, but now he was ready to retreat to the Coyote and his saloon business.

When he got back to Buzzard's Bluff, he went to the sheriff's office first to tell him what Mitchell had said, so he would have an idea of how long he would have to hold Pete. "Well, so far, he ain't budged from his standoff," Mack said. "Every time I crack that door, I hear that pistol cock, so there ain't no worry about havin' to feed him, or anythin' else"

"He's gotta get hungry some time," Ben reckoned, "we'll just have to wait and see. It can't help his resolve to have to look at last night's supper scattered across the floor. He oughta be about ready to take a chance on your word by suppertime tomorrow."

Pete Russell was more determined, or more frightened, than either Ben or Mack had speculated. The jail standoff continued unbroken over the next couple of days and soon became the main topic of conversation in the little town on the Brazos. Mack took longer and longer peeks through the cracked door as Pete became more and more weary and less alert. He reported the different stages Ormond's body was passing through, from rigor mortis when it was stiff as a board until the body went limp again. The skin, what Mack could see through the crack in the door, went from green, to purple, to black, and the corpse's eyes and tongue bulged out to create a hideous façade. While the sight was unnerving to Mack, Pete somehow persevered and Mack was convinced Pete just wouldn't permit himself to look at the body.

In the end, however, it was not the repulsive sight that ended the standoff. It was the smell. After two full days, the body had begun to putrefy, emitting an odor, both strong and unpleasant. Another day passed, and with it, there arose an odor so foul as to be overpowering. The next morning, Ben found Mack sleeping in a bedroll outside the front door of his office. When he asked the reason, Mack said, "Just stand up there next to the door and take a deep breath."

"I figured it had to be pretty soon now," Ben declared. "And he still ain't give up yet?" Right after he said it, he heard what he thought was a cry for help.

"Yeah," Mack complained, "he's give up, but I'm lettin' him holler for a while for settin' in there like a jackass till that corpse stunk up my whole office. He oughta have to sniff it all up by himself."

"Has he tossed that gun out?"

"Yeah, he tossed it through the bars last night, but I let it lay," Mack said. "When I opened the door, the smell liked to knocked me down, so I closed it to keep it from fillin' up my office. That didn't do no good. About three o'clock this mornin', I had to grab my bedroll and come outside."

"I expect we'd best get that body outta there," Ben said. "I'll go see if I can roust Merle Baker out. I doubt he's gonna want to take the body in the condition it's in, but he might have something to clean out the smell. We'll most likely just dig a hole and dump it in it, maybe pour some kerosene on it and burn it. But first, we'll have to rescue your prisoner, bring him outside, and handcuff him to the steps, I reckon. I expect you'd better feed him, too. I'm surprised he can make as much noise as he is. Whaddaya say? You ready to get him? I'll help you if you are."

Mack nodded reluctantly. "One thing I'm gonna do is fix those damn windows over the cells," he said, thinking that the cause of all the trouble that followed.

"I reckon," Ben replied.

The activity at the jail did not go unnoticed by the early risers in the little town, and pretty soon there was a gathering of spectators. Some even ventured close enough to get a whiff of the odor emanating from the cell room. One of these was Tuck Tucker, who walked into Mack's office but turned around immediately. "I think that feller is startin' to turn," he announced to Ben and Mack.

"You think so?" Mack responded. "Maybe we'd best carry him outta there, before he gets too ripe. You wanna give us a hand?"

"Why, sure," Tuck answered. "I'll stay out here and help keep these folks outta the way."

Mack looked at Ben and shook his head, smiling as he replied. "Well, that's what we need, somebody to control the crowd." It amused him to think that Ormond Hazzard would have no trouble clearing a path for them without any help from anyone. With stout determination, they set to their task, first wrapping wet cloths around their faces to keep from gagging on the smell. Ben picked up the pistol Pete had finally discarded while Mack unlocked the cell. Then they marched Pete outside, each of them supporting him by his elbows. He was in no shape to resist, but they cuffed him to the steps as a precaution. Before tackling the job of removing the putrefying body from the cell, Ben gave Pete a dipperful of water, which he gulped down immediately. "We'll see about gettin' you something to eat in a little bit," he said. Too weak to talk, especially since his voice was hoarse from yelling, Pete could only nod as he looked up at Ben. It appeared that he had reached a state where he really didn't give a damn if they shot him or not.

When Merle came with his wagon, he brought a bucket of his own special formula to clean up the area on the floor where Ormond had lain. He also volunteered the use of his wagon to transport the remains out of town to bury them. As Ben had figured, the body was too far gone for Merle to have any interest in taking it to his shop. With the help of two young men in the gathering of spectators, Ben and Mack managed to transfer the body to Merle's wagon.

Meals were restarted immediately for Pete, and he was returned to the cell room but to the cell next to his prior one. There was still odor but not full strength as he had last experienced it. According to Merle, it would take a while. The whole ordeal taught Mack Bragg a lesson, and he had Jim Bowden working on some iron bars for the cell room windows before the day was over.

It was three more days before two U.S. deputy marshals showed up with papers from the Austin office officially identifying them and authorizing them to take possession of the prisoner and the bank's money. They arrived in time for supper one day, stayed in the hotel that night, then had breakfast in the dining room before showing up at the sheriff's office, ready to take possession of the prisoner. By this time, Pete Russell was a little reluctant to leave the hassle-free treatment from the sheriff and the meals from the hotel dining room. Before he left, he made a special effort to apologize to Ben and Mack for all the trouble he had caused in the town of Buzzard's Bluff, starting with his rude behavior to Lacy James that first time in the hotel dining room. "I wish you'd tell her I'm sorry about that and thank her for feedin' me so good while I was in jail."

Ben glanced at Mack, who returned the look with a grin and a raised eyebrow. Pete's apology sounded genuinely sincere. The two deputy marshals seemed to be impressed as well. Not fully educated on Buzzard's Bluff's history with Pete, they could imagine they were escorting an unfortunate victim of the notorious Hazzard brothers. "If he's that contrite when they try him, maybe the judge will go easy on him," Mack remarked as he and Ben watched the deputies leading Pete away.

"Well," Ben remarked, with a sigh of relief, "I reckon I'd best get back to the Coyote to see if Rachel's got any chores she wants done. I've been kinda scarce around there for the past few days and I have to earn my keep."

"Knowin' how Rachel keeps such a tight rein on that place, I can believe you," Mack said. Getting serious for a moment, he confessed. "I'd be a lowdown dog if I didn't thank you for all the help you've been through all this business with the Hazzards and all the rest of it. So thanks."

"Glad I could help," Ben replied. "You had a little too much for one man to handle, and I think it's every citizen's responsibility to help keep the peace." He paused then and grinned. "But next time, call on

Tuck Tucker to help you out. He's your best bet, and he's rarin' to go."

Not surprising, Tuck was the first person Ben ran into when he returned to the Lost Coyote. "Hey, Ben, we was just talkin' about you. Have they picked Pete up yet? I was just fixin' to go down to the jail to see they got him all right." Ben told him that they had picked Pete up and were already riding out of town. "Dad-burn-it, I was on my way down there and everybody here was askin' me questions about them deputies till I couldn't get done talkin'."

Ben glanced beyond the little flame-haired gnome to see the grins on the faces of those gathered near the bar. "Well," he said, "they got underway without any trouble. Matter of fact, Pete was right calm and acted a little bit like he didn't wanna leave Buzzard's Bluff." He walked over to the bar to join the others and told them about Pete's apologies to everybody he thought he might have wronged.

"So now, he's gonna ride all the way to Austin, right?" Tiny asked.

"No," Ben replied. "They're just gonna ride back to Madisonville and put him in jail there tonight. In the mornin', they'll put him on the train and take him to Austin tomorrow."

"'Least, he's gettin' to take a train ride," Ruby remarked. "That's something I'd like to do. I ain't ever rode on a train. Have you, Clarice?"

"Once," Clarice answered, "when the city council bought me a one-way ticket outta Kansas City. I enjoyed it. I was younger'n you then and had a lotta things to learn."

"I don't know how much Pete Russell will enjoy his train ride," Tuck declared. "I don't reckon the ride's so enjoyable when there's a rope waitin' for you at the other end."

Further discussion on the subject of trains was interrupted then when Annie Grey came in from the kitchen to announce that dinner was ready for anybody who planned to eat. She always gave her fellow employees at the saloon a little advance notice before the usual dinner regulars showed up. Also, as usual, Tuck was already there, and Ham Greeley came in the door in time to follow the staff to the one large table in a back corner of the saloon that passed as the dining room. As she often did, Rachel took over the bar so Tiny could go to dinner early. Ben offered to tend the bar in her place, but she insisted that she was a better bartender than he was. He couldn't really argue the point, because she was right, so he joined the others. Everything was peaceful in Buzzard's Bluff again. Even the Golden Rail, the noisy competitive saloon across from the jail, was minus the normally raucous crowd of drifters and ne'er-do-wells that hung out there most of the time. Mack Bragg's jail cells were empty of lawbreakers or drunks. He had a new security bar for his front door and a grillwork of iron bars on the cell room windows that air could pass through but pistols couldn't.

Since it was Wednesday, Annie stayed a little later than she did on other days of the week, so she could bake several trays of what she called her salty bread sticks. They were a favorite of the Wednesday-night poker game in the little side room next to the office. It was a weekly card game with usually the same four players, all leading members of the city council. Mayor Cecil Howard, Postmaster Sam Grier, Dr. John Tatum, and Freeman Brown, the owner of the River House Hotel, always played and were sometimes joined by Merle Baker. It had become a ritual, so Annie always wanted to prepare something for them to have with their whiskey and beer. Most of the merchants in the town would swear that more council decisions were made at that poker table Wednesday nights than at any of the regular monthly council meetings. Tuck Tucker always contended that it was because there was no one at the poker game to ask questions or register complaints.

With no worries for a change, Ben took advantage of the peaceful time to spend some time with his horse and visit with Henry Barnes. After an inspection of Cousin's hooves, he told Henry that he was always pleased with Jim Bowden's shoeing of the big dun gelding. He had said as much to Jim, but he figured, if Henry happened to tell Jim he had complimented his work, it would be worth more to Jim.

When it was time, and he received the signals from his stomach, Ben walked to the lower end of the street to take supper with Lacy James and the other women at the hotel dining room. Seeing Mack Bragg there, he joined him, figuring Mack had most likely already answered all their questions about the farewell to Pete Russell. A once hardened outlaw and gunman who had acknowledged the error of his ways while a resident of the Buzzard's Bluff jail was a story that the women loved to tell. "I wish to hell you hadn't sat down with me," Mack said when they were left alone for a few minutes. "I've had to hear you answer the same questions about Saint Peter Russell that they just asked me. I reckon it is a good story, but how long are we gonna talk about it?" As it turned out, all good stories come to an end.

It was two days after they carried Pete Russell away when Sam Grier's son Robert stopped in town on his way back to his farm and gave them the news. Mack Bragg was having a cup of coffee at the Lost Coyote with Ben when Robert came looking for them. "Ben," he called out as he walked to their table. "I got somethin' to tell you I think you and the sheriff would wanna know."

"Well, sit down," Ben said. "You want some coffee, or do you need something a little stronger?"

"I'll just have some of that coffee," Robert said, then got right to his report. "I was over to Madisonville today to pick up some plants I had ordered at the railroad depot. That fellow you had locked up here that wouldn't come outta his cell." He paused to recall the name.

"Pete Russell," Mack filled in the blank for him.

"Right, that Pete Russell fellow. Well, he killed both of those deputies that were takin' him to Austin."

"What?" Ben recoiled, stunned.

"That's right," Robert said and continued his account to the two shocked lawmen, as well as several others close enough to hear his excited report. "They had him ready to get on the train and they took the handcuffs off him so he could lead his horse up the ramp to the stock car. Well, he just grabbed the gun right outta the one deputy's holster and shot the other deputy before he could pull his gun. Then he told that deputy, whose gun he had, to unbuckle his gun belt and lay facedown on the ground or he'd shoot him. The stationmaster told me he heard the deputy askin' Russell not to shoot him, said he wouldn't try to stop him. And Russell said 'I know you ain't' and put a bullet in the back of that deputy's head. Then he jumped on one of the horses and took off."

It was hard for either Ben or the sheriff to believe what they were hearing. No comment they could make would explain how the story they just heard could have happened. Finally, Mack asked, "What about the bank money?"

"He took it with him," Robert said. "He jumped on a horse that one of the deputies was ridin'. They had a packhorse with the money on it and it was on a lead rope tied to the deputy's saddle. He left 'em layin' there dead and took off for who knows where."

There was nothing said by Ben or Mack for a long few moments while they let Robert's news soak into their brains. Mack was the first to speak again. "I ain't never been so wrong about a fellow in all my life." He looked at Ben, but Ben only shook his head, fully perplexed as much as the sheriff was. "Whaddaya reckon we oughta do?"

"Nothing," Rachel answered his question. She had come to stand behind Ben when she heard what Robert said. "It's no longer your business what Pete Russell does, unless he shows up again here in Buzzard's Bluff. You did your job, Mack. He's the marshals' responsibility now." She turned her attention to her partner then. "And it's certainly none of your responsibility. You don't ride with the Rangers anymore, remember? And I think you tend to forget you're not the sheriff's partner. You're my partner in this saloon." She had known him long enough to know how his mind worked, and she was certain he was feeling it his responsibility to go after Pete Russell.

Also standing close by, as usual, Tuck felt the need to offer his opinion. "Rachel's right, Ben. There ain't no call for you to worry about that two-faced sidewinder. That's the business of the U.S. Marshal in Austin. With all the trouble Pete Russell caused here, with him stinkin' up the jailhouse and all, I know I don't feel sorry for him."

"Reckon not," Ben responded, but he couldn't shake a feeling that a job he had worked on had gone unfinished. Like Mack, he felt he had been tricked into feeling Pete was truly sorry for his past transgressions. And the fact that he had not seen through the ruse was what bothered him most. Now, with the conscienceless murder of two deputy marshals, he felt a strong desire to see Pete pay for his deceit. He glanced up at Rachel, who was eyeing him like a stern mother scolding an unruly child. He couldn't help smiling at her. "Reckon we could get some hot coffee?"

"I'll tell Annie," Rachel said, still not happy with his reaction to Robert Grier's news bulletin about Pete Russell.

CHAPTER 13

"Tore a page right outta your book, Malcolm, ol' buddy," Pete Russell gloated to himself as he held the gray gelding to a spirited pace after leaving the Dallas road and heading west. When he had hightailed it out of Madisonville, he stayed on the Dallas road for about thirty-five miles before he left it to ride cross-country in the general direction of Waco. If they were quick enough to get up a posse, he figured he had stayed on the northbound road long enough to make them think he was heading to Dallas.

He thought of Malcolm Hazzard's long charade as a religious convert that resulted in his early release from prison. It might have been a greater challenge to pull the wool over the judge and the warden's eyes, and Malcolm had won his freedom as a result. But Pete had to give himself credit for causing two deputy marshals to become careless enough to get themselves killed. And the biggest difference between Malcolm's hoax and his was the fact that he was leading a pack-horse carrying over twenty thousand dollars, give or take a dollar or two. *Too bad about Ormond,* he thought.

"Man," he blurted, "he worked up one helluva stink!" He was afraid the sight of the big man's body as it passed through the stages of putrefaction was a picture that might come to revisit him. It bothered him some that he had finally broken down and surrendered the handgun he had held them at bay with. But, he allowed, he was weak from lack of food, water, and sleep. As it turned out, it had been a good thing, for it caused his pitiful state, which, in turn, inspired his charade as a repenting soul, sorry for his crimes. And they bought it, lock, stock, and barrel, even the big stud Ben Savage. "Sorry I ain't gonna get a chance to have another little visit with you, Savage, but I expect I'd best make myself pretty scarce around these parts."

The thought of Ben Savage triggered thoughts of other things he had to consider. He was almost to the eastern end of the road to Waco, the road that went right by the church. Ben Savage knew about the church. He had come there and ambushed him and Ormond, resulting in their capture. Pete thought it might be risky going back to the church now, but it was a place for him to recover his packhorse and trade the gray he was riding. There was also some personal property he left behind when Savage snatched him and Ormond right out from under Reuben Drum and Walt Murphy's noses. Other than the need to ride a different horse, he had to admit that he wanted to plant a seed in Reuben's and Walt's minds that he no longer had the money. It might seem dangerous to return to the church, even for the short time he planned. But there was no reason to suspect that Savage would show up there again. Conversation he had heard between Savage and Sheriff Bragg when he was in jail indicated that Savage was not prone to leave Buzzard's Bluff. He had a business there. Chances were good that Savage had not even heard that he had escaped. And if he had, what would be his incentive to come after him?

He decided it not to be that great a risk to go to the church and reclaim his property. He might have considered the fact that he was now wealthy enough to replace everything he had left at the church. And the best thing for him to do was to ride as far away from Texas as he could get. At this point, he was actually worried more about Walt Murphy than he was about Ben Savage. Walt may not know what happened after he had fled the unsuccessful jailbreak in Buzzard's Bluff. But as sheriff of Waco, he would most likely receive Wanted papers, telling him that one, Pete Russell, had killed two federal deputy marshals and escaped in Madisonville. He didn't know if they would say anything about the stolen money or not. He knew, however, that Walt was obsessed with the money. The fact that he had risked everything to participate in the attempted jailbreak told Pete that Walt was determined to get his share of that money. In view of that, Pete was convinced that he would be dogged by Walt forever, trying to get his hands on the twenty thousand dollars. For that reason, Pete thought it important to return to the church and tell Reuben and the others that he had escaped, but not with the bank money. He would convince them that he had come back to get the possessions he had left behind because he needed them to survive. The first order of business, then, was to hide the canvas bags filled with money.

The place he picked was less than a mile from the church, on the same creek that the church was standing beside. When he came to the point where the road crossed the creek, he turned his horses into the water and walked them about fifty yards upstream to a low rock ledge that created a tiny waterfall. Spotting a fallen tree lying several yards from the creek, he decided that was the place to hide his fortune. So he left the horses beside the creek and carried the canvas bags the deputies had put the money in over to the tree. Using a small hatchet that had belonged to one of the deputies he killed, he carved out a hole underneath the rotting trunk large enough to hold the bags.

After he buried the money and tidied up his work, he went back to the creek, where he waded into the water and pulled some of the larger rocks out of the little waterfall. Then he put them back, but not quite in their original positions, so that it might look like there had been something hidden there at some time. He hoped that his effort was pointless. But in the event someone should think he might have hidden money up that creek, maybe they would see the displaced rocks and think that had been the place. He climbed back on the gray and rode back down to the road, prepared to give another performance to rival Malcolm's.

"Somebody's comin'," Riley Best called back over his shoulder. "One man, ridin' a gray and leadin' a packhorse."

"Can't tell who it is?" Reuben asked.

"No," Riley answered. "Wait a minute! It looks like Pete Russell!"

This was enough to get Reuben up out of his chair and to the door to see for himself. "I swear," he uttered, "it sure is. I thought he was dead or still in jail down at Buzzard's Bluff. That's what Walt said." In a few seconds they were joined by Dora and Paulene and when Pete pulled the gray to a stop at the front door, Reuben said, "Where'd you get that gray?"

"I stole him," Pete answered and climbed down from the saddle.

"We heard you was dead," Riley said.

"For a while there, I thought I was," Pete replied. "And I'm feelin' half-dead now and I'm needin' a drink of likker bad."

"Well, come on in," Paulene said, "and we'll get you one. You look like you been rode hard."

Pete dropped the gray's reins on the ground and walked up the steps. "I'll take care of my horses after I get that drink." They stood aside, then followed him inside where he sat down at the table Reuben had just gotten up from. "You seen Walt Murphy?" Pete asked after he tossed his drink down.

"Yeah," Reuben answered. "He's the one said you was dead. He came here after that day him and the others was gonna break you and Ormond outta jail. And nobody came back from that big ambush with him. Booth Brayer, Charlie Taylor, Dick Flynn, and John Temple; none of 'em made it back here. Walt was the only one and he just made it, himself. He said Ben Savage and the sheriff were all set up and waitin' for 'em when they charged in that jail after you and

Ormond." He paused then to ask, "Where is Ormond? Did he get away with you?"

"No . . . no, he didn't," Pete responded soberly. "Ormond was shot down by Ben Savage and they left me in that jail cell with him for four days, so I could watch him rot. Walt don't know about that because he didn't stick around after Charley and Temple were shot down. He took off like a bat outta hell and never fired a shot at nobody. I'm the only one of us that walked outta that Buzzard's Bluff jail, and I'll tell you why." He went on to tell them the complete story as it actually happened, including the part about his standoff with Savage and Bragg after he got his hands on the gun Ormond dropped. He also confessed to giving up after his body couldn't take it anymore. "So they sent two deputy marshals down there to take me to the train station in Madisonville. And they got the money on the train, but they didn't get me on it. I saw my chance, so I took it. Too bad I had to kill two deputies to get away."

"So, there *was* all that bank money in those saddlebags you and Ormond wouldn't let outta your sight," Reuben said. "I knew it. We all did. Ain't that right, Riley?"

"It sure is," Riley confirmed.

"Me and Ormond knew you knew it, too," Pete said, smiled, and shook his head as if in sad lament. "And we was tryin' our best to hold onto every penny of it. Nothin' against you boys, but we just figured we was the ones who robbed that bank. And we'd already lost their brother and his share of the money along with him." He slowly shook his head again. "And now I'm broke as I was before the whole thing got started, and I'll have every lawman in the state of Texas after me. So I came back here to pick up my stuff and that 74 Sharps single-shot rifle I left here. I got a feelin' I'm gonna be eatin' a lot of wild meat for a while, at least till I can run across a little money somewhere." He paused to see how they were takin' his sorrowful tale. "I've got a right fine gray geldin' out there I'd like to trade, if anybody's interested in pickin' up a good horse. I don't need to be ridin' that gray right now, if you know what I mean."

"I know what you mean," Reuben responded. "I'm always lookin' for a good trade, and you're right, they'll be lookin' for a man fits your description, ridin' a gray horse. You're gonna stay the night, ain'tcha?" Pete said he had planned to, so Reuben said, "I'll take a look at him in the mornin'. We're glad to have your company, ain't we, girls, even if you're a little light in your pocket." They giggled appropriately.

"Oh, I didn't come lookin' for a handout," Pete said. "I intend to pay for my keep here, just like before. I've got fifty dollars I hid in the sack of cartridges for that Sharps rifle. As long as you ain't give my stuff away, I can pay for tonight." When that brought a sudden look of awkwardness to the faces of both Reuben and Riley, Pete asked, "You still got my possibles, ain't you?"

"Why, sure, your stuff's still here, even though we figured you and Ormond had cut out for good when you took your saddles and your saddlebags, too." Reuben was quick to assure him. "But I don't know what to tell you about your fifty dollars. I have to admit, we looked in that sack just to see what was in there and saw them cartridges. But there weren't no money in there."

"No money?" Pete exclaimed. "Did you look real good? 'Cause I rolled it up and stuck it under all the cartridges." When they both shook their heads solemnly, he said, "Well, if that don't beat all. The only person who knew about it was Ormond. That son of a gun, I was gonna buy supplies with some of that money."

"Tell you what," Reuben said, "you don't worry about what you owe for tonight. I'll give you credit for whatever you eat or drink and I'll pay for any transaction you have with either of the girls. How's that? Maybe we'll make it right when we get to horse tradin' in the mornin'."

"That's more than fair," Pete allowed. "I always knew you was an honorable outlaw. We'll talk trade in the mornin'. Right now, I'd best go take care of my horses."

"Reckon who got that fifty dollars?" Riley asked after Pete went back outside. "Everybody looked through all that stuff they were carryin' on their packhorse. It coulda been anybody."

"I weren't lyin' when I said I looked in that bag of cartridges," Reuben said. "Maybe he was right when he said Ormond musta got it. Most likely took it before they ever got here."

Out behind the church, Pete pulled the saddle off the gray and the packsaddle off the roan, then he turned the two horses out to graze with the few other horses there at the present time. He congratulated himself again for tearing another page out of Malcolm Hazzard's book. He never hid any money in an ammunition bag that he could remember, but he would enjoy himself at Reuben's expense for one night before moving on. He was not really concerned about the law tonight. He figured there hadn't been enough time for them to get on his trail. When he went back inside, he planned to ask when Reuben expected to see Walt again.

"I expect he'll show up around here in the mornin'," Reuben said when Pete asked him the question. "We ain't seen him since the night after that business at Buzzard's Bluff. And he usually stops by every two or three days, just to see who mighta turned up here. He likes to keep close watch over who comes and goes here at the church."

"Well, I hope he does," Pete said. "I'd like to hear what happened outside the front door of the jail that night."

By the time breakfast was over the next morning, there was no sign of Walt Murphy, much to Pete's disappointment. But he had some horse trading to do with Reuben to take care of, so they walked out to the corral and Reuben took a good look at the gray Pete wanted to trade. "I gotta admit, I'm tryin' to find the real reason you're lookin' to trade this horse, but I can't find anything wrong with him," Reuben finally conceded.

"I wouldn't try to pull nothin' on you, Reuben. Like I told you, this horse belonged to a U.S. deputy marshal, and those fellers usually ride a good horse. I rode him hard all the way from Madisonville. He never balked once, and I never had occasion to cuss him. I would keep him for myself if I could change his color. But it's my bad luck that so many people saw me ride off on that gray, and your good fortune that I have to trade him."

"I believe you're shootin' straight with me," Reuben replied. "You can see what I've got to trade here in the corral. Those two in the corner, the sorrel and the blue roan, belong to Riley. The rest of 'em are mine, except that brown over there. That's the packhorse you left here when you and Ormond took off. You look over the others and tell me which one you wanna look at."

"First, I wanna remind you, me and Ormond wasn't plannin' to take off that night. We was *took off* by that dry-gulchin' Ben Savage. We just thought we had too much money to leave layin' around while we was out lookin' for our horses. And I'll admit, we weren't sure you and the other boys didn't have somethin' to do with our horses missin', just so you could take a look in our saddlebags. That said, why don't you keep that packhorse I left here and I'll just keep the one I borrowed from that deputy in Madisonville? And that'll take care of what I owe you for last night and today, all right?"

"Fair enough," Reuben answered, "and you take your pick of my horses and we'll swap even."

"That sounds like a fair-enough deal to me," Pete said. He watched the horses for a few minutes longer before declaring, "That red dun looks like a sound horse to me."

"If it was me, I'd take a look at that chestnut." The voice came from behind to surprise them. "Lester used to think that was his pa's best horse." They turned to meet Walt Murphy as he walked up to the corral. They had not seen him come up to the front of the church. "Riley said you two was out around back horse tradin'," Walt went on.

"He was gonna be my second choice to look at," Pete responded, noticing that the mention of his son brought an instant frown to Reuben's face.

"I ain't surprised you're lookin' to trade horses," Walt said, "but I am surprised to see you back here. Tell you the truth, I thought you were most likely dead, you and ol' Ormond, too. Then, I swear, this mornin' I got a telegram that said to be on the lookout for Pete Russell, escaped prisoner, killed two deputy marshals, ridin' a gray horse. Never figured I'd ever see the likes of you again. Thought you'd be headin' for Indian Territory."

A slow smile spread across Pete's face. Walt had already received notification, as had all the other town sheriffs in the area. But he didn't say anything about the missing bank money. He wondered if the sheriff was playing a little game with him, or if there had been no mention of the money. "After that night in Buzzard's Bluff, when you and the boys came to break me and Ormond outta jail, I figured *you* mighta headed for Injun Territory."

"That was a bad deal, all right," Walt replied. "They were set up, waitin' for us. Ben Savage was waitin' for Booth and Flynn when they walked into the Lost Coyote. Maybe the rest of it was my fault because Charlie and Temple were ready to run, but I made 'em go back with me to try to get you and Ormond outta there. But they had that jail set up in ambush, too. Charlie and Temple both went down right away, leavin' me by myself to try to get to you. I tried, but I found out I couldn't, so I had to shoot my way outta there."

"Is that what happened?" Pete asked. "It ain't exactly the way the sheriff and Savage told it to me, after Savage shot Ormond. They said they shot Charlie and Temple when they broke in the front door, and all they saw of you was your horse hightailin' it outta town."

Walt matched Pete's grin with one of his own. "Well, now, that's just what they would likely say, ain't it? I expect you and Reuben and Riley oughta be damn glad I was able to get away from there without being recognized. It mighta been the end of me, but it'da been the end of the hideout here at the church, too." He looked over at Reuben. "That wouldn'ta been too good, would it, Reuben?" Then he quickly turned his attention back to Pete. "Since you killed them two deputies and got away on one of 'em's gray and his packhorse, too, I hope it was carryin' all the bank money."

His comment brought a laugh and a grunt from Pete and he replied. "His saddle and the one that came off the packhorse are layin' inside the back door of the church. You're welcome to all the money you find in 'em."

Reuben spoke up then. "I had to lend him a little credit to pay for his supper," he declared. "That's why we needed to strike a deal on a horse trade."

"Well, I'm glad to see you got away from them deputies," Walt said to Pete. "I expect you just missed bein' the main guest at a necktie party for killin' that bank guard in Giddings."

"It was Malcolm who shot that bank guard in Giddings," Pete responded at once.

Walt smiled. "That don't make much difference now, does it? You sure as hell shot them two deputies in Madisonville and there were plenty of witnesses to say you done it. How long you figurin' on hangin' around here at the church?"

"I don't know," Pete answered. He had no intention of telling Walt exactly when he was going. He was still not sure if Walt knew he had the money, or if he was still just fishing in hopes of finding out. "Not long, that's for sure," he said. "There's bound to be some folks lookin' for me pretty quick."

"I think you're smart not to hang around here," Walt said. "There's too many folks that know about the church now. Ben Savage is one of 'em."

"I hope to hell Ben Savage does show up here," Reuben interrupted. "It'd be the last place he ever set foot on."

"That's right, Reuben," Walt responded, "and I'd like to help you welcome him. But I'm afraid he wouldn't come alone, so Pete best not be here if that happens." Back to Pete then, he suggested, "If you're wantin' to lay low for a day or two longer while you decide where you're headin', I know one place where nobody would look for you." When he thought he saw a spark of curiosity in Pete's eyes, he went on, "My place." When the spark immediately went out, he hurried to explain. "I ain't talkin' about my jail. I'm talkin' about my cabin. Reuben'll tell ya. I've got a little cabin about a mile upriver from town. Ain't nobody gonna be lookin' for you there."

"I swear, Walt, you'd do that for me?" Pete asked,

hoping not to sound too facetious. "You bein' a sheriff and all, I wouldn't wanna put you in a position to lose everything, if the marshals find out you helped me." Walt shrugged, as if it was of no concern to him. "I'll tell you what," Pete continued, "I'll decide in the mornin' what I'm gonna do. I'll let you know then, all right?"

"Whatever you say," Walt answered. "Which one of the horses you gonna take?"

"I'm gonna pick the red dun I think." He looked at Reuben, Reuben nodded his okay, and the deal was struck. *He ain't sure* Pete thought, still smiling at Walt. *He thinks I've got the money, but he's not sure.* "I'll throw my saddle on him and take him for a little get-acquainted ride, so he'll be ready to go tomorrow."

"I'm gonna drink up a little bit of Reuben's coffee, then I expect I'd best get back to town, so my deputy don't get the idea he can take care of the town all by himself."

"That sounds like a good idea," Pete said. "I could drink another cup, myself."

CHAPTER 14

"That's what I thought, you lyin' sack of dung," Walt Murphy muttered aloud when he saw the red dun gelding, with Pete Russell on his back, leave the small barn behind the church at a casual lope. Leading a packhorse after him, he headed down the path to the road. "Wait till tomorrow, are you? I swear, it's gettin' to where you can't find an outlaw you can trust. Now we'll see where you hid that money. And when we find it, we'll divide it all up between the devil and me. Maybe by now there's a reward posted for you dead or alive. That'll add a little more to the pot. Too bad the bank money ain't ever gonna be found." He climbed aboard the buckskin gelding, and when Pete disappeared around the last bend before reaching the Waco road, Walt came out of the trees on the ridge above the church. At a lope, he rode down to the path and pulled up at the bend before following Pete. After taking a look toward the Waco road and spotting Pete heading east on it, he held the buckskin back to let him get out of sight. As soon as he thought he was far enough behind to keep from being spotted, he set out on the road, looking right away for fresh tracks. When he was sure they were the tracks just made by Pete's horses, he knew he could tail him without being seen.

He had not ridden a mile when he came to the spot where the road crossed the creek. Checking the road up ahead, there was no one in sight, so he rode on across the creek, but pulled up abruptly when he discovered no tracks on the other side. His instant reaction was to look quickly right and left, fearing he had ridden into an ambush and expecting a shot at any second. He released his breath then, relieved that he had not done what he had momentarily feared. Pete had taken to the water. Upstream or down? That was to be decided next. So he looked in both directions and decided on upstream because the growth of trees and shrubs looked heavier up that way. Before he turned the buckskin's head, he heard the voice behind him. "Where you headin', Walt? Waco's back the other way."

"Damn, Pete, I didn't expect to run into you," Walt responded, trying to act totally surprised but not alarmed. "I get over this way once in a while when I come over to visit Reuben. There used to be a bunch of cattle rustlers that liked to camp on this creek. I ran 'em out, and I like to keep an eye on the place to make sure they ain't come back. What are you doin'? Tryin' out that dun you just traded for? I don't think you have to worry. You got a good horse." He looked beyond him at the red dun and the packhorse, standing in the trees on the other side of the creek and wondered how Pete got behind him. He was evidently expecting to be followed. "You gonna ride over and look at my place on the river tomorrow, like we talked about?"

Pete graced him with that slow smile that Walt had seen a lot earlier in the morning. "You know, Walt, I ain't known you for very long, but it seems like I've known you for a long, long time. I think it's because I've run into so many liars in my line of work. There ain't no money in those packs you're lookin' so hard at right now. Why don't you step down and go look in 'em to see for yourself? I ain't got that bank money. You're doggin' me for nothin.' "

"Well, I believe I will step down," Walt said. "You see, in my line of work, I've most likely run into more liars than you have." He threw his leg over and dropped to the ground, the buckskin's big body effectively blocking Pete's view of Walt's hand drawing the Colt Peacemaker from his holster by the time his feet touched down. As he walked around the horse to face Pete, he fired the first shot while his arm was underneath the buckskin's neck. When the startled horse reared back, Walt placed the second shot a couple of inches below the first one. Pete dropped to his knees without any attempt to draw his weapon. "And that's my way of dealin' with liars," he said and shoved Pete over on his side. "Then I'll take a look at them packs."

Before searching for the money, he took hold of Pete's wrists and dragged him back up in the trees with his horses. Then he tore the packs open only to find no sign of the money. He searched the saddlebags next with the same result. Frantic for a moment, he then calmed himself by reminding himself that he had just followed Pete here when Pete left the church. He had not had time to get his treasure from its hiding place. "Of course," he told himself. "He hid it. He didn't have it at the church, and the reason he stopped here was to make sure I went on by before he went to get it." He turned to look upstream again. "And I'm bettin' you hid it up that way somewhere," he said to Pete's corpse. "Then I'm gonna put you in the ground where nobody can find you." He thought again of a possible reward offered for Pete, dead or alive, but it wouldn't be as much as that bank money. And it wouldn't be worth the cloud of suspicion he would forever be under.

Satisfied that no one would likely see the body, he rode up the stream, leading Pete's two horses. As he walked the horses, he scanned the banks carefully to pick up any signs of tracks that would tell him where Pete had left the water. He found what he was looking for just short of a low rock ledge that formed a small waterfall. Climbing out of the creek then, he dismounted and left the horses to graze near a fallen tree. There were tracks there but no sign of any continuing on past the waterfall, or reentering the water above it. He stopped and looked at hoofprints reentering the creek below the little ledge, then it occurred to him that something didn't look right. It was as if a couple of the bigger rocks had been moved. *It's under the rocks!* He thought at once and immediately waded into the water. They were heavy, so he could only lift one of them at a time. After he had dislodged them, he could see they were definitely out of place, but he found himself staring at a hard, sandy creek bed with no sign of any digging. It only served to infuriate him, especially when his common sense belatedly told him, if it was gold, maybe he would hide it in the creek. But it was paper money, so he wouldn't have hidden it in the water.

Where then? He felt as if Pete's ghost was laughing at him. Frustrated, he walked over to the fallen tree and sat down to empty the water from his boots. Then he took his socks off, cursing Pete Russell as he did, and wrung them out. As he stared at the stream of water he wrung from his socks, he noticed the water seeped right into the ground between his legs. Curious, he took his boot and raked it across the ground. It was loose dirt, like dirt that had been spread on the ground. He threw his head back and roared with laughter. "Hell, I'm settin' right on top of it!" It took no more than a few minutes to brush away Pete's attempt to disguise his hiding place.

Once he had uncovered the buried canvas sack, and with trembling hands, untied the knotted drawstring, all the aggravation over the rocks in the creek vanished, replaced by the giddy childish delight of Christmas morning. He knew he had been right about the money, and Pete had made it easy for him to claim the money all for himself. That had been his plan all along. He had never intended to share with any of the others. It was only right that he should claim it all for himself, for he had taken the greatest risk to obtain it. He had risked his whole career as sheriff in addition to his life, had he been discovered. As he sat on the log, counting his treasure, a comical thought came to mind. "Maybe I oughta split it with Ben Savage. He gunned down damn-near everybody that I woulda had to kill to claim it all. Too bad I can't at least send him a thank-you letter for takin' out my partners." Of the original conspirators in the plan to take the bank money, only two others remained, Reuben Drum and Riley Best. It wasn't necessary to kill them, since they would think Pete had disappeared and taken the money with him. The same applied to Frances, Dora, and Paulene, so he was now in the clear as long as he didn't start spending money like a newly rich man. And he planned to be extra careful about that, allowing himself simple pleasures until he decided to leave Waco for good.

After he dug a shallow grave for Pete, he led his newly acquired horses back to his cabin on the Brazos River. In the game he was playing for the stolen bank money, he now found himself on the other side. For he was now in possession of the prize, and his worries were all toward how to protect it from others. Since most of his time was spent in town, there was the problem of leaving his cabin unguarded during the day. He was there at night, leaving his deputy, Wayne Price, to sleep in the sheriff's office and keep his eye on the town at night. Now, with his new role as possessor, he had to be concerned for his money during the day, while he was in town.

He had made provision for his valuables in the form of a large square hole, three feet deep in the floor of his small barn, where he kept his horse. He lined sides and bottom of the hole with pieces of tin roofing he got from the contractor who built the bank in town two years ago. The hole was covered with four-inch planks and a door with a heavy padlock and hidden by a covering of dirt and hay. At the present, there was a small amount of cash in the hiding place, his part of a stage robbery by a couple of Reuben's guests, and several handguns he had confiscated during arrests.

He couldn't help worrying about the safety of his hiding place as he cleared away the dirt and hay, thinking how easily he had discovered the hiding place that Pete had fashioned. His was much more disguised, he told himself. It would be much harder to break into even if you did happen to find it and he also had the plus factor of everyone knowing it was the sheriff's cabin. That alone was enough to make a robber stop and think, he figured. When the money was dropped into his safe-box, except for a sizeable roll for his pocket, he covered it all up again. With his money safely secured, he hoped, he then rode into town and took all three horses to Graham's stable. He didn't want to leave them at the cabin while he was away, and Graham's was where he always kept the buckskin when he was in town.

"Hey-yo, Sheriff," Bob Graham sang out. "Looks like you got yourself some new horses. You wantin' me to take care of 'em?"

"That's right, Bob," Walt answered. "I'll leave the buckskin here as usual, but I'll wait till I find Wayne to see if I'm gonna need to keep my horse saddled. These other two, I'm fixin' to leave with you now and I'll decide what I'm gonna do with 'em."

"Wayne was just in here a little while ago, lookin' for you," Bob said. "You been horse-tradin' this mornin'?"

"That's right," Walt answered. "That's why Wayne

couldn't find me. I thought I told him I was gonna see this fellow about sellin' me these horses this mornin'. I knew he was lookin' to sell 'em and I wanted to get to him before somebody else found out. Did Wayne say there was anything urgent he needed me for?"

"Nah. He said there weren't no trouble, he just wondered why you hadn't come into the office yet."

"He's a good man," Walt declared, "just young, that's all. He's gonna make you folks a fine sheriff if the time comes when I decide I've had all of it I want." He paused a moment to watch Graham take the reins of the two extra horses and lead them toward the corral. Then he wheeled the buckskin back toward the street.

Deputy Wayne Price looked up from the desk when the door opened. Upon seeing Walt, he jumped up from the desk immediately, feeling uncomfortable about having been caught sitting in the sheriff's chair. "Walt!" He exclaimed, "I was just lookin' through the latest Wanted papers."

"Don't get up," Walt said. "You look like that chair fits you pretty good. I swear, I think I forgot to tell you I'd be gone a little later than usual this mornin'. Everything all right?"

"Quiet as can be," Wayne answered. "I had to go over to the Reservation and run Clem Grady outta the Hog's Breath before somebody shot him. He musta slept on the front porch last night after Peewee had to throw him out. This mornin' he was back in there as soon as they opened the door, threatenin' to kill Brady John. He's in the back cell. And we got a wire that said that fellow that shot those two deputy marshals in Madisonville got away with that stolen money from the bank. The bank's offered a two-hundred-dollar reward for recovery of all or part of the money."

"Is that a fact?" Walt replied. "I knew that jasper got away with that money. I don't expect we'll hear much about him or that money again." He shook his head and commented, "Two hundred dollars, that would make it worthwhile to keep your eyes open for that jasper, wouldn't it?"

"You know, Walt, I was thinkin' about that fellow. You suppose he might show up over there at that church ol' Reuben Drum runs?"

"Nah, he won't show up over there," Walt replied. "Every outlaw in Texas knows we keep an eye on Reuben. Nobody but the down-and-out drifters show up over at the church, hopin' to get a free meal. That's why I let him stay there—keeps some of the drifters outta town." He winked at Wayne and added, "Besides, I rode by there this mornin', just to make sure."

Wayne chuckled. "I shoulda known you'd check that out—thought maybe that's where you were this mornin' when you didn't come in when you usually do."

"I'll tell you something else I'm been thinkin' over," Walt said. "Maybe we've let that bunch of drifters lay around that old church buildin' long enough. What you just wondered about might just happen one day in spite of what I think of the old man. He might start attractin' some bad characters over there just four miles from this town. There ain't but two or three people there now, and it might be the time to do

something about that place once and for all. I expect
we could get a posse of our citizens together to go
over there and hit 'em one night before they knew
what was comin'—burn the damn buildin' down and
shoot any of 'em that tries to put up a fight." He was
lying when he said he had been thinking it over. In
fact, it had just occurred to him that at this point it
might be best to get rid of Reuben and anyone who
could ever testify against him. And that included the
two women in residence there.

"Doggone, Walt," Wayne responded. "I think that's
the very thing we oughta do. I've been worried about
that place, and I know I ain't the only one in town
who thinks it's a bad mark against the town. We could
round up some vigilantes and close that place for
good."

The more they talked about it, the more Walt felt
inspired to act. "I suspect it wouldn't have to be a vigilante raid. I think, if I talked to the mayor and the
city council about the dangerous situation out there,
they might authorize an official posse to do the job.
I'll talk to the mayor today."

In contrast to Walt Murphy's description of Reuben
Drum, the old man had not lost all the fire in his
gizzard at all. He had lost his only son and none of
the outlaws he had given shelter to would take up the
cause to avenge his loss. Instead, they hatched daring
raids with the sole purpose of getting their hands on
that stolen bank money. This morning had been the
final straw. Pete Russell had shown up there after his

escape, no doubt bringing federal marshals on his tail. Then Walt Murphy showed up and it was obvious to Reuben that Walt suspected that Pete had gotten away with the money. When Pete packed up and left, Riley Best stood on the church steps watching him until he rode out of sight. Not three minutes later, Riley reported that he saw Walt ride down from the ridge behind the church and set in behind Pete. Reuben walked outside to join Riley, and a short time later, they both heard two shots that couldn't have been more than a mile or so away. He told Riley at the time that it might be the last they saw of Walt, if those shots meant what he suspected. And he was concerned about the future of his church. The more he thought about it, the heavier the lack of vengeance for his slain son weighed on his mind. So he made a decision. If nothing else, he swore he would take his vengeance on Ben Savage himself. It was his responsibility as Lester's father.

There was nothing further from the mind of Ben Savage than the possibility of Lester Drum's father seeking to take his life in payment for that of his son. He was doing his best to readjust his life to that of a saloon owner, now that the gunfights were over in Buzzard's Bluff and the action taking place was far from his town. There were still things that bothered him and people he thought were getting away free and clear who definitely shouldn't. Walt Murphy always came to mind to top that list. He was still of the opinion that it was Walt who rode away on that buckskin horse. And that didn't sit well in his craw. But he had decided to let the law agencies take the responsibility and do their jobs—this after countless lectures by his business partner.

There had been no more news about Pete Russell there in the little town of Buzzard's Bluff. Whether he had been caught or not was of no concern now to Sheriff Mack Bragg. He was more concerned about drunks causing problems on the streets of the town. And Ben guessed that was good. Annie Grey still came in early every morning to have coffee with him, and her husband and Rachel still joined them a little later. He should have been content with the way things were, but he was not. The job with Walt Murphy had not been completed. Murphy had not been arrested for his part in all the killing and attempted jailbreaks. And in Ben's mind Walt Murphy was the biggest crook of all. Ben had no use for any man who wore the badge of an officer of the law and took the oath to honor it, then operated on the other side of the law.

"Whatcha thinking about, Mr. Savage?" He turned to see Rachel coming from the kitchen, a cup of coffee in her hand.

"I was wonderin' if you were gonna come outta the kitchen with some coffee for me," Ben answered, "but I don't see but one cup in your hand."

"Liar," Rachel replied, "you're still thinking about that bunch that tried to break Pete Russell outta jail and the one that was wearing the mask who got away."

"Now, why would you think that?" he responded, pretending a little indignation.

"'Cause you haven't been thinking about anything

else ever since we heard about that fellow getting away from those deputies," she answered. "Here, you can have my cup, and I'll go get another one."

"No, thanks," he said. "You probably put about two spoonsful of sugar in yours. I'll get my own." He got up from his chair. "You need to drink your coffee like a man," he teased.

"Do I look like a man?" She came back at him.

"Only when you wear your hair up in a knot," he countered, then quickly skipped out of her reach when she threatened to throw her coffee at him. He got no farther than the kitchen door, where Annie was waiting with a cup of coffee for him. "How'd you know I was comin' to get a cup of coffee?" He asked, immediately thinking about Rachel's insistence that Annie possessed special forewarnings of things about to happen.

"Everybody knew it, as loud as you two were yakking about it," Annie answered and extended the cup toward him. "No sugar, right?"

"Right. Thank you very much," he replied and took the cup.

"You're welcome," Annie said. "Maybe it'll take your mind off Walt Murphy." She spun around and went back to her kitchen. "I heard her say that, too," she said as she walked away.

"Wait a minute," he mumbled as he walked away. *I was thinking about Walt Murphy, but neither one of us mentioned his name.* He didn't say anything about it to Rachel when he went back to join her at the table. It would only get her started on the subject. They sat there a while watching the customers that came and went. As they did, it caused him to wonder why he didn't take the opportunity given him to enjoy a peaceful life, now that the dangerous situation had been settled. *You're a fool if you don't,* he told himself. *It's time to put the Walt Murphys of this world out of your mind and enjoy the situation you've got now.*

Tuck Tucker came striding in the front door then, looking as if he'd come to take charge, as was his usual custom. Seeing Ben and Rachel sitting at the table near the kitchen, he strode back to engage them. "You seen Ham Greeley? It's time for his daily whuppin' at the card table." Things were back to normal in the little town of Buzzard's Bluff . . . but for how long?

Tuck went over to sit down at his usual table and pulled a deck of cards out of his pocket. "Whaddaya drinkin', Tuck?" Tiny called out from the bar. "The usual?" When Tuck said he was thinking about a glass of beer, Tiny asked, "Beer? That ain't your usual drink.

"I know, but I'm a little bit off my feed, so I'm gonna take it slow and ease into the hard stuff later."

Back at the table near the kitchen door, Rachel laughed and commented. "I never knew Tuck was ever off his feed." She laughed again, then stopped when she looked at Ben when he didn't laugh at Tuck as well. His mind was far away, she realized when she looked at him and he seemed to be looking out in space. "Doggone you, Ben Savage, you're going to Waco."

"What?" He responded, not fully back from his thoughts.

"Waco," she repeated. "Waco and Walt Murphy,

you're going back there. Don't tell me that wasn't where your mind was."

"I'm sorry, Rachel, there's something I've got to find out, or I ain't ever gonna have any peace of mind."

She shook her head as if disgusted. "I guess there just ain't no cure for what you've got. When are you leaving?"

"Before long," he said.

CHAPTER 15

"Are you sure you wanna do this?" Riley Best questioned Reuben again. "This feller you're goin' after ain't no ordinary gunslinger. I can tell you that for a fact." He patted his shoulder that was still in the healing stages even now. "Lester went to throw down on him first, but Savage beat him with time to spare to put a bullet in me, too, before I could pull my iron. I ain't takin' his part, I'm just sayin' Lester drew first and Savage did what anybody would do. That's all." Looking at the somber face of the gray-haired man, he could guess that Reuben wasn't hearing anything he was saying. "Reuben," Riley pleaded. "I know you're grievin' the loss of Lester. I am, too. Lester was a good ol' boy, and I was right sorry I couldn't do nothin' to keep him from gettin' shot. It was just bad luck, that's all there was to it. So why don't we just call it that and don't go lookin' for more bad luck? You'll have a full house here in no time. Things will be just like they was before Pete Russell and Ormond Hazzard led Ben Savage up here."

Reuben continued to clean and oil his Colt Peacemaker while Riley tried to persuade him to reconsider his plans. He didn't utter so much as a grunt in response to Riley's pleas until he had finished cleaning his gun, reloaded it, and slipped it back in the holster. Then he looked Riley square in the eye for a moment before turning to one of the two women sitting close by, listening to Riley's plea. "Dora, honey, pour me a drink of that rye whiskey." Turning back to Riley then, he said, "I heard every word you said and I know you're afraid I'm gonna get myself killed. I 'preciate that, but the man took my son's life. It don't matter to me who drew first. He killed my boy, and he's gotta pay for that." He interrupted himself to take the glass of whiskey from Dora. "Thank you, honey." Back to Riley then, he continued. "I tried to get one of you boys to gun Ben Savage down for Lester and me, but there wasn't nobody interested in doin' it. And I'm sorry for that now because I know it wasn't nobody else's responsibility to avenge my kin. It's my responsibility to do it for Lester. I know what you're thinkin', but I ain't as old as you think I am. And Ben Savage won't be the first gunslinger I've come up against. I've made a few widows in my day and I'm still here to talk about it. So I'm goin' to Buzzard's Bluff, and that's all there is to that. There may be snow on the roof, but that don't mean there ain't a fire in the stove," he quoted. "Besides, it don't take much strength to pull a trigger."

Paulene pulled her skirt up to wipe a tear from her eye with the hem of it. "That's the sweetest story I ever heard, I swear."

Riley was distracted from Reuben's lament for only a moment to give her a look of disbelief before returning his attention to the old man. Losing some of his patience with Reuben at this point, he said, "I ain't sayin' you ain't able, Reuben. I just don't think you're considerin' the fact that you ain't as young as you used to be, and it's been a long time since you've had to pull a trigger."

"You've had your say, and I 'preciate what you're tryin' to tell me," Reuben said. "But I've made my peace with myself that that's what I've got to do. So tomorrow mornin' I'm headin' outta here to Buzzard's Bluff. And me and that saloon ranger are gonna settle this thing between us." He watched Riley's reaction and when he saw him slowly shaking his head, he asked, "Are you gonna try to stop me?"

Riley shook his head again. "Nah, I ain't gonna try to stop you. Hell, I'm goin' with you." He looked at Paulene. "You girls be all right here by yourselves for a couple, maybe three days?"

"Yeah, we're big girls, ain't we, Dora? We'll be all right," she replied. "You go do what you need to do, then get yourselves back here. But ain't you already had enough trouble with Ben Savage, Riley? You still ain't healed up from the last time you crossed his path. Ain't you afraid you might be shot on sight?"

"There's that chance, I reckon, but only if he sees me first. Ain't nobody else in Buzzard's Bluff that's ever seen me, so I'll try not let Ben Savage see me at all. Now, I reckon if we're goin' first thing in the mornin', I expect I'd best go make sure my horse and tack is in good shape to ride."

Reuben left the room with him, still telling him he appreciated his support, but stressing the fact that he didn't have to plan on calling Ben Savage out, himself. The women watched until they had left the room before Paulene expressed her thoughts about their plan. "If that Ben Savage is the rip-snortin'est gunslinger they say he is, this is the last we'll see of Reuben and Riley. And if they don't come back alive, we'll turn this place into the hottest gol-danged whorehouse in Texas. Those cowpokes that go to the Reservation over in Waco will be comin' to the church to get their religion."

As they had declared, Reuben and Riley, with one packhorse, rode away from the church the next morning. After a good breakfast, prepared by his cook, Frances Wright, they set out for Buzzard's Bluff. Dora and Paulene saw them off with wishes of good hunting and words of caution. Grateful for Riley's accompaniment, Reuben was confident he was up to the task he had set for himself. Riley, on the other hand, was not sure he wasn't crazy for returning to the town where the man lived who very nearly killed him. He was important for one reason right from the start of the mission, however, for Reuben had never been to Buzzard's Bluff and didn't know which road led to the town. Once they were on the road to Buzzard's Bluff, however, Reuben said he was going to need some .45 caliber cartridges for his Colt, Army single-action Peacemaker. Riley also carried a Colt, but it was configured to use .44 caliber cartridges, so he suggested that Reuben could buy his cartridges at Cletus Priest's store, halfway between Waco and Buzzard's Bluff. Riley's suggestion surprised Reuben and he said as much. "Ain't that the place you said you got shot?"

When Riley shrugged, Reuben went on, "And that woman blasted Slim Dickens?"

"That's the place," Riley admitted.

"Ain't you afraid they'd shoot you on sight?"

"I don't think they would," Riley answered, although a little uncertain of it. "When me and Lester and Slim was there, we never had no quarrel with Priest or his wife. Our quarrel was with Ben Savage. Savage cut me and Lester down, and Slim was fixin' to shoot him, but Priest's wife unloaded her double-barrel shotgun on him before he got off a shot. I don't fault the woman for doin' it. Savage was most likely a friend of her and her husband's. She most likely thought Slim was gonna kill her and her husband, too, after he was done with Savage. When they found out I wasn't dead, they coulda finished me off, but they didn't. The woman bandaged me up and Savage let me go." He paused a moment while he recalled the situation. "He told me to stop and rest my horse before I rode him all the way back."

Reuben took a few moments to consider all Riley had said. "I reckon you could be right," he finally allowed. "I need the cartridges and I druther get 'em before we get to Buzzard's Bluff." So they decided they would stop at Cletus's store.

They sighted the rustic cabin sitting by a healthy creek, ten miles past the spot they had picked to rest their horses. "Best let me ride on ahead of you," Reuben suggested, "just in case they see you and decide not to take no chances." Not absolutely sure himself, Riley gave no argument and let Reuben lead the way up the path to the store.

"Cletus, lookee yonder!" Jenny Priest called from the front window, where she had gone when she happened to catch sight of two riders coming from the wagon road when she walked past.

Responding to the excitement in her voice, Cletus walked over to the window beside her. He squinted to try to see who the riders were but didn't recognize them. "Who is it?" he asked.

"I don't know who the feller in front is," she answered, "but look at the one behind him. Ain't that the feller that got shot in here, that I put a bandage on? It looks like him to me."

Cletus squinted harder to get a better look. "Blamed if you ain't right. That is that feller! Ben Savage let him go, and now he's showin' up here again." They exchanged worried expressions, both thinking Riley had returned to take his vengeance on them for the deaths of his two friends. "Well, they've come to the wrong place to even any score they think they got a right to," Cletus said. "Grab that shotgun!" He went to the stockroom door and reached inside to get the Henry rifle propped up just inside the door. Then he joined his wife, who had already positioned herself behind the counter. With shotgun and rifle lying on the counter, aimed at the door, they awaited the arrival of the two visitors.

So far, so good, Riley thought as they pulled up before the front steps and dismounted. Seeing no sign of anyone outside the store, they walked up the three steps to the porch and entered the store. They stopped dead still just inside the door, halted by the sight of the two weapons pointing at them. "Can I help you?" Cletus asked.

Afraid to make a sudden move, both men stood frozen for what seemed a long silent moment before Reuben responded. "You always greet customers like this?"

"Only the ones who brought trouble with 'em when they was here before," Cletus answered, watching Riley closely.

Noticing, Riley spoke up then. "We ain't bringin' no trouble this time. I ain't forgot you doctored by shoulder and neck, ma'am," he said to Jenny. "Reuben, here, needs some .45 cartridges, and I need some chawin' tobacco if you've got any. I thought I owed you the business. Then we'll be on our way."

The sincerity in his voice caused both Cletus and Jenny to hesitate. "Well, sure, I'd be glad to sell you some forty-fives, and I've got tobacco, too. How much do you need?" When Reuben replied that he could use two boxes, Cletus pulled his Henry off the counter and leaned it against the shelf behind him while he took the cartridges off the shelves above. Jenny aimed her shotgun away from them but left it on the counter as a deterrent in case they had any mischief in mind. After filling Riley's request for chewing tobacco, Cletus took payment from each of them and saw fit to apologize. "Sorry we said howdy like we did, but when we saw it was you, we was afraid you'd come to blame me and Jenny for what happened here that time."

"No," Reuben answered him. "Like Riley said, our

quarrel ain't with you folks. Our quarrel is with Ben
Savage. He killed my son in your store." His statement
caused Cletus and Jenny both to become tense once
more, until they picked up their purchases off the
counter and headed for the door. "Good day to ya,"
Reuben said upon leaving.

Husband and wife remained stationed behind the
counter until they heard the horses leaving, then they
both hurried to the window to watch them out of
sight. "Well, ain't that somethin'?" Cletus asked. "Gave
me a start when I saw 'em ridin' up here." He paused
to think about it before remarking, "That was too bad
that old feller's son was killed, weren't it? Wonder
which one of them two that got killed was his son?"

"Clabber," Jenny spat, "don't matter which one.
They both deserved to get shot."

Reuben and Riley continued along the road to
Buzzard's Bluff before making camp for the night at
a wide stream that showed signs of many campers
before them. They figured they would have about a
twenty-five-mile ride to make Buzzard's Bluff the next
morning. As they took care of the horses, Reuben
wondered aloud, "Reckon Dora and Paulene will be
all right till we get back?"

"I don't see why not," Riley replied. "Two tougher
women ain't ever been born."

"Less you ain't countin' that Priest woman back
yonder at the store," Reuben said.

* * *

Riley and Reuben were deep in their slumber about an hour past midnight, enjoying the night sounds of the crickets by the peaceful stream, while far behind them the three women at the church were sleeping as well. It was Dora who was first stirred from her bed by the smell of smoke that seemed to be coming in the windows from outside the building. She lay there for a little while, and when it didn't seem to go away, she got up and went into Paulene's room to awaken her. "What is it?" Paulene asked, trying to clear the sleep from her head.

"Smoke," Dora said. "I smell smoke. Something's on fire somewhere."

"You sure?" Paulene asked, hoping Dora had been dreaming. Then she smelled the smoke as well. Before she could say anything else, she was startled by the sound of crashing glass in several windows out in the church area almost simultaneously. It was followed by the sound of horses loping around the building with yelling and pistol shots like those heard in an Indian raid. Dora screamed and Paulene jumped up from her bed. "They're burnin' the place down! We gotta get outta here!" She wrapped a blanket around her and handed one to Dora, who was too terrified to move. "Come on!" Paulene yelled at her. "We gotta get outside!"

When they ran outside the room, they found great parts of the area converted to a saloon in flames and the shooting seemed to increase. They realized at once that the shots were aimed at the windows as the raiders rode around and around the church. Their attackers were trying to kill the occupants of the building. First thoughts of putting out the fire were soon abandoned when it became obvious that it was already too far along. The old building was going up like kindling. "If we don't get outta here, we're gonna burn up with it!" Dora cried in panic.

The best exit left to them was out through the kitchen, so they plunged through the smoke-filled room to the small cubby between the kitchen and the back door where the cook, Frances Wright, slept. Dora opened the curtain that served as a door and found the terrified little woman curled up in a corner of the small room. "Frances!" Dora cried, "come on, we've got to get out of here!" She didn't wait to make sure Frances was following and rushed to the back door behind Paulene.

When Paulene opened the door, it created a draft that pulled a black plume of smoke out with the two terrified women, who stopped on the steps when one of the raiders pulled his horse to a stop before them. "Walt Murphy!" Paulene blurted. "You double-dealing double-crosser! What are you doing?"

"Who else is in there?" Walt asked. "Where's Reuben and Riley?"

"Why don't you go in there and look for them?" Paulene spat back at him.

"Maybe I will, slut." He raised his pistol and put a bullet in her breast. Dora screamed when she saw Paulene collapse on the steps. Terrified, she turned and tried to run back into the burning building. Another shot from the sheriff slammed the young girl between her shoulder blades and she went face-down on the kitchen floor at the feet of Frances Wright. The frail little woman, frightened speechless, backed into her room. Walt kicked the buckskin hard and galloped around the back corner of the building before some of his posse rounded the corner.

The surprise assault on the outlaws' hideout continued for only a short time when it soon became obvious that there was no opposition and anyone inside must surely have perished. The posse of eight, led by Sheriff Walt Murphy and his deputy, gathered at the back of the burning building to assess the results of their actions. Their main attention was naturally drawn to the body of the woman lying on the back steps. "This is just plain bad luck here," Walt was quick to try to allay their feelings of guilt for having killed a woman. "She shoulda give up right at the start and she wouldn'ta got shot. We was all shootin' into that buildin'. Ain't no tellin' whose shot was the one that kilt her, so it ain't nobody's fault. I couldn't tell for sure, but I thought there was some shots comin' outta there, too. Since I'm the one leadin' this party, I'll shoulder the blame for the woman's accidental death."

"Ah, it weren't your fault no more than any of the rest of us," Bob Graham said. "Like you said, it was an accident. Shots was flyin' everywhere. It's a wonder we didn't shoot one another. She didn't have no business runnin' with outlaws, anyway."

"She ain't the only one," Wayne Price announced. Standing closer to the steps, the deputy was peering through the open door when a draft sucked some of the smoke from the kitchen. "There's another body layin' just inside the door. I swear, Walt, it looks like another woman."

"Oh, my goodness," Walt was quick to exclaim, "that is sorry luck. Them poor women shoulda tried to come outta there with their hands up. None of us here woulda shot a woman, even if they was whores. What about that little space back of the kitchen where the cook sleeps? Can you see that far?"

"I can't see in it," Wayne said, "but if there's anybody in there, they ain't alive. That whole space ain't nothin' but a ball of flames."

"Them poor women," Walt repeated. "They shoulda got outta there. We'll give 'em a decent burial."

The posse stood around for a while to watch the fire destroy the old church building, but it was obvious that it would be some time before it finished the job. "Looks like it's gonna be a while before this is done," Walt told them. "You've all responded to the town's needs and you've done a good job. We won't have to worry about a gang of outlaws holed up right outside our town no more. It's awful late now, so I reckon you all wanna get back to your homes. Me and my deputy will stay here till daylight, so we can make sure there ain't nobody else in there." That seemed to be the choice for most of the posse. Two of them, feeling regret for the deaths of the two women, volunteered to dig a grave for them. They remained long enough to do that with a pick and shovel they found in the small barn, then they, too, returned to their homes.

When the sun came up the following morning, the sheriff and his deputy roused themselves from their beds of hay in the barn to find only smoky remains left of the old church. It was their job to carry the two bodies out of the ruins and drop them into the single grave left there for that purpose. Wayne grabbed the shovel and started filling in the grave. "Too bad Reuben Drum wasn't here," he said. "I know you were plannin' to arrest him and anybody else that was here." He threw a few more shovelfuls of dirt on top of the women, then remarked, "I figured he was gone, since there weren't no horses in the corral."

"Yeah, I figured you most likely noticed that, too," Walt said. "I think Reuben will get the message that he's done here when he gets back. If he gets back—he mighta took to heart what I told him the other day when I said it was time to pick up his mess and take it somewhere else."

"I'll bet that's what happened," Wayne said. "Looks like he left it all to those two women there. It was sure bad luck for them, wasn't it?"

"Yes, it was," Walt answered, "and I feel bad about that. But with a posse like that, all fired up and rarin' to go, everybody was shootin' off their guns and bad things almost always happen to innocent people. While you're finishin' that grave, I'll take a look through what's left of the church to make sure there ain't nobody else layin' in there. Then, I expect we'd best get back to town to make sure everything's all right back there." He walked through the ruins of the church while Wayne was laboring over a grave big enough for the two unfortunate women. He couldn't tell his deputy that the late-night raid was not the success in his mind as it seemed to be for Wayne and the eight volunteers. True, they had destroyed the popular hideout, but Walt was counting on dealing Reuben and Riley the same hand he dealt the two prostitutes. Both men knew about the bank money. They knew Pete Russell had come away from Madisonville with it, and he suspected they knew he went after Pete. He would know for sure if they showed up in his town again, looking for a share. If they did, they wouldn't get away a second time. And with them gone, there was no one else to tie the missing money to him.

Why wasn't Reuben there last night? That was the question puzzling him now as he poked around the burnt-out remains of what had been Reuben's room. *Hell,* he thought, *Reuben was always there. He never left the church.* Who could have tipped him off and told him a raid was planned for last night? He didn't decide to propose the raid until yesterday. The thought caused him to turn and look at his deputy, laboring away with the shovel. *Is he as naive as he lets on?* After a moment studying the young man, he decided he wasn't capable of deception. Back to the destroyed church then, he poked around the flooring that wasn't consumed completely, looking for any signs of a hidden safe. He was disappointed to find no trace of Frances Wright, but at least she had not been there to witness the murders of the two other women. Her absence at the time of the raid troubled him, however, for she had no other home that he was aware of. *The outhouse,* he thought, *what if she was in the outhouse?* Then he remembered that he and one of the other men had kicked the outhouse over after checking to make sure no one was in there.

The morning was equally unusual in the small cabin occupied by Billy and Betty Wells and their two small children. During the night just passed, they had a surprise visit from Betty's Aunt Frances, who had walked almost four miles to their small cabin just short of the bridge over the Brazos. A hardworking young man, Billy did some farming, but his main occupation was raising hogs. He made a living providing pork products to the hotel and small restaurants like Jake's Rib House. As the only relative Frances had in Texas, Betty did not see her aunt very often and never in the middle of the night with a story she swore them to hold secret. Barely able to talk at first, so frightened was she, then gradually recounting her night of horror, she told them how she escaped the fate that Paulene and Dora shared. When Dora fell dead at her feet, the result of Walt Murphy's second shot, she could only back into her cubby to hide again. It was soon she realized, however, that if she remained there, she would surely perish. So she forced herself to sneak back by the kitchen door and wait until none of the riders were right behind the church. Taking her life in her hands, she then ran from the burning building to the outhouse, which was lying on its side. She managed to open the door and crawl inside, and she remained there until the posse had gone home, leaving only the two lawmen and two volunteer grave diggers for Paulene and Dora. She hid in the overturned outhouse until Walt and his deputy made their beds in Reuben's barn, after the gravediggers had gone. Only then had she summoned the courage to sneak out of her hiding place and run for her life.

She had no place to go, so Billy and his wife assured her that she was welcome in their home for as long as she wanted. "I could use some help with little Gracie and Francine," Betty insisted, "and you can certainly help with the cooking."

"I'll help you any way I can," Frances said. "I may be little, but I can work hard as anyone."

"Then it's settled," Billy said. "You just stay right here." This even after hearing Frances's story about the sheriff murdering the two women. Like most folks around town, he knew Walt Murphy had some rough edges on him, but he wouldn't have suspected him capable of blatant disregard for human life.

Chapter 16

Ben didn't linger long over breakfast for a couple of reasons. He wanted to leave before Tuck came in for breakfast, and he knew he'd get another lecture from Rachel on letting the law take care of the law's business. With Tuck, it would be the opposite. He would likely suggest that he should accompany him to Waco. He ate the breakfast Annie fixed for him in short order, thereby being subjected to a shorter dose of Rachel's insistence that he was needed there at the Coyote. He knew, in fact, that he really wasn't. She ran the business and everyone at the Coyote knew it. He helped in any way he thought he could, but there was very little call for him to do anything as far as operating the saloon. He was sure that Rachel was just concerned for his safety, and he appreciated that, but it sometimes felt like his wings were being clipped. So he gulped the last of his coffee and said, "I ain't sure, three or four days, I reckon," when Rachel asked. "There's just a couple of things I wanna check on, that's all."

He almost bumped into Tuck when he went out

the door. "Mornin', Tuck," he said and walked on down the steps.

"Where you goin'?" Tuck asked at once.

"Down to the stable," Ben answered and kept walking, his saddlebags over his shoulder and his rifle in hand. "Annie just pulled a fresh pan of biscuits outta the oven. Better get in there quick, if you want a hot one," he said over his shoulder, leaving Tuck to stand there undecided. He loved hot biscuits, but he was curious about the saddlebags and rifle. To Ben's relief, he went on inside to the biscuits and an explanation from Rachel and Annie.

He made good time on the cool clear morning, and Cousin seemed in the mood for traveling. So when he approached the little creek he often stopped at, about ten miles north of Buzzard's Bluff, he was undecided whether to stop or not. *Just long enough for Cousin to get a drink of water,* he thought, since the dun was showing no signs of fatigue. When he got closer to the creek, he realized someone was camping there, just off the road. He saw some horses near the bank and smoke from a small fire about twenty-five yards from the road, but no sign of anyone about. Only slightly curious, but cautious as a manner of habit, he scanned the banks on both sides of the creek before he caught sight of someone lying on his belly beside the creek.

Not sure if it was a body he was seeing, or someone lying in ambush, he immediately reined Cousin back and pulled his rifle out of his saddle scabbard. It paid to be ready, whichever it was. Then he saw the body move, lifting his head from the water and getting up on his knees. The man wiped his mouth with the back of his hand and reached on the ground beside him and picked up a canteen. Ben had to grin when he realized the man had just filled his canteen and decided to get a long drink from the creek while he was at it. An older man, as his white hair testified before he plopped a faded Boss of the Plains hat down on his head, he was unaware of the approaching rider.

Cautious now he might startle the old-timer, Ben decided he'd best announce his presence. He dropped his rifle back in the saddle scabbard and called out a howdy. The reaction of the old man was predictable. He spun around, dropping his hand on his sidearm, looking frantically for an assailant. Ben put his hands in the air. "Whoa, partner!" He called out. "I mean you no harm. I'm just passing through on my way to Waco."

The old man made no move for a few moments, apparently deciding if he had anything to fear from this stranger or not. Finally, he answered Ben's call. "Well, your horse don't make a helluva lot of noise, so I reckon you kinda caught me by surprise. Come on ahead, then, I ain't got no right to say you can't use the road, have I?" He chuckled, more embarrassed than frightened. "Tell you the truth, I can't hear as good as I did when I was your age."

Ben nudged Cousin and continued along the road until he reached the old man, who was standing close to the road now. "You travelin' all by yourself?" Ben asked.

"No, there's two of us," he said. "My partner's gone a-ways down this creek. I keep listenin' to hear a shot from that direction."

"Why is that?" Ben answered, more interested now. "Have you had some trouble?"

"No, no trouble," he quickly replied. "When we pulled up here, 'bout a half hour ago, we run up on a couple of deer, drinkin' water right in the middle of the road. My partner's younger'n me, so I told him, 'You run down that creek and see if you can get a shot at one of 'em. I'll stay here and build a fire and water the horses.' Well, I'm still waitin' to hear a shot that'll tell me what's for dinner."

"I reckon you were lucky to run up on deer this late in the mornin'," Ben allowed. "They musta been lookin' for a place to lay low and didn't know it was the middle of the road."

"Maybe so," the old man allowed. "But ignorant deer taste just as good as smart ones. If you ain't in a hurry, you can stick around to see if my partner has any luck and you can help us eat some venison."

"Why, that's mighty neighborly of you, and I'm tempted to take you up on that. I ain't had deer meat in quite some time." He was tempted, but he had other things on his mind. "I expect I'd best keep on goin', since I'm figurin' on makin' Waco tomorrow. Thank you just the same, though."

"You'd be welcome," the old man said. "I notice you ain't leadin' no packhorse, so you must be travelin' light."

"I am at that," Ben said, "but, like I said, I'll be in Waco tomorrow. I might pay a visit to Jake's Rib House to make up for travelin' light. You ever eat there?"

"Nope, never have, but I've heard of it," the old man said.

"I best be gettin' along," Ben said. "I hope you hear that gunshot pretty soon. If I hear it before I get outta earshot, I might turn around and come back."

"You do that, young feller. We'd be glad to share."

It was fully three-quarters of an hour before Riley emerged from the trees hugging the bank of the stream, clearly disappointed. "I got just close enough to get a glimpse of 'em about a quarter of a mile downstream, but I didn't have a shot. I followed them damn deer for two miles, I bet, and never got close enough to shoot. I really wanted me some deer meat, too."

Disappointed as well, Reuben said, "And I ain't even got any bacon cookin', either. I was countin' on that deer meat so much that I ain't got any coffee started. I spent half the time jawin' with some jasper that came by on his way to Waco."

"Who was he?" Riley asked.

"I don't know," Reuben replied, "just some jasper. Seemed like a decent enough feller, though. We just passed the time of day. I told him you was off chasin' a deer."

"Is that right? Wonder what he woulda thought, if somebody told him he was jawin' with Reuben Drum?" Riley asked and they both chuckled. "Hand me that coffeepot and I'll go get some water."

After leaving the old man by the creek, Ben rode for another fifteen miles before stopping to give Cousin a rest by a wide stream. He decided he would be there long enough to build a little fire and make some coffee while the big dun gelding grazed and drank. Thinking back on his chance meeting with the old man at the creek, he appreciated the meeting with a fellow traveler that would gladly share his food with a stranger. *And I didn't even ask his name,* he thought. *Doesn't matter. Odds are I'll never run into him again.* When Cousin was rested, Ben's mind was back on the mission he had set for himself. At this point, he was only a short ride from Cletus Priest's store, and he had considered stopping by there on his way to Waco. Thinking about it now, he decided he would skip it, since his horse was freshly watered and rested. Maybe he would stop there on his way back to Buzzard's Bluff.

It was close to noontime when Reuben Drum and Riley Best pulled up short of Henry Barnes's stable. "Before we go ridin' down to the Lost Coyote Saloon, you ain't told me just exactly what you're plannin' to do."

"I told you already," Reuben insisted. "I'm gonna walk in that saloon and tell 'em I come to see Ben Savage. And when he comes out, I'll tell him I've come to kill him, just like he killed my boy. He can face me like a man, or I'll shoot him down where he stands."

"Damn it, Reuben, I've told you how fast that man is. If you face that man in a showdown, he'll cut you down like a cornstalk."

"He might," Reuben allowed, "but he'll have to be pretty damn accurate to stop me with one shot, and I know I'll get one in him before I'm done."

"Maybe," Riley admitted. "It's hard to say what you'll do when that bullet hits you. And it sounds to me like we took a long ride just so you can commit suicide. If that's what you were thinkin', you coulda just told me and I coulda shot you back in Waco. And me and the women coulda give you a proper funeral."

Reuben gave his younger friend a patient look, the kind a father gives his son. "Did you think I was really plannin' to dry-gulch this gunslinger? I want him to know why I'm fixin' to kill him. I brought you with me 'cause I don't know what he looks like, and if I saw him outside the saloon, I wouldn't know it was him. I figure I don't need you to go in the saloon lookin' for him or you're liable to get shot when he saw you. So you find you a place outside where you can watch to see if I come out and we'll high-tail it outta here when I do."

"Whatever you say, old man," Riley replied. "Looks like nothin' I say is gonna keep you from gettin' your crazy head blown off, is it?"

"Reckon not," Reuben said with a grin. "I don't deny I might be a little bit crazy, but don't call me old." He gave his horse a touch of his heels and started down the street. "That looks like a saloon right down there on the right."

After passing the stable, they saw the sign that told them the saloon was the Lost Coyote. There was no one in the blacksmith shop across the street from the saloon, so Riley pulled his horse to a stop there, as Reuben directed, and stood watching as Reuben rode up to the saloon. In Riley's mind, Reuben looked older than he had the day before. And while he disagreed with what he was doing, he thought he understood why. It made him feel kinda sad because Reuben had always been mighty good to him when he was down and out. Another thought struck him then. What will happen to the church with Reuben gone?

Who would take the reins? *Not me,* he said to himself. *With Reuben gone, I'm done with it.*

Reuben tied his horse at the rail and stepped up on the porch. He paused a second to ease his forty-five up and down in the holster a couple of times to make sure it was riding easy. It had been a long time since he had been called upon to do so. Ready then, he stepped inside the bat-wing doors and stood for a few more moments to look the room over. More than half the tables were empty, and most of the customers were eating dinner. It struck him that it was relatively quiet for a saloon. However, there were a couple of men standing at the bar. Near the kitchen door, a woman sat alone, speaking occasionally to a short, red-haired man who seemed to be bouncing back and forth between a couple of the tables, talking to the men seated at them. He acts like he's in charge, Reuben thought, but he wasn't the picture he had painted in his mind of the owner of the saloon. So, he walked on over to the bar.

"Howdy," Tiny greeted him cheerfully. "What's it gonna be? You lookin' for a drink of whiskey or just wantin' to eat dinner?"

"Right now, I'll just take the whiskey," Reuben answered. He watched the room while Tiny poured.

"Ain't seen you in before," Tiny said. "You new in town?"

"That's right," Reuben answered. "I'm just passin' through. I'm lookin' for Ben Savage. Is that him over at that table?"

"Him?" Tiny responded with a chuckle. "No, that ain't Ben. That's Tuck Tucker. Ben's outta town, but

Rachel Baskin's here." He nodded toward her. "She's Ben's business partner, if you're lookin' to talk about business." Although Reuben wasn't dressed as a salesman, Tiny thought Reuben might be trying to sell something to the saloon, so he looked over toward her and called, "Rachel," and motioned her over before Reuben could stop him. Rachel came over promptly, and Tiny said, "This gentleman is looking for Ben. I told him Ben's outta town."

Rachel favored Reuben with a smile and said, "That's right, Ben's out of town, and I expect he won't be back before three or four days. I'm Rachel Baskin, Ben's partner. Is there something I can help you with?"

Properly flustered by now, Reuben apologized. "I'm sorry to bother you, ma'am, but your bartender called you before I had a chance to explain." He hastily made up his story as he told it. "I just had a message to give Ben Savage from a friend of his. I was gonna tell him Robert Diamond is planning to be in town here next week and he hopes to see him." Robert Diamond was the first name that popped into his mind. It was an alias he had once used.

"Well, I can tell Ben that," Rachel said. "I'm sorry you missed him, and it wasn't by much, because he just left town this morning. But I'm afraid he won't be back for three or four days. And with Ben, we're never sure it'll be that soon. I hope he'll be back to see his friend, though. Robert Diamond, I'll be sure to tell him."

"Thank you, ma'am," Reuben said politely while trying to settle with his disappointment in the failure of his planned showdown with Ben Savage. Undecided as to what he should now do, he asked, "What's that you're serving for dinner? It looks pretty good."

"That's fresh venison," Rachel said. "That's today's special, something we don't have very often. Our cook's husband killed a deer this morning. He's butchered it for us, and we're frying up a mess of it while it's still fresh, and he's gonna smoke the rest of it. Would you like to try some?"

He couldn't think of any reason not to, since his whole mission had failed, so he said, "Yessum, I think I would. Let me go outside and call my partner and I'll be right back." He turned and headed for the door, then stopped and came back to leave a coin on the bar for his whiskey before heading for the door again.

"I thought he was a whiskey drummer or somethin'," Tiny said, "else I wouldn'ta called you over here."

"I declare, Tiny," Rachel replied. "How many drummers do you see coming in here dressed like that with a big ol' six-gun strapped on? He coulda been somebody wanting to settle an old score with Ben." She looked toward the door and wondered aloud, "You ever hear Ben talk about a friend named Robert Diamond?"

"No, but I expect there's a heck of a lot we don't know about Ben's past," Tiny said. "And that gray-headed old man didn't hardly seem like a gunslinger," he said in his defense.

Outside the saloon, Reuben walked out into the street and waved to Riley, signaling him to come. Riley promptly came to him at a lope. "He ain't here," Reuben said. "He's outta town for three or four days.

Tie the horses up and we'll have us some dinner here. They're servin' deer meat today. Said the cook's husband had better luck than you did."

Relieved to hear the news, Riley dismounted and said, "Now, that surely suits my taste. You sure they said three or four days, right?" It would be hard to pass up fresh venison, but it would be worse to get caught eating it, if Ben Savage walked in.

CHAPTER 17

Once again, Ben entered the town of Waco, Texas. On this occasion, he had already decided his first stop should be Bob Graham's stable, where Walt Murphy kept his horse. Ever since Henry Barnes's comment on the day of the ill-fated jailbreak, he knew he had to go to Waco. Henry noticed unusual markings on the lower legs of the buckskin the masked outlaw rode by his stable in his escape. He hated to admit it, but that was almost the only reason to take the trip to Waco. If Walt Murphy's horse had similar markings, it wouldn't prove anything, but it would be hard to accept it as coincidence in Ben's mind. If he was lucky, he might get a chance to see Walt's horse at Graham's stable. If he was even luckier, he might see the buckskin tied out front of the sheriff's office.

When he rode past the sheriff's office, however, there was only one horse tied out front and it was a flea-bitten gray, so Ben kept riding until he reached Graham's. "Ranger Ben Savage, if I remember correctly," Graham greeted him cordially. "Did you ever track down those two men you were lookin' for?"

"As a matter of fact, I did," Ben answered. "I was just passin' through on my way back home and saw you standin' out here, so I thought I'd stop and say howdy."

"Well, that's mighty neighborly of you," Graham started, then paused when a thought struck him. "Too bad you weren't here a couple of nights ago. You coulda gone with us on a vigilante raid. A bunch of us raided a nest of outlaws on the other side of the river and burned 'em out." When that caused a raised eyebrow on Ben's face, Graham went on. "It was all official, ordered by the town council and led by Sheriff Murphy. We went stormin' over there and cleaned out a hangout for outlaws that's been there for several years."

"The church?" Ben asked.

"Right, the church," Graham answered, remembering their earlier conversation. "Then you know we oughta done this a long time ago."

That was a big surprise to Ben, knowing the setup Walt Murphy enjoyed in partnership with Reuben Drum. "Was anybody arrested?" He wondered aloud.

"No, there wasn't anybody arrested. There wasn't anybody there but a couple of women and they was killed by stray shots, I reckon, 'cause none of us was shootin' to hit anybody. And that part of it was a shame. We never meant for somethin' like that to happen. They just didn't come outta there when they should have, right in the beginnin' when the fire was first started."

There were a lot of different thoughts running through Ben's mind after hearing Graham's account of the raid. One thing for sure, that raid would never have taken place without Walt Murphy's okay, no matter what the mayor and the council wanted. So Ben had to think that it was most likely Walt's idea. The next question was, why wasn't Reuben there? Did Walt warn Reuben of the raid in advance? Or was he not warned and the sheriff was surprised when he wasn't there? While he thought about that, he steered Cousin over closer to the corral. After a moment, he said, "That's a fine-lookin' buckskin. He looks like that one the sheriff rides." He wanted to say more when he saw the short black sock marking on the front left leg, but he waited for Graham to confirm it.

"That is Walt's buckskin," Graham said.

There was little doubt left in Ben's mind now. Walt was in that bunch that attempted to take the money from Sheriff Mack Bragg's office—at least that buckskin was there. After all the arrests and killings, there were few left to split the money. If Reuben Drum was killed there would be even fewer to divide the cash with. So, where was Reuben? And where was the money? Did Pete Russell bring it to the church? It was too complicated to try to descend on Walt Murphy alone. He had to have a little patience and see if there were more answers to his questions. He said so long to Bob Graham and turned Cousin toward the sheriff's office.

When he walked into the sheriff's office, he was greeted by Wayne Price, who was sitting in the sheriff's chair behind the desk. "Ben Savage!" Wayne exclaimed. "I didn't know you were back in town."

"Howdy, Wayne," Ben returned the greeting. "I just rode in a little while ago, and I thought I oughta stop by and see how you and Walt are doin'. Where is the sheriff?"

"Walt's where he is most every day about this time, Jake's Rib House," Wayne said with a grin.

"I reckon I shoulda figured that out," Ben chuckled. "How come you didn't go with him?"

Wayne shrugged. "I like them ribs Jake cooks, but I don't want 'em every day, like Walt does. I reckon I like beef a little better'n pork."

"I heard you had a little barbecue at the church the other night," Ben commented.

"Yes, sir, we sure did," Wayne replied, "burnt the place to the ground. Ain't nothin' left of that place no more."

"I remember Walt tellin' me that first day I rode into Waco that those drifters out at the church didn't cause the town any problems. Matter of fact, he said you didn't bother 'em because it kept 'em from comin' into town."

"That's what we used to think, all right," Wayne replied. "But Walt was talkin' to the mayor and some of the council, and they decided we'd better put them outta business before we started havin' real trouble. Like that fellow, Pete Russell, that you arrested. Walt figured he might show up at the church after he killed those two deputy marshals and ran off with the money. Come to find out, he didn't. We figure he went straight on up to Dallas. Like Walt says, we'll never see that jasper or the money, either, here in Waco."

"I expect Walt's right," Ben agreed. "I heard there were no arrests durin' that raid on the church. Was anybody killed?"

"Well, none of the outlaws. There wasn't anybody

there but two whores, and we found one of them layin' on the back steps and the other'n layin' on the kitchen floor. They was shot. We figure it had to be by ricochets or stray shots 'cause nobody shot at either one of 'em. That was the only thing that went wrong that night. I was the one who got close enough to see the body on the floor between the back steps and the kitchen. Walt was worried about another woman that stays there. She's the cook. Frances Wright's her name, but she wasn't there. Don't know why she wasn't there. Maybe she was with Reuben and whoever else was supposed to be there."

"You say you saw both bodies of the women," Ben wondered. "The woman you saw lyin' between the back steps and the kitchen, which way was she lyin'?" When Wayne looked as if he didn't understand, Ben asked, "When she went down, did it look like she was runnin' toward the back steps, or runnin' away from the back steps?"

Wayne paused to remember the scene as he had seen it. "I reckon she was runnin' away from the steps, like she was runnin' back in the church 'cause her head was toward the kitchen."

Ben let his mind create a picture of one woman being shot down on the steps and the other one seeing it happen and running for her life. No doubt they could have seen and heard everything that went on at that outlaw camp, but now there was no one to question Walt Murphy's word but Reuben Drum and anyone who escaped with him. There was no doubt in his mind now that Walt had instigated the raid to quiet Reuben Drum about his partnership with him. Or maybe it was to make one less partner to share the bank's money, if he gets his hands on it. "What about the cook?" he asked. "She ever show up anywhere?"

"Not that we know of," Wayne replied. "Trouble is, nobody knows anything about her, whether she's got any kin around here or not. All we know is when that buildin' burned down, there weren't no trace of her a-tall. So she musta been gone before we got there. We figure she mighta come back the next day, saw what had happened, and took off for home, wherever that is."

What the hell is he doing back here? Walt Murphy paused when he glanced toward the front door, his fork halfway to his mouth. The image of the big Ranger was one he hoped he'd never be bothered with again. Quickly recovering his wits then, he stuck the fork in his mouth and chewed the pork gristle thoughtfully as he watched Ben approach his table. "Ben Savage," he greeted him, "what brings you back to our town? Are you on the trail of that feller Pete Russell?"

"Howdy, Walt," Ben replied. "No, I ain't really on that job anymore. But I was just curious enough to take a little ride up this way to check with you in case he mighta had some tie-in with that bunch out at the church."

"Yeah, we heard Russell escaped, but we ain't seen hide nor hair of him here," Walt said. "Don't know why he would come here, though. The last time he did, he got himself arrested and hauled back to Buzzard's Bluff with you." He made an effort to chuckle, as if amused by the fact that Ben had snatched Pete and Ormond right out from under his nose. "You gonna eat some ribs?" he asked then when Jake looked over at him from behind the counter.

"Yeah, might as well," Ben answered and nodded toward Jake. Then told him coffee when Jake asked what he wanted to drink.

"Wouldn'ta done Pete Russell much good if he had gone to the church," Walt went on when Ben pulled a chair back and sat down. "The church is burnt to the ground, and if he was there, he ain't there now. Matter of fact, there ain't nobody there anymore."

"That's what I just found out," Ben said. "I stopped by your office and Wayne told me about your vigilante raid over there. But he said there wasn't anybody in the building when you burned it down except two women, and they didn't make it outta there."

"That's right," Walt replied, "and that's just a damn shame. But I'm sure I don't have to tell you about the trouble you can have when you're dealin' with a bunch of half-drunk citizens on a vigilante raid. It's a wonder they didn't shoot some of their own raidin' party."

"I wonder why Reuben Drum wasn't there," Ben commented. "It was my understandin' that he was always there. Hell, he was the one runnin' the place, wasn't he?"

"That's right. I ain't got no idea why he wasn't there, myself. Maybe he decided he was gettin' to be too much of a nuisance and it was time to move before I arrested him." They were interrupted briefly when a tired-looking woman set a plate of food down before Ben. "Thank you, Grace," Walt said, then made a quick introduction. "This is Grace Shaw. She's Melvin's wife. Melvin, that's Jake's brother."

"Ma'am," Ben said and nodded. She made no response and turned away to return to the kitchen.

"I'da told her who you are, but it wouldn'ta done no good. She's deaf as a stump. She can figure out some things you're sayin', if she's lookin' right at you. Jake told Melvin she's just playin' like she's deaf, so she won't have to take any orders from him." He paused to chuckle, then continued. "So, whaddaya aimin' to do now, since Pete Russell ain't here in town and he ain't at the church? Dallas is my guess. Are you gonna ride up there to look for him?"

"Nope," Ben answered. "He ain't my responsibility anymore. I was just curious about the church, since he and Ormond went there once before. I expect I'll just start back to Buzzard's Bluff in the mornin'."

Walt smiled, pleased to hear it. "Well, sorry you made the trip for nothin'. I wish that jasper hadda come back here with that money. The bank was offerin' a nice reward for the return of it."

"It wasn't really any trouble to ride up here," Ben said between bites of grilled ribs. "I wasn't doin' much back there at Buzzard's Bluff. Since our little attempted jailbreak, it's been quiet as can be. We were just glad we didn't lose both of those bank robbers while they were in our jail and we killed most of the party tryin' to break 'em out." He shook his head and swore. "One of 'em got away, though. He musta had a wide yellow streak down his back, 'cause when the shootin' got hot and his partners got cut down, he turned rabbit and lit out." Ben watched Walt carefully to see if he showed any sign of anger. "Henry Barnes owns the stable up at that end of town. He said he ain't ever seen a man so scared, beatin' on that poor horse for all he was worth. Henry said he felt sorry for the horse—said it was a fine-lookin' horse—think he said it was a buckskin." Walt's gaze was steady and unblinking. Ben guessed that he was struggling to show no emotion. "You might wanna keep your eyes open for any stranger ridin' a buckskin," Ben suggested.

A smile slowly broke out on Walt's face and he responded. "Maybe I'd best keep an eye on myself while I'm at it. I ride a buckskin."

"You do? You weren't down in Buzzard's Bluff a few nights ago, were you?" Ben joked and laughed.

"Well, if I was, I wouldn't hardly tell it to a Texas Ranger," Walt japed in return, no longer nervous. Their discussion was interrupted then when Jake came over to talk.

"How were the ribs, boys?" Jake sang out. "Walt better like 'em, 'cause if he don't, I'll lose half my business."

Happy to change the subject, Walt said, "They were just as good as ever, Jake. Reckon you've still got my business. How 'bout you, Ben?"

"As good as any I've ever eaten anywhere, maybe better," Ben allowed.

"Good, glad to hear it," Jake said. "I was afraid for a little while last night I wasn't gonna have enough. I get my meat from Billy Wells and he was late with my supply. Melvin had to ride over the river early this mornin' to help him finish killin' hogs. If he hadn't, the sheriff's dinner mighta been pretty late."

"What's the matter with Billy?" Walt asked. "Is he sick or somethin'?"

"Nah, Billy ain't sick. Melvin said somethin' about his wife's aunt, or somebody, landed on his doorstep by surprise and he had to do some quick work to make a place for her. Said it wouldn't happen again. I told Melvin he shoulda told Billy it better not, or we'll start buyin' hogs from somebody else."

Ben was not watching for any reaction by Walt from Jake's hog supply problem, but he just happened to catch a sudden twitch in the sheriff's eyebrows and his eyes seemed to freeze wide open. It was only for a few seconds, but Ben was convinced that something Jake had just said had somehow struck a nerve. As if to confirm it, Walt glanced at him, then quickly back at Jake. Only a couple of minutes passed after that before Walt announced that he had to get back to his office, so Wayne could go to dinner. "Hate to run off on you," he said to Ben, "but I had a pretty good head start before you came in."

"No problem a-tall," Ben said. "We don't want that young deputy of yours to miss his feed. Matter of fact, you go along, I'll pay for your dinner. I figure I owe you."

"That's mighty neighborly of you, Ben, 'preciate it." He got up and walked out the door.

"Tell Wayne to come down here to eat," Jake called after him, and Walt just waved his arm in reply without looking around. Jake looked back at Ben and said, "Wayne just comes in once in a while. I wish he liked ribs as much as Walt does. I could use the business."

"I expect I'll finish this cup of coffee, and I'll get goin', myself," Ben said to Jake. "It was mighty fine eatin', and that's a fact." Something had lit a fire under Walt having to do with Jake's story about someone named Billy Wells, and Ben was interested in finding out a little more about him. "I'm glad you got your meat this mornin'," he commented as he paid for Walt and himself. "I'da been disappointed to miss one of your dinners."

"Thank you kindly," Jake replied. "Hope you come back to see us again."

"I'm sure I will, whenever I'm in town. How far did your brother have to go this mornin' to help Billy Wells butcher hogs?"

"Oh, it weren't that far," Jake said, "just on the other side of the river. Billy's got a little farm less than half a mile past the bridge."

"Is that right?" Ben asked. "I swear, I've traveled that road several times before and I don't remember seein' a hog farm that close to the bridge."

"Well, you wouldn't hardly notice it, I reckon, less you were lookin' for it. You can't see much of the farm from the road and there's just a little sign beside the path to the house. It ain't even got Billy's name on it. It just says, 'Pigs.'"

"You know," Ben said then, "that coffee tastes mighty good. I believe I'll have another cup. I'm not in any hurry."

"How 'bout a slice of pie with it?" Jake suggested. "Betty made an apple pie this mornin'."

"Well, now, that really sounds good to me," Ben replied. He decided to kill a little time, enough for Walt to go to the stable to saddle his horse. He had a strong feeling that Walt was in a hurry to go somewhere. And if his hunch was right, he wouldn't worry about trying to trail him, because he already had directions to Walt's possible destination.

Chapter 18

Billy Wells stopped as he was walking from the barn on his way to the house, a movement in the edge of the trees where the path cut through from the road having caught his eye. He paused there to watch a rider on a buckskin horse emerge from the pines that stood between his house and the road. "Walt Murphy," he muttered unconsciously. After hearing Frances Wright's account of the night when she had fled the church, he felt an immediate moment of panic. A visit from the sheriff was something he had dreaded and hoped would not occur. His initial instinct was to run to the house for his shotgun, but he feared it was too late for that. He was caught in the open, and if the sheriff saw him run, he might simply shoot him down. He had no choice other than to play innocent for the sake of his wife and kids. Knowing now the evil the sheriff was capable of, playing dumb might be his and his family's only chance for survival. He turned to face him as he rode into the yard. "Well, afternoon, Sheriff Murphy," he greeted him. "What brings you out this way?"

"How do, Billy?" Walt responded. "I understand Frances Wright is stayin' with you and your wife. I thought I should come out and tell her about a fire at that old church she was doin' some cookin' for, in case she was thinkin' about goin' back there."

"Oh?" Billy replied, trying to think of the best thing to say. "She's in the house, Sheriff. I reckon I can tell her you've come to see her. I know she'll be sorry to hear about the fire."

When Billy remained standing there, Walt said, "Why don't you just do that?"

"Right," Billy replied. "I'll just do that." He turned and started for the house, only to stop again. "Can I get you a drink of water or somethin'? Make you some coffee?" As soon as he said it, he realized how awkward it was.

"No thanks, I just et," Walt answered. "I'll just have a word with Frances."

With no other choice, Billy continued on toward the house, with Walt on the big buckskin plodding close behind him. Inside the house, Betty and her aunt were already aware of the sheriff's arrival. Frightened, Frances backed into a corner of the kitchen, sank down on the floor and sat there hugging her knees. Seeing her aunt so terrified, Betty took another look out the window and said, "I'll be damned . . ." and took Billy's shotgun down from its pegs over the fireplace. "You just stay here till we see what he wants." Then she took a post beside the kitchen door with the shotgun beside her, just inside the door, where it couldn't be seen.

Billy stopped at the foot of the kitchen steps and when Betty opened the door, he said, "Hon, Sheriff

Murphy is here and he wants to talk to your aunt about that place she was cookin' for. He said they had a fire in that old church and he thought he oughta let her know. I reckon she'll be surprised to hear that." He hoped his wife was catching the vague phrases he was using to tip her off.

She understood what he was trying to tell her, so she responded. "Well, that was mighty nice of Sheriff Murphy to go to that trouble. Afternoon, Sheriff," she called out to Walt then. "Aunt Frances has been down with the miseries for a couple of days, so she's lyin' in the bed. I'll see if I can get her up. I know she'll wanna hear about that fire."

"I don't wanna cause her no trouble, if she's ailin'," Walt said. "I'll just be a minute. I can come in, or she can just come to the door."

"I'll get her to the door," Betty said. "I think she can stand up that long." She went at once to her aunt and quickly told her what to do. "You don't have to worry. You just remember, you weren't there that night. You just act surprised and don't be afraid. I'll have that shotgun right beside me, and the first sign I see of mischief, I'll blast him outta the saddle. All right?" Frances nodded rapidly and let Betty help her to her feet. Then with Betty's arm for support, she walked to the kitchen door to face the man who had murdered Dora and Paulene.

"Afternoon, Frances," Walt said, still sitting in the saddle. "I'm sorry you're ailin', but I figured I oughta let you know the church burnt down night before last."

He watched her carefully for her reaction, but she gave him the best performance she could manage.

"Burnt down!" she exclaimed dramatically. "How did that happen? Did everybody get out all right?"

He wasn't sure, so he hesitated, still watching her closely. "No, I'm afraid I've got some bad news about that. Both Dora and Paulene didn't get out in time, and we had to bury 'em right behind the barn."

"My Lord in Heaven," Frances gasped. "What are Reuben and Riley gonna do now?"

"I ain't seen either one of 'em," Walt replied. "They weren't there. I reckon they decided to move on somewhere else."

"Maybe they figured it was gonna happen any day, so they left before it did," Frances said. "Thank you for comin' to tell me."

"I thought you deserved to know," Walt said, suspicious again, thinking her statement about them thinking it was going to happen might imply that she knew the fire was deliberately set. He knew that he hadn't said how the fire was started. He decided there was too great a possibility that she was lying and knew he had raided the church. He couldn't take a chance on her spilling her guts about the raid and the murders, whether she was lyin' or not. She knew too much. He could feel an itch in his trigger finger to pull his .44 and silence her now, but there were too many witnesses, including two small children. He would have to kill every one of them and that might be too much to handle. It would be best to do it at long range, he figured. There was too much daylight left, so he decided he would leave now, then come back later and set up in the trees with his rifle after it began to get dark. She was bound to seek the outhouse before going to bed, and that was when he would silence her.

It would be much easier to ride back up the road unseen after dark. "Well, that's all I came to do," he said. "I'll get on back to town. I hope you get to feelin' better." He wheeled the buckskin. "Billy," he acknowledged and rode back up the path toward the road.

Kneeling on the ground with the barrel of his Winchester 73 protruding through the branches of a laurel bush, Ben relaxed his grip and let the front sight drop from its position on the middle of Walt's back. He had held it there for the entire time the sheriff sat talking to Frances Wright, ready to squeeze the trigger at the first show of aggressive movement on the sheriff's part. It appeared that Walt had bought Frances's story, and from where Ben knelt, the poor woman appeared barely able to stand. He pulled his rifle back out of the bush and walked to the edge of the trees to watch Walt leave.

Following the path back up to the road, Walt didn't hesitate. He turned toward Waco and headed straight back toward the bridge into Waco. He had been too far away to hear the conversation at the back door of the house. But whatever he told them didn't appear to upset any of them. Ben didn't know what had actually happened at the church that night. Most of what he had learned had come from Wayne Price. But he knew it was Walt's idea, and Walt had led the attack. It was his theory that Walt wanted all parties connected to the stolen bank money eliminated, so he could keep it all. He felt strongly that Pete Russell was more than likely dead and probably by Walt's hand. He needed to be able to prove it, and the only source that might give him a clue was the frail-looking little woman he had just witnessed Walt talking to. There was no doubt Walt had been concerned about the woman, enough so that he had taken a ride out there to find her.

Ben climbed on his horse and made his way to the edge of the trees where he could see Walt riding down the road toward town. He waited until the sheriff was out of sight, then turned Cousin back on the path that led to the house. Billy was still standing at the foot of the steps at the kitchen door, talking to his wife and her aunt, when Betty alerted him of the arrival of another visitor. Billy turned to look toward the path, and when he saw it was a stranger, he muttered, "I hope to hell he's lookin' to buy a pig."

Looking over her husband's head from the top step, Betty looked at the big man and commented, "He don't look like he's lookin' for a pig." She looked at Billy and asked, "Now what?" Frances stepped back inside the door.

"Howdy," Billy greeted Ben, somewhat guardedly.

"Howdy," Ben returned, looked at Betty and said, "Ma'am," with a nod of his head. "I'd like to get a little information if I could. My name's Ben Savage . . ."

"Ben Savage!" Frances gasped from inside the kitchen door before he could finish. "Oh, my Lord, my Lord!" Her reaction immediately alarmed Billy and Betty.

"Yes, ma'am, Ben Savage," he replied. "I'm a Texas Ranger, and I just wanna talk to the lady inside the door. I'm tryin' to get to the bottom of what happened to those two women at the church night before last.

It's my guess that she was in that church when they set it on fire. Am I right, ma'am?"

Frances didn't answer the question. She was interested more in one of her own. "Reuben Drum and Riley Best went to Buzzard's Bluff to kill you! Did you kill them?"

"No, ma'am, I haven't seen any sign of Reuben Drum or Riley Best, and I wouldn't recognize them if I had. Why were they gonna kill me?"

"Because you killed Lester, Reuben's son," Frances said, no longer hiding behind the edge of the door.

Ben looked at Billy and asked, "Mind if I step down?" When Billy invited him to, he stepped down out of the saddle. "I'll admit I killed Lester Drum," Ben replied. "I didn't know his name at the time, but it wouldn't have made any difference if I had. He gave me no choice. I don't take kindly to any man who draws a weapon on me. The reason I'm here right now is to make sure you're all right. I know that Walt Murphy led the raid on the church to kill Reuben Drum and everyone else there." At this point, he was bluffing because he had no proof backing that statement up. "I know that the sheriff killed the other two women that night. What I don't know is why he didn't shoot you. You were in that building when he set it on fire. Why did he let you go?" He was gambling on her reaction to his remarks, and she responded pretty much as he had hoped she would.

"He didn't let me go!" Frances cried at once. "I had to hide behind the kitchen pantry while those men rode around and around the church like wild Indians. When the sheriff told Dora and Paulene to come on out the back door, I started to go, too. But before I got out into the kitchen, he shot Paulene down on the back steps. And when Dora saw that, she turned around and ran back into the church, but he shot her down, too. I ran back to my bed to hide again."

There it was, a complete witness report of the murders. The only thing better would be if she had written it all down and signed it, he thought. "Wayne Price told me you weren't in the church when they checked the ruins the next mornin'. How'd you get out?" Not withholding anything once she had begun, she told him about taking an opportunity to escape and hide in the overturned outhouse. "One last question," he said. "Did anyone else see Walt shoot the two women?"

"No," she answered, eager to tell him. "They were all on the other side of the church when he stopped his horse by the back door. They were all shootin' their pistols up in the air, so I reckon they didn't notice his two shots."

That was good news to Ben to know that the citizens of Waco who had volunteered to ride as vigilantes were not a party to the murders. He was also glad to hear that Wayne Price was not a party to the executions, because he was of the opinion that Wayne was basically a good man. He had thought from the beginning that Wayne had no idea his boss was as crooked as any outlaw in Texas. "Well, I wanna thank you, ma'am, for answerin' my questions, and I'm glad that you were able to get outta that fire alive. I expect you told the sheriff just now that you weren't there at all that night. Right?"

"I did," Frances answered. "I guess he believed me. He didn't shoot me." She hesitated for a moment before saying, "You'd best watch out for yourself, 'cause Reuben went to Buzzard's Bluff to kill you. Riley Best tried to talk him out of goin' after you, but Reuben's determined to take his vengeance on you. Riley ended up goin' with him."

"Thanks for the warnin'," Ben told her. "I'll try to keep an eye out for him." He stepped back up into the saddle then. "I intend to charge Walt Murphy with these crimes. If it comes to trial, I'll call on you folks to testify." Judging from the expressions on Billy and Betty's faces, they weren't too enthusiastic about that. But Frances was nodding her head vigorously, and she was really the only witness he needed. *I hope to hell I can keep her alive to testify,* he thought as he turned Cousin back up the path.

Following the path through the screen of pines that hid the house from the road, he cleared the edge of the trees and came face-to-face with Walt Murphy. Startled, both men reined back hard to confront each other. Walt, maybe the more surprised of the two, spoke first. "Ben Savage, what are you doin' here?" He had at first planned to come back after dark to finish the job and shoot Frances when she went to the outhouse. But before he got to the bridge over the Brazos, it occurred to him that, if the woman was ill, she probably wouldn't come outside in the dark. She would use a chamber pot. Feeling stupid for not considering that to begin with, he turned around, thinking he would just have to wait for a shot at her while it was still daylight.

"Maybe I should ask you the same thing," Ben replied in answer to his question.

"I'm on some official business of the sheriff's office," Walt said, "to make sure Frances Wright wasn't in that fire at the church. I'm wonderin' what business a saloon owner from Buzzard's Bluff has up here."

"None that I can think of, but I ain't here as a saloon owner," Ben retorted. "I'm here in my official capacity as a Texas Ranger, and it looks like I'm gonna have to place you under arrest for the murders of two women. And before you start thinkin' it's just my word against yours, Frances Wright *was* in that building when you set it on fire and shot Dora and Paulene." Walt realized then that he wasn't bluffing. And before he thought to react, Ben was holding his six-gun on him. "Don't try it, Walt. It would be a mistake," Ben warned when the sheriff started to reach for his .44. "It's best for you to make it easy on yourself, so I don't have to put a hole in your chest. And that's just what I'll do, if you make one move I don't like." He motioned with the Colt and said, "Now, reach across with your left hand and pull that pistol outta the holster with nothin' but your thumb and forefinger and drop it on the ground.

Walt did not move to do as Ben instructed. Instead, he sat there, a sneer of defiance on his broad face. "You're a little outta your territory, ain't you, Ben? I'm the law in these parts."

"Do like I told you," Ben replied, "or I'll take a corpse back to town."

Walt still remained motionless. "If I don't, are you just gonna shoot me as I'm settin' here?"

"That's exactly what I'm gonna do. When I bring a body in, they don't ask me if you put up a fight or not, so you'll just make my job easier, if you insist on suicide."

"Tell you what, Ben, ever since you rode into town that first day, I've been wonderin' what kinda man you really are. There ain't nobody out here in the woods but you and me. Why don't you put that gun away and we'll settle this thing like real men? Just you and me, man-to-man, and we'll decide who deserves to die and who deserves to live. Whaddaya say, Ranger, have you got the guts to face me?"

"All that would prove would be which one of us is the dumbest," Ben answered. "Now, stop wastin' time and get rid of that gun, like I told you." He aimed his six-gun at Walt's chest.

"All right," Walt said, "you've got the upper hand. Don't get itchy fingered on me. You know, if you shoot me, or if you take me to jail, then over twenty thousand dollars of cash money ain't never gonna be found. Right now, I'm the only one who knows where it is. Half of that money could buy you a lot of whiskey for that saloon of yours."

"I'm done talkin'," Ben said, impatiently. "If you don't throw that gun down, I'm gonna start shootin' pieces offa you."

"All right, all right," Walt blurted, "but you're passin' up a damn big payday. And all you have to do for it is go on back to Buzzard's Bluff and leave us be." Ben answered with the cocking of his weapon. "I'm doin' it," Walt exclaimed and reached across his body with his left hand as Ben had ordered. "Two fingers, see," he said, holding the hand up high for Ben to see. Then, thinking to distract Ben with the left hand, he suddenly reached for his pistol with his right hand.

Expecting it, Ben put a round in his right shoulder, causing him to drop the pistol on the ground. "Damn you!" Walt exclaimed painfully and clutched his shoulder while Ben slid off Cousin and hurried to take control of Walt's reins.

"I warned you," Ben said as he dropped the buckskin's reins to the ground, then quickly reached up and pulled Walt's left hand away from his shoulder and handcuffed his hands behind his back.

Only then recovering from the sudden shock of having been shot, Walt bellowed, "Free my hands! You damn maniac, I'll bleed to death if you don't do somethin' to stop this bleedin'."

"I expect you're right," Ben replied, "so we'd best quit wastin' time and get you back to town where we can get you some help." He picked up the sheriff's handgun and stuck it in his saddlebag.

"Are you crazy?" Walt roared. "You can't take me back to town like this. I'm the sheriff!"

"You ain't no more," Ben said, realizing Walt was having trouble believing he could be arrested. "That's the only place I can take you where you can get a doctor to fix you up. The only other place woulda been the church, but you burnt that to the ground and killed everybody there. Remember?" He took up the reins to Walt's horse and climbed back into the saddle. "Just relax and enjoy the ride back to town," he advised as he led the buckskin out to the road and turned toward town.

Finding it hard to believe what he had just witnessed, Billy Wells backed slowly out of the patch of bushes he had hidden behind. His rifle in hand, he made his way back through the trees to the house, where his wife and her aunt waited to hear the cause of the shot they had heard. Fully expecting Billy to report that Ben had been shot as he rode back to the road, they were astonished by his report. "It was the sheriff and Savage, all right," he blurted excitedly. "Ben Savage shot Walt and arrested him, and he's takin' him back to town—to jail, I reckon."

"Are you sure?" Frances responded.

"I'm sure, all right. I heard the whole thing," Billy assured her. "It looked like Walt was shot in the shoulder. He was still on his horse, though."

"Walt Murphy arrested," Frances marveled. "I can't hardly believe it." To Reuben Drum and all the occupants at the old church hideout, Walt was the ultimate authority and would never be challenged.

"Maybe this will bring a new day to Waco," Betty speculated hopefully.

CHAPTER 19

News of the arrest swept rapidly along the main street of town, leaving an astonished collection of shopkeepers and customers in its wake, as Sheriff Walt Murphy was led slowly up the middle of the street. His hands in irons behind his back and one sleeve of his shirt soaked with blood, he sat stiffly in the saddle, looking neither right nor left. Not certain how fanatic the sheriff's supporters might be, the formidable Ranger leading him rode with his rifle in one hand, the butt resting on his thigh, with the barrel pointing straight up. When they came to the sheriff's office, the Ranger and his prisoner stopped and tied up at the hitching rail. But the wave of amazing news continued on past to the end of the street.

Deputy Sheriff Wayne Price was at Bob Graham's stable when the news reached that far. Stunned, he was not sure he could believe the rumor, so he hurried back to the jail as quickly as he could. Charging in the door, he found, to his amazement, Sheriff Walt Murphy standing in front of one of the cells, stripped of his gun belt, his hands cuffed behind him, his shirt bloodied, and Ben Savage holding a ring of keys in one hand, a six-gun in the other. "Walt?" Wayne exclaimed "What . . . ?" That was as far as he got before Ben interrupted him.

"Deputy, glad you're back," he said and tossed the keys to the startled young man. "Here, see if you can find a key to this cell. We'll get him inside and send for the doctor to come take a look at that wound. Who do you fetch to doctor your prisoners?"

Wayne stood speechless for a few moments, staring at Walt. When Ben started to repeat the question, he blurted, "Doctor Griffin, that's who we usually send for."

"Well, send somebody for him," Ben said. "Walt's gonna need to have him take a look at that shoulder."

Finally recovering from his shock upon first seeing his boss in this condition, Wayne responded. "I'll send for him, but do you mind tellin' me what's goin' on?"

"Right," Ben replied. "Sorry, I shoulda told you that to begin with. He's under arrest for the murder of Dora Somebody and Paulene Somebody on the night you fellows set fire to the church."

"But those deaths were accidental," Wayne protested.

"That's right," Walt interrupted. "Tell this fool. You was there. You saw how everybody was shootin'. Ain't no tellin' whose shots hit those women."

"Did you see those women get shot?" Ben asked, ignoring Walt's outburst, and Wayne said that he, himself, didn't actually see the women get hit. He said there was a lot of shooting going on just for effect, and a lot of it may have been a little careless. Ben continued, "Well, I've got a witness who did see them get shot, both of 'em by your sheriff, here. Ain't that right, Walt? Shot one of 'em down when she walked out on the back steps and the other one in the back when she tried to run back inside. My witness was still in the church when that happened, and she saw it all." He paused a moment to let Wayne digest that, before going on.

"Nobody's gonna believe that old woman," Walt charged. "Everybody knows she's half crazy. If she wasn't, she wouldn't be livin' with a gang of outlaws. And every one of them outlaws at that church would lie to try to stop me from roundin' 'em all up."

Wayne was still standing there, wearing his confusion on his face, so Ben continued. "I'm also chargin' him with attemptin' to break two prisoners out of the Buzzard's Bluff jail. His buckskin horse was identified when he escaped after the jailbreak was prevented, and I'm bettin' we'll find a mask made out of a sack in his saddlebags when we check 'em. On top of that, there's a little thing about drawin' his weapon on a peace officer." He nodded toward a sulking Walt Murphy and said, "That's how he got the wound in his shoulder." When Wayne remained dumbfounded by what he had just heard, Ben asked, "So, now, how 'bout that doctor?"

"Right," he replied, but still stood there as if waiting for Walt to say something. When he failed to, Wayne unlocked the cell door and left the key in the door, then walked outside to send someone for Dr. Griffin. He was right back within a few minutes to report that the blacksmith's son volunteered to fetch the doctor. It was in time to see Ben removing Walt's handcuffs.

"Good," Ben replied. "While we wait for the doctor, let's go in the office and talk about a few things."

Wayne dutifully followed him into the office, and Ben closed the cell room door behind them. "First, I know this is kind of a surprise to spring on you, so I'd like to tell you everything I've got on Walt, so far. I know he hired you, so you most likely don't like turnin' on him like this, but Walt's been takin' advantage of the town of Waco for a long time. He's gone too far now, when he starts killin' innocent people just because he thinks they know too much." He went on to tell Wayne about the stolen bank money he was sure Walt had in his possession. When he was finished, there were very few questions left for Wayne to ask.

"So, what are you plannin' to do with him now?" Wayne asked.

"As far as I'm concerned, you're the sheriff here now," Ben answered. "So, I'm leavin' him here in your custody until the Federal Marshals pick him up and take him to trial. It's a tough way for you to start off as sheriff, with him right under your nose, but if you're made of the kind of steel I think you are, you'll handle it. And right now is the time when you've got to stake your claim for the job of sheriff and show your city council you're ready to do it. So, whaddaya say, do you wanna be sheriff?"

"I reckon I do," he said at once. "I'll sure as hell try to impress Mayor McNeal and the rest of the council."

"Good man," Ben told him. "There's also the question of over twenty thousand dollars of stolen money that belongs to the Bank of Lee County. Walt's got it hidden somewhere. If we can find it, it needs to go back to the bank. You got any idea where he might have taken that to hide?"

"I ain't got any notion," Wayne replied. "He's got a

cabin up the river a mile or so. Maybe he hid it there somewhere."

"If you tell me how to find that cabin, I'll go see if I can find where he hid the money," Ben said. "If I find it, I'll turn that over to you, too, and you can collect the reward money the bank's offerin'."

"Why would you do that?" Wayne asked.

"Just a little spendin' money to get you started off right in your new job," Ben said.

They were interrupted then by the arrival of Dr. Fred Griffin. He looked surprised to see Ben and Wayne standing there talking. "The blacksmith's boy said you sent for me to tend the sheriff's bullet wound," Griffin said to Wayne. He seemed a little unsure of the message.

"That's right, Doc," Wayne replied. "He's in the cell room. I'll go with you." Before leading the doctor into the cell room, Wayne glanced at Ben for approval and got a nod to let him know he should be guarding the prisoner while he was with the doctor.

The door between the office and the cell room had been closed for no longer than a couple of minutes when the front door opened and a slightly built man, wearing a frock coat and a derby hat, walked in. He stopped in the doorway for a long moment to gawk at the big broad-shouldered stranger standing by the desk before he entered the room. "I'm Mayor John McNeal," he stated, before asking, "Where's Sheriff Murphy?"

"He's in there with the doctor and Deputy Price," Ben said, nodding toward the cell room door.

"Who are you?" McNeal asked and Ben identified himself as a Texas Ranger. "I heard that Sheriff Murphy was led up the street with his hands cuffed behind him. Was that you?"

Ben nodded and said that it was. He realized that he was just getting the first of a great many reactions of shock from the citizens of the town. Walt had obviously established himself as an invincible guardian of the town and its laws. "Yes, sir, Mr. Mayor, that was me. Ben Savage, Texas Ranger," he said, showing McNeal his badge. "We've been on to Sheriff Murphy for quite some time now and I think we've finally got enough evidence to convict him." He was lying about the Rangers investigating Walt before, but he thought that made it sound more official. "I have to tell you, sir, you've got yourself an honest, outstandin' deputy in Wayne Price. You're lucky he's qualified to take over the job of sheriff when the marshals come to pick Murphy up." He went on to tell the mayor about Walt's involvement with the outlaw element and the extent to which he was willing to go to satisfy his greed.

McNeal shook his head while he thought about it. "You mean that little raiding party he organized against those outlaws in that old church building—a raid that I gave my okay to—was really just an attempt to kill some witnesses to his deceit?"

"I'm afraid so," Ben replied, which caused the mayor to shake his head again. "You ain't the only one he's fooled, so I wouldn't be too hard on myself, if I was you." He went on to tell the mayor about the stolen bank money. "Walt's got it hid somewhere, so we'll try to find it. In the desk drawer, there's a sizeable roll of money I took off him when I arrested him. I suspect it's part of that bank money, unless you folks pay your sheriff a helluva lot more than other towns do."

It was obvious that the explosion of facts presented to the mayor were almost too much for the slight man to believe about a man who had held his trust. Ben feared that McNeal's knees were going to fail him before they finished talking. "Can I see Sheriff Murphy?" McNeal finally asked, as if he needed to see Walt to believe all he had just heard.

"I don't see why not," Ben said. "He's right in there where the doctor's workin' on him." He went over and opened the cell room door for him. McNeal walked in to find Walt sitting on a bunk facing him while Dr. Griffin fashioned a sling to support his arm.

"It's all a bunch of hogwash, John!" Walt blurted when he saw the mayor. "I didn't do none of that stuff that saloon ranger said I did. They're just tryin' to get rid of me. You need to tell 'em to let me outta here, or the whole town's gonna go to hell."

"Be still!" Dr. Griffin barked, "unless you wanna put this damn sling on yourself."

Walt ignored him. "John, you know I'm the only reason we've kept the peace in this town, and ain't nobody can do it but me. Who you gonna believe, me or this damn saloon ranger that just drifted into town?"

"Finish the damn thing yourself!" Dr. Griffin said, when Walt wouldn't hold still. He got up from the stool he had been sitting on, wrapped his instruments in a towel, and dropped them in his bag. He looked at Wayne, who was in the cell with him, his gun drawn. "Let me out. He's gonna be all right. I got the bullet out, and if he doesn't do anything to stress it, it'll heal just fine." When he walked past McNeal, he said, "I'll send you my bill for fixin' him, just like I always do. I don't care if he is the damn sheriff." McNeal turned around and followed him out, still finding it difficult to believe the sudden turn of events.

Ben remained in the cell room until Wayne had locked Walt's cell, then he came out to the office with him. Both the doctor and the mayor were waiting for them. "Why does Walt keep calling you a saloon ranger?" McNeal asked Ben, thinking that maybe Walt knew about a drinking problem Ben had.

Suspecting as much, Ben smiled and answered. "Because I'm half-owner of a saloon in Buzzard's Bluff. If you're ever down that way, drop in for a drink at the Lost Coyote. If you're worried about my authority to arrest Walt Murphy, it's easy enough to check. Go to the telegraph office and wire Ranger Headquarters in Austin and ask about my status."

"What tha . . .?" Riley Best started and pulled his horse to a stop in the middle of the road. "Reuben! Lookee yonder!"

Reuben Drum reined his horse to a stop beside Riley's and strained to see what Riley was looking at. "Where?" He asked. "I don't see nothin'."

"That's just what I'm talkin' about," Riley replied. "You don't see nothin' and we're supposed to see the church from this spot on the road."

"I swear, you're right," Reuben said. "What the hell happened?" They both kicked their horses and set off for the path to the church at a gallop. As soon as they reached it and followed it around the grove of trees near the wagon road, they saw the reason they hadn't seen it from the road. "Oh, me. Oh, me." Reuben could only repeat over and over as he gazed at the blackened ruins of what had been his domain, his little kingdom. "What happened?" He asked, then his next thought was, "What have them three women done?" For whatever it was, they were successful in destroying everything he had acquired since finding the old church building. He looked at Riley, who could only shake his head in wonder. They rode on up to the ruins and dismounted.

"What the hell?" Riley blurted when he saw the outhouse lying on its side. The little barn was unharmed, but when he began looking around back of it, he discovered what appeared to be a fresh grave. "Look here, Reuben!" he called out, and when the old man joined him, he asked, "Don't that look like a grave to you?"

"It sure does," Reuben agreed, "and I think I got a pretty good idea who's in it." While Riley had been looking around the barn and the outhouse, he had been taking a closer look at the church building. "I think them three women are in that grave. You look at the church buildin'. There's a helluva lotta tracks around the whole buildin', like a bunch of horses ridin' round and round it, and there's somethin' that looks like bloodstains on the back steps." He gave Riley a solemn look. "There's bad business here, and I think whoever burnt this place down was after me and you."

"Ben Savage?" Riley asked.

"No, hell no," Reuben responded. "If it'da been

him, he'da been tryin' to arrest us. It was Walt Murphy. There ain't no doubt about it, we know for sure now he killed Pete Russell and he's got that money. You saw him ride after Pete that day. And now he came out here to make sure he didn't have to split it with me and you. It can't be anybody else."

"I reckon you're right," Riley said. "And I bet he weren't too happy when he found out me and you was gone." He turned to look again at the grave. "I swear, that's just a damn shame about them three women. They didn't deserve to be treated like that."

Reuben was thinking the same thing. "I reckon I owe Walt Murphy for this little piece of business."

"Whaddaya think we oughta do?" Riley asked. "He's kinda put us outta business here."

"He's wiped us out here," Reuben answered, "so I reckon we'll just have to go set up in his territory till we decide what we're gonna do. If we can get our hands on that money, we can do whatever we want." When Riley immediately asked if he was talking about going to Waco, Reuben explained what he meant. "We can go to the part of town we've always gone to, the Reservation. Me and you can go to the Hog's Breath. Brady John will give us a room and he can tell us what Walt is up to. It oughta be easy enough to lure him down to that part of town to take care of a little trouble. Then he'd be in our territory again." He took another long look at the new grave. "I swear, it'd be a lotta work, but I'd like to dig that grave up just to be sure it's who I think it is in there."

Riley shrugged. "Maybe not so hard as you think. It's fresh-dug dirt, and it ain't been dug that long. I'd like to see, myself. If there's somebody else buried here, it might tell a whole different story. I'll get the shovel outta the barn."

Riley was right, the dirt was not packed at all and the grave had not been dug very deep, so in spite of his healing wound, he managed to help Reuben with the digging. It was a distressing sight that greeted them when they uncovered Dora and Paulene. In a hurry to cover them back up, it took some determination for Riley to keep probing until he was sure there were only the two bodies buried there. "Well, where the hell's Frances?" Reuben asked. "There ain't no other graves around here. You reckon they carried her off with 'em?"

"What for?" Riley asked. "Frances is as old as you are. What would they want with her? She must notta been here, or if she was, she musta got away, somehow."

"If she did, I bet I know where she went," Reuben said. "She's got kin here in Waco."

That surprised Riley. "I never heard Frances say she had any kin anywhere, much less in these parts. Are you sure about that? Looks like she woulda mentioned it."

"She didn't want nobody to know 'cause she didn't wanna take a chance on anybody from the church botherin' 'em. She's got a niece and her husband livin' not quite four miles from here."

"I thought you told us that she just wandered in one day, needin' a place to stay," Riley said.

"She did," Reuben replied. "She saw this place and thought it was a church, so she came in and said she didn't have no place to go. When she found out where she had really landed, she didn't care if we were outlaws. She told me she would cook for me, if I'd let her stay."

"Well, I'll be doggoned," Riley responded, "if that ain't somethin'." He thought about it for a minute, then asked, "Why didn't she stay with her niece?"

"She was afraid they weren't fixed to take care of an extra mouth to feed. Her niece's husband had just got started on a little piece of land he wanted to raise hogs on. And at that time, he hadn't got anythin' started but two little girls that was needin' to be fed. So she just walked away one day, and this is as far as she got."

"Well, I'll be . . ." Riley marveled. "I'da never figured that about Frances. Tell you the truth, I never thought much about where she came from, anyway. Just thought she came with the church, I reckon." He thought about it for another moment, then dismissed it. "You reckon we oughta go to her niece's house and see if she's there?"

"That's what I'm thinkin'," Reuben answered. "If she is, she can tell us what happened here."

"This is really a sorry piece of business," Riley said, taking another look at the blackened remains of the old church. He rubbed his belly and added, "I was lookin' forward to gettin' a good dinner when we got here, too."

Billy Wells was standing on the next to the bottom rail of the fence around one of his hog pens, watching his pigs gobble the slop he had filled the trough with, when he heard a horse whinny behind him. He turned to see the two riders entering the yard, the third visit by strangers in the last two days. Once again undecided if he should be alarmed, he decided his reception would have to be friendly, since he was not armed. He stepped down from the fence and turned to meet them. "Howdy," he offered when they pulled up before him.

"Howdy," Reuben returned, not at all sure he had found the right place, since he didn't know Frances's niece's name or the name of her husband. There was little doubt, however, that he had found a pig farm. "I'm lookin' for a woman who works for me, name of Frances Wright. She's got a niece around here somewhere, but I ain't sure exactly where. If she's here, I surely would appreciate it if you'd tell her that Reuben and Riley are lookin' for her. We've been away for a couple of days and came back to find our place burnt to the ground. I'm hopin' Frances is all right and thinkin' maybe she can tell me what happened."

Billy wasn't sure what he should do. He had no way of knowing if Frances would want to talk to these two strangers or not. Much to his relief, however, he was saved from making the decision by a call from the kitchen steps. "Reuben!" Frances called out and Reuben and Riley both turned their horses toward her, so Billy followed along behind them. Betty came out the kitchen door to join her aunt, after ordering Gracie and Francine to stay in the house. "I don't think Reuben will do you any harm," Frances said to Betty. "He's always treated me good."

"I'm glad to see you're all right," Reuben said. "We just came from the church. What happened there? How'd it catch fire?"

"Walt Murphy," Frances said. That was all that was necessary to confirm what Reuben had already surmised, but he stood silent while she told him every detail about the vigilante raid and the outright murders of Dora and Pauline.

"How many of 'em were there?" Reuben asked.

She told him she wasn't sure, but there were at least six or eight of them. "I could hear a little bit of what they were talkin' about, and I think they were all men from the town. I know for sure the deputy sheriff was with 'em. He stayed with the sheriff after the rest of them went home."

"Vigilantes," Reuben snorted in disgust. Her report of the ensuing visits, first by Walt Murphy, then by Ben Savage, was of special interest to him, especially that of Walt's arrest by Savage. He turned to Riley and commented, "That sorta changes things, don't it?" He turned back to Frances then. "Me and Riley has got some thinkin' to do about what we're gonna do right now. But it looks like you landed right side up." He nodded to Billy and Betty in turn. "'Preciate you folks takin' care of your aunt."

"This is my niece, Betty, and her husband, Billy Wells," Frances said, belatedly. "And those two little devils with their noses pushin' the screen-wire outta the door are their daughters."

"Pleased to meet you folks," Reuben said. "We're gonna miss your aunt's cookin', ain't we, Riley? We'll thank you kindly for the information. We'll not trouble you any further."

"It wouldn't be polite of me, if I didn't offer you something to eat," Betty suddenly spoke up, much to Billy's surprise, as well as that of Reuben and Riley. "I bet you ain't had any dinner, have you?" As astonished as any of them, Frances's eyes opened wide, lifted by her raised eyebrows. She realized then that Betty had been surprised by the respectful politeness exhibited by the gray-haired outlaw.

"No, ma'am," Riley was quick to answer her. "We ain't et yet. We was figurin' on gettin' some of Frances's good cookin', till we found the place burnt down."

"We wouldn't wanna put you folks out," Reuben said. "You sure weren't expectin' two hungry coyotes to show up here."

"No trouble a-tall," Betty said. "Aunt Frances and I were just fixin' dinner when you showed up. We've got plenty. We'll just throw a few more potatoes in the pot and slice off some more ham. We made enough biscuits to feed twenty people. So you might as well join us for dinner." She glanced over at her aunt, who was beaming with delight.

"Well, me and Riley can't hardly turn down a kindly invitation like that," Reuben said, then paused a moment to look in Billy's direction. "Is that all right with you, partner?"

"She's the boss," Billy replied with a chuckle. So the Wells family sat down to dinner with one of the most fierce outlaws in Texas. It delighted Frances Wright, and she knew it would be a story repeated often by Billy Wells to his grandchildren when Gracie and Francine were grown up and starting their own families.

As Betty had claimed, there was plenty of food, a

fact that Frances very much appreciated when she recalled how little they had when she had left their house to find the church. Walt Murphy and Ben Savage were forgotten for most of the meal, until it was finished and the two outlaws remembered that they had places to go before nightfall. So they thanked their gracious hosts and said their good-byes. "Let me know if you get set up again," Frances said to Reuben as they were leaving. "Billy and Betty may be tired of havin' me around, and I might be lookin' for a cookin' job." Reuben said he would. As Frances and Betty watched the two outlaws ride away, Frances felt inspired to comment, "When you're visitin' with Reuben Drum, it's hard to imagine he's killed eleven men."

"Yes, it sure is," Betty replied. "I wish you hadn't told me that."

Chapter 20

Anxious to have a look in Walt's cabin, Ben started up the river right after Walt was settled in his cell. The directions Wayne gave him were somewhat vague, to the extent that Ben wondered if Wayne had ever been to the cabin. He followed the road along the Brazos until reaching the trail that forked off to the east, crossing the river at that point. That much was fairly simple, but he found that there were several homesteads along the trail that hugged the riverbank. Reduced to guesswork, he had to ask for help from someone, so he turned Cousin toward a farmer following a mule and plow around a field. The farmer saw him approaching, so he halted his mule and waited. "Howdy-do," he said. "You look like you're lost."

"I am at that," Ben replied. "I'm lookin' for Sheriff Walt Murphy's cabin, but his directions ain't that good. Am I even close?"

"You're close, but Walt ain't gonna be there this time of day," the farmer said.

He seemed a bit cautious to Ben, so he thought he'd best flash his Ranger's badge. "You're right, he ain't there. He's in the jail. I know where he is, it's his cabin I can't find. My name's Ben Savage. I'm a Texas Ranger, workin' with Walt on a job, and I'm goin' to fetch something from his cabin. Do you know where it is, Mr. . . ." He paused and waited for the name.

"Johnson," the farmer replied, "Bud Johnson. You're on the right trail. There's another farm past mine. That's Roger Stewart's place. Walt's place is the next one you'll come to. It'll be easy to spot. Ain't none of the scrub and trees cleared, just a cabin and a barn settin' near the water. You'll see it, soon as you pass the last cleared field."

"Much obliged, Mr. Johnson." He wheeled Cousin away and went back to the trail. Just as Johnson had said, he came to a tract of land that had never been cleared of trees beyond what must have been felled for logs to build the cabin. There was one small patch of grass on one side of the cabin that might support one horse for a short time. It made Ben wonder why Walt bothered to keep the cabin up, why he just didn't stay in town. *Well, he's got a permanent place in town now,* he thought. He rode up to the front of the cabin and dismounted, leaving his reins around the saddle horn. "There you go, Cousin, you can go get yourself a drink of water, then if you're hungry, you've got a whole pasture all to yourself," he said, looking at the small grass clearing.

He pulled a pry bar he found in the sheriff's office out of his saddle sling where it had been riding with his rifle and let the horse go to the water. As he had expected, there was a large padlock on the door and a sign above it that read, THIS CABIN PROPERTY OF SHERIFF WALT MURPHY. He took a look at the door hinges, which seemed fairly stout, then looked at the door hasp. The hasp was definitely the weaker spot, so he went to work on it with the pry bar. In a short time, he wedged the nails holding the hasp out, leaving the big padlock to remain on the hasp and the door free to open.

He walked into the dark interior of the small cabin and stood there for a few minutes just looking around him. Then he went around the main room and opened all the shuttered windows to get some light inside. Then the search began. He scoured the walls and floors, searching for some indication of a secret hiding place. He checked the stones in the hearth and fireplace, looking for a loose stone, anything that would give him a clue. There was nothing, no place to hide a large sum of money. There was not much in the way of cookware, but he looked in every pot, pan, and bucket he could find. He turned the bunk upside down. He inspected the rafters overhead for shelves or boxes. There was nothing. He finally decided the money was not there. "That leaves the barn," he said.

It wasn't much of a barn with only one stall, but big enough to hold two horses, if necessary. There was a small hayloft that ran only about half the length of the barn and a feed and tack room. *Not much of a barn,* he repeated to himself, *but I reckon he didn't really have any need for one.* Walt kept his horses in town. It appeared there was nothing to see in the barn, so Ben turned around and walked back to the door. He stood in the open door and looked back inside, not at all surprised that he had found no hidden money. The whole barn was of a rather shabby construction. Ben guessed that it had been originally built as a temporary barn, with plans to build a more solid structure later. Figuring he had wasted his time in coming out to the cabin, he took only a brief look around outside the two buildings before climbing back into the saddle and heading back to town. When he thought about it, he decided the sheriff would not likely hide the money in a place where he didn't spend the night.

Seated at the desk that was now officially his, at least temporarily, depending upon how he handled the job during these critical days, Wayne Price tried to ignore Walt's calls to him. Finally, he got up and went into the cell room to see what his prisoner wanted. "I can't believe you're treatin' me like a low-down outlaw," Walt said when Wayne came in the room. "You oughta know me better than to believe all that crap Ben Savage is tellin' you. He's got you and the mayor, and everybody else thinkin' you can believe everything that crazy old woman says. Use your brains, Wayne, she's Reuben Drum's cook. Of course, those outlaws will try anything to get me."

"I don't know, Walt." Wayne hesitated. "But I think you'd best just set there a while till we get everything straightened out. I'll get you a cup of coffee." He offered, then paused, about to go back out the door, when he thought to ask, "What did you ride out there to see that woman for?"

"To try to find out where Reuben Drum was, since he wasn't at the church that night," Walt answered. "Where's Ben Savage gone? What's he doin' now, with me locked up in my own jail?"

"He rode out to your cabin to see if you hid the

money you took from Pete Russell somewhere out there," Wayne replied.

"I swear, I shoulda known that would be the first thing he'd be lookin' for. He thinks I've got the money Pete Russell has took all the way outta Texas by now. And he's got you thinkin' it, too. What about Reuben Drum and Riley Best? Have you been back out to the church to see if they've showed up yet?"

"No, I reckon I didn't expect them to come back to the church after we burnt it down," Wayne replied.

Walt shook his head as if disappointed in him. "Dang it, Wayne, somebody oughta already been watchin' that place. You need to let me outta here, so I can help you take care of this business. You've got too much for one man to handle."

"I can't do that, Walt, you know that. Besides, I'll have Ben Savage to help me when he gets back from your cabin. And you've got a wound in your shoulder, anyway."

"Shoot!" Walt responded. "You ain't likely to see that jasper again. When he finds out there ain't no money out at my cabin, I expect he'll figure out that Pete Russell's still got it, and it's gone from these parts forever. Then there won't be any use for him to hang around, if he ain't got a shot at a big payday. He's most likely on the road to Buzzard's Bluff right now. Listen to me, Wayne. You've known me a helluva lot longer than you have that jasper, Ben Savage. All I'm askin' for is a chance to hunt Reuben Drum and Riley Best down before they find a place to set up another outlaw camp near our town. You know you can trust my word. Just unlock this cell, and I'll work with you to make sure we don't have any more men like Reuben Drum campin' in our front yard."

"If you do, Wayne, then I reckon I'll have to shoot him again to keep him from runnin'." They both turned to see Ben enter the cell room.

Alarmed at first, Walt quickly got his emotions under control. "Well, Ranger Ben Savage," he brayed, "I don't see you carryin' no big sacks of money. Looks like there weren't no money out at my place, just like I already told you." He glanced at Wayne and winked.

"It looks like I ain't found your hidin' place yet. That's more like it," Ben answered him. "It's just gonna take a little more lookin'." He shifted his attention to Wayne. "It's gettin' close to suppertime, so I reckon you're gonna have to feed your prisoner. Who feeds him?"

"Damn, that's right," Wayne responded. "We have an arrangement with the hotel dinin' room to feel our prisoners. I didn't even think about tellin' 'em we have one tonight." He shrugged, embarrassed. "It bein' Walt and all, I just didn't think about him bein' a regular prisoner."

"Reckon we oughta feed him, anyway?" Ben japed.

"I reckon," Wayne replied. "All I have to do is tell Mary Jane how many to feed and she knows what time we feed 'em. And she sends the meals down here. I'll take care of it right away."

"I'm gonna see if I can get a room in the hotel tonight," Ben said. "I'll tell Mary Jane for you, if you want. Matter of fact, I'll eat supper there while I'm at it. Or maybe you'd like to go to supper early. If you do, I'll watch the jail for you."

Wayne signaled Ben to follow him with a nod of his

head, then promptly walked out of the cell room. When they were in the office, he confided, "You go ahead. I don't feel like I can eat anything for a while. My stomach don't seem to wanna settle down."

"Walt workin' on you?" Ben asked, guessing that the young man was caught between his civic duty and his sense of loyalty.

"Yessir, a little bit," he confessed. "It's just still hard for me to believe Walt Murphy's sittin' in there in that cell, and I'm the one responsible for keepin' him there. You s'pose there's any way we got this all wrong and Walt ain't done what we think?"

"Nope," was Ben's simple answer. "Walt's capable of some of the most low-down things you can think of. He's just been good at not gettin' caught—until now. Are you gonna be able to do the job you got dropped on you?"

"Yessir, I'll do it. I might not like it, but I'll do it."

"I figured you would, and I knew you could," Ben said. "I'll go along and get myself a room in the hotel. I'll tell Mary Jane about Walt, although I expect she already knows. Then after I eat, I'll come spell you. Maybe you'll be ready to eat something by then."

"Hey, Brady," bartender Buddy Suggs yelled, "look who's comin' in the door."

Brady John, owner of the Hog's Breath Saloon, looked toward the front door. "Well, I'll be go to hell . . ." he drew out. "Reuben Drum." He rose to his feet and walked to meet the gray-haired man, who at that moment, spotted him and returned the smile on his weathered face. "Reuben, you old sidewinder, you ain't been here in the Hog's Breath for two years, I bet."

"That's a fact, I reckon," Reuben responded. "I had me a hole that was just right. There weren't no reason to leave it, not till they burned me out of it, that is."

"I heard about that," Brady said. "I was wonderin' if you came out of it all right, but here you are, lookin' mean as ever." He paused to look at Riley, who was standing there grinning at the reunion of the two old friends.

Noticing, Reuben said, "This here's Riley Best. Me and him's all that's left of the Reuben Drum gang."

"Howdy, Riley. I'm Brady John. Me and Reuben go back a long way. You two come on over and set down at my table." He looked over toward the bar. "Buddy, bring us a couple more glasses."

Buddy, wearing a broad grin on his face, had anticipated the request and was already on his way to the table with the glasses. "How you doin', Reuben?" Buddy asked when he set the glasses on the table. "This is a rare occasion, seein' you in town." He nodded to Riley. "Matter of fact, I ain't seen you or any of the other boys from the church in a while. We used to call you boys the deacons, didn't we Brady?"

"I ain't had no reason to leave the church, till Walt Murphy fixed me up with one," Reuben declared. "So now, I expect it's time I started settlin' up my accounts while I've still got a steady hand."

"You know Walt's locked up in jail, don't you?" Brady said.

"Yeah, I heard that," Reuben replied. "I found Frances Wright where she was hidin' out, and she told me that feller from Buzzard's Bluff, Ben Savage, shot him and arrested him. Savage is the next one on my list. He killed Lester, and he's gotta pay for that."

"That is sorrowful news," Brady said. "I'm right sorry to hear that."

"Savage is pretty much the reason there ain't none of us left but Reuben and me," Riley commented. "I was with Lester when he got shot." He reached up and placed his hand on the bandage showing at the back of his collar. "He ain't nobody to get careless around," he stated.

"So, whaddaya gonna do?" Brady asked.

"Well," Reuben started patiently, "I'm needin' a room for Riley and me." He paused right away to assure Brady. "I ain't broke. I can pay for the room."

"I wasn't even thinkin' about that," Brady insisted. "Of course, I've got a room for you upstairs. If I didn't, I'd kick somebody out. You know that."

"I told Riley we could count on you," Reuben said. "Then, I'm gonna just keep my eyes open and bide my time. I'm bound to get a chance to catch Ben Savage sooner or later. I don't know about Walt, but I'll be waitin' for a chance to save the judge the trouble of hangin' him."

When Brady suggested they take a drink to that, he refilled the glasses, and they all tossed the fiery liquid down their throats. "Like I said, Walt's in jail, but I think Ben Savage is still in town." He was distracted then when the huge frame of Peewee Burns came in, nearly filling the front door. "Was Peewee workin' for me last time you were here?" Brady asked Reuben, and Reuben shook his head, so Brady raised his hand

and signaled Peewee to come over. In a few seconds, the simple giant was hovering over the table. "Peewee," Brady said, "this is Reuben Drum, a fellow you've heard plenty about." Peewee nodded obediently and Brady continued. "This fellow with him is Riley Best. They'll be stayin' upstairs for as long as they want. They're my special guests."

"Yessir," Peewee responded with a foolish grin that almost reached the bottom of a long gash, still in the process of healing.

Noticing that their attention was attracted to the fresh injury, Brady chuckled and informed them that the injury was a result of Peewee's first and only meeting with Ben Savage. "It still hurts him to breathe too deep," he added. "Doc says his ribs got cracked." His comment immediately caused the grin on Peewee's face to fade away.

"He's back in town again," Peewee said. "I just saw him goin' into the hotel dinin' room." He was astonished by the reaction his simple statement caused the two men sitting at the table with his boss.

Reuben's whole body seemed to go rigid, and Riley exchanged a wide-eyed stare of alarm with him. Sensing the tension just created, Brady asked, "What are you thinkin', Reuben?"

"Like I said, a minute ago," Reuben replied, seeming to calm his nerves a little, "I'm bound to get a chance sooner or later. I like sooner, so I reckon I've had my drink and now I'm goin' to the hotel to see what's for supper."

"Maybe Peewee better go along with you," Brady suggested, but Reuben insisted he didn't want anyone mixed up in it with him.

"This is my debt to pay for Lester. I don't want nobody to get in the way—just me and Mr. Ben Savage."

"The hell you say," Riley interrupted. "You need me to go with you. You don't even know what Ben Savage looks like. You ain't ever seen him."

That caused Reuben to hesitate for a few moments when he realized Riley was right. Still he was not sure he could trust Riley to stay out of it after he spotted Savage for him. It had become more and more important to him that he should face this man who had taken his son's life. It should be a direct challenge to face each other and settle it for the sake of his son. "I've had him described enough," he said to Riley. "A big man, wearin' a Ranger's badge, there won't be that many people in the dinin' room to make it hard to pick him out."

"What if that deputy is in there, too, and they're both wearin' a badge?" Riley insisted. "How you gonna know which one to call out then?"

"Wayne Price ain't that big," Peewee spoke up, eager to see anyone call Ben Savage out. "And he's a lot younger feller than that big ranger."

"I don't think I'll have any trouble tellin' 'em apart," Reuben decided. "And there ain't no use gettin' anybody else in trouble over it."

"What if you call him out and he don't answer your call?" Riley questioned. "He might just say, 'You're under arrest, Reuben Drum,' and hauls you off to jail."

"If he don't answer my call to face me, I'll shoot him down, anyway," Reuben insisted. "Besides, he don't know I'm Reuben Drum. We ain't ever met."

Riley gave up. "I reckon you're gonna do what you wanna do."

"I always have," Reuben replied with a smile on his face. "I can't see any reason to change now."

Riley thought back on their trip to Buzzard's Bluff. He had tried in vain to talk the old man out of going after Ben Savage. It looked like this time Reuben was going to push it to the edge. He offered only one additional word of caution. "Take any advantage you can, and don't underestimate this man. Remember, I've seen him in action. He's big, but he ain't slow."

"I've been practicin' a little bit, and neither am I," Reuben boasted. "I'm wastin' time here. I'll see you after supper. If you wanna do somethin' to help me, you can throw our stuff in our room. Then I reckon we'll take the horses to the stable." Without waiting for comment or complaint, he got up from the table and headed for the door, striding like a man who was confident in what he was about to do.

CHAPTER 21

Mary Jane Reynolds greeted Ben cordially, and at his request, seated him at a table by the outside door. Like so many hotel dining rooms and restaurants, there was a weapons table on the other side of the door from his table, and he felt he would like to be handy to his six-gun with the tense situation in town at present. She told him he could sit anywhere he wanted, since he was a lawman, and the rule didn't apply to lawmen. He thanked her just the same, but since he was not wearing his badge, he thought to save her the trouble of having to explain to other guests why he was allowed to wear his weapon. She thanked him for his consideration. "You'll be too busy explainin' to the folks why the food doesn't taste good," he teased.

"Is that so?" She came back at him. "Maybe you might not wanna ask me why yours tastes kinda funny when I bring it to you." As he suspected, she already knew about Walt Murphy's arrest. "Everybody in town knows about it," she said with a light chuckle. "If you ask me, it was a long time coming." She was interrupted then when a tall gray-haired man walked in the door and paused to read the sign on the little table by the door for sidearms. He seemed reluctant to remove the Colt .45 he wore on his hip.

Mary Jane saw his indecision and went to the table to meet him. Thinking that possibly he was unable to read, she said, "We just ask it of everyone, to leave your firearm on the table until you're ready to leave."

"I can read," he said, but seemed to take no offense.

"Oh, I didn't mean to imply that you couldn't," she was quick to say. "It's just the rule for everybody." Still, he hesitated, making no move toward giving up his handgun.

Taking notice of the impasse by then, Ben took a look at the tall, slender man and immediately recognized him. Without getting up out of his chair, he said, "He's all right, Mary Jane, he's a friend of mine." To the man, he asked, "Did you and your partner ever get to eat that deer he was huntin' north of Buzzard's Bluff?"

Reuben looked down at him then, taking a closer look and recognizing Ben as well. "Nope, we had to settle for sowbelly again that day." He chuckled in spite of the serious mission he was undertaking. Even as he made the remark, he scanned the room from one side to the other, as if searching for someone.

It was obvious to Ben that the man was uneasy about something. Maybe, he thought, he was fearful of someone, so made a suggestion. "Why don't you sit down here with me and you can keep your gun on the table with mine?"

Patiently waiting for the man to make a decision,

Mary Jane said, "I think that's a very good idea. I'll have Nancy bring you something to drink and you can both sit there and watch your guns." Undecided what to do, since he didn't see a likely prospect for his planned vengeance, Reuben reluctantly surrendered his gun and sat down at the table.

"Looks to me like you're lookin' for somebody," Ben commented. "Was somebody supposed to meet you here? Maybe your partner?"

"No, I'm lookin' for a feller that's supposed to be in here eatin' supper," Reuben answered, "but I don't see nobody."

"Who are you looking for?" Mary Jane asked. "I know just about everybody in this town. Maybe he's come and gone already."

"Don't know if you'd know this one or not. He ain't from here," Reuben said. "Ben Savage."

"Ben Savage?" Mary Jane exclaimed. "You're sitting at the table with him."

Stunned, Reuben Drum's nervous system seemed to shut down completely. Unable to move or speak, he simply sat there, eyes wide open and mouth agape.

Seeing the man was in obvious distress, Ben asked, "Why were you lookin' for me?"

Still distraught and grappling with this totally unforeseen situation, Reuben could only blurt out his intended purpose. "To kill you," he uttered with complete lack of emotion.

"To kill me?" Ben echoed, astonished. When Reuben did not respond further, Ben said, "Most folks just come in here to eat. Why do you wanna kill me?"

Gradually recovering from his initial shock, Reuben answered. "Because you killed my son."

"Who was your son?"

"Lester Drum," Reuben answered, obviously confused to find his intended challenge to a duel had resulted in nothing more than a calm discussion.

"Well, I'll be . . ." Ben started. "So you're Reuben Drum." He paused for a moment before continuing. "I'm sorry for you havin' to lose your son. But I've gotta be honest with you, Lester didn't give me any choice. He went for his gun while I was standin' at the counter of Cletus Priest's store. He didn't give any warnin', just decided to shoot me. You'da done the same as I did. When somebody's fixin' to kill you, you just try to kill him first, right? Well, that's what happened, but maybe if we'd had a chance to talk it over, like you and I are doin' right now, we mighta decided there wasn't any sense in either one of us dyin'. I reckon we'll never know about that, will we?" He paused to see if Reuben would respond with anything to say.

He didn't, but he couldn't help remembering that Riley's version of the shooting was pretty much the same as that just given by Savage. *That don't matter,* he told himself, just as he had when Riley told him. Someone had to pay for Lester's death.

Ben continued, figuring the longer he could talk, the better his chance of avoiding gunplay. "So now you come in here lookin' to kill me because I was faster than Lester was that day. That don't hardly seem right to me. He came after me, and that's the real reason your son is dead. I didn't wanna kill your son, or anybody else's son, and I'd rather not have a shoot-out with you."

When Ben finally finished talking, nothing more was said for a long moment. Fully as stunned as Reuben, Mary Jane stood staring at the two potential duelists, and Nancy seemed paralyzed while holding two cups of coffee over the table. Reuben obviously didn't know what to do at this point. The challenge hadn't gone at all as he had imagined, so Ben sought to defuse it further. "You wanna go ahead and set that coffee down, miss?" It was enough to shake her out of her trance. She put the cups on the table, then quickly stepped back in case six-guns started blazing, this in spite of the fact that the weapons of both men were on the weapons table. "Now, Reuben," Ben went on, "you seemed to me to be a reasonable man when I talked to you back on that creek north of Buzzard's Bluff. I don't know about you, but I'm kinda hungry right now. Why don't we have ourselves a good supper before we do anything else tonight? I'll pay for it. Hell, there ain't no reason we can't enjoy some of that stew I see on those other tables, no matter what we decide to do after supper. Whaddaya say?"

"Now, that's a real civilized idea right there," Mary Jane at once agreed. "A good supper can fix a lot of things. Nancy, go fetch a couple of plates of that stew, and don't be stingy with it. And don't forget the biscuits." Nancy hurried away to do as she was instructed. Mary Jane turned back to the two men at the table. Neither man made a move toward the weapons table, but she was not at all confident that it meant sudden violence could not break out at any minute. She made another suggestion that she thought might help keep the peace. "Should I send someone to fetch Deputy Sheriff Price?" A flicker of alarm immediately registered in Reuben's eye.

"No," Ben said, "I don't think so. Wayne's got a prisoner to watch. Besides, he's new in his job as sheriff and he's liable to wanna arrest somebody. And nobody's done anything to get arrested for. Have they, Reuben?"

"Well, not so far," Reuben answered honestly. Talk was interrupted then by the arrival of Nancy with two plates heaping with beef stew. Reuben hesitated, as if there might be something hidden in the stew, but Ben attacked his with great enthusiasm. So Reuben followed his lead, and pretty soon, they were both concentrating on the food in front of them.

Ben paused to give Reuben a grin and say, "It ain't like fresh deer meat, but it's pretty damn good eatin', ain't it?"

"It sure is," Reuben agreed before he could catch himself.

Quick to respond, in an effort to help Ben prevent a shooting in her dining room, Mary Jane replied. "Why, thank you, sir. We're always happy when we please our customers." She stepped away then when Nancy motioned. "What is it, Nancy?" Mary Jane asked.

"Nothing, really," Nancy replied. "I just thought that while we're not real busy, I could run down to the jail and take Walt Murphy's supper to him, since Cal isn't here right now."

Mary Jane answered her with a knowing smile. Cal Booker, her cook's thirteen-year-old son, usually delivered the prisoners' meals to the jail. "Cal should be back in just a little bit. Charlotte just sent him to the store for something." When Nancy made a pouty face, Mary Jane laughed and said, "Well, all right, if you want to, you can take the prisoner's supper to him."

Overhearing their conversation, Ben said it wasn't necessary for Nancy to do it, because he was going back to the jail when he was finished eating and he would carry Walt's supper to him. "No problem at all," Mary Jane replied to Ben. "You go ahead and take the plate to him," she said to Nancy. No use in making him wait." Nancy went at once to the kitchen to fix a plate and Mary Jane said aside to Ben, "She's got a tremendous crush on Wayne Price, and he doesn't have a clue." She turned her attention back to the gray-haired outlaw then who was still peacefully eating. "You need some more coffee?" Reuben shook his head and continued to work away at the generous plate of food before him. She left them briefly when a man and his wife came in, and she led them to a table as far as possible from the one where the outlaw and the ranger sat.

When she returned to the table by the door, Ben had removed his napkin from his shirt collar and folded it on the table. Since Reuben was still polishing off the last biscuit, Mary Jane cheerfully announced, "I'm declaring Reuben Drum the winner of this contest. He's still going strong." She gave Reuben a big smile and said, "You can tell everybody you beat Ben Savage in a contest."

"Can't argue with that," Ben said at once, well aware of Mary Jane's efforts to help him prevent a gunfight, "fair and square." He was still very much alert to the possibility of an attempt by Reuben to go through with the assassination he had planned.

The older man was licking his fingers and tidying up his mustache after his big meal with no outward indication that he was still of a violent nature. When Reuben took the last gulp of his coffee, Ben declared, "Well, I reckon I'd best pay up and get on back to the jail, so Wayne can come to supper." He watched Reuben closely for any signs of renewed aggression, but there were none evident. The older man seemed at peace with himself. Ben glanced at Mary Jane and shrugged. It appeared their attempt to tame the offended father had succeeded. So, Ben got to his feet and paid for the two meals, leaving Reuben with no further comment.

After Ben walked out the door, Reuben got up from the table, and without a word to Mary Jane, retrieved his .45 from the weapons table, and followed Ben out the door. He didn't holster his gun, which caused Mary Jane to wonder, so she followed him outside. Much to her horror, she saw Reuben calmly raise the weapon and take dead aim at the broad back of the unwary Ranger walking away from the hotel. "Ben!" She screamed.

He didn't know why he dropped to the ground when he heard her scream. It was simply an unthinking reflexive action on his part. But he heard the bullet snap over his head while he was still in the air and the sound of the shot when he hit the ground. Knowing he had only seconds before the next shot, he rolled over on his back even as he hit the ground and fired one shot while his six-gun was still holstered. He was lucky. His shot caught Reuben in his thigh, spinning him around to drop on one knee and giving Ben time to draw his weapon and cock it. Scrambling to his feet, he rushed back to the wounded man in time to knock the .45 from his hand before he could cock it again. With the life-or-death moment past, Ben's strongest emotion was one of anger at himself for being so stupid, for thinking he had talked the old man out of his original plan to kill him. "Really?" he demanded as he looked down at Reuben. "In the back? I oughta go ahead and shoot you in the head, you yellow dog!" He aimed his six-gun at Reuben's face. He held it there for only a few seconds, however, until he took control of his anger. "All right, let's get you up from there. Can you walk, if I help you?"

"I don't know," Reuben replied weakly, so Ben handed Reuben's pistol to Mary Jane and asked, "Can you hold this for me?" She nodded and he thought to say, "And thanks for the warnin'." She nodded again, still wide-eyed in shock at having witnessed the shooting. Back to Reuben again, he said, "Might as well walk you on over to the doctor before I take you to jail." He turned him toward the doctor's office and started to walk, but Reuben had too much pain to put any weight on the leg. Ben picked him up on his shoulder and carried him to Dr. Griffin's office. "I'll pick up the gun later," he yelled back at Mary Jane, who was still standing there cautiously holding the weapon as if it was a live thing. With Reuben over his shoulder, he didn't want to worry about keeping two guns out of his reach, and he had already stuck his own gun in his belt, instead of back in the holster where Reuben might be tempted to try to grab it.

When he reached the doctor's office, he was met with the cynical smirk of Dr. Fred Griffin. "Another one? I suppose I oughta start payin' you a percentage for bringing in gunshot wounds. First one was the sheriff, who's this one? Never mind, just bring him on in here and dump him on the table. Is he violent?"

"Not anymore," Ben answered, "but I'll stay here with you while you work on him to be sure he don't cause any trouble."

After Dr. Griffin examined Reuben's wound, he determined that the bullet was embedded deeply in the muscle next to the bone. "I'm going to have to do some cutting to get that thing outta there. I'll have to knock him out for a little while to keep him still. He's not going to be out for long, and when he comes to, I might need you to hold him down." Staying with him was no problem, since Ben was in no particular hurry to get back. Wayne might want to go to supper, but with Nancy down at the jail, he might not be in any hurry at all. Reuben wasn't very enthusiastic about being knocked out, so Ben held him down while Griffin held a cloth with chloroform on it under Reuben's nose. It didn't take long before Reuben relaxed, and the doctor could go to work. Griffin worked quickly, but the surgery added to the time Ben was away from the jail, unaware as he was to the events taking place while he had been occupied at the dining room and now in the doctor's office.

Wayne had been surprised to see Nancy arrive at the sheriff's office carrying a plate of food for his prisoner. "When did you start deliverin' prisoners' food to the jail?" Wayne had asked.

"I don't, usually," she had replied with a sweet smile for him. "I just thought I'd do it today, since we've got a new sheriff and he hasn't come in the dining room in a while."

He could feel himself flush, although he fought hard not to show it. "Well, I ain't officially the new sheriff yet, but if they do give me the job, I expect I'll be eatin' in the dinin' room pretty regular."

"Well, we'll be pleased to serve you," Nancy said sweetly. "Mary Jane said you usually give 'em coffee or water, so we don't have to carry a pot down here."

Before Wayne could answer, there was a shout from the cell room, interrupting their conversation. "Hey, Wayne, is that my supper? Bring it on in here. I'm 'bout to starve to death."

"I'm sorry," Wayne apologized to the young woman. "I left that door cracked, so I could hear anything goin' on in there."

Curious to see Walt Murphy locked up in a jail cell, Nancy went to the door and eased it open a little farther, enough to see in the cell room. It was also far enough for Walt to see her face. "Well, hello there, Nancy, darlin'. Did you bring me my supper? How come Cal didn't bring it? You just wanted to see for yourself if they really had the sheriff in jail, didn't you? Well, I'm right here, just like they told you, and I'm ready to eat whatever you got with you. Bring it on in."

"You'd best let me have that plate," Wayne told her. "You can stay here in the office."

"It's just ol' Walt and his usual nonsense," Nancy replied. "I'm not afraid to go in there with you to protect me. I ain't ever seen the inside of a jail before," she said excitedly.

"All right, if you really want to, but there ain't

gonna be nothin' for you to see. I'll just put the plate on the bench he uses for a table and come right back out of the cell." She gave him the plate of food and slipped inside the cell room door behind him. From a peg by the door, Wayne took a ring that held the cell keys. "You know what you're supposed to do, Walt," he said as he inserted the key.

"Oh, right," Walt said. "I forgot, go to the back of the cell. I'll tell you the truth, I just got a happy feelin' when I saw you two young people come in. I almost forgot I was in jail. I almost forgot I was wounded, too, till it started painin' me again. You just go ahead and do it like you've done it before." He backed away to the back of the cell. "I always enjoy the food from the hotel, but I'm hopin' maybe tomorrow you might send me some ribs from Jake's." He looked quickly back at Nancy. "That ain't sayin' nothin' against the food Charlotte Booker cooks at the hotel. Wayne knows. Right, Wayne? I love Jake's ribs."

Walt continued a constant stream of meaningless chatter while Wayne unlocked the cell door, drew his pistol, and picked up the plate from the floor where he had set it while he opened the cell. He had failed to notice until then that the bench was missing from the front of the cell. "Where's the bench? Your table?" Wayne asked, standing just inside the cell, his .44 in one hand and a plate of beef stew in the other.

"Oh!" Walt blurted. "I forgot about my table! I had it back by the bunk, playin' some two-handed cards on it. Here, I'll get it!" He hustled to pick up the bench and hurried to the front of the cell with it. Pretending to favor his wounded shoulder, he seemed about to drop the heavy bench. In an apparently desperate effort to place it near the cell door, he suddenly lunged at Wayne. Using the bench like a battering ram, he drove Wayne backward against the cell wall. While Nancy stood helpless, Walt easily overpowered the startled young man, forcing his arm backward until he could no longer grip the gun. When it dropped from his hand to land on the floor, Walt threw Wayne aside and picked up the weapon. Lying stunned on the floor, his shirt covered with beef stew and blood running from a cut on his forehead, Wayne's worst nightmare was unfolding right before his eyes.

Gripped by the frightening turn of events, Nancy let out one short scream before Walt stopped her. Pointing the gun at her, he ordered, "Shut up!" That was all it took, for she could no longer make a sound had she even tried, as she stared at the gun in his hand. Back to Wayne, who was trying to get up from the floor, Walt stated, "You've got a lot to learn, son, before you're ready to take over my job. I'm back in charge now, and if you don't do exactly like I tell you, I won't hesitate to put some daylight in your head." He motioned to Nancy then. "You come on in the cell, honey." When she hesitated, he snapped, "Now, damn it, or I'll shoot you down where you stand!" As soon as she walked into the cell, Walt stepped outside and locked them in. He placed the key ring back on the knob by the office door and asked Nancy, "Is Ben Savage up in the dinin' room?" She nodded her head vigorously. It was at that moment they heard gunshots that sounded as if it might have come from that end of the street.

With no way of knowing if they were of any consequence to him or not, Walt hurried through the office to the front door. He opened the door partially and looked toward the hotel. Unable to see the outside door to the dining room from that angle, he had no clue as to the cause of the shots. He didn't see anyone in the street in front of the hotel. His intuition told him it had something to do with Ben Savage, however, and he thought to get ready to welcome him with a hot reception when he returned to the jail. He hurried back to the desk and traded Wayne's pistol for his gun belt and weapon from the drawer. Then he took his rifle out of the gun case behind the desk and his saddlebags out of a cabinet. By that time, he heard some voices of people in the street, so he went back to the door to have another look. There were several of the usual spectators going toward the hotel, bold enough to gawk now that no additional shots were heard. It occurred to him that, with a distraction at the end of the street, it would be the ideal time for him to walk up to the stable and get his horse. It seemed a better plan than his original idea to wait in ambush for Savage at the jail. As much as he would love to surprise Savage with a bullet in his chest, he realized he would still be in the jail after he killed Ben. Then he would run the risk of getting hit with a bullet from some would-be hero in one of the stores.

He stuck his head inside the cell room door just long enough to make sure his two prisoners were secure. Feeling he was on top of his game once again, he couldn't resist japing them one last time. "Don't you young folks do anything improper in there while I'm gone." They could hear him chuckling as he walked back through the office and out the front door.

Outside, there were a few people on the street, but they all seemed interested in seeing what was going on at the hotel. He was pleased to see that no one paid much attention to him as he casually walked toward Bob Graham's stable at the end of the street.

CHAPTER 22

Hearing someone coming in the stable behind him, Bob Graham turned around only to be startled to see it was Walt Murphy. He didn't speak, not sure what to say. His confusion caused Walt to grin when he told him he wanted to saddle his horse. "What the hell's the matter with you, Bob? You act like you're seein' a ghost."

"I swear, Walt, I thought you were in jail," Bob finally stammered. He was afraid to say anything about the fresh blood seeping through Walt's shirt, a result of his action in the jail cell with Wayne.

"Oh, that little misunderstandin's all been straightened out. I'm back in charge again. There was some little somethin' up at the hotel a little while ago, but Ben Savage is up there, so I'm lettin' him handle it."

"I just got back from there," Graham said, still confused. "Ben shot Reuben Drum."

That caused Walt to pause for a moment. "Well, I'll be . . ." he started but stopped to think what that might mean to him. That was why Ben was taking so long to get back to the jail. Maybe it couldn't have happened at a better time. Savage would most likely be tied up for a while with that, giving him all the time he needed to do what he had to do. "I'll have to remember to thank ol' Ben for takin' care of Reuben for me." He headed for the corral. "Right now, I've gotta take a little ride tonight. I'm gonna need a packhorse, too, if you'll lend a hand." Not without his black sense of humor, even in situations like this, he said, "Throw my packsaddle on that big dun over yonder."

"That one?" Bob asked pointing toward Cousin. Walt nodded. "That's Ben Savage's horse," Bob said.

"Right," Walt replied. "I told him I might need to take him. Just throw them packs on him." He took great satisfaction in taking the dun, remembering that it was the theft of Savage's horse that first brought him to Waco. *Let's see if he comes after the horse again,* he thought. *This time, it'll cost him his life.*

Knowing he was helplessly abetting a horse thief and a jail escapee, Bob Graham saddled Cousin with the packsaddle, which had nothing in the packs. For his own safety, he had no intention of trying to stop Walt, certain it would more likely lead to his own death. So he walked Cousin out to the front of the stable and handed the reins to Walt when he rode his buckskin out. Still wearing a contemptuous grin, Walt took the reins and started out on the north road at a gentle lope. Graham stood watching him until he rode out of sight, all the while dreading the encounter with Ben when he had to tell him his horse had been taken. But first, he had to go to the jail to see if Wayne was all right.

He was relieved to find that Wayne was not wounded

or dead, but he was confused to find Nancy in the cell with Wayne. They both tried to explain while he unlocked the cell and freed them. He told them that Ben had shot Reuben Drum, so all three hurried to the hotel to find out what had prompted the shooting. After Mary Jane and some of the customers from the dining room told them how Reuben came to be shot, Wayne and Bob went to Dr. Griffin's office to look for Ben. They found him preparing to transport a wounded Reuben Drum to jail.

As expected, Ben was not at all patient when he was told that Walt Murphy had escaped. "Escaped? How did he escape?" He asked while staring at the cut on Wayne's forehead, but was more fascinated by the food stains all over his shirt. When Wayne had finished his confession, Ben actually felt some compassion for the young man. It was a tough way to learn a lesson in handling a prisoner. "That was just a tough piece of luck," he said. "But you'll sure as hell never repeat that mistake again, right?" Wayne swore that he never would.

Ben was not so dismissive of the news that Bob came to tell him, however. "What?" He demanded in disbelief. "He stole my horse? How could he steal my horse? Were you there when he took it?"

"Yes, sir, I was," Bob admitted. "That's how I know it was him that took it. I told him that dun was your horse, and he said you told him it was all right if he took him."

"That lyin' dog," Ben swore. Walt was offering him a challenge to come and take the horse, if he thought he could. He knew the only reason Ben had come to Waco in the first place was to get his horse back. He knew Ben would come after him. It was an invitation to prove who was the better man. He looked at Wayne and said, "I'll help you take Reuben, here, to the jail." He looked back at Graham again. "And while I'm doin' that, you go to the stable and put my saddle on the best horse you've got, hopefully, one that don't belong to somebody else."

"You can use my gray," Bob said. "He's as strong a horse as you're likely to find." He hesitated before adding, "And there won't be no charge."

"You're damn right there won't be any charge," Ben replied. "Now, let's get movin'." With Wayne on one side and Ben on the other, they made a chair for an uncomplaining Reuben Drum and carried him to jail through a small gathering of spectators still hanging around in the street. Standing a little apart from the others, near the harness shop, one interested spectator followed at a distance until they reached the sheriff's office. Not certain what he should do, Riley Best turned about and headed back toward the Reservation and the Hog's Breath Saloon. He was confident that Ben Savage had not spotted him, but he didn't know what he could do for Reuben now.

Walt rode his horses hard for the short distance up the river, past the Johnson farm and the Stewart farm, never letting up until reaching his cabin in the trees. His first priority was to get his money and supplies for his pack horse. He fully intended to kill Ben Savage, but he wanted to pick his place for the ambush. And there was too much cover around his cabin for Savage to move about in while he was holed up inside the cabin. He had it in mind to head to Houston. He was finished in Waco, also thanks to Ben Savage, so he would collect his money and what belongings he had at the cabin and pick a spot for Savage to catch up. Even though he was sure he had a good start, he wasted no time at the cabin. Satisfied to see the floor of his small barn had not been disturbed since he was last there, he raked the dirt and hay off the thick planks and unlocked the heavy padlock on the door of his safe-box. He quickly packed the money in two canvas bags and loaded them onto Cousin. Then he went into the cabin and got what stores he had of salt, coffee, sugar, flour, dried beans, and bacon. These he loaded on Cousin as well.

In the process of loading his supplies, he checked his money again to make sure the packs were secure. He couldn't resist opening one of the canvas sacks just to take another look at the packs of bills and gloating over the rough path the money had taken before it all landed in his hands. A worrisome thought entered his mind then. His deliberate invitation to Ben Savage to follow him might not have been the smart thing to do. He wished now that he had not stolen Ben's horse and had determined to escape free and clear of the relentless saloon ranger. As much as he wanted the pleasure of killing Ben Savage, he now decided it was best to play it smart and put distance between them. He had friends in Navasota, and that was on the way to Houston. If he wasn't certain he had lost Savage by the time he reached Navasota, that would be his best place to stop him for good. The more he thought about it, the better he liked the idea. He told himself not to dally. It was about one hundred miles to Navasota. He would plan on making it in two hard days of riding, and he had two good horses to do it with. The first thing to do, he decided, was to leave Savage a trail heading north, to make him think he was heading to Dallas, then cut back to follow the Brazos south. In an attempt to buy more time for himself, he lit his lantern and left it on the table to give Ben something more to consider. As soon as he was ready, he climbed aboard the buckskin and led the dun north along the riverbank, going in and out of the shallow water at the edge for a distance of about half a mile. When he came to a grassy plot that looked like a good place to exit the water, he stopped. But instead of leaving the river, he turned his horses around and went back downstream. Heading south now, he left the river when he was about fifty yards short of his cabin, took a wide detour around it, then returned to follow the river south toward Navasota.

Ben knew how big a head start Walt Murphy had on him, but there was nothing he could do to shorten it. Wayne was still obviously shaken over what had happened to him. And Ben felt he had to be sure the young deputy was going to be all right, if left solely in charge of his new prisoner, Reuben Drum. So, by the time he was satisfied that Wayne was going to be confident again, he had already wasted too much time before starting after Walt. At this point, he could only assume that Walt had headed straight for his cabin, since Bob Graham said he rode out the north road after leaving the stable. When he was ready, he left the jail and headed for the stable where he found Bob Graham's gray gelding standing in front, wearing his saddle and bridle, waiting for him. As he approached, Bob came out of the stable leading his packhorse. "I didn't know how long you figured on bein' gone," Bob said. "So I saddled your packhorse, too. There ain't nothin' much in the packs, though. You've got your little coffeepot in there, but there ain't no coffee."

"I don't know, myself," Ben replied. "But I reckon it'd be a good idea to take him just in case." He checked the cinch on the gray, then stepped up into the saddle. Pulling his Winchester out of the saddle sling, he checked to make sure it was fully loaded. Satisfied, he touched his forefinger to the brim of his hat and said, "'Preciate the loan of your horse. I'll bring him back soon as I can."

"Good luck," was all Bob could think to say, thinking there was to be one helluva contest between too strong men. He wished he could witness the meeting, but at a safe distance.

To add to his problems, it was already getting dark by the time Ben rode away from the stable. So, he was forced to take caution as he followed the road north, especially when passing large clumps of trees near the riverbank. In his mind, he saw several good spots for an ambush well before reaching Walt's cabin. A couple were suspect enough to cause him to leave the road and come into the trees from behind to make sure no one was there. He came to the conclusion that Walt's first priority had been to get to his money, so he continued on along the road until he passed the Stewart farm before resuming his cautious approach.

He pulled the gray to a stop when he saw a glimmer of light shining through the thick growth of trees that hid the cabin. Leaving the horses there, he worked his way closer on foot, his rifle in hand. When he had approached close enough to see the entire cabin, he was puzzled to discover the light he had seen was evidently from a lantern inside. His immediate thought was of a trap set up for him to walk in to be shot down. It was a little too obvious, so he suspected some other plan of ambush. It occurred to him then that there had been no sound from the horses, his or Walt's. They were close enough to have whinnied their acknowledgment of each other. So he continued moving around the cabin until he could see the small barn behind it. He realized then that there were no horses there. The purpose of the lantern had been solely to delay him even more. *And it had worked well,* he thought. But to be sure, he moved up to the back window and looked in to see the lantern sitting on the table of an empty cabin.

He wondered then if the stolen money had ever been hidden there at the cabin. So he went inside and took the lantern from the table and went out to take another look in the barn. His question was answered as soon as he entered the rough structure. *Damn, I was standing right on top of it,* he thought, as he stared at the open box in the middle of the floor that had been so well hidden beneath the four-inch planks and the dirt and hay. Knowing with certainty that Walt had not stayed to wait for him, he went back to get his horses. Then, using the light of the lantern, he looked around the cabin and the barn for tracks that might tell him which way Walt had gone. It was not difficult to pick out the most recent tracks leading away from the barn. He suspected they were intentionally made obvious, but he followed them north into the river's edge, picking the trail up at intervals where it came out of the water, only to return. Finally, there were no more places where the tracks left the water and he was convinced that Walt had stayed in the water, turned around, and gone the other way. The time had come to trust his gut feeling, because it was now too dark to try to pick up signs on the banks, even with the lantern. *I don't know where he's heading,* he thought, *but it ain't north. I'm betting my horse on it.* He threw the lantern in the river and climbed out of the water, determined to follow the Brazos south, watching for signs of tracks or a camp.

For the next two days, he followed the trail along the river with only an occasional discovery of tracks that could or could not be those left by Walt. His chase soon became one based on nothing more than the hope that his hunch had been on the mark. On the morning of the third day, he found himself only ten miles north of Wilfred Tuttle's store. He decided that, if Walt had not stopped at Wilfred's, it would be enough to convince him he had made a mistake with his hunch. He would have to search elsewhere, and he didn't know where to start. "Come on, horse," he said to the gray. "Let's go find out if our little trip together has been for nothin'."

* * *

Rosa Cruz sat in a rocking chair on the porch of the old trading post known as Tuttle's Store peeling apples for a pie. A movement through the trees on the river road caught her attention, and she paused to see if someone was approaching the path to the store. In a few seconds, she saw a lone rider leading a pack horse. She continued to watch, thinking there was something familiar about the large man on the horse. A moment later, she cried out, "Ben!" She jumped up from the chair, still holding her pan of apples, and ran to the door of the store. "Ben!" she cried again. "It's Ben!"

Wilfred Tuttle came running out to the porch. "You sure? Where?" Rosa pointed to the path leading down from the road. "Yep, ain't nobody else sets a horse like that." He walked down the steps to greet their friend. Rosa put her pan down in the chair and followed him. "Well, if you ain't a sight for sore eyes," Wilfred declared. "What are you doin' down here in this neck of the woods?"

"I had to get down here to make sure you're still kickin'," Ben joked. He stepped down from the gray to receive Rosa's hug.

"I thought you were settled in Buzzard's Bluff for good," Wilfred said. "How's the saloon business goin'?"

"It's doin' just fine, no thanks to me. I'm lucky to have a level-headed partner to run it, because it seems like I can't get away from bein' a Ranger."

"Well, what you need is to have Rosa fix you up a good breakfast and later on eat a slice of that apple pie she's fixin' to make." He winked at Ben and said, "I bet you ain't had no breakfast this mornin'."

"You'd win that bet, because I don't have anything left to cook," Ben confessed. "I was figurin' on buyin' some supplies from you. I didn't have time before I left Waco."

"Waco?" Wilfred asked. "What was you doin' in Waco?"

"That's a long story I'll tell you over a cup of coffee, all right?" As soon as he said it, Rosa turned and ran back inside to make some. "I'm sorry I don't have a lot of time to visit, but I'm tryin' to catch up with a fellow I think headed this way. Kind of a heavyset fellow, ridin' a buckskin and leadin' a dun." He saw Wilfred's eyes light up immediately.

"A dun like that one you used to ride," Wilfred said. "Late last evenin', he was here, bought a lotta goods from me, more'n I've sold in a while, and he had plenty of money to spend. He seemed like a friendly enough feller. What did he do, rob a bank?"

"Lee County Bank in Giddings," Ben answered. "He didn't actually rob the bank, he ended up with the money when he killed the last of the three that did the robbery. He's done a lot of bad things, but the worst was stealin' that dun you saw him leadin', and that's the reason I'm chasin' him. Did he say where he was headin'?"

"Said he was on his way to Navasota," Wilfred said. "I declare, I thought that horse looked familiar."

"That's why I've gotta catch up with him as soon as I can. Cousin can't stand but so much of bein' treated like a packhorse." Rosa came back out to announce that there was a fresh pot of coffee on the stove and she was making up some corn cakes. She was disappointed to hear that Ben was in a hurry to leave, but he explained. "I'll surely stay long enough to get some of that coffee and eat some corn cakes. When I take care of this business I'm on, I'll make a longer visit on the way back, all right?"

"Promise?"

"Promise," he said. He ended up spending an hour there, which he hated to lose. But Rosa fixed him a good breakfast, he stocked up on some basic supplies he had been out of, and the horses got some extra rest, plus a portion of oats.

"You take care of yourself, Ben Savage," Rosa instructed as he climbed on the gray gelding and started out again.

CHAPTER 23

"Well, I'll swear," Rafer Black sang out when he saw him walk in the door of the Silver Dollar Saloon. "Walt Murphy, what the hell are you doin' in Navasota?"

Walt grinned when he spotted Rafer sitting at a table with another man. He walked over and pulled a chair back. "I figured I'd just stop by and have a drink with my old partner," he said.

"It's been a good while since you took that sheriff's job in Waco," Rafer said. "What happened? Did they find out what you really did for a livin' before you started sheriffin'?" He interrupted himself to nod toward his companion. "This here's Luke Davis." To Luke, he said, "Me and Walt go way back." Walt nodded to Luke, and Rafer shifted his attention back to him. "You still workin' that business at the church with ol' Reuben Drum?"

"Up till a couple of days ago," Walt answered. "The church got burnt to the ground and Reuben's in jail, all on account of one damn Ranger. So it was time for me to leave for greener pastures. I figured I'd head on down to Houston to see what I could get into down there. The only problem is that Ranger ain't satisfied with me just leavin' town. He's wantin' to tie me to some killin's that happened at the church, so he might be on my trail. I figure I'm about ready to light here for a spell to wait for him."

"One Ranger, huh?" Rafer asked. "Don't sound like much of a problem to take care of. What's his name?"

"Ben Savage," Walt answered.

There was an immediate reaction from both Rafer and Luke at the mention of the name. "Ben Savage?" Rafer exclaimed. "I thought he dropped out of the Rangers. I know we ain't seen hide nor hair of him around here anymore. He ain't been too welcome ever since him and another Ranger arrested two men right here in this saloon, then shot 'em before they got 'em back to Austin for trial."

"I reckon you know why I need to do somethin' permanent about him, then," Walt commented. "He wrecked everything I had goin' for me, and I had to run, so I intend to do the same for him."

"You might need a little help," Luke suggested, "if he's as ornery a stud as I've heard people say."

"I could use some help, I reckon," Walt allowed, as if considering the idea. "Tell you the truth, I'm a little bit hampered right now." He unbuttoned a couple of buttons and showed them the bandage on his shoulder. Actually, he had already planned to enlist their help, but he wanted them to think it was their idea. He figured that would hold the price down to something more reasonable. "'Course, I would expect to pay for somebody to take a chance on gettin' shot. I managed to get away with a little bit of money I had saved up for a while." He paused as if adding it up in his head. "I reckon I could come up with a hundred dollars apiece, if you help me stop him."

Rafer looked at Luke and made a face. Back to Walt, he said, "A hundred dollars each would come in handy right now. I'd say you've got a deal, wouldn't you, Luke?" Luke readily agreed.

"Good," Walt said. "Let's have a drink to seal the deal." He turned to give the bartender a signal. "Now, I reckon we'll have to decide how we're gonna set up an ambush for him."

Cal Devine, the bartender, brought a bottle of whiskey over to the table. "I was wonderin' if anybody was gonna buy any whiskey, or if all three of you was just gonna set around polishin' the seats of my chairs."

"Go to hell, Cal, we got business to talk over," Rafer responded.

They sat discussing different approaches to eliminating Walt's problem without landing in jail. The law was almost nonexistent in the town, but the sheriff didn't stand for outright assassinations on the streets without some sign of a duel. So it was a question of one of them calling Ben out, or just shooting him down in a crossfire as soon as he rode into town and then running for it. Rafer and Luke seemed to favor the latter, reasoning that the sheriff wasn't going to chase them if they left town. Walt preferred to have them closer. He had checked into the hotel before he found his two partners in the Silver Dollar, and he wanted them to keep an eye on the entrances to the hotel when he was in his room. It was not an easy setup because they didn't know what time of night or day Ben might show up.

* * *

"Ben Savage," Lem Wooten pronounced slowly. "What brings you to town? Word got around that you weren't a Ranger no more." The owner of the stable had never been especially cordial to Ben.

"That's only partially true," Ben replied. "I'm still a Ranger, I just don't work out of the Ranger company in Austin anymore. I'm followin' the man who rode in on that buckskin in your corral, yonder, leadin' that dun in the corner."

"That a fact?" Lem asked. "What did he do?"

"Well, for one thing, he stole that dun. He's wanted for murder and possession of stolen money and for breakin' out of jail. It's my job to return him to Waco for trial. When did he leave the horses?"

"This mornin'," Lem said. "Left 'em here after he checked in the hotel. I reckon you're gonna cost me a customer, like you always do when you show up in town." Among the charges Ben had said Walt was wanted for, the one that kindled an interest was the one about being in possession of stolen money.

"The last time I came in here, I was ridin' that dun in your corral right now and that's the main reason I'm here today. I'll tell you what, I'll leave my horses with you while I'm in town and I'll pay you for what's owed for his and mine. Fair enough?"

"Fair enough," Lem agreed.

"Eugene Harper still the sheriff?" Ben asked. Lem said that he was, so Ben pulled his rifle from his saddle and started toward the sheriff's office on foot.

Lem stood watching him as he walked down the

street. "He's outta luck if he's hopin' to get much help outta the sheriff," he predicted.

"You're Ben Savage, ain'tcha?" A boy of about fourteen asked Ben when he walked into the sheriff's office. He was sitting behind the desk and seemed not at all surprised to see him.

"That's right," Ben answered, wondering how the boy could know. He glanced toward the cells to notice they were all empty.

"Sheriff ain't here," the boy said before Ben asked. "He had to ride out east of town to see 'bout some missin' cows."

"I didn't think he worked outside of town," Ben said. "Well, when he comes back, tell him I tried to check in with him before I made an arrest."

"I'll tell him," the boy said, then got up and followed Ben to the door to stand and watch as he walked toward the Silver Dollar Saloon. He turned around when he heard the sheriff come in from the storeroom. "He said to tell you he wanted to check in with you."

"Yeah, I heard him," Harper said. "I shoulda told you to ask him who he came to arrest. I bet it might be Walt Murphy. He just rode into town. It's a good thing I saw Savage comin'. He'da wanted me to help him arrest Murphy, or whoever he's chasin', and I ain't even had my dinner yet."

Ben decided it a good idea to check the saloon before looking for Walt in the hotel, and the saloon most likely to attract him would be the Silver Dollar. It was close to dinnertime, but Walt might be inclined to have a drink before he ate. He stepped inside the door, holding his rifle in his right hand, and paused by the door to survey the room. There was no sign of Walt Murphy. He made one more sweep across the broad barroom, and when his gaze swept back, it came to rest on the eyes of Cal Devine. The bartender graced him with a wide smile. "Well, Mr. Ben Savage, welcome back to Navasota. If you're lookin' for Sheriff Walt Murphy, he ain't here right now. You didn't miss him by much, though. Him and his two bodyguards left here to go to the hotel. I expect he'll be right glad to see you."

"Who are his two bodyguards?"

"Now that wouldn't be too sportin' of me to give out the names of our customers, would it? I mean, even if I did know."

"Much obliged," Ben said and walked out the door, heading for the hotel. He trusted what little information he had gotten from the bartender because he knew Cal just well enough to believe he owed allegiance to the owner of the Silver Dollar and no one else. To Cal, it was much like a game of checkers between the lawmen and the outlaws and whoever won was of no consequence to him. So now, he was confident that Walt had hired two men to help with his ambush and was planning to hole up in the hotel until they did the job for him.

When he started down the street, he noticed a man seemingly loitering around the front entrance to the hotel. He stepped inside a store doorway to take a longer look at the man and decided he could be one of the two men Walt hired. On a hunch, he left the doorway and walked down the side of the store to the alley behind the buildings. When he approached the back of the hotel, he hugged the rear wall of the barbershop next to the hotel while he watched the back entrance. After a few seconds, he spotted him, a second man generally fitting the description of the man by the front entrance. He had been sitting on the other side of the back steps and got up, evidently to stretch before sitting down again.

The bodyguards, Ben thought, for what other reason would the two men have for standing at the front and back doors? To get by them without tipping anybody off was not going to be easy. The thought had no time to age before he saw the way. There, actually on the side of the building, was another back door. This one led to the kitchen. That would be his entrance.

Still hugging the barbershop wall, he slid along it to the corner of the building where he could quickly slip around it and be out of the view of the backdoor guard. As soon as he slipped around the corner, he waited, his rifle trained on the back corner of the main hotel building. When no one appeared to challenge him, he walked across the narrow alley, up three steps, and went in the kitchen door. "Don't mind me, ladies," he said to the cook and one of the waitresses, both of whom were stopped in their tracks to gape, surprised. He walked on through the kitchen and stopped at the dining room door to see if Walt was there.

As he scanned the room, his gaze stopped on a woman near the inside door that led into the hotel. She was staring openly at him with an authoritative look about her, obviously wondering what he was doing in the kitchen. Ben figured she was likely the dining room manager. He decided it best to approach her in his capacity as a lawman, so he walked straight to her. "Afternoon, ma'am, I'm Texas Ranger Ben Savage," he said. "Are you the manager?"

"Yes, I'm the manager," she replied, "Mildred Deaton. What can I do for you?" She eyed the rifle in his hand openly.

"I'm concerned about the safety of one of the hotel guests. There have been some threats against his life. Walt Murphy, he checked in this mornin', and I thought I was supposed to meet him here for dinner."

"Oh, my goodness," Mildred reacted, somewhat distressed that some form of violence might be threatening her dining room. "There must be some mistake. There's only been one new guest that's checked in this morning and that was Mr. Thompson."

"Thompson," Ben echoed. "That's right, we were goin' to use that name this time. He hasn't been in to eat yet, has he? I'm supposed to meet him here."

"He's not coming here for dinner," Mildred said. "Mr. Thompson made special arrangements to eat in his room. Blanche should be about ready to take it up to him now."

"I don't know why he didn't think to tell me about it," Ben said, with a frustrated shake of his head. I reckon I'll have to sit and watch him eat in his room. If it's about ready, I'll just wait and go up with Blanche." He gave her a smile then and said, "I think your other guests will be more comfortable without me and my guns sittin' down here."

"I think so," she replied. "I'm glad you appreciate that. I'll see if Mr. Thompson's dinner is ready." She went to the kitchen and had no sooner gone through the door when she came right back out with Blanche following her.

Blanche took another look at the big man who had surprised them when he came in the kitchen door and signaled him to follow her with a nod of her head. He stepped quickly in front and opened the door for her. "Thank you, sir," she said sweetly and led him down a hallway to the back stairs. "Mr. Thompson's in the best room in the hotel," she commented as they climbed the stairs. "He must be somebody important to have so many men guarding him."

"Oh, he is," Ben replied.

"He must have plenty of money, too, to take that room."

"Oh, he does," Ben responded. *Only, it ain't his,* he thought.

When they reached the second floor, Blanche led him all the way back to the front of the hotel where the rooms overlooked the street. "Here we are," she said, "room number one. I'll bet he'll be surprised to see you."

"I expect he will," Ben said. *And so will I, if his name's really Thompson.*

Blanche rapped on the door and promptly received a reply from inside. "Who is it?"

"It's Blanche, Mr. Thompson. I brought you your dinner." They heard the sound of the key turning in the lock. Then, before Ben could stop her, Blanche said, "One of your guards came up with me."

Immediately irritated to think one of the men had left his post by the door, Walt jerked the door open, ready to berate the guilty party. When he found the doorway filled with Ben Savage, he was too startled to react quickly enough to avoid the butt of the rifle that knocked him flat on his back. Although he was still holding the pistol he had drawn as a precaution, his hand was pinned to the floor by Ben's boot, while the muzzle of the rifle barrel was only inches from his face. "Hello, Walt, I believe you ran off without askin' me if you could borrow my horse." Walt could only stare up at him, his eyes glazed, unable to speak as yet.

Equally startled, although uninjured, Blanche was also unable to speak for a few long moments. When she could, she asked, "Should I leave the tray, or bring it back later?"

"Just set it down on that table over there," Ben instructed. "And you just sit down beside it." At this point, he didn't want her to run all over the hotel yelling about what she just saw. "There ain't no reason for you to be scared. I'm a Texas Ranger and this man is a wanted criminal. I'm placin' him under arrest." With his free hand, he freed the pistol from Walt's hand, then rolled him over and cuffed his hands together. As an added precaution, he pulled a sheet off the bed and used it to bind Walt's feet together, then left him there while he searched the room for the stolen money. It wasn't hard to find. Two canvas bags were sitting beside the bed with a pair of saddlebags on top of them. Each bag had an article of clothing on top of the money to disguise it. When he was checking the saddlebags, he heard Blanche speak.

"Mr. Stephens and Mildred were talking about the bags of clothes he brought with him," she commented. "They said he musta been one helluva clotheshorse. Mr. Stephens said he acted like he had a lotta money and he reckoned rich folks could afford all the clothes they wanted."

Pleased to see that Blanche seemed to be calm now,

Ben asked, "Who's Mr. Stephens?" When told he was the owner of the hotel, Ben asked. "Is he here now?" She said he was. "Can you go get him for me and not say anything to anybody else about what's goin' on up here?" She nodded and went immediately to do his bidding. He thought it best to let her keep thinking the sacks held nothing more than clothes.

When Blanche returned with John Stephens, Ben identified himself as a Ranger and told him who Walt really was. "I'm tryin' to arrest this man without upsettin' your hotel guests, but he's got two more outlaws with him. You mighta noticed 'em—one at your front door, one at the back. They were supposed to keep any lawmen like me from gettin' to him. I can take care of the other two men, but I could use a little help from you." When Stephens immediately reacted as if he wanted no part in it, Ben assured him. "The only thing I want you to do is to go down to the jail and get Sheriff Harper to come back to take the other two men to jail."

"Just tell Harper to come get them?" Stephens wanted to be sure.

"That's all—and tell him he'll need two pairs of handcuffs."

When Stephens left the room, Blanche took a look at the trussed-up prisoner, then asked, "Anything else I can do for you?"

He had been trying to decide how he was going to handle the two guards, and she seemed almost excited to be involved at this point. So he asked, "Would you be afraid to go to the back door and tell the man sittin' outside that Mr. Thompson said come up to the room?"

"No, I can do that. He ain't hardly going to do

anything to me for that. I'll do it!" She started for the door at once.

"There's one standin' by the front door, too," Ben said.

"I'll tell him, too," she said and was off, excited to be part of the arrest.

"Don't you come back after you tell 'em," he called after her. "I don't want you to get in the way of any shootin'." He heard her acknowledge as she hurried down the stairs.

Around two minutes later, Rafer Black came up the front stairs to the second floor to find Luke Davis in the hallway, coming from the back stairs. "He send for you, too?" Rafer asked. "Did that little gal say what he wanted?"

"Nope, just that he said he wanted to see me," Luke answered.

"Well, if he's decided he don't need us to take care of that jasper, it's too late to get his money back 'cause we're doin' our part of the deal," Rafer said. "Come on, we'll see what he's got in mind. That's the room there with the door wide open."

They walked on up to the room and walked inside to be stopped by the sight of Walt Murphy lying against the front wall, his hands locked behind his back, and his feet bound together. "What tha . . . ?" was as far as Rafer got before the door slammed behind them.

Both men jumped as if hearing a gunshot and started to react with gun hands reaching for their weapons. "I wouldn't," Ben warned. "First gun outta the holster gets shot. I'm Texas Ranger Ben Savage, and I wanna see your hands up in the air. Now!" He added when there was a show of reluctance from Rafer. When they did as he ordered, he pulled their guns out of their holsters. "Now, sit down over there against that wall. Cross your legs, Indian style, and sit down."

"Whaddaya arrestin' us for?" Luke asked. "We ain't done nothin'.'"

"Attempted murder," Ben answered, "aidin' Walt over there with tryin' to ambush an officer of the law. I will have to admit it, though, you ain't any good at it."

They didn't sit there very long before they heard footsteps in the hall outside the door, followed seconds later by a loud knock. "This is Sheriff Harper! Open up in there!"

"It ain't locked, Sheriff, come on in," Ben called back. The door opened slowly as if the sheriff was afraid it might be a trap. "Looks like you took care of that cattle rustlin' problem," Ben said.

"What cattle rustlin' problem?" Harper started, then quickly replied, "Oh, right, yeah, that got took care of. What's goin' on here, Savage? What do I need two pair of cuffs for?"

"For those two gentlemen sittin' on the floor over there. They're yours. By my authority as a Texas Ranger, I'm leavin' those two in your custody and recommendin' they spend two or three days in your jail for planning to kill an officer of the law. That one's mine." He pointed to Walt. "I'm takin' him straight back to Waco for trial. He's the only one I came after. He broke jail in Waco. I'll be startin' back with him tonight."

Harper stood for a few moments looking down at the two men sitting against the wall. "Rafer Black and Luke Davis," he pronounced with unhidden contempt. "If you two ain't a pair of jokers. I knew, if you hung around town long enough, you'd find a way to cause me trouble." He nodded toward Walt. "You don't want me to hold that one, too?"

"Nope, I know he's anxious to get back to Waco as fast as he can, so we'll head out that way just as soon as I pack up the horses."

"Suit yourself," Harper said. "I'll take care of these two—always like to help the Rangers when I can." As he said it, he was thinking he'd most likely hold Rafer and Luke overnight and let them go tomorrow and to hell with Ben's recommendations. He didn't want the bother of two prisoners. Had he known the big Ranger better, he might have known that Ben suspected as much. And that was the reason he planned to ride straight west to Austin with Walt, instead of north to Waco. There was no use taking a chance on the two small-time outlaws deciding to come after him.

Ben thanked Harper for his cooperation and waited for him to take his prisoners out of the hotel before he got Walt ready to go. John Stephens was standing by the front desk when Ben marched Walt to the front door. He stopped Walt there while he asked Stephens if he had Walt's bill ready. Surprised, Stephens opened the register and quickly came up with a total for the time Walt was there. "Mark it paid for me and sign it," Ben said. Then, while Walt stood there sneering, Ben fished in his pockets for a roll of money and paid Stephens. When he had his receipt, he placed the saddlebags on Walt's shoulders and wedged the largest of the canvas sacks between his locked arms behind his back. Carrying the other sack, himself, he herded Walt out the door and up the street to the stable.

CHAPTER 24

"Damned if he didn't do it," Lem Wooten muttered to himself when he looked out toward the street and saw Ben marching Walt toward the stable. Of special interest to him now were the saddlebags on Walt's shoulders and the canvas bags both he and Ben carried. The remark Savage had made about possession of stolen money came to mind. *He must have robbed a bank,* he thought. "You fixin' to leave?" Lem called out.

"Just as fast as I can load up," Ben answered.

Lem didn't go at once to get the horses. Instead he stood by the entrance to the stable and gawked at the prisoner and the canvas bags. "What's in the sacks?"

"Nothin' that would interest you," Ben replied. "Let's get the horses."

"Right," Lem responded, but he continued to stare at Walt, whose face was half-covered with drying blood from the cut across his forehead, the result of Ben's rifle butt. Almost as if reading Lem's thoughts, Walt glanced down at one of the sacks, now on the floor at his feet. He glanced back up to meet Lem's gaze and slowly nodded. "Right," Lem said again when Ben turned toward him, about to tell him again. "I'll bring that dun up and let you saddle him. Which one do you wanna put your prisoner on?" Ben told him the buckskin. "Looks like you opened up his head pretty good," Lem went on. "You want me to get a pan of water, so he can wash some of that blood outta his eyes?" He gave Walt a hard, unblinking stare.

"No, he's all right," Ben said, "just bring up the horses."

Aware now that Lem was offering a proposition of help, conveyed solely by the exchanges of glances, in exchange for part of the money in the bags, Walt immediately complained. "How 'bout it, Savage? You're holdin' all the cards. What's it gonna hurt to let me clean some of this blood outta my eyes? You can unlock my hands long enough to do that. Hell, I can't hardly move my shoulder, and you'll have your gun on me. If you don't wanna do that, you can wash my face for me."

Ben hesitated, wondering what Walt might be up to. He decided, however, that there wasn't much Walt could do. If he made a move to escape, he would shoot him. "All right, if that will make you more comfortable." He looked at Lem then and said, "Get him a pan of water and a rag."

"Right," Lem said again. "I'll be right back." In a few minutes, he returned with a large pan. "I got a big'un. This is one I use when I'm doctorin' a horse." He didn't exaggerate. The pan was large enough to hide the pistol he was holding on the side away from Ben. "I'll set it down on that shelf by the side of that stall there. He can wash up there." He laid the pan down carefully, keeping the loaded revolver hidden behind it. Then he stepped away from it.

"All right, Walt," Ben said and turned him to face the pan on the shelf. "I shouldn't have to warn you. Any funny moves and I'll shoot you down." He unlocked the handcuffs and drew his six-gun. "Walk straight to that shelf and wash up."

Walt did as Ben instructed, although confused by Lem Wooten's actions. He had been sure he and Lem had communicated a deal and he had expected Lem to simply shoot Ben without warning. As soon as he reached the pan of water, however, he understood Lem's thinking. He would provide the weapon, but he didn't have the guts to shoot the Ranger. *The yellow dog,* he thought. He might have paid him a couple of hundred dollars for shooting Savage, but now, he would give him about twenty dollars for the use of the gun. *Maybe more,* he reconsidered when he thought of the pleasure he was about to receive when Ben Savage was shot down by his hand. He felt the shiver of a thrill race through his veins when he anticipated the moment when Ben realized he had been outfoxed. With his back toward Ben, he splashed some water on his face with his left hand while his right hand held the pistol behind the pan. "You know, Savage, I figured me and you was meant to stand and face each other and find out for sure who's the best man." Ben didn't comment. "That would be the kinda shoot-out folks would talk about for years."

"Hurry up and get finished with that," Ben replied. "I don't wanna spend all night gettin' you on your way to prison, or a hangin', whatever the judge decides." He glanced over at Lem again. The stable owner, seemed extremely fidgety, biting his lower lip nervously, and continued to edge backward as if expecting something to happen. Ben wasn't sure why, but something prompted him to take a couple of steps to the side as Walt appeared to finish.

"Just me and you, Ben, and two six-guns," Walt announced as he turned and fired. His shot missed by a foot while Ben's struck him in the center of his chest.

Walt stared down at the hole in his chest in total disbelief. He raised the pistol again but seemed unable to hold it steady and couldn't think to cock it. The last sight that reached his fading vision was the muzzle of the six-gun that fired the fatal shot that struck him in the forehead. He stumbled backward against the shelf, knocking the pan of water off to fall with him to the floor.

Not a word was said for a long moment before Lem managed to blurt, "I don't know where in the world he got that gun."

"You don't, huh?" Ben replied and swung his gun around to point at him. "Get down on your knees." When he did, Ben took a coil of rope off a peg by the stall. "Put your hands behind your back." He tied Lem's hands and feet and left him there while he saddled the horses and packed up the bags of money, not willing to risk another attempt by Lem to claim some of it. When he was packed up and ready to leave, he told him. "Somebody will likely come along and untie you. I hope I'm halfway to Waco by the time they do. I oughta take you to prison for what you tried to do, but I don't feel like botherin' with you. Your penalty for tryin' to help him kill me is you got the job of buryin' him."

* * *

As he had planned to do before, he took the road north out of Navasota but turned sharply west once he was out of sight. He proceeded to take the stolen bank money directly to Austin, where he made his report on the fate of Walt Murphy to Ranger Captain Randolph Mitchell. His biggest regret was the promise he had given to Rosa Cruz to visit her and Wilfred on his return trip, but he would endeavor to make that up some other time. He had already been gone from Buzzard's Bluff long enough to cause Rachel to think she had lost another partner.

He led the extra horses he had acquired up to the north end of town to leave them at the stable. Henry Barnes walked out to meet him. "Well, Ben, I'm glad to see you back in town. Looks like you picked up some extra horses."

"Howdy, Henry. I'm mighty glad to be back. Yep, I picked up a couple of horses. I've gotta take that gray back to Waco in a few days, whenever I feel like makin' the trip. I borrowed him from a fellow who owns a stable there. I'm keepin' that buckskin for a while, although I think he makes Cousin feel kinda jealous. Anything happenin' around here?"

"Nothin' I can think of that's worth talkin' about," Henry replied.

"Good," Ben said. "I oughta be just about on time to eat whatever Annie's cooked for dinner."

"Wait till we put these horses away and I'll go with you," Henry said.

When the horses were unsaddled and turned in the corral, they walked down to the Lost Coyote, just in time to meet Ham Greeley coming from the other direction. "Hey, Ben!" Ham greeted him. "You just get back?" When Ben said he did, Ham whooped, "Hot damn! I can't wait to tell Tuck you're back in town." He turned around and hurried back toward the harness shop to announce it to Tuck. He knew it would really get Tuck's goat not to be the one to make the official announcement.

Keep reading for a special preview!

A MacCallister Christmas

From bestselling authors William W. *and* J. A. Johnstone
*comes a special action-packed holiday western tale of peace
on earth and bad will toward men . . .*

Ever since he left Scotland to start a new life in
America, Duff MacCallister has stayed true to the
values and traditions of his clan in the Highlands.
But as Christmas approaches, he yearns to
reconnect with his family—even the ones he hasn't
met yet. This year, two of his American cousins—
twins Andrew and Rosanna—will be joining Duff
for the holidays at the Sky Meadow Ranch. That is,
if they manage to get there alive . . .

The twins' train is held up by not one but *two* vicious
outlaw gangs. The Jessup gang has been using the
Spalding gang's hideout to plan the robbery. The
Jessups just lost two of their brothers in a bank job
gone wrong—courtesy of Duff MacCallister—
and they're gunning for revenge. Together, these
two bloodthirsty bands of killers and thieves are
teaming up to make this one Christmas the
MacCallisters will never forget. But Duff's ready
to deliver his own brand of gun-blazing justice,
holidays be damned . . .

Look for *A MacCallister Christmas*, on sale now.

PROLOGUE

Dunoon, Argyll, Scotland, present day

"'Tis because o' that television show that yer here, isn't it, lassie?" the old woman asked as the young American couple came up to the counter to pay for the lunch they'd enjoyed in this picturesque little café.

The young woman smiled and said, "Is it that obvious?"

"Ye look a wee bit like the girl who plays the daughter, ya ken."

"You really think so?" The young woman blushed, obviously pleased by the comparison.

"Oh, aye. In fact, ye look as if ye have some Scots blood a-flowin' in yer veins."

"I do! A little. I don't really know how much."

"Enough that I'd consider ye a good Scottish lass. We need to figure out what clan. Once we ken what yer colors are, ye can go next door to me sister's shop, where she sells all sorts o' goods decorated with all the clan colors . . ."

While that conversation was going on, the young man had handed over his credit card. He took it back from the old woman now as she handed him his receipt along with it. His wife said eagerly, "I don't really know anything about the clans. Well, other than what I've learned from watching TV."

"Then ye've come t' the right place. I'll teach ye everything ye need to ken. What is't ye Americans call it? A *crash course*?"

"Yes, that's right."

While his wife leaned over the counter to continue the spirited conversation with the woman who ran the café, the young man stepped through the door to the narrow cobblestone street to wait for her. He had a hunch it might be a while.

"Snagged another'un, did she?"

The voice came from the young man's left. A burly older man sat there, puffing on a pipe, bundled up against the day's chill with his cap pulled down on his gray hair.

"I beg your pardon?" the young man said.

The older man took the pipe out of his mouth and pointed with the stem at the café entrance. "Aileen in there. She can spot the tourists and the TV fans and manages to send about half of 'em in her sister Isobel's shop. 'Twouldn't surprise me if she gets what you Americans call a *kickback*."

"Annabel really does enjoy that show," the young man said with a smile. "We've been all over the Highlands during the past week. Saved up to take this trip for a couple of years."

The older man moved over on the bench and nodded curtly to the empty space. The young American sat down and held out his hand.

"I'm Richard van Loan."

"Is that an English name?"

"Dutch, I believe. I've never been into genealogy all that much."

"I've nothin' against the Dutch, so I'll shake yer hand. Graham McGregor is me name. 'Tis a pleasure to meet ye, lad."

"Likewise," Richard said. He looked around at the old buildings that fronted the narrow street. Eastward, between some of those buildings, a narrow slice of the Firth of Clyde was visible, the water a deep, deep blue on this cloudy day.

"You have a beautiful city here."

"'Twas not always so large. Me grandfather told me it grew like wildfire after the port was put in and the steamers began comin' up the firth, and James Ewing built Castle House next to old Dunoon Castle. A'fore that, 'twas just a country town, Dunoon, spelled a bit different than today. Me great-great-grandfather Ian McGregor had a pub here, the White Horse."

"Sounds like it would have been a wonderful place to visit," Richard said.

"Dinna ye go talkin' about such things! Ye would never believe how many tourists show up in the Highlands searchin' for some magical place where they can go travelin' through time!"

Richard laughed. "Really? Well, people take these things seriously, I suppose."

"Aye, they do. Yer wife . . . I'd wager she's a wee bit in love wi' tha' braw laddie on the TV."

"Oh, I don't know about that—"

"But he's not the only hero t' come from Scotland,

ye ken. Why, there was once a lad from right here in old Dunoon who was every bit as big and bold and handsome, an' even better in a fight! Me great-great-grandfather Ian was his friend, ye ken, before he left to go t' America and become a famous frontiersman, like in yer Western movies."

"Your great-great-grandfather became a frontiers-man in America?"

"No, th' lad I'm tellin' ye about! Duff MacCallister, tha' was his name. Duff Tavish MacCallister. Did ye ever hear of him?"

Richard shook his head slowly and said, "No. No, I don't think so."

Annabel came out of the café, pointed at the shop next door, and said, "Richard, I'm going to be in there for a while looking around. Are you all right out here?"

"Yes, I'm fine," he told her. "Take your time."

"She will, ye ken," Graham McGregor said after Annabel had vanished into the shop. "Take her time, that is. Lassies always do."

"Yes, I've been married long enough to know that. You were saying about this fellow Duff . . . Tell me more about Duff MacCallister."

"I reckon I can do that," Graham said, nodding. "Old Ian filled me grandfather's head wi' stories, and he passed 'em on to me when I was naught but a tyke." He paused, obviously thinking about which story to tell, then went on, "I know a good one. Lots o' ridin' an' shootin' an' fightin', like in them movies I was talkin' about. It started in th' month o' December, long, long ago, in a frontier settlement, Chugwater, Wyomin' . . ."

CHAPTER ONE

Chugwater, Wyoming . . . back then

Duff MacCallister took off his hat and raised his arm to sleeve sweat off his rugged face.

"If I dinna ken what day 'tis, I'd say 'twas the middle o' summer, not December!"

"Not that long until Christmas," Elmer Gleason agreed. "It's unseasonably warm, that's for sure."

The two men had just finished loading a good-sized pile of supplies, including heavy bags of flour, sugar, and beans, into the back of the wagon they had brought into town from Sky Meadow, Duff's ranch farther up the valley. Both were in shirtsleeves, instead of the heavy coats most men normally wore at this time of year in Wyoming. In fact, Duff had rolled up the sleeves of his shirt over brawny forearms.

He was a tall, broad-shouldered, tawny-haired young man, originally from Scotland, but now, after several years here in Wyoming, a Westerner through and through. He had established Sky Meadow Ranch when he arrived on the frontier, brought in Black Angus cattle, like the ones he had raised back in Scotland, and built the spread into a large, very lucrative operation that took in thirty thousand acres of prime grazing land.

Elmer, a grizzled old-timer who had lived a very adventurous life of his own, had been living on the land when Duff bought it, squatting in an old abandoned gold mine at the northern end of the property. People believed the mine was haunted, but what they had seen was no ghost, just Elmer.

Since Duff had made that discovery, the old-timer had become one of his most trusted friends and advisors. He worked as Sky Meadow's foreman, and Duff had even made him a partner in the ranch with a ten percent share.

Now, with the supplies Duff had purchased from Matthews Mercantile loaded, Elmer licked his lips and said, "I reckon we'll be headin' down to Fiddler's Green to wet our whistles before startin' back to the ranch? A cold beer'd taste mighty good on a day like today."

"Aye, the same thought did occur to me," Duff said. "Go ahead, and I'll catch up to ye. I'll be makin' one small stop first."

"At the dress shop?" Elmer asked with a knowing grin.

"Perhaps . . ."

"Go ahead. I'll be down there yarnin' with Biff when you're done. We can talk about the weather, like ever'body else in town is probably doin'."

Duff lifted a hand in farewell and turned his steps along Clay Avenue toward the shop where Meagan Parker sewed, displayed, and sold the dresses she made, which were some of the finest to be found anywhere between New York and San Francisco, despite the unlikely surroundings of this frontier cattle town.

Meagan's talents were such that she could have been in high demand as a designer and seamstress anywhere in the country, but she preferred to remain in Chugwater.

Duff MacCallister was a large part of the reason she stayed.

Duff and Meagan had an understanding. Neither of them had a romantic interest in anyone else, and because of financial assistance she had rendered him in the past, she was also a partner in Sky Meadow.

The ranch was named after Skye McGregor, Duff's first love back in Scotland. The young woman's murder had been part of a tragic chain of circumstances that resulted in Duff leaving Scotland and coming to America. A part of Duff still loved her and always would. Meagan knew all about Skye and Duff's feelings for her, and she accepted the situation, so it never came between the two of them.

Someday they would be married. Duff and Meagan both knew that. But for now, they were happy with the way things were between them and didn't want to do anything to jeopardize that.

Now that Duff wasn't lifting heavy bags and crates into the wagon, the day didn't feel quite as warm to him, although the sun still shone brightly in a sky almost devoid of clouds. A couple of times earlier in the fall, a dusting of snow had fallen, but it wouldn't have been unusual for several inches to be on the ground by now.

A little breeze kicked up as Duff walked toward Meagan's shop. He lifted his head to sniff the air. There was a hint, just a hint, of coolness in it.

Maybe that was a harbinger, Duff thought, an indication that the weather was going to change again and become more seasonable. Even though a man would have to be a fool not to enjoy the pleasant weather—it wasn't a raging blizzard, after all—with Christmas coming, it needed to *feel* like winter. That little tang he had detected put some extra enthusiasm in Duff's step. He was in a good mood, and he didn't think anything could change that.

Four men reined their horses to a halt in front of the Bank of Chugwater, swung down from their saddles, and looped the reins around the hitch rail there. Hank Jessup, the oldest of the group, turned to the other three and said, "All right, Nick, you'll stay out here with the horses."

They all had the same roughly dressed, rawboned appearance, and their facial features were similar enough that it was obvious they were related. Hank, with his weather-beaten skin and white hair, could have been father to the others, based on looks, but in actuality he was their older brother. Half brother, anyway. Late in life, their father had married a much younger woman and somewhat surprisingly sired the other three—Logan, Sherm, and Nick.

They had willingly followed Hank into the family business of being outlaws, and they had come to Chugwater to help themselves to an early Christmas present of however much loot was in the bank's vault.

"You said I could go inside this time, Hank," Nick complained. "I always have to watch the horses."

Sherm said, "It's an important job, kid."

"You're our lookout, too," Logan added. "You've

got to warn us if any blasted badge-toter comes along and starts to go in the bank."

"Yeah, yeah," Nick muttered. "I guess so."

Hank said, "And you're watching the horses because I say so, that's the most important thing." He squared his shoulders, nodded to Logan and Sherm. "Come on."

The three of them stepped up onto the boardwalk and headed for the bank's front door. They didn't draw their guns yet, because they didn't want to alert people on the street that anything unusual was going on.

Nick lounged against the hitch rail, handy to the spot where the reins were tied so he could loosen them in a hurry if he needed. This wasn't the first bank robbery he and his brothers had pulled. Sometimes the boys came out walking fast, still not wanting to draw attention, and sometimes they came on the run, needing to make as rapid a getaway as they could.

Inside the bank, Hank glanced around quickly, sizing up the situation without being too obvious about it: two tellers, each with a single customer, one man and one woman. A bank officer, probably the president, was seated at a desk off to one side behind a wooden railing. The man had a bunch of papers spread out on his desk and was making marks on one of them with a pencil, pausing between each notation to lick the pencil lead.

No guard that Hank could see, but it was entirely possible those tellers had guns on shelves below the counter, and the bank president probably had an iron in his desk drawer, too.

Question was, would they be smart enough not to try to use them?

Hank wouldn't mind gunning them down if it came to that. Wouldn't mind at all.

He exchanged a glance with his brothers and nodded. No time like the present.

Hauling the gun from the holster on his hip, Hank yelled, "Stand right where you are! Nobody move, or we'll start blasting!"

Meagan was sitting at a table with several pieces of cloth in front of her when Duff came into the shop. She had three straight pins in her mouth, taken from a pincushion close to her right hand. She looked up at him and smiled.

"Careful there, lass," he cautioned. "Ye dinna want t' be stickin' pins in those sweet lips o' yours."

Deftly Meagan took the pins out of her mouth and returned them to the pincushion, which allowed her to smile even more.

"I certainly wouldn't want to hurt my lips," she said, "when I have such an important use for them."

"Oh? And what would that be?"

Meagan stood up and came toward him, a sensually shaped blond beauty. Because of the unseasonably warm weather, she wore a lightweight dress today that hugged her figure, instead of being bundled up.

"This," she said as she put her arms around Duff's neck and lifted her face so he could kiss her. He did so with passion and urgency.

After a very enjoyable few moments, Duff stepped back and said, "I have some news this morning. Elmer and I stopped at the post office on our way t' the mercantile, and a letter was there waiting for me."

"Well, don't keep me in suspense," Meagan said. "Who is it from?"

"My cousin Andrew. Ye've heard me speak of him many times."

"Of course. He's the famous actor. He and his twin sister, both."

Duff nodded and said, "Aye, Rosanna. The pair o' them were actually the first of my American cousins I ever met, when they came to Glasgow to perform in a play called *The Golden Fetter.* Andrew had written to me then, introducing himself and asking me to come see the play and meet him and Rosanna. Fine people they are."

"Being MacCallisters, how could they be anything else?"

"Aye, 'tis true, we are a fine clan. I've seen them a number of times since then, in New York and elsewhere, and back in the summer, I wrote to Andrew and invited him and Rosanna to spend Christmas at Sky Meadow if they could arrange their schedule to make it possible. In his letter I received today, he says they've been touring, but they're ready t' take a break from it and pay me a visit for the holidays."

"Duff, that's wonderful news," Meagan said. "I'm looking forward to meeting them. When will they be here?"

"Andrew is no' sure yet, but 'twill not be for another few days, at least. He assures me they'll arrive before Christmas."

"And what about your cousin Falcon? Didn't you tell me that he's coming for Christmas, too?"

Duff grinned and said, "Falcon told me he would *try* to make it. Wi' Falcon, ye never can tell what wild adventure might come along an' drag him away. So if he shows up, I'll be mighty glad t' see him, of course, but I willna be surprised if circumstances prevent that."

"Well, I hope he's able to come," Meagan said. "It would be almost like a family reunion. Isn't he Andrew and Rosanna's brother?"

"Aye, youngest brother. Falcon is the baby of the family, although I doubt he'd appreciate bein' referred to as such. Andrew and Rosanna are ten years or so older than him."

"Aren't there other brothers and sisters?"

Duff waved a hand and said, "Aye, spread out all over the country, they are. One o' these days, they need to have a proper MacCallister family reunion."

"I'll bet that would be exciting," Meagan said with a smile. "There's no telling what might happen."

"Och, lass, are you for sayin' that th' MacCallisters attract trouble or some such?"

"Well, now that you mention it . . ."

Duff chuckled and pulled Meagan back into his arms for another hug and kiss. He stroked a big hand over her blond hair and said quietly, "'Tis something else I'd rather be attractin'."

"Oh, you do, Duff. You definitely do."

He was about to lower his lips to hers for another kiss when gunshots suddenly rang out somewhere down the street. The sounds shattered the warm, peaceful day and made Duff jerk his head up again.

Those shots were concrete proof of what Meagan had just said. No MacCallister could go very long without running into a ruckus.

"I'll be back," Duff said over his shoulder as he charged out of the dress shop.